'Izzie'

'Izzie'

A Child of the Cut

Rupert Ashby

Paper Cut Books

To the families who spent their time
living and working on the nation's canal system.

First published in 2013

British Library Cataloguing in Publication Data

A catalogue record for this book is available from the British Library.

ISBN 978 0 9575135 0 1

Paper Cut Books
(part of Half Cut Theatre)
10 Lichfield Avenue
Werrington
Peterborough PE4 6PF
www.halfcuttheatre.com

Edited, designed and produced by

Priory Ash Publishing
2 Denford Ash Cottages
Denford
Kettering
Northants NN14 4EW
www.prioryash.com

Printed and bound in Great Britain

The author is donating 50 per cent of the profit
from the sales of this book to

Foxton Inclined Plane Trust

www.fipt.org

Acknowledgements

While most of the characters in this story are entirely fictional, Sister Mary Ward was definitely real. She looked after the health of the boat people from her cottage by the canal at Stoke Bruerne for many years. For further information about her see http://clutch.open.ac.uk/schools/stokebruerne99/Sister_Mary.html

Writing a novel is more than the author sitting at a computer for hours, getting the story from head to hard disk. It is that, but it also involves much more. From its inception to final production many other people are involved, and the book you are holding could never have existed without them.

Will Adams at Priory Ash gave his clear, no-nonsense advice on the mechanics of getting into print and how to market the finished book.

Rosamund King at Brent Archive kindly dug out the Bombing Maps of Kensal Green, together with a host of newspaper cuttings relating to the area during the Second World War.

Dr Betty Chambers MBE not only loaned her thesis covering education in the 1930s, but also let me borrow a number of primers that were in use during the period.

Frank Harris shared his knowledge of Blisworth during the Second World War.

Douglas Abrahams, fellow guardsman of Frank Harris, and formerly of the Household Cavalry, provided details of the Changing the King's Guard during the war years.

Charlotte Rodriguez posed for the cover photographs and transformed Izzie from the page to a real person.

Jennifer Wickham became my first 'public' reader and critic.

Edith Coole proofread the final version, spotting the 'typos' and bad grammar.

Jane, my wife, has supported the whole project, offering advice, alterations – and sometimes improvements – from beginning to end.

To all of these – and to any whom I may have inadvertently missed, my heartfelt and sincere thanks.

For me, this has been a labour of love, but it could never have come to fruition without their invaluable help.

Rupert Ashby
Peterborough
October 2012

Contents

Preface

I first became interested in canals while spending boyhood holidays with my grandparents at Blisworth on the Grand Union. One evening, when I was about seven or eight, my grandmother and I went to the then Blisworth Hotel to hear an evening of arias. A distant family member had been involved in a production of an opera in Northampton. I cannot now remember whether it was *La Traviata* or *Il Trovatore*, but the principals were performing excerpts at various villages around Northampton to raise some money for their society.

My grandmother was not a fan of opera but thought that, as Uncle Bob was involved, she ought to go. On the way home I asked her if we could go via the canal towpath, to which she agreed. It was getting dark by then and we were passed by a pair of narrowboats. They were fully loaded with coal, and travelling by night to save time.

I could not take my eyes off them! I was totally fascinated. That evening had two major effects on me. It ignited a lifelong passion for the history and culture of this country's canal network – and it put me off opera for life!

I like to think that Izzie, or someone like her, may have been on one of the loaded boats I saw that night. I hope you will enjoy reading about her life.

Chapter 1

Book learnin'

'Isobel Margaret 'Orne,' recited the tall, dark-haired woman, whose weather-beaten face gave her the appearance of being older than her thirty-five years. In one hand she held a fully loaded shopping bag, while the other was being held tightly by a serious-faced, dark-haired young girl. The words were addressed to a younger woman, seated at a high desk, who wrote down the name with a pen on the page of a book. The older woman watched, still struggling to fully believe that she was doing the right thing for her daughter, and conscious of the fact that the child's father would certainly not view it in the same way. She watched the pen, intrigued, as the marks were made on the page. But she had little understanding of what they meant. She vaguely recognised the last group of markings as indicating the word 'Horne', her surname, as she had often seen them on other pieces of paper. But she had no idea how or why they represented her name. Watching the younger woman writing, but having no knowledge herself of what was being written, she was convinced. She was certain that she was doing the right thing by enrolling her daughter at the school – and she would take whatever criticism was inevitably going to come her way from her husband.

'And what is Isobel's date of birth?' asked the younger woman, looking up.

'Twelfth o' May, nineteen twenny-eight,' Maggie Horne answered, returning to the matter in hand.

At the mention of the date, Izzie's mind went back to her last birthday, in the spring. It had been the best one ever! She had woken up and remembered that it was her special day, her birthday! Today she was ten! Her mother and father had pretended they had forgotten.

'You know what day it is, don't you?' Izzie had said as they were preparing to move off.

'It's Tuesday, ain't it?' her father had answered.

'Yeah, but it's summat else an' all, ain't it?'

'Is it?' her mother had asked.

'Don't say you're both forgot it's me birthday!' Izzie had looked upset.

'Oh, it's your birthday today, is it?' her father had asked. 'Are you sure it's today?'

'Course I'm sure!'

'You better 'ave this then,' her mother had said as she reached into the cupboard and handed her a small parcel wrapped up in brown paper.

"Appy birthday, Izzie, love!' Her father had given her a kiss.

'An' many 'appy returns!' Her mother had done the same. Izzie had taken the parcel.

'Oh, you!' she had said as she realised they had been teasing her. 'Makin' me think as you'd forgot!' She had carefully unwrapped the paper to reveal two lace handkerchiefs, beautifully embroidered with the letter 'I'.

'Oh!' she had gasped as she saw them. 'They're ... they're beautiful! Oh, thank you, Mam and Dad! Thank you ever so much!' Then there had been more kisses and hugs.

'I thought that were the right letter for your name, but I ask' the woman in the shop, just to make sure – bein' as it were a bit fancy, like,' Maggie had explained.

'I ain't never gonna use these. I'm gonna put 'em in me bag wi' me treasures!'

'Whatever for?' her father had asked, incredulously.

'Well, they're far too pretty to go blowin' your nose on, ain't they?' she had replied.

'That's a lovely idea, love.' Maggie had agreed with her.

'Well, I dunno!' her father had exclaimed. 'I been married to one woman for fourteen year, and I'm 'ad another woman, a daughter, for ten o' them year, an' I'll still be blowed if I can ever understand 'em!' Amid the laughter, they had all gone about their daily duties to 'get 'em ahead.'

Later, Izzie had done as she had said she would and had put her new handkerchiefs away with her 'special treasures'. These were various things she had collected over the years because she thought they were pretty or sentimental. They consisted of some pebbles with fine patterns on the surface, some shells from birds' eggs, an old brooch that had been Maggie's mother's, and one or two other odds and ends to which she attached some value. There was also a fragment of lacework that had once been part of a piece that her father's mother had made to keep the flies out of the boat horse's ears! She kept all these in a little cloth bag that always hung on a hook over her bed. She had made it a few years before when her mother had been teaching her to sew.

Their meal that night had been Izzie's favourite – sausages and mash followed by treacle sponge.

'So, how old does that make you, Isobel?' The young woman's question brought Izzie abruptly back to the present.

'Ten!'

'Very good. Now, Isobel, my name is Miss Roberts and, as you know, I'm the teacher at our little school here. When you come into school tomorrow morning, you can hang your coat up over there.' She pointed to a row of iron coat-pegs screwed to a piece of wood attached to the wall. 'And your desk will be that one there.'

Isobel – or Izzie, as she had always been known – followed the pointing finger to one of the twelve small desks that were arranged in four rows of three. This particular one was at the front of the row next to the wall by the coat-pegs.

'Now, Mrs Horne, if you will just sign here, please.' She dipped the pen in the inkwell on her desk and indicated a dotted line at the bottom of the page in the book.

'I jus' want what's best for 'er – give 'er a better start in life 'n what we 'ad, like,' Margaret Horne said as she took the proffered pen.

'Of course, you do, Mrs Horne,' Miss Roberts agreed. 'It's a very praiseworthy thing to do for your daughter, and I'm sure we'll get on just fine, won't we, Isobel?'

'Yes, Miss Roberts,' replied the girl. Her mother took the pen and, holding it rather awkwardly, scrawled 'X' on the line next to where Miss Roberts's finger was pointing.

'Thank you,' said Miss Roberts, and wrote some more words alongside the mark.

Her first impressions of her new pupil were good ones. Isobel Margaret Horne seemed to be a cheerful, respectful and obedient child. Although she had seen her around the Wharf for many years, Izzie had always avoided her gaze. She did not appear to have the sullen streak that she had noticed in some of the children who had been brought to her, who had made it obvious from the start that they regarded attending her lessons as a complete waste of their time. Time that they would far rather spend running around and causing havoc outside on the Wharf.

During the enrolment procedure Izzie had been looking around the schoolroom. It was housed in a small brick building next door to the Company's Wharf Office. It had been built originally as a secure storeroom. But that had been many years ago, back in the days when the Wharf had been very much busier. There had been no requirement for a secure storage area for a number of years now.

Standing here in the schoolroom, it did not appear to her to be the boring place she had often thought it was when she had peered at it through the windows. There were pictures on the painted brick walls, some that the children had painted, and others, more professional-looking, in frames. Perhaps her recent change of mind may have had something to do with it, but Izzie decided that she quite liked the look of this schoolroom, and she realised that her mother had been right when she had often said in recent months, 'You're gittin' too ol' to waste all your time, messin' about on that Wharf!'

✳

It had been the sight of children playing on the Wharf back in the days when the canal was much busier that had prompted a certain Miss Henrietta Watts, a retired schoolteacher, and a redoubtable lady, to approach Emily Roberts's father, Horace. At that time he was the young assistant to the clerk responsible for running the Company's business at the Wharf.

'I say! Young man!' she had called to him as she had entered the

Wharf Office on a warm June afternoon back in the 1920s. Horace was in the office on his own as the wharf clerk had gone to the head office for a meeting with the manager. Horace looked up from his desk and observed a tall, slim lady in her late sixties. She had grey hair, severely combed back and secured in a bun, and she wore a pair of tortoiseshell-framed spectacles. She was dressed very precisely in a navy blue jacket and skirt – good quality clothes – and it was immediately obvious to Horace that she was not from one of the boats.

He rose from his desk and greeted her. 'Good afternoon, madam, and what can I do for you?'

'I have observed a group of children playing outside your office here,' Miss Watts began, 'and I was wondering if you could kindly explain to me why – this being about the middle of the summer term – they are not in school?' Horace invited her to take a seat, and then informed her that these were the children from the boats. Due to their parents' peripatetic employment they were always on the move.

'Schooling, in the usual sense of the word, is not, therefore, a viable proposition,' he concluded.

Miss Watts sat and listened patiently to his explanation. When he finished, she thanked him for the information and rose to her feet. Turning, she said half to him and half to herself, 'We must see what we can do about that!' and walked out of the office, leaving Horace more than a little confused.

A few days later she returned to the Wharf Office with what she said she firmly believed to be 'a viable proposition'.

'I think that was the phrase you used, young man.' She smiled at Horace over the tops of her spectacles. Next she proceeded to explain her plans to him and the wharf clerk, both of whom sat like small boys in her class, giving her their full attention.

'If your Company can provide me with an empty boat, and if they can make sure that it is weatherproof,' she began, 'I will undertake to fit it out, at my own expense, as a kind of "floating classroom". I can then teach the children from any boats that happen to be tied up at the Wharf for as long as they are here. Additionally,' she continued, 'I propose that I should run the school for half a term on a voluntary basis, with no payment. After that period, your Company and I can review the situation. If the school is proving to be a successful venture, then I would request to be paid a modest salary – nothing too grand – just sufficient to cover my expenses, plus a little more. If it is not a success, then the Company can have its boat back again and I will simply disappear and go off into a peaceful retirement.' She paused momentarily. 'Any questions?'

The two men were so impressed with her clarity of vision and the power of her argument – not to mention her strength of character – that the wharf clerk immediately agreed to put forward Miss Watts's proposal to his manager. This he did the same day, adding to it both his and Horace's strong recommendations that it should be accepted. He also laboured the point that if there was a school at the Wharf then it would enable both himself and Horace to spend more time on their work and less having to leave the office to prevent the boat children trespassing and generally misbehaving because they were bored and had nothing else to do!

An appointment was made and two of the managers from the Company's head office duly arrived at the Wharf. After a brief discussion the managers agreed to everything Miss Watts suggested. The two arguments that clinched it were Miss Watts telling them that if the Company did not accept her proposals, it would be 'responsible for breeding another generation of illiterates', and also that 'Any education is better than no education at all.' One of the managers confided to the wharf clerk afterwards that he had never felt so intimidated since his own school days!

The following week the Company arranged for a rather ancient, but freshly cleaned, narrowboat to be towed up to the Wharf and moored at the end. An hour or so later, two carpenters arrived with the necessary materials to erect a cabin roof, sides and a floor over the length of the hold. In the meantime, Miss Watts set about begging and borrowing old desks and spare books from the schools in the neighbourhood. After some weeks of hard work, negotiating, cajoling, pleading and cadging, she proudly announced that she had managed to acquire everything she needed to start, and that the school was open and ready for business. All she needed now were pupils.

So the school had begun and proved to be an immediate success. At certain times, when there were maintenance stoppages and the like, and the Wharf was full of boats, the children had to share desks because there were so many of them attending the classes. After the first half-term Miss Watts was put on the Company's payroll. She often told Horace that she felt far happier and much more fulfilled teaching the basics of reading, writing and arithmetic to her ever-changing class of boat children than she would ever have been finding some sort of charity work 'or whatever else retired single ladies find to do with their time'.

These days, however, Miss Watts was no longer in charge. She had passed away in her late seventies a few years previously, leaving the school with no teacher. But Horace, who had by that time become the wharf clerk, had a daughter. Her name was Emily, and she had trained as a teacher at St Peter's Training College in Peterborough. She was also not particularly happy at the elementary school where she was currently working. She was full of enthusiasm and her ideas were too modern for her headmaster. It seemed an obvious move for her to take over from Miss Watts. Horace 'had a word' and the job, with an increased salary, was hers.

In more recent years the boat that was being used as the schoolroom had started to leak and was getting beyond repair. Horace had noticed, however, that another result of the fall-off in trade was that the secure storeroom next to his office was hardly ever used any more. So one day the store room was cleared, cleaned from top to bottom and repainted throughout. Books, desks and other equipment collected by the school over the years were all moved, lock, stock and barrel, out of the boat and into the storeroom, which, from that day on, became the new schoolroom. The old boat was towed away and burned.

As wharf clerk it was Horace's responsibility to issue the 'orders' to the captains. These 'orders' were the information the captains needed to tell them where they were to take their boats to load, what the loads were, and where they were to be delivered, together with similar details for any return loads they may be fortunate enough to get. These return loads, or 'back loads' as they were called, were much sought after as the wages for travelling empty were less than when running loaded, and wages for 'laying in' – tied up and 'waiting for orders' – were lower still. These days, thought Horace, as he sat at his desk, there were precious few return loads to be had. There was little enough in the way of loads at all. He looked through the papers on his desk for the umpteenth time that day. There were still no new orders for any of the half-dozen pairs of boats he could see out of his office window. Neither these days was there an assistant wharf clerk to help him. The trade had reduced so much that one person was able to do all the work.

Horace, a portly man in his fifties, was liked and respected by the boatmen and their families, but they all knew that he took his job very seriously. When there were new orders to be issued or any information to be given out, Horace made sure that he dotted all the i's and crossed all the t's to make sure they fully understood what he was telling them. Bill had returned from Horace's office on more than one occasion, saying, "'e's a good man, Mr Roberts, but 'e never uses one word when 'alf a dozen'll do!'

Next door, his daughter Emily turned her attention to Izzie's mother.

'You know, we start at nine o'clock, sharp, Mrs Horne, so we like all the children to be here by about five to.'

'She'll be 'ere,' Maggie Horne nodded.

'I don't suppose you've any idea how long you'll be here at the Wharf?'

'No. Sorry. We're jus' waitin' for orders, see.'

'That's fine. I'm quite used to that. We'll just do the very best we can for Isobel while she's here. I'll see you again tomorrow, Isobel.'

Emily Roberts smiled when they had gone. 'Good for you, Mrs Horne!' she said to herself. She knew from earlier conversations with Maggie that she was keen on her daughter going to school, but that her husband was against it. She realised that Maggie had gone against his wishes and was prepared to stand up to him.

In the early autumn evening sunshine Maggie and Izzie saw that there were still five other pairs of boats moored along the canal, as there had been for nearly a week. In her mind's eye Maggie could see this Wharf as it used to be – back in the days before first the competition from the railways and then road transport had decimated the trade that had been the monopoly of the canals. When she was Izzie's age there were so many more boats tied up here – as far as the eye could see in both directions along the cut, as the canal was called by those who made their living on it. They would arrive during the day after finishing a run, pick up their orders for the next one, and be away again the following morning. The space they vacated would be filled by others arriving later that day, which would do the same. In Maggie's mind there could be no doubts, the trade was dying – and that was why she believed it was so important for Izzie to have some kind of an education.

Maggie and Izzie walked quickly from the schoolroom and back along the Wharf towards the pair of boats that were their floating home.

Each of the two boats was seventy feet in length and seven feet wide, hence they were called 'narrowboats.' One of them was equipped with a diesel engine and was known, as all canal boats with engines were, as 'the motor'. The Hornes' motor was called *Zeus*. The other boat of the pair did not have an engine and was towed on a rope behind the motor. This was known as 'the butty', and the Horne's was *Aphrodite*. All the Company's motors were named after Greek gods and the butties after goddesses. Usually, when they were on a run Maggie looked after *Aphrodite* while her husband steered *Zeus*. *Zeus's* cabin was rarely used except for storage because, although neither Izzie nor her father could smell it, Maggie always insisted it stank of diesel.

As she and Izzie approached the boats Bill Horne's tousled head appeared from *Zeus's* engine compartment. He was a well-built, stocky man in his late thirties, his lined, weathered boatman's face topped by a shock of unruly black hair. Izzie could feel her mother's tension as she gave her husband a peck on the cheek.

Izzie's father was a good man, a hardworking man, but a man with a stubborn streak. He had always maintained that the lack of work on the cut was only a temporary downturn, that it would pick up again in a year or two, and that the trade would continue to flourish well on into the future – in fact, for ever.

'That shoppin' took you a long ol' while today, didn't it?' he commented as they approached.

'Well,' Maggie began hesitantly, knowing full well what was coming, 'I stopped off at that there boat kids' school on the way back…,' she paused and took a deep breath, ''an' I signed our Izzie up.'

'You what?' Bill exclaimed, stopping what he was doing and staring at his wife. 'You done what? You signed our Izzie up for book learnin'? What the devil do she want wi' bloomin' book learnin'? Answer me that!'

Maggie sensed that yet another prolonged session of 'words' on the subject of their daughter's education was about to start, so she handed the bag of shopping to Izzie.

'Go an' put these 'ere away for us, will you, love? There's a good girl.' Izzie did as she was told and took the purchases on board and down into the tiny back cabin of *Aphrodite* to put them away in the cupboard.

Only eight feet in length, the boat cabin was home to all boating families. It was entered from the rear deck by means a pair of narrow double doors in the middle of the rear bulkhead, while a sliding hatch in the cabin roof made access and egress possible. A short flight of two or three steps led down into the cabin. Each cabin was fitted with a coal-fired kitchen range on the left-hand side, which provided heat and cooking facilities. Forward of the range was a cupboard, the door of which was hinged at the bottom so that it could be let down to form a table. It was in this cupboard that Izzie busied herself putting away the shopping.

But she could still hear her parents arguing. Her mother was saying, 'It won't do the girl no 'arm an' it ain't like she's got owt else to do while we're tied up 'ere an' waitin' for orders, now 'as she? An' besides, she says to me as she's changed 'er mind now an' she wants to go to school!'

'Now, you look 'ere, Maggie 'Orne,' retorted Bill. 'Neither you nor me never 'ad no book learnin'. We was both born on the boats an' we growed up on the boats an' we works on the boats. You don't need no bloomin' book learnin' to work on the boats. Our Izzie were born on the boats an' she'll grow up on the boats an' she'll git wed to a boatin' man an' she'll carry on workin' on the boats. So she don't need no bloomin' book learnin' neither, I tell you. She's only sayin' as she wants to go to the school now cos you're been on at 'er so much about 'er goin'! Tellin' 'er as 'ow she ought to go!'

'I jus' want what's the best for 'er.'

'An' you think I don't? I'm tellin' you! She don't need no bloomin' book learnin' while she's on the boats!' he repeated.

'But what if she don't wanna stay on the boats? What if she wants to go on the bank? What then?'

'Never 'appen!' Bill replied. 'Never 'appen! She's a child o' the cut, is our Izzie. She got cut water for blood, that one. Jus' like you an' me 'ave. She'll stay on the boats. You mark my words.'

'That's if there'll be any boats left for 'er to stay on.' Maggie knew she was now treading on dangerous ground, but decided to press home her point. 'Every time we ties up 'ere there's more an' more pairs waitin' longer an' longer for orders. I tell you, Bill, the trade's dyin'! It's dyin' right under your bloomin' nose, only you're too damn stubborn to see it!'

'I'm tol' you afore not to talk like that! Don't you never let me 'ear you talkin' like that again!' There was real anger in Bill's voice now. 'Like I tol' you time an' time again, there'll allus be work on the cut – allus! The trade'll pick up. You see if it don't. An' all this talk of a war – that'll make the cut busy again! Our Izzie'll be on the boats till she's an ol' woman.'

'Well, let's jus' say as signin' her up for that there school's give 'er a bit o' choice, then.' This was Maggie's parting shot as she turned away and disappeared into *Aphrodite*'s cabin to check on the cooking. Bill was about to say something else but realised he would have been addressing thin air so, thinking better of it, he just muttered 'Bloomin' book learnin'!' under his breath and returned to rubbing down *Zeus's* engine, which was mounted just forward of the cabin in what was known as 'the engine 'ole'.

After a short while the meal Maggie had left cooking during her shopping trip was ready. The cupboard door was let down to become the dining table and laid up for the meal. Bill came in and the three of them sat round it and tucked into mutton stew and dumplings.

As she ate, Izzie looked around the familiar little cabin that had always been her home. The tiny kitchen range was on the go practically all day, as her mother always managed to cook the dinner at the same time as she was steering the boat. Consequently, the cabin was always warm on cold days, and on warm ones leaving the sliding hatch in the roof and the doors open for a while soon cooled it down.

Opposite the range, on the right-hand side of the cabin, was the side bed, a built-in, fixed seat that doubled as a bed at night. There was a small stool as an additional seat. The steps doubled as a coal box and her father would often sit there after he had finished his day's work, a mug of tea in his hand.   Forward of this part of the cabin was what looked, at first sight, like an open area. What appeared to be a cupboard on the left-hand side of the boat was, in fact, hinged down at night to form a double bed, the cross bed. A curtain, hanging between the cupboard in the main cabin and the bed, was pulled across at night to divide the cross bed from the rest of the living quarters.

'So there's no orders again today, then?' Maggie asked, as they were finishing their meal. Her voice was quiet and calm, the earlier argument on the back of the boat forgotten.

'Not yit. I dropped by the office earlier, but Mr Roberts said as there wasn't nuthin' for any on us yit. Any'ow, Arthur an' Sam was both 'ere afore us, so we know as we're gonna 'ave a bit of a wait, like.' Izzie sat quietly and continued to eat her meal, relieved that the issue of her going to school had been forgotten.

Later that evening, when Bill and Maggie were settled in the cross bed, which in the down position took up the whole of the width of the small cabin, Izzie made herself comfortable on the side bed.

Because she had never known any other arrangement, she had never minded not having her own private space. Once the curtain had been pulled over, she found she could escape into her own little world. She could lie there in her bed, listening to the range singing away beside her, with a feeling of happiness, contentment and security. Lying there on this particular night she tried to imagine what it was going to be like starting school the following day. Miss Roberts had seemed to be a very kind and gentle lady.

She loved both her parents dearly and hated to see them arguing, but she was really looking forward to her first day at school tomorrow. It was going to be a big adventure, and although she had never told anyone else the real reason for it, she had within her a burning ambition. As of two months ago, more than anything else in the world, Izzie was dying to learn how to read!

Chapter 2

Difference of opinion

Izzie was aware of her parents' difference of opinion about the future of the canals. Her mother was convinced that competition from the railways and improvements in road transport would inevitably be the death of the canals. 'Every time I go shoppin' there's more an' more cars an' lorries everywhere,' she often said to Bill. Izzie had noticed that there seemed to be more and more goods trains on the lines that ran close to the canal. Her mother was certain that the lack of orders was a sure sign that the decline in the trade had already begun, and that it would get worse and worse until there would be nothing left to carry by water. The boatmen and their families would be out of a job and would have to find other employment – and accommodation – on the bank. Izzie realised that it was her mother's real fears for her future on the canals that had prompted her to suggest that she should go to the school on many previous occasions.

Her father's views were the complete opposite. He always maintained vehemently to anyone who was prepared to listen that the situation that they faced was only temporary and that in due time the trade would pick up again. All the business that had been lost to the railways and the road hauliers would come back to the cut when customers realised how much more reliable it was.

'If summat's gonna sit in a ware'ouse for weeks afore it's used there ain't no need for gittin' it there any quicker, is there?' was the question he always asked. 'An' you can shift an 'ell of a lot more wi' a gallon o' diesel on a boat than you can on a lorry,' he usually added, confident that the trade would carry on well into the future.

Consequently he could see no point at all in a school for boat

24

children because he firmly believed that the best schoolroom for boating people was the great outdoors, learning from experience about the wonders of nature. He had learned about the natural world from his own father, whose enthusiasm for the subject had been so strong that it had rubbed off on his son. Bill's speciality was the identification of different birds that were found along the cut. Very often when they were travelling along a rural stretch he would suddenly point towards a spot in the hedgerow and say, 'Look, our Izzie! It's a buntin'!' And she would follow his pointing finger with her eyes and see the bird that he was indicating. With her father's tuition, over the years, she had become almost as adept at recognising types of birds as he was.

At other times, when they were tied up in the evenings, after the engine had been turned off and everything was quiet, Bill would suddenly raise a finger to his lips, indicating that they should listen. The only sound they could hear would be a bird singing, and he would say, 'That's a warbler, that is.' He could recognise all the birds that inhabited the canals, the hedgerows and the surrounding fields by sight and by song. He considered it his God-given duty to pass this information on to his only child in the same way as his father had passed it on to him.

Bill was also adept at predicting the weather. Often the boats would be travelling along during a morning when the canal would be bathed in bright sunshine, and they would feel the warmth of a summer breeze. Izzie would make a comment to her father about it being such a lovely day. Bill would look carefully around at the sky, sniff loudly, and, after a short pause, reply, 'See them clouds up there, our Izzie? You mark my words, it'll be rain be night!' and it usually had been!

He had set about teaching Izzie how she, too, could recognise the different types of cloud. He did not know any of their proper names, nor did he know the science behind why they behaved the way they did, but he pointed them all out to her. He carefully described what each of the different types looked like and pointed out their individual features. He explained to her how to observe certain cloud formations in particular areas of the sky. He taught her how to look at them and see how, when both the direction and strength of the wind were taken into consideration, they could be the portents of the weather to come – good or bad.

He knew the countryside around the canals very well too. 'The countryside's like a great big larder!' he often said. At certain places where they stopped he would take Izzie out with him after dark and show her how to set snares for rabbits. Then the following morning they would get up very early, retrace their steps and see how many rabbits, if any, they had managed to catch. More often than not, because of Bill's knowledge gained from years of experience, they were richly rewarded. Initially, Izzie had felt a bit sorry for the poor rabbits, being caught and dying in this way, but these sorrowful thoughts were soon banished after her mother had skilfully converted them into a tasty stew or, better still, a rabbit pie!

'That's all the learnin' you need when you lives on the boats, our Izzie,' her father would often say when talking about his 'country skills', often adding, 'An' you don't wanna go fillin' your pretty little 'ead wi' none o' that there bloomin' book learnin'. It won't never do you no good!' And for most of her ten years she had been more than happy to agree with him.

The Wharf itself was nothing grand. It was basically a broad area of brick sets, with repairs here and there in concrete, with the buildings, all erected around the same time and all in red brick, set back from the water's edge. Viewed from the canal there was the Wharf Office, roughly in the centre of the buildings, with the little schoolroom to its left. Beyond that was a gap between two buildings where a road provided access for vehicles. This road led away behind the Wharf buildings, then turned to the left to join the main road. Close to the road was the wet dock and the dry dock, where the Company's boats were repaired, maintained and painted. Just beyond the docks, at the far end, stood the diesel pump where the motors could refuel. Next to the office in the opposite direction was what had originally been built as a stable block back in the days when the boats had been drawn by horses. Nowadays it was used as a store for many items that had accumulated over the years, such as old office furniture, but mainly spare parts for boats and their engines. Then came a narrow alleyway that led to the road. This was bordered on the other side by a coal store for the boats' ranges and for the office fire during the winter months. Finally, there was The Boat Inn, the pub that was used mainly by the boat crews.

Standing by the wall of the schoolroom was an old wooden barrel. It had been there for years, so long that no one could now remember who had put it there or why. But similarly, no one had felt inclined to take it away just in case it had been put there for some purpose.

It had a sort of purpose for Izzie. Despite all that her father said about 'bloomin' book learnin'' she had occasionally been sufficiently curious to want to have a peep through the windows of the schoolroom. Because of the building's previous use the windows were high up in the wall, well above eye level, so it was necessary to climb onto the barrel to see in. Looking through the windows, Izzie had observed some of the other boat children, all of whom she knew, sitting at desks in straight rows – and every single one of them, despite Emily's best efforts, was looking fed up, as all of them in their heart of hearts would rather have been on the cut.

In the past, every time her mother had suggested that she might go to the school her father, predictably, had always strongly objected, repeating yet again that boating folk had no need for education.

Izzie held an inordinate amount of respect for her father's opinion in all things. Up until recently, recalling what she had seen through the schoolroom window, she had always readily agreed with him on this matter, rather than going along with what her mother had suggested. 'I don't wanna sit in no row o' desks in no stuffy ol' schoolroom doin' no book learnin'! she had thought.

The children who attended the school often chided the few, including Izzie, who did not. Jeering at them, they implied that the real reason they did not go to school was that they were far too stupid to learn anything and that they would all grow up knowing nothing! Izzie put this attitude down to envy. She knew very well that they would much rather spend their time playing about on the Wharf.

'What are you learned today, then?' they often asked the pupils as they left the schoolroom at the end of the day. Whatever the answer, the retort was something along the lines of, 'That'll come in 'andy when you're workin' down Braunston, won't it?' At which point they would fall about laughing to the obvious discomfiture of the others. Perhaps because they were all tired after a day in school, they never realised the joke until it was too late. One of them always fell for it as they walked back to their boats.

Izzie knew that the teacher's name was Miss Roberts and that she was the daughter of Mr Roberts, who worked in the Wharf Office. She had sometimes seen her arrive at the schoolroom in the mornings and leave again in the evenings. On warm days she had seen her sitting outside the schoolroom at lunchtimes, eating her sandwiches with her father, but she had never spoken to her, just in case she might be asked awkward questions as to why she had never attended her school.

Of the few children who did not go to the school, Izzie was aware that some of their parents were of the same mind as her father. One or two of them were in the same situation as she was where mother said they should go but father said they should not – and father's word was law. With the others, it seemed that their parents had no inclination to send their offspring to school, leaving them to spend their time at the Wharf playing games or generally messing about.

To be fair to Izzie, at ten years of age she had grown out of playing. When she had finished her daily jobs on the boats, if it was not raining nor too cold, she would take herself off for a walk along the towpath, trying to identify for herself the species of birds just as her father had taught her. At first some of her expeditions had been more successful than others. Back in those days she would sometimes return, saying, 'I 'eard a fieldfare jus' down that way a bit this mornin', Dad!' Only to be told, 'Not this time o' year, you never, our Izzie!' But, nowadays, more often than not, he would congratulate her on birds she had identified.

Because of the nature of her father's work, Izzie knew the boat children, played with them, chatted with them, but they were never together long enough to become close friends.

If the weather was bad she usually stayed aboard *Aphrodite*. Her mother had taught her to sew, knit, embroider and crochet, and over the years she had become proficient in all of these. When new ones were required, she was proud to crochet the intricate edgings for the shelves by the range.

Their boats and the cans on the roof were decorated with traditional roses and castles. Her father had shown her how to paint them. She practised painting on her own special bowl. The Hornes' boats were both brightly painted in the Company livery of red, blue and yellow.

Although she spent many hours on her own, Izzie was not a lonely girl. She was content with her own company, to be with her patents, or to enjoy watching the cut go by.

As she had her jobs to do on the boats – polishing the brass and whitening the ropes – she had often wondered if she could have found time to fit in schooling as well – even if she had wanted to go. But that was then. This was now. Now, against her father's wishes, she was going to school. Now she would make time to go – and fit in her jobs. Now she was going to learn to read.

Chapter 3

Deaf to the written word

Izzie was sitting in the schoolroom, eager and excited, by ten minutes to nine the following morning. Her father had, rather grudgingly, wished her well as she and her mother had stepped off *Aphrodite* to walk the short distance along the Wharf to the schoolroom. Maggie had taken her inside and left her in Miss Roberts's care. Izzie had hung up her coat where she had been shown the previous day and had sat down at 'her' desk. Miss Roberts had welcomed her and introduced her to the rest of the class. There were only four other children there and Izzie already knew every one of them. There were the two Johnson boys, Raymond and Thomas from *Hephaestus* and *Nike*, Ivy Cox from *Eros* and *Clotho*, and Janet Beech from *Apollo* and *Gaia*. They had all smiled at her as she had taken her seat.

'What're you doin' 'ere?' Raymond asked. Izzie ignored him.

The problem for Emily Roberts was that all five of her charges were not only of different ages, but also of different abilities and at different stages of learning. Nine-year-old Ray Johnson and his brother Tom, two years younger, had already been to the school during two previous lay-overs. Ivy was ten, the same age as Izzie, and already knew the basics of reading and writing, while Janet, who was only five, had started at the school only a couple of days before Izzie. Emily chose a suitable book for Ivy and told her to read it quietly. She then set the boys an arithmetic exercise and devoted most of her time that morning to Janet and Izzie. She started at the beginning – it was all new for Izzie and revision for Janet.

Halfway through the morning there was a break in lessons of a quarter of an hour. It was raining hard, so before Emily went next door to see her father she told the children to stay in the schoolroom. As soon as she had gone, Ray Johnson shouted over to Izzie, 'Didn't think we'd ever see you in 'ere!'

'Allus said as there weren't no point in learnin', you did!' his brother added.

'I can change me mind, can't I?' Izzie retorted. Ivy came to her support. 'Leave 'er alone! She got as much rights to be 'ere as you two 'ave!' And with that the subject was dropped. The boys started to make darts from scraps of paper while the girls chatted quietly. Janet was eager to tell Izzie what school was like.

�֍

By the time she walked out of the schoolroom at the end of that first day Izzie was really beginning to wish that the orders her father and mother were awaiting so desperately would never arrive. She had enjoyed herself so much! She and Janet had sat together for most of the morning while Miss Roberts had been telling them about something called the alphabet, and how to recognise letters and the sounds they made. Then she showed them how letters could be put together to make words. In the afternoon they had all done some money sums. Miss Roberts gave them all some cardboard 'coins' and asked them to add and subtract different amounts. Emily was no longer surprised to find that, although none of her pupils could read a single word when they started their schooling, they were all very competent when it came to counting money! They played shops, taking it in turns to be the shopkeeper. At the end of the day they sat quietly while Emily read them a story.

When Izzie arrived back on *Aphrodite* she was bubbling over with excitement at all the wonderful things she had done at school, and she was also very anxious to show her parents how she could write the letters she had learned.

Izzie was aware that if there were no orders for them for too long the family budget would start to get tighter. But she had enjoyed her first school day so much! So it was with mixed feelings that she asked her father, 'Is there any orders come through today, Dad?'

'No, love,' he sighed. 'Not yit.' Despite her father's melancholy,

Izzie was delighted to be able to go to school again the following day.

When she walked in she found that Ivy was not there. Arthur Cox, her father, had received his orders late the previous afternoon and their boats had left early that morning. The day followed much the same pattern as the previous one, and Izzie began to learn how to put letters together herself to make simple words. Miss Roberts gave her a little notepad and a couple of pencils to practise writing the letters and words back at home on the boat.

After they had eaten that evening, she proudly showed her mother and father what she had learned. With two days of schooling, she had already learned how to write her own name! She gripped the pencil tightly, then slowly, and a little awkwardly, carefully saying the name of each letter as she formed it, wrote 'isobel' on a page of her notebook.

Bill looked at it for few seconds and grunted. 'Bloomin' book learnin'!' he muttered. 'Don't mean nuthin' to me. I'm goin' to The Boat.' And with that he put on his coat and cap, kissed his wife on the forehead and disappeared up the steps.

Izzie was not surprised by his response but she was a little hurt. Maggie explained that she should not be too upset by her father's reaction. It was just that he did not really understand. After all, Maggie explained, Izzie, as a girl of a mere ten years of age, had just done something very special. It was so special that neither her mother nor her father, nor any other member of her family, had ever been able to do it, not even as grown-ups.

'You're actually writ your own name!' Her mother was obviously very proud. 'Never in your life will you ever 'ave to scribble a cross on any bit o' paper an' then watch while someone else writes by your mark to say as it's you as 'as writ it – never!' Maggie was overjoyed at what she considered such a great achievement, and she told her daughter so.

'You dunno 'ow iggerant it makes you feel sometimes,' she continued, 'like when I 'ad to put a cross in that book to git you into the school. You won't never 'ave to do that cos now you can write your own name!' After a pause, she added, 'Don't you never tell your Dad as I said so, but I tell you what I reckon, an' it's this.

I reckon as underneath all that bluster an' goin' on about "bloomin' book learnin" an' such, I reckon 'e's jus' a little bit jealous on you – 'e'd never admit it, mind!'

A couple of days later the long-awaited orders arrived. Izzie came home from school to be told that they would be leaving early the following morning. She knew that it was necessary for them to leave the Wharf, but she was so sad that she would not be going to school again, not for the next little while, at least. She really liked Miss Roberts and she knew from what her teacher had said that she was getting on well with her lessons – particularly her reading. Over the past two days she had learned much more about the sounds the letters made and how they combined to make words. That afternoon, Miss Roberts had shown her a book with pictures of animals. Each picture had the name of the animal printed underneath it, and she had spent time with Izzie, explaining how the names were made up from the letters of the alphabet. Izzie had enjoyed this very much and was keen to get back to school to look at the rest of the book.

'We're loadin' coal up by Coventry an' takin' it to some pickle factory as is right on the cut, down London way,' Bill told her with a gleam in his eye. He was happy to have some work again. 'We could've got 'em ahead tonight but the coal yard won't be ready for us till late mornin' the day after tomorra.' It was then that Izzie had a sudden thought.

'I'll be back in a minute,' she called as she scampered back along the Wharf in the direction of the schoolroom. All the way there she was praying to herself that Miss Roberts would still be there and would not have left for home. She arrived, a little breathless, just as her teacher was putting on her coat and preparing to leave.

'Isobel! What is it?' Emily was surprised to see her. Panting to get her breath back, Izzie managed to tell her that they would be leaving early the next day.

'Well, it's very nice of you to come and tell me and to say "goodbye", Isobel, but you really needn't have bothered. I'm used to the children I teach leaving and starting at the school nearly every day.'

'It weren't that, Miss Roberts.'

'What was it then?' Emily Roberts asked. There was a long pause, then Izzie suddenly blurted out.

'Can I take me picture book wi' me while we're doin' the run ... please?'

Emily was amazed. Most of the children who came to her school were only there, it seemed, to get them out from under their parents' feet, and to stop them causing mayhem on the Wharf. Most of the time they made no secret of the fact that they did not want to be at school at all and certainly had no interest in learning anything.

This young lady, Isobel Horne, though, she was different. She was very different. Emily had noticed it soon on her very first day in school. She was actually interested in what Emily was teaching her. She was enthusiastic in all the lessons, but she was particularly excited about reading.

'Why, of course you can, Isobel.' Izzie went over to the bookcase and took out the book.

'Thank you ever so much, Miss Roberts. I'll bring it back when we're next this way, I promise.' She smiled as she made her way towards the door.

'Isobel!' called Emily. Izzie stopped in her tracks.

'Yes, Miss Roberts.' She turned to face her teacher.

'I'd like you to tell me something, please, if you can?' Izzie was wondering if she had done something wrong.

'What, Miss Roberts?' she asked, warily. 'Tell you what?'

Emily Roberts looked very serious. 'Why is it, Isobel, that you want to learn to read so badly?'

For a few moments Izzie looked at the floor, thinking hard, wondering if she should actually explain her reasons. She had never told anyone why she was so very keen to learn to read. She had not even told her mother. 'Me Mam'd think I were bein' a bit silly if I were to tell 'er!' she thought. But Miss Roberts was not her mother. Miss Roberts would understand. 'She won't think as I'm bein' a bit silly.' So when she slowly lifted her head to face her, Emily noticed that there was a slight reddening of her cheeks.

'Me Mam's ask me lots an' lots o' times if I wanted to go to school, but me Dad allus said as I didn't need no book learnin', as

'e calls it, an' it were a waste o' time, so I weren't bothered. But
then ... well ... summat sorta 'appened.'

'What was that?' Emily asked, intrigued.

'I dunno 'ow to tell you, really... It were a bit funny ... I s'pose.'
Emily Roberts winced inwardly for the umpteenth time. She had
long given up the unequal struggle of even attempting to correct
the boat children's spoken grammar.

'Well, tell me anyway – funny, or not.'

'Well ... I ain't never tol' nobody this afore – never – not even
me Mam! It were one day ... a couple o' month back now...,' Izzie
began rather hesitantly. 'We was tied up in Brum an' I were out
shoppin' wi' me Mam... She wanted to go an' git some meat, but
when we got to the butcher's there was so many folk in the shop as
she tol' me to wait for 'er outside in the street... Any'ow, while I
were stood there, waitin' for 'er, like, I were lookin' round about
me, lookin' up an' down the street. An' then I seen the shop as were
agin' the butcher's.'

At this point Izzie took a deep breath and an unstoppable torrent
of words began to tumble from her mouth, almost falling over each
other as she spoke. It was obvious to Emily that this young girl was
speaking from the darkest recesses of her heart.

'It were a bookshop, see, Miss Roberts, an' it were that chock full
o' books! There was rows an' rows on 'em, all on shelves an' that! I
'adn't never seen so many books altogether in one place afore. An'
I jus' stood there, lookin' at 'em through that shop winder, an' I got
to thinkin' to meself, like. An' I thought, when you says summat,
well, you jus' says it, like, don't you? You says the words once – an'
they're gone, ain't they? They're gone for ever. You can only sorta
git 'em back if you says 'em again. An' if it's a long time after, well,
you might 'ave forgot what it was as you said, any'ow. But if them
words as you said ... if they was summat that were sorta ... well ...
sorta important, summat really important, like, well, you don't
want 'em to be gone for ever, do you? You don't wanna forgit 'em.
You wanna keep 'em. You wanna keep 'em ... like ... for ever!
Well! If you knows 'ow to write them words, then you can write 'em
down on a bit o' paper, an' then they're there for ever, ain't they?
An' then anybody as knows 'ow to read can come along later, an'

they can read them words as you writ down. An' they can come an' read 'em for years an' years after. They can even come an' read 'em long after you're dead an' buried. An' then they git to know what it was as you said, all them years afore.' She paused for breath.

'An' lookin' at all them books in that there bookshop, I reckon as there must 'ave been a awful lot o' really important words as were said an' what needed to be writ down, a awful lot! But if you can't read them words as they writ, then they might as well not 'ave writ 'em down at all, might they? Like ... like when somebody says summat, only you can't 'ear 'em cos of the noise o' th' engine.' She paused for breath again, and when she spoke again it was in a more measured tone.

'So I says to meself, right there an' then, I says, "One day," I says, "I dunno 'ow I'm a-gonna do it, but one day I'm a-gonna learn 'ow to read proper, like. An' then I'm a-gonna come back 'ere – right 'ere – to this 'ere bookshop, agin' the butcher's in Brum, an' I'm a-gonna go in an' I'm a-gonna buy me a book an' then I'm a-gonna take it 'ome wi' me, an' then I'm a-gonna sit down an' then I'm a-gonna read it – an' I'm a-gonna read it all the way through!" Back then, o' course, I didn't know 'ow I were ever gonna learn to read, but some'ow ... some'ow, I jus' knew as one day I would...' Another pause.

'So that's why I wanna learn 'ow to read, Miss Roberts, so as I can read some o' them books. That's why I tol' me Mam as I wanted to come to your school. I were so 'appy when she brought me 'ere.'

Emily could feel tears pricking the backs of her eyes as she looked down at the very serious-faced young lady standing in front of her. She took a step backwards and sat down at her desk.

'Deaf to the written word!' she murmured, as she realised in amazement that she had never before, in all her teaching career, encountered such insight, such depth of thought, nor such single-mindedness in any of her many pupils. She was completely astounded by what she had just heard from the mouth of this ten-year-old boat girl.

'I better go,' Izzie said, looking out of the window. 'It's startin' to git dark.'

'No!' Emily Roberts stood up. 'Just wait a moment, please,

Isobel.' She walked over to a tall cupboard that stood in a corner of the schoolroom. Opening the cupboard, she spent a few moments searching inside. When she turned round there was another book in her hand.

'Take this one with you, as well, Isobel. It's for you to carry on with when you've finished the one you've already started.' Izzie's eyes widened with delight.

'Oh, thank you, Miss Roberts! Thank you ever so, ever so much! I'll bring 'em back. Honest, I will.'

'I know you will, Isobel, I know you will. Now, have a good run, won't you? Who knows? One of these days when you're somewhere at the other end of the country, you might even be able to write me a letter to tell me how your run is going!'

'I might jus' do that one o' these days. Bye, Miss Roberts – an' thank you again!' She ran back to *Zeus* and *Aphrodite*, beaming all over her face and clutching her precious books. As she approached the boats, her father was checking on the side cloths in readiness for the following day's loading.

'Where'd you 'ave to rush off to in such a 'urry, young lady?' he asked her. Hiding the books behind her back so that he would not see them, Izzie managed to sound quite convincing.

'Oh! I jus' went to say "bye-bye" to Miss Roberts cos we'll be gone long afore she gits 'ere tomorra, won't we?'

'Ah! That we will. Be gittin' 'em ahead first thing, as soon as it's light, love.' Bill was cheerful.

Izzie walked along the Wharf and stepped down into *Aphrodite*'s cabin. She whispered to her mother about how Miss Roberts had lent her some books to help with her reading while they were away.

'Where can I 'ide 'em so me Dad won't find 'em?' she asked her mother a little desperately.

'Give 'em 'ere!' Maggie said, taking the books and giving her daughter a conspiratorial wink. She pulled open the knife drawer below the cupboard and put the books right at the back of it. Already there, Izzie noticed, were the notepad and pencils she had brought home a few days before. ''E'll never think o' lookin' in there. But jus' you make sure as 'e don't see you readin' 'em, or 'e'll be off about your bloomin' book learnin' again!'

37

✳

The following morning they were out of bed, washed and dressed by half past five. Bill disappeared into *Zeus's* engine hole. After a few minutes all was ready. He flicked out the pedal on the enormous flywheel and gave it a good, strong push with his foot. Nothing happened the first three times he tried, but at the fourth attempt the engine caught and burst into life. The reassuring 'bomp-bomp-bomp' from the exhaust chimney on top of the cabin told them all was well. The engine was running. They would soon be on their way.

The boats had been moored, as they usually were at the Wharf, 'breasted up' – tied up to each other side by side. *Aphrodite* lay nearest to the towpath with *Zeus* tied up on her outside, so while Bill had been attending to the engine Izzie and Maggie had untied *Aphrodite's* fore and aft mooring ropes and were standing on the towpath holding the ropes to keep both boats close into the bank. As Bill emerged from the engine hole and took up his steering position on *Zeus's* rear deck, Maggie and Izzie climbed aboard *Aphrodite*.

Zeus had a very small rear deck called 'the counter'. At the back of it, connected directly to the rudder, was the tiller by which the boat was steered – a metal bar in the shape of a swan's neck angled up from the deck, then turned to form a handle for the steerer. The butty stern was very different and had changed little since the horse-drawn days. It was rather longer than the motor stern with a gunwale on each side. Unlike the motor, the butty was steered by means of a long, heavy wooden tiller, tapered at one end and curved. It was detachable from the 'ellum' or stern post at the back of the boat, with the thicker end inserted into the ellum post curving downwards so that the steerer could stand inside the rear doors and be comfortable. However, when the boats were moored it was replaced curving upwards, leaving clear headroom for easier access to the cabin.

Maggie took hold of *Aphrodite's* big wooden tiller and turned it to the steering position while Bill and Izzie loosened the ropes that bound the boats together. Izzie took care of the rope at the fore end while Bill attended to the stern. When the boats were separated, Bill turned his attention to *Zeus's* tiller and speed control while Izzie remained at *Aphrodite's* bow. Bill eased the motor gently forward and when *Zeus's* stern was almost level with *Aphrodite's* fore end, he threw Izzie the free end of the 'short snubber'. Catching the end of the rope with practised ease, Izzie quickly attached it to the dolly on the front deck. As Bill continued to take *Zeus* forward, the slack in the rope was gradually taken up and, as it tautened, *Aphrodite* eased away from the bank. With Maggie's expert steering, the butty followed *Zeus* in the semi-darkness along the crowded cut without so much as a touch on any of the other boats. Once the pair was under way, Izzie made her way back to *Aphrodite's* cabin, where she put the frying pan on the range and began making bacon sandwiches for their breakfast. They always had bacon sandwiches when they set off with new orders!

It was just beginning to get light when Izzie walked sure-footedly along *Aphrodite's* top planks to the front deck with her father's mug of tea in one hand and his bacon sandwich in the other. She called to him and he reduced speed a fraction to allow *Aphrodite* to catch up just close enough for his daughter to pass him his breakfast.

'Thanks, love,' he said after his first swallow of tea.

'Everythin' goin' awright, Dad?'

'Ah!' Bill returned the speed control to its normal running position, his mouth full of bread and fried bacon. 'We'll be up at that coal yard by 'leven tomorra.'

They travelled on along, passing under 'Skew Bridge', skewed because it had been built at an angle to accommodate a road. The canal there rounded a tight bend, making it something of a challenge for the novice steerer. Bill and Maggie, though, were far from novices and had negotiated Skew Bridge – and the bend – many times before. When they passed under it in the opposite direction, returning to the Wharf, it always made Izzie's heart lift. Skew Bridge was special. It meant that they would soon be tying up. She always felt very happy and contented when they were at the Wharf; perhaps because that was where she had been born; perhaps because, apart from the pair of boats, it was the nearest thing she had to somewhere she could call 'home'.

Because she felt so happy there, Izzie always had mixed emotions when beginning a run. She was pleased because she knew her father would be happy having work to do, but she was also sad to be leaving the Wharf. Part of her was happy to be on the move again, but, as she looked back over her shoulder at the Skew Bridge, another part of her could not wait until they passed under it again on their way back. And now she had another reason for wanting to be back there – the school, Miss Roberts – and her burning ambition to read.

The following morning, as dawn turned into day, a watery sun rose in the sky. It was going to be cool, typical of early autumn. Izzie was snug in *Aphrodite*'s cabin. She had taken the animal picture book from the back of the drawer and was studying it intently. Her mother cast an occasional glance down into the cabin, proud to see that Izzie was so enthusiastic about learning to read. Had she been aware of the effect of leaving her daughter to wait outside the butcher's shop in Birmingham, she would have been even more convinced that she had made the right decision to take her to the school.

After a while Izzie stood up and held the book in front of her mother. 'Look, Mam. It's a picture of a cat. An' that's what that says – c-a-t, "cat"!'

Maggie was a past mistress at multi-tasking. She could steer the butty, cook, and pay attention to her daughter all at the same time. 'That's clever!' she commented.

Izzie turned a page in her book. It was a picture of a dog. 'That word there says d-o-g, "dog"!'

Maggie smiled and Izzie felt very proud. 'Why don't you cover up the picture with your 'and an' see if you can read the word wi'out lookin' at the picture?' she suggested.

Izzie turned to the next page. 'C-o-w – co-ooh?' Izzie queried. As she showed her mother the page, her hand moved away from the picture.

'That's a cow, ain't it?' Maggie said.

Izzie looked. 'C-o-w, "cow",' she said.

And so the journey passed with Izzie working out the names of the animals in her book, then looking at the pictures to see if she was correct. Then she turned to the other book Miss Roberts had given her. It was similar, but instead of animals it had pictures of clothes.

'Look, Mam. See – c-o-a-t, "coat". I reckon if that 'cuh' were a 'buh' instead, it'd say "boat".'

'Well, I dunno, but I reckon you could be right at that!' Maggie smiled contentedly. Her husband was happy. Her daughter was happy. What more could she want?

A distant queue of waiting pairs came into view as *Zeus* and *Aphrodite* approached the coal yard near Coventry. It was a yard they had passed many times before, but this was the first time they had to load there for many years. As they joined the back of the queue, Izzie heard a distant church clock chime eleven times and thought, 'Me Dad might not be able to read or even write 'is own name, but 'e can judge 'is times on the cut almost to the minute! Both Bill and Maggie were relieved to see that on the right-hand bank of the canal was a hopper for loading the coal.

Izzie watched as the coal was lifted into the hopper by a bucket elevator, a continuous belt with buckets attached to it that carried the coal up from the ground and emptied it into the hopper. A man on a bulldozer was busy pushing the coal into a pile from where two more men were shovelling it into the buckets. Loading by hopper, Bill and Maggie would avoid the backbreaking work of shovelling the coal by hand. Nearly all of the seventy-foot length of both boats was taken up by the hold where the cargo was carried, a space that took a lot of filling!

By the time their pair was nearing the head of the queue it was nearly a quarter to twelve. Swinging *Zeus's* stern towards the bank, Bill told Izzie to get the orders Horace had given him from the ticket drawer. With the orders in hand, she jumped off and went to the hut next to the hopper.

'Mornin',' the man in the hut greeted her.

'Mornin',' she replied, handing him the orders. He read: 'Steerer Horne with *Zeus* and *Aphrodite* ... order for fifty ton to go to ... Blake's Pickles.' He looked at Izzie.

'Horne?' he said again. 'My God! You were a little baby last time your Dad came and loaded here! And look at you now!' Izzie smiled, a bit embarrassed. The man checked his book.

'Ah, here you are!' He wrote something, then looked at his watch and entered the time. Pushing the book towards Izzie, he handed her his pen.

'Sign here, please, young lady.' Izzie took the pen and carefully wrote 'isobel'. He took the book back and looked at what she had written.

'Very good!' he said as he wrote 'Horne' after it. 'Tell your Dad to load up next.' He wrote out a loading note and gave it to Izzie with the orders.

'Thanks, Mister. Bye!' she said as she left the hut and jumped back on board.

As they came to be loaded she crossed over to *Aphrodite* and closed the doors and slide. She saw the man who was controlling the hopper – his face was black with coal dust. As he released the coal into the boats, great clouds of the stuff billowed into the air.

Between them, Bill and Maggie skilfully manoeuvred their boats so that first *Zeus* then *Aphrodite* were properly loaded to ensure that the boats 'swam' properly, with a minimum of redistribution required. Bill was proud that he and Maggie had this skill. They had had years of practice. 'We do awright as a team, me an' the missus,' Bill thought.

Soon they had put away their shovels, turned at the winding hole just beyond the coal yard, clothed up the sides to protect the cargo, and started on their way.

The sky gradually clouded over and a light drizzle began to fall as they worked through the shallow lock at Sutton's Stop to start their long journey across to the Grand Union Canal, then on down to London. Despite the weather, Bill looked back at Maggie, a broad grin on his face, and she smiled back at him. Maggie looked down into *Aphrodite*'s cabin at Izzie, who was practising how to write the names of the animals in her book. As Izzie looked up from her studies, they too, exchanged a smile. The weather may have been wet and the air may have been cool, and autumn may have been lumbering inexorably into winter, but to all three of them it felt so good to be travelling with a full load once again.

Chapter 4

The pickle factory

When they were on a run Izzie missed the Wharf, and although she was happy with her own company she missed having the other children to talk to. This time, although she had only been there a matter of a few days, it surprised her how much she missed the school and, as the pair made its way along the canal, she wondered what new things she would have been learning, had she still been there.

However, when they were travelling with a load her father was happy, which meant that her mother was happy. On a run they all had set tasks. Izzie's jobs consisted of looking after the brasses and rope. Most metalwork on the boats was brass and it was a point of pride with boatmen that this was always kept polished. There was also an elaborate display of ornamental rope work which had to be regularly whitened to keep it looking smart and decorative. However, when they were approaching a flight of locks Izzie had another job – 'lock wheeling'.

Working locks was a tiring business made easier if the flight they were approaching was 'for' them, meaning the water was at the right level and the gates open ready for the boats to go in. If the locks were 'against' them, the far gates would be open and had to be closed before the paddles could be wound with the windlass to get the water to the right level. The boatmen called a flight where the locks were 'for' them 'a good road', while a flight 'against' them 'a bad road'.

Some distance ahead of each flight, as they approached a bridge hole, Bill would slow *Zeus* down, lift the rickety old bicycle from its home in front of the engine hole and drop it onto the towpath. Izzie rode the bike to the first lock to make sure it was ready for the pair to go straight in as soon as they arrived.

Lock wheeling was tiring work. To begin with it was hard cycling along the bumpy towpath. The bike was an old-fashioned type with no gears and 'sit-up-and-beg' handlebars. Having set the first lock, Izzie then waited for the boats. Once they were safely in the lock, it was time to get to work again, closing the gates behind the boats and drawing the paddles. She then had to pedal along to the next lock where the whole process was repeated throughout the entire flight. Only when the last lock in the flight had been set and the boats had passed through it could Izzie rest.

All the while she needed to keep a lookout for boats approaching from the opposite direction. Once, she had made the mistake of setting a lock for her father's pair, only to see another pair coming the other way that were very much closer to the lock that she had just set 'against' them! Neither the boatman nor his wife were very happy about this state of affairs and had informed Izzie so in no uncertain terms. They had also remonstrated with Bill and Maggie when they passed them. Bill had explained that Izzie was still learning, but the experience chastened her so that she never made that mistake again!

If the flight consisted of broad locks – wide enough to take two boats side by side – the pair would be 'breasted up' while Izzie prepared the locks. Both boats could then be steered by either Bill or Maggie, leaving the other free to help Izzie to work the paddles and gates. In narrow locks, however, there was only room for one boat at a time, so *Zeus* would go through first and *Aphrodite* would have to be 'bow hauled' through afterwards by Maggie or Izzie using the ropes.

Izzie had been lock wheeling from as soon as she was old enough to wind the paddles, open and close the gates and ride the bike. Like all the other children of the cut, she had built up her strength as she had grown. She had become used to the work although it was hard at times. In fact, on sunny days she found that she enjoyed it. She was not as enthusiastic when it was cold and windy or raining, but on this day the rain had passed over and there were a few rays of sunshine poking through the clouds. It was mild and Izzie was very happy with life.

Eventually the pair cleared at the last lock. Bill lifted the bicycle back onto *Zeus* and, as Izzie stepped aboard *Aphrodite*, her mother handed her a hot cup of tea.

'You'll be needin' this after all them locks, love.'

'Thanks, Mam.' Izzie ducked down into the cabin to sit down for a rest. It had been a long flight and the gates had been heavy to move.

Her mother had left the cupboard open with the packet of tea on it. As Izzie sipped from her mug, she looked at the packet. There were two words on it. She knew the second of them must be 'tea' because that was what was in the packet, so she tried to sound out the letters of the first word. 'M-a-z-a-w-a-t-t-e-e!' she said. 'That sounds like a rum ol' word!' she thought. 'I must remember to ask Miss Roberts about that 'un when I gits back to school.'

✳

Some days later, when they were sitting in the cabin after their evening meal, Izzie asked her father when he thought they would arrive at the pickle factory.

'Late tomorra af'noon if we gits a good road. I reckon as 'ow we'll tie up there overnight an' then unload come the morning.'

The following afternoon Bill noted the number on one of the bridges and shouted back to his wife that their destination should shortly be coming up on the left. As he did so, he slowed the motor down so that the pair would be easier to stop. As they rounded the next bend he noticed a red-brick building set back from the water's edge with a large expanse of concrete in front of it. It was a building they had passed many times on previous runs, but this was the first time they had had to stop there. The building had a tall chimney at one end that was belching out black smoke into the darkening sky, and there was a strong smell of onions and vinegar in the air. 'I reckon as that'll be the place!' Bill shouted.

'Smells like it might be!' Maggie shouted back. They steered the boats towards the towpath. Bill gave *Zeus* a burst in reverse, then dropped her into neutral. He and Maggie stepped onto the bank, each with a rope. As the ropes tautened, the pair of boats came to a halt tucked in close to the bank. Izzie stepped off the boat and took her father's rope. While she and Maggie held the pair on the ropes, Bill went off in search of someone at the works.

After a few minutes he returned with a man in overalls. 'This is the place!' he shouted. 'We can tie up 'ere!' His wife and daughter secured the ropes they had been holding to some metal mooring rings concreted into the side. Bill introduced the man as Tom Speechley, the works manager.

'You'll be all right there till mornin',' Tom said. 'I'll send a couple o' me lads down wi' shovels just after eight o'clock. They'll 'elp you with the unloadin'.' This was something of a relief to Maggie as at many places where they delivered coal it was down to the boatman and his crew – her – to shovel the coal out of the holds and onto the wharves. That was heavy work, and with only one man and one woman working the shovels it took a very long time to empty two full boatloads of coal – around fifty tons!

While Maggie was preparing their meal with Izzie's assistance, Bill decided that, as they had never tied up in this part of London before, he would go for a walk. He was back after a short while with news that there was a cinema nearby and suggested an evening out at 'the pictures'. Izzie was very excited. Going to the cinema was real treat that only ever happened on the rare occasions when they were tied up overnight near a picture house, and then only if her father could afford to take them. Maggie enjoyed the cinema too. It made a change from spending the evening on the boat or in a pub. After they had eaten, they quickly got themselves ready and walked through the busy streets the short distance to The Hippodrome. The film showing was called *Bringing Up Baby*. It was very funny and Izzie laughed so much that at one point she was convinced she would burst! Having had such an enjoyable evening, it was a very happy family who strolled back to the boats late that night, Bill and Maggie arm in arm, and Izzie walking next to them.

True to Tom Speechley's word, at five past eight the following morning two strong-looking young men, carrying shovels, approached the boats. Maggie and Izzie were washing up the breakfast things and Bill was standing ready, leaning on his shovel, waiting for them. 'Where are we puttin' it?' he asked.

One of the men pointed to an area of the concrete wharf in front of the factory. 'Just 'ere'll do. Then we can barra it over as we wan' it.'

'Best git started, then,' Bill replied, burying the blade of his shovel in the mound of coal in *Zeus*'s hold. The other two followed his lead.

Unloading coal was one of the dirtiest and most tiring jobs a boatman ever had to do. The weather was fine so Bill and the other two did not get soaked while they were working, but a light shower would have settled the coal dust and would have saved them from working in a permanent cloud of the filthy stuff.

After about an hour Maggie appeared carrying a tray with three steaming mugs of strong tea on it. The faces of the three men lit up at the sight, and they took a short rest while they drank. She repeated this at regular intervals until one o'clock, when she announced that a meal was ready. The men from the pickle factory, who they now knew as John and Dick, put down their shovels and started to make their way back towards the factory.

'An' where do you two think you're off to, then?' Maggie called after them.

'Gettin' our sarnies, love,' Dick called back.

'You can't be doin' 'eavy ol' work like this on san'wiches!' Maggie retorted. 'Git yourselves back over 'ere. I'm made enough for all on us.'

The two men stopped, looked at each other, then turned and made their way back to the boats. 'This is very kind o' you, Mrs…?' John began.

'It's Maggie, an' it's very kind o' you to be 'elpin' my Bill wi' all the unloadin'! If you two 'adn't been 'ere, I should've 'ad to 'ave done it. Now, come on board, both on you. It'll be a bit of a squash, but I reckon as 'ow we'll manage.'

It was indeed a bit of a squash with all five of them in *Aphrodite*'s tiny cabin, but they coped. John squeezed onto the side bed with Bill and Maggie, while Izzie sat on the stool and Dick on the steps, all balancing their plates on their knees. The men were very hungry after their morning's exertions and the stew and potatoes disappeared from their plates in no time. Maggie then reached across to the range and produced a large spotted dick and a bowl of custard.

'My favourite!' Dick exclaimed. 'Named after me, you know!'

'Now you come to mention it,' John laughed, 'you are a bit of a spotty 'Erbert, ain't you?'

''Ark at 'im!' Dick addressed the others. ' I tell you, wi' mates like 'im, a bloke don't need too many enemies – an' that's the truth!' Another round of tea followed as the laughter continued.

'That was lovely, Mrs ... er Maggie!' John said as he drained his mug.

'An' you two needn't be bringin' no san'wiches tomorra neither,' said Maggie. 'D'you wan' another cup?' After second mugs of tea all round, the men reluctantly left the snug cabin and returned to their work with the shovels.

All through the morning Izzie had taken advantage of her father's being busy outside and, when she was not helping with the cooking or the endless mugs of tea, she had been studying her books. She had no way of knowing how well she was doing, but she had an idea that with each page she was taking less and less time to make out the word and check it against the picture. Most times she was correct, 'So I mus' be doin' it awright!' she thought.

The men worked steadily through the afternoon, with more cups of tea provided by Maggie and Izzie, and *Zeus* had been emptied by dusk.

'Same time tomorra?' called Bill as the men shouldered their shovels and prepared to go home.

'We'll be 'ere, Bill, mate!' John replied. Bill came back on board, his face and hands black with coal dust. Maggie had a kettle of hot water ready for him to wash.

'We're done awright today,' he said as he dried himself. 'We're unloaded the motor in a day. They're good lads, them two are.'

'They liked my tea!' Maggie answered.

'Ah!' Bill agreed, 'an' your stew an' your spotted dick!'

'Tomorra,' she continued, 'will you ask 'em if there's any slipper baths near 'ere? You'll be needin' a bath after unloadin' all this 'ere coal – an' me and Izzie could wi' one an' all.'

'I'll ask 'em, love.'

The main building of the pickle factory had originally been a warehouse, used for storing cargoes back in the days when the canal was much busier. As a result, the wharf was long enough for the boats to be moored in line, one behind the other, rather than breasted up. So when John and Dick arrived at eight o'clock the following morning, the three men began working straight away on emptying *Aphrodite*.

Between the seemingly endless supply of tea and preparing a midday meal for five, Maggie went into the pickle factory and asked Tom if she could use the telephone. He showed her into his small office, where she rang Horace Roberts. 'They'll 'ave finished the unloadin' by tonight, Mr Roberts,' she told him. Back at the Wharf, Horace mentally braced himself for the question he knew was coming next. 'Is there a chance of any back load?' Maggie asked, more in hope than in expectation.

'Afraid not, Maggie,' Horace apologised. 'You'll have to come back up here empty and wait for orders as usual.'

Maggie finished her call, thanked Tom for the use of his telephone and went to convey the news to Bill. He clicked his tongue and looked up at the sky. 'Ah, well!' he said, and went back to his shovelling.

After they had finished their midday meal Bill enquired about the slipper baths.

'I walk right past 'em on me way 'ome,' said Dick. 'I can easy show you where they are.'

So, at the end of the day, as soon as *Aphrodite* was empty, they all picked up soap and towels and walked with Dick to the baths.

A little while later, Izzie was relaxing in the rare luxury of a hot bath. She was not sorry to hear that they would be returning straight to the Wharf without having to go elsewhere to pick up a return load, because that meant she would soon be going back to school. She could not wait to show Miss Roberts how well she had progressed.

❋

The next few days, as the pair was making its steady progress back to the Wharf, could not pass quickly enough for Izzie. For the first time on a run she whiled away the time by looking at the signs and notices they passed on the way. She could not read all the words, but some of them she was sure she had worked out. Her book with pictures of clothes in had a picture of a coat so she knew the sounds that 'c', 'o', and 'a' made. When they passed a yard with piles of coal in it and she spotted 'coal' written on the merchant's sign, she realised that that was what it said. When she saw it she again remembered the name of the pub at the Wharf, The Boat Inn. She had been right! If 'c-o-a-t' spelled 'coat', then 'b-o-a-t' must spell 'boat'. It all seemed so logical as the letters fell into place and made sense. There was the odd problem – how did 't-h-e' end up as 'the'? She resolved to ask Miss Roberts about this when they got back. She wrote these words down in her notebook too, together with other words she had seen and thought she had worked out.

As they were leaving London they met a pair of Pickford's boats. She knew they were Pickford's because of the colours and way they were painted. This time, however, she paid careful attention to what was written on the side. She knew from her animal book what 'p' and 'i' were from the picture of a pig, and she also knew the sound 'c' and 'k' made from the picture of the duck. What she could not work out, though, was how 'f-o-r-d-s' came to be 'fuds' – something else to go in her notebook and to ask Miss Roberts about on their return to the Wharf!

Eventually, early on a cold, dreary evening, Izzie caught sight of the spire of a familiar village church. To her this church spire was special because, in her mind, it fulfilled the same purpose when they approached the Wharf from the south as the Skew Bridge did when they were coming from the north. It was a sign that she would very soon be back home, tied up again at her beloved Wharf.

Soon after passing the church, the pair nosed into the Wharf and was secured. Both Horace and his daughter had gone home, so they would both have to wait until morning – Bill to ask for any orders, and Izzie to go back to school.

Emily Roberts's face lit up in a broad smile as her star pupil entered the schoolroom just before five to nine the following day. Izzie proudly handed back to her the books she had borrowed.

'I'm read all these 'uns, Miss Roberts. Thanks for lendin' 'em to me.'

As the rest of the day went by, Emily discovered that her pupil had, indeed, worked very hard at her reading while she had been away and was thrilled to see how much Izzie had learned. During the day she told Izzie that the words she had looked at so far were all called 'nouns' and that they were words for naming things. Izzie understood. Miss Roberts then spent some time explaining that there were other words she needed to learn called 'verbs', which were what she described as 'doing' words. She also told Izzie that when words are put together properly they make something called a sentence.

'Every sentence,' she said, 'has to have at least one "naming" word and a "doing" word in it.'

Izzie had to think about that and asked some questions, but eventually, towards the end of the day, she thought she had grasped it. Miss Roberts told her that 'Birds sing' was a sentence. After a few moments' thought, Izzie asked. 'Is "Dogs bark" a sentence an' all?'

'Yes, it is! Well done, Izzie!' her teacher responded. Izzie asked her about the problems she had had in reading the signs she had seen – 'the' and the last part of 'Pickfords', among others. Miss Roberts told her that these were 'funny' words that she would explain more about the next time they were tied up at the Wharf.

Far too soon it was time for school to end. 'See you tomorra, Miss Roberts!' Izzie called as she left.

'See you tomorrow, Isobel,' Emily responded with a smile.

The result of her father's encounter with Emily's father was not so happy. 'Nothing at the minute, I'm afraid, Bill,' Horace told him. 'I'll let you know as soon as anything comes in.'

Bill returned and told Maggie. She was about to say, 'What did I tell you? The cut's dyin'.' But she stopped herself, seeing that her husband was upset and realising that it would only lead to yet another argument.

It was mid-afternoon a few days later when Horace tapped on the side of *Aphrodite*'s cabin. 'May I come aboard?' he shouted.

'Ah! Come on in, Mr Roberts,' Bill called back as he stood up and pushed open the cabin doors. Horace stepped inside. "'Ave you got summat for us?'

'I have!' Horace seemed cheerful, 'and I think you're going to like it. That pickle factory run you just did with the coal from Coventry – it looks like it's going to be a regular run, at least for a while, anyway. I had a telephone call from a Mr Speechley, was it?'

'Ah, Tom Speechley – 'e's the works manager bloke.'

'Well, he says he was really impressed with how quickly you got the coal down there. Oh, and there was something about some most acceptable dinners for a couple of his men.' Horace smiled at Maggie.

'Them lads of 'is worked damned 'ard. You can't expect 'em to work as 'ard as that on a few san'wiches, now, can you?' she said.

'I don't expect you can,' Horace continued. 'Anyway, apparently that first run you did was for a sort of trial for a new customer at the pickle factory. Well, the customer was pleased with the result and has given them a big order. Mr Speechley says he thinks it might be a Government order. He doesn't know much about it, but he says that from an odd bit of a conversation he overheard his boss having on the phone, he thinks that it might be something to do with this war that's probably going to happen.'

'I'm 'eard a lot o' folk goin' on about a war,' Maggie chipped in. 'What's it all about, Mr Roberts?'

Horace settled himself down for a long explanation. Bill and Maggie looked at each other and smiled. Mr Roberts always enjoyed giving long and detailed explanations!

'Well...,' Horace began to explain as he sat down on the step, 'it's the Germans. Their Chancellor – that's like their President – he's called Herr Hitler and he's what they call a Nazi. Well, he's got some notion into his head about some bit of land or other. It's called the Sudetenland, or something like that. Now, at the minute, this piece of land belongs to Czechoslovakia, but this Hitler chap, he thinks it should really belong to Germany. Of course, the Czechs are objecting to this and saying it's theirs and they intend keeping hold of it. But Hitler's saying that they pinched it from Germany in the first place and if they don't give it back then he'll just march in there with his army and take it back off them by force.'

'Do you think this 'Itler bloke'd do that?' Maggie asked.

'I think he would. He's already sent his troops into Austria and declared that from now on Austria's not an independent country any more. It's part of Germany now, he says!'

'Yeah, but 'ow's all that 'appenin' over there goin' to affect us an' what we're doin' over 'ere?' Bill asked.

'Well, Mr Chamberlain says he doesn't think there's going to be a war. He seems to think that what this Hitler chap's getting up to in mainland Europe is those countries' affair and it's up to them to sort it out between themselves. He doesn't seem to think we should get involved. But then there's Winston Churchill!'

'I'm 'eard of 'im, an all,' Maggie said.

'Well now, he sees it very differently from Chamberlain. He's convinced that Hitler won't just stop there,' Horace continued. 'He thinks that, once the Nazis have got their hands on this Sudetenland place, they won't be satisfied with that. He thinks they'll try and take over the whole of Czechoslovakia next. Then he says after that they'll want to take over Poland too, and he doesn't think they'll stop there either. He's absolutely sure that Hitler wants to take over all of Europe … and that includes us, over here in Britain!'

'I don't much like the sound o' that – 'e sounds a right nasty piece o' work, this 'Itler bloke!' Maggie interjected.

'Well, Churchill, he's convinced that there's definitely going to be a war. Some of the other MPs, though, they're saying he's got it all wrong and they're calling him a "warmonger" and suchlike.' He paused for a while. 'Personally, though, I think he might have a point.'

Horace removed his glasses and, taking a clean white handkerchief from the breast pocket of his jacket, proceeded to polish them. Bill took advantage of Horace's pause in the explanation.

'An' you say Tom Speechley reckons as that's what this 'ere pickle factory contract's all about?'

'I don't know for sure, but I suppose it could be.'

'Git off!' Bill snorted. 'What would the Government want wi' pickled onions if they're s'posed to be gittin' ready to fight a war? If they are gittin' ready to fight a war, that is. It'd be guns an' bullets an' stuff like that as they'd want – not pickles. I bet you any money you like it's nowt but a bloomin' rumour. The cut's allus rife wi' rumours – allus 'as been!'

'Well, I don't know. Perhaps they want pickles for making some gas or something?' Horace surmised.

'Didn't the Germans use some sort o' gas agin' our soldiers in the last war?' Maggie asked.

'Yes, they did,' said Horace. 'Mustard gas, it was called. I remember seeing some of the chaps who'd been affected by it. Horrible stuff it was!' He stood up to leave. 'But anyway, rumour or no rumour, war or no war, you're due to load up with coal up near Coventry again in three days' time.'

'Thank you, Mr Roberts. We'll be there!'

Izzie learned the news of their imminent departure when she returned from school later that afternoon. 'At least,' she thought, 'this time I can tell Miss Roberts a 'ole day afore we 'as to go.'

Although their world often appeared to be a long, thin ribbon of water, isolated from the outside world, Bill and Maggie, like others in the country, had noticed unusual preparations as they passed through the towns on their runs. Both of them remembered the Great War all too clearly and were uneasy at the thought of another conflict. Izzie had asked a few questions and had watched the newsreel at the cinema, but she seemed unconcerned. Having discussed the matter before she came home, her parents had decided that they should not risk frightening her by saying anything about the possibility of a war.

Izzie gave Emily the news when she arrived in the schoolroom the following morning. During the day Emily told Izzie about how, when two letters appear together, they sometimes make a different sound from when they are written separately, such as 'ar', 'er' 'or' and 'th'.

'I'll look out some more books for you to take with you, Isobel,' Emily said. Having looked at the words Izzie had written in her notebook, Emily was able to select books that would consolidate what she had already learned, then move her on to the 'doing' words. As Izzie reached for her coat from the peg at the end of the school day, Miss Roberts handed her five new books. 'Five?' exclaimed Izzie.

'Well, you're getting on so well now with your letters and the sounds they make that you're starting to read through them a lot more quickly than you could before. Five books should see you through your next run, I think.' Izzie looked at the books. 'Read these two first,' Miss Roberts said, holding up two of the books. This one is all about the "doing" words we talked about, and this one is all about the "funny" words that I was going to talk to you about the next time you were tied up, but you've got on so well in the last couple of days that I think you might be able to cope with them now. These other three books are little stories with pictures for you to move on to when you've finished the first two.' She opened one to show Izzie. 'You see? There is a picture with a sentence or two written underneath it. The sentence describes what's happening in the picture.'

'Oh, yeah!' Izzie exclaimed. She thanked Miss Roberts and ran back to the boats.

She noticed that her father was sitting on *Zeus*'s cabin roof, busy splicing a rope, so, quickly running down into *Aphrodite*'s cabin, she hid her books at the back of the knife drawer as she had done previously.

'You're got some more books, then?' her mother asked her in a half-whisper. Izzie told her what Miss Roberts had said about her progress.

'That's really good, love!' Maggie said. 'I'm real proud on you! Perhaps one o' these days you might even learn me to read an' write a bit, an' all.'

Just then Bill entered the cabin, so the subject was immediately dropped. 'It's gonna be a cold 'un tonight,' he said as he sat down. 'Winter's comin' awright – an' it's comin' wi' a vengeance!'

Izzie looked out through the hatch. It was just beginning to get dark. The sky was so clear that she could see the stars beginning to appear. As she looked upwards a chill breath of wind blew in through the hatchway and made her so cold that she shivered.

'Shut them doors up an' keep the warm in, gel,' her mother said. Izzie did not need to be told twice.

They left for the coal yard near Coventry early the following day and were loaded up and on their way to London by late afternoon a couple of days later. John and Dick were again on hand to help with the unloading when they arrived and the boats were soon turned round and making their way back to the Wharf, again, unfortunately, empty.

Izzie spent more time with her books. The last two books Emily had lent her were about animals – one about a cat and the other about a dog. Each page had a picture on it of the animal doing something and a sentence below it describing what was happening in the picture. She opened the book about the cat. There was a picture of the cat chasing a mouse. Pointing to each word with her finger, as Miss Roberts had taught her she read slowly, 'The ... cat ... runs ... after ... a ... mouse.' On the next page the cat was chasing the mouse through an open door. 'The ... cat ... d-o-e-s...,' she read. 'That's one o' them tricky words!' she thought. Why's "d-o-e-s" sound like 'duz'? She continued to read, '... not ... like ... a ... mouse ... in ... the ...house.'

'I'm readin'!' she said aloud as she turned the page. Although there were only eight pages in the book, she was thrilled that she had managed to read each one. 'I'll save th' other book about the dog till tomorra,' she said to herself as she put them carefully back into the drawer. 'An' I reckon as Miss Roberts'll be pleased, an' all.'

After another run to the pickle factory they arrived back at the Wharf in time for Christmas. All the crews tried to get back to the Wharf for Christmas, if possible, because the Company organised and paid for a party for the children at The Boat on Christmas Eve. The lounge bar of the pub was furnished with long tables where they sat for their Christmas party tea. Maggie and most of the other mothers went along to help serve the food, while their menfolk got themselves quietly mellow in the public bar. After they had eaten, some games were organised and Martha, the landlord's wife, played the piano. Izzie looked forward to the party every year, especially to what she thought was the best part of the whole afternoon.

After the tea and games, everyone was told to sit down and be very quiet. When all were quiet and still they would hear a knock at the door. Martha would say, 'I wonder who that could be?' and go to open the door. To a great deal of cheering and shouting, Father Christmas would walk in, carrying his sack of Christmas presents for the children.

This year, Izzie was sitting expectantly, watching for the door to open as usual. Only, this year, she was just a little bit disappointed. The door opened and in walked Father Christmas with his sack as he had done every year as far back as she could remember. Only this year, it was different. This year she recognised him. It was not Father Christmas at all, it was Mr Roberts, dressed up in a bright red suit and wearing a false white beard! When he gave her her present she was tempted to say, 'Thank you, Mr Roberts.' But then she noticed the awe and wonder in the faces of the younger boys and girls around her. And in that fleeting half-second she remembered feeling exactly the same when she had been their age. So instead, she smiled at Mr Roberts and said, 'Thank you, Father Christmas.'

Chapter 5

Frozen in

S oon after Christmas they were on their way to Coventry again. The journey to the coal yard was uneventful, other than to confirm to them that over Christmas the weather had become much colder. The boats were loaded and turned round so that they were quickly under way on the long run back towards London and the pickle factory. Izzie had noticed that since they left the Wharf each morning her father had made sure that *Zeus's* range was alight so that he could be warm. The weather remained cold and wintry for the whole journey to the pickle factory. The unloading went as smoothly as before. Although the hard work of shovelling the coal kept the three men reasonably warm, they were grateful for the regular cups of hot steaming tea that Maggie and Izzie supplied. They were even more grateful still to sit in *Aphrodite's* snug, warm cabin and devour a hot meal at lunchtime. At the end of the second day both of the boats were empty and they headed for the 'winding hole' a little further on to turn the boats round.

The procedure used for turning a boat was known as 'winding' (pronounced as in 'tinned' not 'find'), because the wind was used to help to turn the boats. With craft seventy feet long this was impossible within the normal width of the canal and had to be performed at a junction or a specially constructed 'winding hole' where the canal was wide and deep enough to take the length of the boats. Bill and Maggie turned the boats round with practised ease.

Again, when Maggie called Horace Roberts there were no return loads available, so they set off empty straight back to the Wharf.

Bill watched what he called 'snow clouds' coming and going in the skies above them. He was pleased to see them pass over without

59

any significant snowfall. There were occasional flumes of snow and a thin covering of ice on the canal in the morning.

When she woke two days into the return trip, Izzie noticed that there were intricate patterns of frost on the inside of the glass in the porthole just above her bed. She touched them with her finger and immediately pulled her hand away again as it was so cold. Bill opened the back doors to discover that as far as the eye could see the canal was frozen over and covered to a depth of about six inches with snow. He muttered an oath under his breath as he stepped up onto *Aphrodite's* counter. Picking up the long pole from the cabin roof, he swung it up vertically and brought the end down hard onto the snow and ice that covered the water. The pole went through the snow, then bounced up as it hit the ice.

'We won't git far in this!' he said angrily, as he threw the pole back down onto the cabin roof. He came back inside and slammed *Aphrodite's* hatch tight shut. They sat round the table, basking in the heat from the fire in the range, but really wishing they could be out in the cold – and on the move. The depression they all felt pervaded the whole of the tiny cabin. 'Trouble is,' Bill said. 'We ain't near no towns nor villages along this 'ere stretch. If I'd knowed it were gonna freeze as 'ard as this last night I'd 'ave made sure as we stopped a bit closer to somewhere.'

'P'raps it won't be for long.' Maggie tried to cheer the mood up a little.

'Or it could be for weeks!' Bill replied as a worried look flashed across his face. The rest of the day took an age to pass. By evening they were ready to eat – not because they had been busy, but because they needed something to do to relieve the boredom. Izzie felt frustrated because, with her father there, she dared not get her books out. 'A 'ole day, an' I could 'ave been doin' me readin'. What a waste!' she thought.

Her mother dished up stew, then, just before they began to eat, she lifted the saucepan from the range and poured what was left into a basin, covering it with a plate. She stood it inside the cupboard.

'What are you doin' wi' that, Mam?' Izzie asked.

'You wasn't ol' enough to remember the last time we was froze in miles away from anywhere, was you? We're got no idea 'ow long we're gonna be stuck 'ere, see? An' we don't wanna run out o' food now, do we? So we all 'as to eat a bit less to make it last longer – that means no second 'elpin's. We're none of us gonna be workin' so we won't need so much to eat neither,' her mother explained.

'An' if we 'adn't been carryin' coal on the way down an' we'd ... well ... kept a bit back, like, then we'd 'ave to watch 'ow much of it we was puttin' on the stove an' all,' her father added.

To all of them, but especially to Izzie, the next three days seemed like a lifetime. Frequent snow showers and temperatures constantly below freezing meant that they only left the warmth of the snug cabin for absolutely vital necessities. Otherwise, they stayed where they were and kept themselves warm. Izzie was anxious to read her books, but she did not want to start a discussion about 'book learnin'' in such difficult circumstances. She grabbed her chances when she could. When her father went out to make sure *Zeus* was all right and to check over the engine, she took her book from the knife drawer and managed to read the odd page or two before he returned.

Every morning for each of those three days, as soon as he was washed, shaved and dressed, Bill repeated the same ritual with the long pole, swinging it high in the air and bringing it down onto the frozen surface. And every morning for each of those three days there was the same depressing result. The pole bounced off the surface of the hard, solid ice. Izzie began to see the wisdom of her mother's thrift with the food that they had left to eat. As they could not move the boats, they were unable to get to any shops to replenish the provisions in their dwindling larder.

Another thing that seemed strange was that the boat did not rock from side to side as they moved about the cabin. Izzie had never known it so still except when it had been in dry dock. Held firmly in the grip of the ice, it remained level, even when all three of them were on the same side of the boat.

Early on the fourth morning, as Bill made his way onto the counter, Izzie noticed a slight movement of the boat, and as she woke she thought she could hear some creaking and cracking. Again Bill lifted the pole from the cabin top and brought it down onto the icy surface of the canal. But unlike the previous times there was a cracking noise as the pole punctured the ice. Bill was surprised how little effort it took to push it through the ice and straight down to the mud on the canal bed. He looked up at the trees and saw that the snow was melting on the branches, and as he turned round to replace the pole he saw that the same thing was happening to the snow on the cabin roof.

'I reckon as 'ow we might git 'em ahead today!' he shouted excitedly. 'We might 'ave to put some more blackin' on the bow when we gits back to the Wharf, but I reckon as we can cut us a way through this 'ere ice if it don't git no thicker nor this!'

Zeus's engine was coaxed into life and they were soon under way again, all three of them wrapped up warm against the cold and with both of the ranges alight and burning well. The ice sang as it cracked and scraped along the sides of the boat. Izzie stood on the front of *Zeus*, pole in hand, pushing away the bigger sheets of ice.

Considering that the surface of the water was covered with great sheets of floating ice up to three or four inches thick, they made good headway through the day. The weather may have been freezing cold, but it felt so good to be moving again, and as they progressed it became more obvious that the thaw had set in. When they arrived at the next village they tied up for an hour while Maggie and Izzie disappeared to the shops to replenish their much diminished food supplies.

When they ate that evening Bill appeared to be deep in thought. As Maggie cleared the plates away, he said, 'I been thinkin'. We don't wanna lose this 'ere pickle factory job on account o' bein' late, now, do we?'

'Weren't our fault the cut were froze over, were it?' Maggie asked.

'No, I know that, but you remember what Mr Roberts said. Tom Speechley liked us doing the job 'cos o' the good time we made,' he replied. 'So I been thinkin' – we could make up some o' the time we're lost if we could run a bit later at night. What d'you reckon?'

'What? Run in the dark, you mean?' Maggie asked, a little uncertainly. 'You know I don't like runnin' in the dark – an' you ain't never been that keen on it, neither!'

'Yeah, I know,' he tried to reassure her, 'but it ain't like we dunno this bit o' cut, is it? We're done this road a good many times afore. It could mean as we could git back to the Wharf an' then on to the coal yard wi'out losin' too much time.'

'I s'pose so,' said Maggie, still not totally convinced. Bill, however, took her answer for agreement. 'Right!' he announced. 'That settles it, then. We'll push on till around ten o'clock or so tonight an' again tomorra night an' we'll see 'ow far we can git.'

Overhearing this conversation, Izzie was excited by the prospect of running at night. She hoped she might be allowed to stay up later and was disappointed, when, despite her protests, she was packed off to bed at the usual time. Once tucked up in bed, though, she found that the gentle movement of the boat relaxed her. The noise of *Zeus*'s engine was far enough away not to disturb her and she was soon off to sleep.

In the morning she could see that her parents were both bleary-eyed, but that they were also pleased with the progress they had made. 'Another ten o'clock finish tonight an' tomorra an' we'll be nearly back up to time!' Bill announced triumphantly.

The next night, as Izzie was beginning to drift off to sleep, her parents began to take the boats up the flight of locks at Buckby. She had pleaded with them again to be allowed to stay up, saying she could help by lock wheeling. Both her parents had agreed, however, that riding the ancient bike on the towpath on a dark, frosty night would be far too dangerous, so, reluctantly and under protest, she had gone to bed.

Zeus and *Aphrodite* had been 'breasted up' before they had entered the flight of broad locks. They negotiated the first locks successfully and headed northwards as a goods train rumbled past them on the nearby line, its white smoke hanging in the chill air, and the glow from its firebox lighting its cab.

'Ready for the next 'un!' shouted Bill. While he was holding the pair steady in mid-channel, Maggie walked on up the towpath to draw the paddles and open the gates. Unfortunately, they had a 'bad road'. The last boats to use the flight had been travelling in the same direction, so the locks were all 'against' them. This made Maggie's job longer, harder and, in the dark, more dangerous. She had to cross over the gates twice at each lock.

Her eyes had become accustomed to the inky, black darkness that surrounded the pair. It was punctured only by *Zeus*'s headlamp, which lit only a small area directly in front of the boat. Bill was listening intently over the sound of the engine, to ascertain which stage of the locking operation his wife was performing. He heard the sound of the first of the top gates banging shut, then Maggie's footsteps along the lock side. She came into the range of the headlamp briefly as she crossed over the gates, her breath visible in the frosty air. As she disappeared into the darkness again, Bill heard more footsteps, then the sound of the second top gate slamming home against the first. Then there were yet more footsteps before he heard the sound of a set of paddles being drawn. The water rushing out of the lock drowned the sound of his wife's boots on the gates as she crossed to draw the paddles on the other gate. He increased the speed control on the engine and worked the tiller to counteract the water rushing towards him as the lock began to empty. Unable to hear his wife's footsteps over the sound the torrent, he realised when another surge of water hit the boats that she had raised the other set of paddles. Eventually, in the dim light, he saw one of the gates slowly open. He waited patiently until they were both open, then gently eased the pair into the chamber. The gates were closed behind him and he heard Maggie drawing the set of paddles in the first of the top gates. Again came the noise of rushing water as it poured through the paddle holes under pressure. Again he adjusted the engine speed to counteract the effect of the waves of water entering the lock.

Then, above the sound of the rushing water and of the engine, he plainly heard the sound of a scream – his wife's scream – a scream that was suddenly cut short by the sound of a loud splash!

'Maggie!' Bill shouted as he grabbed a spare windlass and leapt from *Zeus*'s counter and onto the bottom lock gate. He shinned up the lock gate and ran as fast his legs would carry him up to the top gates. Peering into the lock, he quickly realised exactly what had happened. His wife had slipped on the icy gate and fallen into the canal – but above the closed top gate! There was but one thought in Bill's mind. Drop the paddles and stop the torrent of water surging into the lock through the paddle hole and pray that he would be in time! He grasped the freezing metal of the paddle rod with his bare hands and jerked it round. Swiftly lifting the pawl, he let go of the rod, allowing the paddles to drop free.

'Please, God, don't let me be too late!' he breathed.

The metallic rattling of the rack-and-pinion lock gear exploded like gunfire in the cold stillness of the night. But there was no loud, comforting 'clunk' as the wooden paddles fell to rest in their closed position. Instead, the paddle gear stopped part of the way down. Bill knew immediately what was blocking their path. The strong current of water flowing into the lock far below the water line had swept Maggie through the paddle hole in the gate where she had become firmly wedged.

'Oh my God!' he murmured. 'I'm too bloody late!'

Izzie had awakened with a start. She sensed something was wrong. The boat rocked violently as Bill leapt from *Zeus*'s counter. She jumped out of bed, pulled on her boots and put her cardigan on over her nightdress. She climbed out of the cabin into the darkness to hear her father's desperate scream.

'Izzie! Izzie! Run an' fetch the lockie! Quick! Your Mam's drowndin'!'

From somewhere – she never knew where – she found the strength to clamber up the lock gate and onto the lock side. She ran up the towpath as fast as she could go, totally oblivious to the freezing temperature and the ice beneath her feet. Breathless, she arrived at the little lock-keeper's cottage and hammered hard on the door with both fists, shouting at the top of her voice for him to come and help. It seemed like an age before a light appeared inside and the door opened.

'Quick!' Izzie yelled at him. 'Me Mam's drowndin' in the lock!'

For a middle-aged man the lock-keeper was very agile. Quickly, he pushed his feet into his boots and picked up his coat and his windlass. Passing the windlass to Izzie, he threw his coat on over his pyjamas as he ran close behind her. Back along the towpath, Bill had raised the paddles in both of the bottom gates and was prodding in the canal by the top gates with the long pole. As they approached he yelled, 'Quick! She's stuck in the paddle 'ole!'

Then there was nothing any of them could do but watch and wait. As the water level in the lock dropped with agonising slowness, the moon made a sudden appearance from behind a cloud. By its pale, silvery light Izzie could just see, with water forcing its way around it, the lower half of her mother's lifeless body sticking through the hole in the lock gate. At first, she could not believe what she was seeing with her own eyes. 'Them legs stickin' through that 'ole in that gate can't be me Mam's legs, surely! But then ... who else's could they be?' Izzie first half-spoke, half-breathed the word, 'Mam?' And then, as the awful truth hit home, she screamed it. 'Mam!!'

As the lock-keeper pulled her away and hugged her to him, the tears came. Izzie cried into that lock-keeper's old overcoat as she had never cried before. He held her close and tried to comfort her. Izzie was aware that he was talking but she could not make sense of the words. The lock-keeper raised his eyes from Izzie's tear-stained face. He looked across the lock at her father. Bill was kneeling on the freezing cold lock side, looking down at the visible half of his wife's body, unaware of the temperature, unaware of everything else around him, his shoulders heaving in uncontrolled and uncontrollable sobbing, as he simply repeated, over and over to himself, 'Maggie!'

Chapter 6

Bad business

Two days later there was a letter awaiting Emily on her arrival. It had been left there by Arthur Cox, who had acted as postman.

'dear mis roberts

mea mams ded she ~~downd~~ drownd in bugby loks the uther nite mea dads sortin out the funral its goin to bea at brornstun i op you can cum the locky is elpin me rite this

from isobel horne'

Emily already knew about Maggie's tragic death. Horace had gone straight round to the schoolroom to tell his daughter when the news had come through the previous day. Even so, when she read the letter tears welled up in her eyes as she realised the effort Isobel must have put into writing this letter at a time that must have been the saddest and most desperate moment of her young life. When she had suggested that Izzie could write to her she had never imagined that the first letter her pupil would ever write would contain such tragic news. Collecting her thoughts and dabbing her eyes, she hurried next door to show the letter to her father.

'Bad business!' Horace said as he read it. 'Bad business!'

'It's Isobel I feel so sorry for, losing her mother at such a young age,' Emily said.

'She always struck me as being very fond of her mother.'

'She was. It was Mrs Horne who brought her to school – going against Mr Horne's wishes.'

'Bill Horne's going to find it hard too. But he's a capable chap and I have no doubt he'll manage. But it'll take him a while to get over his grief. I've told him to come back here when he's ready. I doubt it'll be until after Maggie's funeral.' Horace had already made arrangements for another motor to tow *Aphrodite* back to Braunston where she would await *Zeus*. The motor would be arriving later, carrying a very, very special cargo.

The news of Maggie's tragic and untimely death was spread, as they knew it would be, over the entire length of the canal by the 'towpath telegraph'. As pairs of boats met each other, all would have received the news, 'Maggie 'Orne's drownded in Bugby locks.'

✳

The day after Maggie's death her body was taken away. There had to be an inquest and Bill and the lock-keeper were summoned to attend. When they returned, Izzie was watching from *Zeus*'s counter. She saw them having a brief conversation outside the lock-keeper's cottage. They shook hands and her father trudged slowly along the towpath towards her. She could see from his face that he had been crying.

'What 'appened, Dad?' she asked.

'It were a bit like bein' in court,' he said as he climbed aboard. 'There were this bloke sittin' there as they call a coroner, an' 'e were askin' me a lot o' fool questions about 'ow your Mam died.' They stepped down into the cabin. Sitting down, he continued, 'I 'ad to go through the 'ole bloomin' story again! It upset me, I can tell you, goin' over it all again. Tellin' 'im as 'ow I 'eard 'er slip off the gate, an' ev'rythin'.' He lapsed into silence, his head in his hands. Izzie put her arm round him.

'Must 'ave been 'orrible for you, Dad,' she said.

Her father looked up. 'I ask' 'im at one point – I says, "Are you tryin' to say as you reckon as I pushed 'er in?"'

'What did 'e say to that?' Izzie asked.

'Oh, 'e said summat about 'e 'ad to consider "all the possibilities". Any road, at the end of it all, 'e give 'is verdict – 'e said it were "death be misadventure", whatever that means!' Again he fell silent with his head in his hands. Realising he needed to be on his own for a while, Izzie quickly made him a cup of tea, then walked to the lock-keeper's cottage and knocked on the door.

'Come in, Izzie,' the lock-keeper's wife said, opening the door and giving her a big hug as she entered. 'I'm so sorry about your Mum. We didn't 'ave a lot to do with each other, but she always smiled and waved to me if I saw 'er on the flight.'

'I loved me Mam!' said Izzie, as she began to weep again.

'Course you did, love! Course you did! And it's cruel that she should 'ave been taken from you so young!'

'Is your 'usband 'ere?' Izzie asked, drying her eyes.

''E's out the back, love. You can go through if you want.' Izzie made her way to the back yard where she found the lock-keeper chopping wood.

''Allo, Izzie,' he greeted her, sadly. 'I tell you something! That Dad of yours – 'e's a brave man, and no mistake.'

'Yeah?' she answered, not sure what he meant.

'Let's get inside out of the cold,' he said, burying his axe in a log. They went into the warm kitchen of the cottage.

'Sit yourself down, Izzie,' his wife said. The lock-keeper took his pipe from the mantelshelf over the kitchen range and lit it.

'Standing there in that coroner's court,' he said, 'and answering all them questions – and all so soon after your Mum's death, too? I don't think I could 'ave done it. I don't – honest!'

'Must 'ave been really 'orrible for 'im. Why do they 'ave do all that?' Izzie asked.

'Well, you see, when there's a sudden death in circumstances like your Mum's, it's the coroner's job to find out exactly 'ow it 'appened – to make sure there was no, what they call, foul play. Do you know what that is?'

'Does it mean as somebody might 'ave pushed 'er in?' The lock-keeper's wife gasped at Izzie's answer, but said nothing.

'That's the kind of thing, yes. Well, the coroner 'as to ask a lot of questions and 'e 'as to ask a lot of people – 'e 'as to ask the folk who were there when it 'appened, the doctor and anybody else who was involved, so 'e can get a picture in 'is mind of 'ow it all occurred, so 'e can be sure there was no foul play.'

'Is that why me Dad 'ad to go through it all agin? It's real upset 'im!'

'I know it 'as!' he replied. "E was a bit tearful all the way back on the bus. You'll 'ave to look after 'im a for bit, you know.'

'I reckon as we'll 'ave to look after each other,' Izzie said.

'That's the ticket! You look after each other.'

'Thanks for all what you done … you know … th' other night.' She almost wept again.

'Just doing my job, love. That's all.'

'Well, thanks anyway,' she said, getting to her feet. Izzie went to shake hands with him, but instead the lock-keeper gave her a hug. With tears in her eyes his wife hugged her too on her way out. As they watched her walk back to *Zeus* the lock-keeper and his wife looked at each other.

'It's a bad business!' the lock-keeper said, shaking his head.

'What nice folks!' Izzie thought as she made her way back to the boat.

✳

Early in the morning on the day of her mother's funeral, Izzie helped her father to place the top planks across the hold in a neat row just behind the mast – the pride of place. They were both wearing their best clothes. Soon afterwards there was a knock on the side of *Aphrodite*'s cabin. Bill opened the doors. Standing there were six friends of his, all smartly dressed. They were all boatmen themselves, who had known Maggie well.

'It's time,' Bill said to Izzie. She and her father walked with them to the next bridge and up onto the road. Looking into the distance, Izzie saw the hearse approaching slowly. When it arrived, the undertaker shook hands with them both and enquired where *Zeus* was moored. The six men took the coffin and hoisted it onto their shoulders.

'Are you ready, gentlemen?' the undertaker asked. They nodded. And so the sad little procession wound its way along the towpath. All thoughts of keeping contracts and of making up lost time were now forgotten. *Zeus*'s engine was already running, ready and waiting, to take her captain's lady on her final run. Maggie's last journey was to be from Buckby to Braunston because, as Bill had told Izzie, 'Our family's allus been buried in Braunston.'

The undertaker led the way, followed by the six boatmen carrying Maggie's coffin. Bill and Izzie walked slowly behind it, clutching each other's arms tightly, each of them trying to be strong for the sake of the other. Izzie had put on her best dress. 'It's only navy blue. It ain't black, but it's the only "best" dress as I'm got,' she thought. 'But I don't reckon as me Mam'd mind too much about that. Any road, you can't see much on it under me coat.' Bill, too, looked smart in his jacket and his waistcoat with his watch and chain in the pocket.

When the coffin bearers were alongside they gently eased Maggie's coffin onto the planks. Much of the hold was already covered with a host of flowers and tributes, and another undertaker, following the procession, was carrying more of them. Maggie had been a well-known and popular person in the close-knit community of boating folk.

Bill and Izzie stepped onto the counter. Two of the coffin-bearers loosened the ropes and Bill, grim-faced, took up his position at the tiller. The drizzle that had been falling all night eased slightly as they pulled away from the towpath. Maggie Horne was coming home.

Bill knew that on this run, every lock would be set 'for' them. Every set of lock gates would be open and ready for them to enter and men and women from other boats would be there to close and open gates and draw and close paddles. Izzie would not be required to be a lock wheeler today.

Neither had Bill had to organise anything. It had all been done without his asking, and, indeed, without his direct knowledge. It was the boat people's way of showing their respect for one of their own. Margaret Violet Horne was guaranteed a 'good road' on her last run on the cut, a 'good road' straight through to the yard at Braunston.

Not a single word passed between Izzie and her father throughout the entire length of the journey, nor yet between them and the people operating the locks for them. At a time like this mere words were neither adequate nor necessary. A bow of the head or a gesture of the hand was all that was needed. Izzie stood next to her father, her eyes fixed on her mother's coffin, sad thoughts crowding her mind.

They met no other boats in Braunston Tunnel. Bill knew they would not, and when *Zeus* arrived at Nurser's Yard six more boatmen were waiting, also in their best clothes, ready to carry Maggie on her final journey up the road from the yard and over the bridge. The procession then turned right and headed up the steep hill to the church. Maggie was to be buried where previous generations of both hers and Bill's families and the families of many other boat people had been buried – high on a hillside overlooking the Northern Oxford Canal, as it wove its picturesque way through countryside and away into the distance towards Rugby.

Many of the boat people had stayed over in Braunston for an extra day or two to attend Maggie's funeral. Horace and Emily Roberts had motored from the Wharf to be there too. Izzie was so pleased to see Miss Roberts in the congregation that she nearly ran up to greet her – but just managed to stop herself as she remembered where she was and why she was there.

For Bill and Izzie the service passed by in a blur. In his address, the Rector of Braunston said complimentary things about Maggie and, even though they had only met each other once or twice, he spoke as if he had known her well. Soon they were following her coffin out onto the hillside where it was carefully lowered into the freshly dug grave. The Rector said more prayers, then invited Bill to throw the first earth onto the coffin. After he had let his handful of earth fall, he stood at the graveside for a few moments, his head bowed. Then, sniffing back his tears, he returned to his place. The Rector indicated it was Izzie's turn. Unsure of what she was expected to do – she had never been to a funeral before – she stood at the edge of her mother's grave, and dropped in her handful of earth, as she had seen her father do. Then she simply stood there, looking down at the strange wooden box. The box that she knew contained her mother's dead body and, with tears streaming down her face, she spoke very quietly between sobs.

'Goodbye, Mam… wherever you are… You knows as I love you… I'll allus love you!'

Bill, the only person near enough to hear her, stepped forward and put his arm round her shoulders. Horace whispered something to the rest of the group at the graveside. Everyone else nodded in agreement and moved a little further away leaving Bill and Izzie alone together to say their final goodbyes to Maggie in private.

A little while later, as they walked slowly back to the churchyard gate with their arms around each other, Horace and Emily approached them. Horace solemnly offered their condolences.

'Thank you both for comin',' Bill replied. 'Me an' Izzie, we really 'preciate it. You're both very welcome to come an' join us in the pub for a pint, if you'd like.' Horace thanked him but explained that they had to get back.

'Telephone me sometime over the next couple of days and we can discuss what's going to happen in the future, Bill,' he said.

'Ah, I will that,' Bill replied. 'I need to think on that a bit.'

While Bill and Horace were talking, Emily took Izzie to one side and asked her how she was feeling. Izzie said, 'Awright. I'm tryin' to be strong for me Dad's sake, but I miss me Mam so very bad.'

Emily took a clean handkerchief from her handbag and gave it to Izzie as fresh tears started to fill her eyes. 'You will, Isobel. You will,' she said.

Nearly everyone who had been at the church – and a few more besides – congregated at the pub by the canal after the funeral. They all made a point of having a quiet word with Bill about the happy memories they had of Maggie – and they all wanted to buy him a drink, so he managed to get through many more pints – not to mention double whiskies – than were good for him.

Later, as the boat people began to drift away in twos and threes, the sound of boat engines being started was heard. The canal at Braunston was beginning to return to life. The close-knit community of boat people had stopped work for a while to honour one of their own, a popular and well-loved wife and mother who had so sadly and so tragically died. Each one of them was aware that such an accident could quite easily befall any one of them at any time. Risks like walking on icy gates and lock sides were part and parcel of their lives. Sadly, deaths like Maggie's were not a rare occurrence. But, risks or no risks, the life and the work of the canal had to go on. There was work to be done. There were boats to be loaded and loads to be carried and delivery times to be met. Life on the canal outside the comfortable, welcoming warmth of the pub was quickly returning to normal.

As Izzie sat on a stool next to her father, sipping her lemonade, she began to realise that their lives, hers and her father's, were never, ever going be the same again. 'It were bad enough that terrible, terrible night at Bugby locks when me Mam drownded, but today! Today!' she thought to herself. 'Today's been the very worst day o' me 'ole life!' She recalled staring at the coffin on the front of *Zeus* as they had travelled from Buckby, knowing her mother's lifeless body lay inside. She remembered watching as it was lowered slowly into the ground. She thought again about how she felt inside as she looked down at the coffin in the grave and dropped her handful of soil onto it. 'Everythin' seems so … so final, some'ow!' There was no room for any doubts any more. Slowly, as she sat there, hearing – but not hearing – the other boat people talking, it began to hit Izzie that, although she had known her mother was dead from the moment on that fateful night when she had run back to the lock with the lock-keeper, although she had known then, she had not – not until today – really realised what it would mean to her and her father. 'Me Mam's never gonna come back … ever! From now on, it's jus' us! Jus' me an' me Dad!

Chapter 7

George Andrews

It was fairly late morning the following day when Bill surfaced. He overslept – the result of his overindulgence the night before. Having washed, dressed and eaten breakfast, his hangover was slowly beginning to abate. Izzie had woken earlier. Without the so-called 'benefits' of strong drink to send her to sleep, she had endured a fitful night, punctuated by nightmares about that awful night at Buckby. She had got up early but, without her mother there to organise things, it still felt strange. 'What would me Mam've done?' she asked herself. Then she made a decision. 'I'll go up the village an' git some shoppin'.' She felt almost as if she was doing something wrong, taking money out of her mother's purse. 'I s'pose that's summat else I gotta git used to now!' she thought, as she picked up her mother's shopping bag and set off up the long hill to the village.

It was the first time she had ever been shopping completely on her own – something else that felt strange. The very fact that she was doing it on her own was a stark reminder that her mother was no longer there. But it also made her feel quite grown-up as she purchased what she knew she and her father would require from the shops.

She walked back along the towpath to *Aphrodite*, now safely reunited with *Zeus*. Lifting her mother's bag, now heavy with shopping, onto the boat and pushing back the slide, she stepped down into the warm, snug cabin. Her father looked up at her, his eyes still tired from both his grief and his hangover.

'Izzie, love! Where you been?' he asked.

'I'm been up the village to get a few bits an' pieces as I thought we'd want,' Izzie replied.

75

'Come an' sit down 'ere a minute, love. You can put them things away in a bit. I need to 'ave a word wi' you first. It's summat important.' Izzie put the shopping bags down on the floor and sat next to him. 'Now,' he began, a little too seriously for her liking, 'some time, either today or tomorra, I gotta ring Mr Roberts up, an' I gotta tell 'im … well, I gotta tell 'im … sort o' what me plans are, like.'

'What plans?' Izzie asked, innocently.

'Well…,' Bill hesitated, 'plans for the future, like – our future … yourn an' mine, now your Mam's gone, an' that.' Izzie's worried look turned quickly to a smile.

'Oh, there ain't no need to worry about that, Dad! I can steer the butty! I'm done it afore when me Mam were poorly that time, ain't I?'

'Ah!' Bill replied. 'That's as maybe. But, you see, the comp'ny wouldn't 'old wi' it. They wouldn't allow for a ten-year-old girl to do the steerin' on the butty – not reg'lar, like. It were different when your Mam were ill cos that were like … an emergency. An' it were only for the odd day or two any'ow – but reg'lar? No! It'd be agin' the rules, do you see?'

'Well, the rules is daft, then!' Izzie exclaimed angrily.

'So 'em may be,' Bill agreed, 'but they'm the rules all the same.'

'But I seen lots o' kids o' my age steerin' butties – an' motors an all – an' some on 'em as is even younger 'n me!' she protested.

'So you might 'ave done! So you might 'ave done! On big companies' boats, not on ourn,' explained her father.

'Whassit matter whose comp'nies' boats they are?'

'Well, some of th' other boat comp'nies, the big 'uns, like, they 'as different rules 'n our 'un. An' their rules allows for young 'uns to steer.'

'Why don't our Comp'ny allow it, then?'

'Well,' he began, 'it's all to do wi' what they call th' insurance. Mr Roberts explained it to me some while back. See, the Comp'ny pays over some money every year to another firm what's called an insurance comp'ny. So, say, if a boat gits sunk or a load gits damaged or summat like that, then th' insurance comp'ny pays some money out to our Comp'ny. So nobody don't lose nuthin'. Do you see?'

'Don't the big comp'nies pay no insurance, then?'

'They do. They all do. But our Comp'ny's only a littl'un, see. An' they 'as to be careful to keep the money as they 'as to pay out on things down as low as they can. So they've agreed wi' th' insurance comp'ny as they'll be charged less money in return for promisin' as 'ow nobody under sixteen year ol' steers a boat – unless it's an emergency.'

Izzie could not escape the logic of the reasoning. But then came the sudden realisation of the effect these insurance rules would have on them, now her mother was dead.

'So what's all that gonna mean for us, then?' she asked, wide-eyed, and fearing the worst. 'What's all that gonna mean for you an' me, eh Dad?'

Bill looked even more serious now. When he spoke, he spoke slowly and deliberately, and there was a catch in his voice that Izzie recognised. She had heard it often in the last few days when he had been speaking to friends about her mother, and she had come to realise that he was fighting to hold back his tears.

'I never thought as I'd ever 'ear meself sayin' it, our Izzie! Never! An' I gotta say, it 'urts me more 'n I can tell you to say it, it does that! An' I'm sorry, love, but there ain't no easy way o' sayin' it neither.' He paused and took a long deep breath, and as he shifted his gaze so that he did not have to meet his daughter's troubled eyes, he spoke quietly and even more slowly. 'It means ... it means as 'ow we'll 'ave to go on the bank!'

'What?' Izzie exclaimed, her worst fears realised. 'You mean ... you mean ... give up the boats? Leave the cut? Live in a 'ouse?'

Bill nodded gravely and Izzie could see moisture in the corners of his eyes.

'But ... but that ain't fair!' she shouted. She thought she had cried until she had no more tears left, but now she felt them welling up in her eyes again.

'I'm sorry, Izzie love.' Bill put his arm round her and tried hard not to show his own worries and fears at the prospect of giving up the only job – the only way of life – he had ever known. 'But that's the long an' the short on it. That's jus' about 'ow it is, see?'

Izzie sat quietly for a moment, then, standing up, she dried her eyes on the sleeve of her cardigan. 'I ... I'm jus' goin' outside for a bit. I'll put that shoppin' away when I gits back.'

'Awright, Izzie love, but don't you go an' git cold out there, now,' Bill called after her as she disappeared through the back doors. He realised that she needed some space and time on her own to try to come to terms with what he had just said.

She did not walk very far. Stepping onto the towpath, she ambled slowly along and through the next bridge hole, where she stopped. Leaning against the cold brickwork of the bridge, she stood staring into the distance, her mind in a turmoil. She tried hard to comprehend the bombshell her father had just delivered, to make some sort of sense of the tragic turns her life had taken over the past few days. In just over a week she had not only lost her mother, but now it looked as if she was about to lose her home too, the only home she had ever known.

'Why me?' she asked herself, almost out loud. 'What terrible, terrible sin am I ever done as God should 'ave took it into 'is 'ead to punish me so 'orribly, like this? And at that very moment, a really awful thought jumped into her mind. 'Surely it couldn't 'ave been that? No! Surely not that! But...,' she thought, 'Can it 'ave been that? Summat ... summat to do wi' me wantin' to learn to read so bad?' She pondered on the wretched thought.

'It could be that, couldn't it?' she thought. 'After all, it were me Mam as signed me up to go to school in the first place – an' she done it wi'out me Dad knowin'. An' now it's me Mam as is dead. Did God punish 'er for takin' me to the school by gittin' 'er drownded? An' is this my punishment – 'avin' to leave the cut? Me Dad's been agin me goin' to the school an' learnin' to read all along, right from the beginnin' – 'e's never thought no different nor that – an' 'e's still 'ere... So ... so does that mean as in God's eyes me Dad's been right all along an' I shouldn't never 'ave gone to that school?'

She spent what seemed like an age leaning against that bridge, unaware of the freezing brickwork, believing that not only the death of her mother, but also the loss of her home and of her father's livelihood were all her fault – and her fault alone. She was to blame. She was to blame for all of it! She convinced herself that if she had not been so enthusiastic about learning to read, that her mother would still be alive and the family's future on the boats would be assured. Instead of which, everything was going to change. And it was all going to change for the worse – much, much worse!

She covered her eyes with her hands as she began to sob quietly, weighed down by the intolerable burden of guilt she felt pressing down on her shoulders. She looked at the cold murky water and considered jumping into the canal, putting an end to it all, drowning herself! One thought stopped her. 'I dunno if me Dad could 'andle two deaths so close together.'

But then, like a shaft of sunlight piercing a dark cloud, a gleaming light of sense and reason broke through the misery and grief of her thoughts.

'No!' she shouted out loud. 'It couldn't 'ave been that!' she began to reason. 'Lots o' boat kids is learnin' to read now, an' their Mams is all still alive! An' any road, the Bible's a book, innit? An' you got to know how to read if you gonna read that, ain't you? So God can't think as 'ow it's a bad thing to learn to read, now can 'e?

''Ow do, Izzie!' She had been so wrapped up in her grief, her guilt, her thoughts, that she had been totally oblivious to anything else that was happening around her. She looked up to see who it was who had spoken her name. It was a young boatman called George Andrews, a man in his late teens whom she knew vaguely. Being older than her, he had kept his own company and had not mixed with the children. He had walked along the towpath towards her – the pair of boats that he worked with his grandfather was tied up a little further along the canal.

'I 'ope as 'e never 'eard me shoutin' out "No!" like that!' she thought. ''E'll think I'm turned into some mad woman!'

If George had heard her, he was too good-mannered to mention it, and he put the redness around her eyes down to the fact that she had been crying over her mother.

'Is your Dad aboard?'

''E's on the butty. Why?' she replied.

'I need to 'ave a quick word wi' him.'

Izzie watched as George started along towards *Aphrodite*. He took a couple of paces then suddenly stopped and turned back to her.

'Er … me an' me Grandad was ever so sorry to 'ear about your Mam,' he said. 'We couldn't git to the funeral cos we only got in las' night.'

'Tha's awright. Thank you,' she said as George walked to *Aphrodite* and rapped on the cabin side with his fist.

'Bill? Bill 'Orne! It's me, George Andrews. Can I come aboard? I need a word wi' you!'

From inside the boat Bill's voice answered, 'Yeah, come on in.' His head appeared through the slide as he opened the doors for George.

'Another 'un come to say 'ow sorry they are!' thought Izzie. 'But it don' 'elp, do it? It don' bring 'er back!' She stood there a few moments longer. 'I ain't goin' back yit,' she said to herself as she wandered further along the towpath. She walked up past the locks and on towards the tunnel. As she approached the tunnel mouth, she knew that the towpath there would be very wet. It was always wet there because high up to the side, hidden behind a steep bank and a row of bushes, was a reservoir that supplied water to the Braunston summit level of the canal. She walked along slowly, being careful where she put her feet. At a point not far from the tunnel mouth she stopped. Standing there, with her feet on a dryish patch of grass, she looked into the mouth of the tunnel. She stared blankly into the murky darkness that swallowed up the canal after a mere few yards.

The all-consuming blackness inside the tunnel held no fear for her as it may have done for those from 'off the bank'. She had been travelling through tunnels ever since she had been a baby. On some days, if it was a bright, clear early morning when no boats had gone through, it was possible to look into the black mass inside the tunnel at Braunston and just make out the minuscule pinprick of white light that was the other mouth of the tunnel, nearly a mile away. But on this day the weather was too grey and overcast. Mist was forming, and as a number of boats had passed through the tunnel there was also coal smoke and diesel fumes. No matter how hard she peered, no matter how hard she stared, she could not make out the tiny speck of light. All she could see was the black, black darkness.

'That's jus' about what me life's like now,' she thought, sadly. 'A long dark tunnel what I can't see the end on! I dunno what me Dad's gonna do on the bank – 'e ain't never done nuthin' but boatin' – and we ain't never lived nowhere 'cept on the boats. I dunno what sort o' job 'e could git – 'e don't know nuthin' about nuthin' as ain't boatin'.' She let out a deep sigh and slowly turned round. Avoiding the worst of the puddles, she began to trudge, slowly and sadly, back to the pair of boats that was only going to be her home for another day or two at the very most.

※

As she got closer to *Zeus* and *Aphrodite*, she heard a most unexpected sound. 'What's that? Laughin'? Tha's the las' thing I 'spected to 'ear! Me Mam 'ardly cold in 'er grave, an' on top o' that 'avin' to give up the cut! An' me Dad's in there wi' that George bloke … an' they're laughin'? What on earth can they possibly be laughin' at at a time like this?' she wondered. Certainly, the sounds she heard getting louder as she approached *Aphrodite* were happy ones. Izzie could not help feeling upset. She thought that George and her father were being, somehow, disrespectful to the memory of her mother. The boat rocked slightly as she stepped onto the counter.

'That you, Izzie, love?' her father called out cheerily.

'Yeah.' Izzie pushed back the slide. 'What are you pair so 'appy about?'

'Come on in 'ere, girl! You an' me, we're got some good news for a change!'

Izzie, unable to conceive of any news on this day that could possibly be described as 'good', stepped down into the cabin and sat down on the step. The first thing she noticed was her father's whisky bottle on the table. 'This 'as gotta be summat special!' she thought. ''E only ever gits 'is whisky out if it's summat really special – an' I'd 'ave thought 'e'd put enough drink away yesterday!'

'George, you jus' tell our Izzie what you're jus' tol' me.'

George turned to Izzie. 'Well, you know me an' me Grandad runs *Worcester* and *Dolphin*, don' you? I'm been 'is crew ever since me

Gran died,' he told her. 'But now, well, me Grandad's gotta go in the 'ospital, an' it looks like 'e's probably gonna be in there for a long ol' time – 'e's gotta 'ave a operation, see,' George continued. 'Well, I can't work a pair on me own, anymore 'n your Dad can, can I? So I jus' been askin' 'im if I could come on 'ere wi' you two, an' steer the butty for 'im, like.'

Izzie's sad face slowly split into a grin. She looked from George to her father. 'Do that mean what I think it means? Do it mean as we don't 'ave to give up the boats? We don't 'ave to go on the bank?' she asked excitedly.

'That's exackly what it means!' her father replied, grinning from ear to ear. 'You an' me'll 'ave the butty cabin like we allus 'ave, an' George can sleep on the motor!'

'Don't forget,' Izzie said, 'me Mam allus reckoned as it stank o' diesel!' She laughed and the others joined in.

'So everybody wins,' George added, smiling as well. 'You gits to keep your boats, an' I gits to earn a livin'.'

Izzie decided there and then that she liked this George Andrews. She liked him a lot! He and she were going to get along just fine!

'An' aside from that,' George added, 'I reckon it's about time as I started out on me own a bit. I mean, sometimes the way me Grandad talks to me, you'd think I were still a nipper!'

'I know exackly what you mean!' said Izzie, smiling at her father. Her thoughts returned to the way she had been feeling a few minutes earlier, standing on that sodden towpath. She may not have been able to see the far end of the canal tunnel, but now? Well, here was George! And she could clearly see a very bright light shining at the end of her own personal tunnel.

Chapter 8

A good man to be with

Later that day George arrived with his belongings and stowed them in *Zeus*'s cabin. Bill telephoned Horace Roberts and explained the new arrangements.

Horace was happy with the situation. 'You were fortunate to find an experienced crew so quickly,' he told Bill. 'I was very much afraid we were going to lose you.'

'Not yit awhile, Mr Roberts! You ain't gonna git rid o' me that easy!' Bill joked.

'I know young George. He's a good man, and he'll be a good crewman for you. It'll help him out as well.'

All three of them gradually settled into what was, in some ways, a new, but in others an established routine. Bill steered *Zeus*, as he always had. George was happy to take *Aphrodite*, as he had previously steered the butty for his grandfather, and Izzie continued with her familiar tasks of polishing the brasses, whitening the ropes and preparing the locks.

During those days and weeks after her mother's funeral, Izzie was struck by the difference in the ways the other boat families reacted to them. When they were tied up with other boats for the night, the men were very much 'matter of fact', chatting and joking with Bill. Their wives, she noticed, smiled at her more and hugged her more often. Some of them would present her with a freshly baked cake or a packet of sweets. Others would tell her that she had to be brave and be 'a little mother'.

Devoid of the niceties of adult conversation, the children were more direct.

'Your Mam's dead, ain't she?'

''Ow did it 'appen?'

'Was you there?'

'Did you see 'er stuck in the paddle 'ole?'

They all took a ghoulish interest and wanted to hear all the gory details. Izzie did not want to reply.

No one talked to Izzie about Maggie. Wrapped up in his own grief, not even Bill wanted to talk to Izzie about her mother and she wished he would. Sometimes, when she was unable to get to sleep, or when she woke in the night, troubled by bad dreams, she often heard her father sobbing quietly on the other side of the curtain. She knew that he, like her, was hurting inside. But she knew she could do nothing to help him.

Only George talked to her about Maggie. He brought her name into their conversations, mentioning her naturally, and asking Izzie how her mother did certain things. Without ever seeming to pry, he asked her what her mother had enjoyed doing – and what she did not like! He never asked too much, and with his knowledge born of experience he knew exactly what to say. Izzie valued these moments and took comfort from them.

As soon as the first opportunity arose, Izzie had a quiet word with George. Having first made sure that they were out of her father's earshot, she explained, 'You know Miss Roberts as does the school at the Wharf?'

'Mr Roberts's girl? Yes,' George answered.

'Well, cos we don't git to the Wharf much now, she's lent me some books to read while we're on the run, but me Dad don't 'old wi' it. 'E reckons as learnin' to read's a waste o' time. 'E goes on an' on about "bloomin' book learnin'", as 'e calls it.'

'Oh ah!' George smiled.

'Point is, I don' wan' 'im to catch me at me books, see? I don't allus git time. Sometimes I'm too busy. Sometimes me Dad's in the way. Sometimes I don't git a chance for days on end. But I'm gonna learn to read cos...' For a moment she thought about telling George about the bookshop, but then she thought better of it. 'Cos it's important. So, I'm gonna be readin' 'em on the butty, an' I don't want you goin' blabbin' to 'im as you're seen me, OK?'

George nodded wisely and smiled again. He was more than happy to play along with her little subterfuge. 'Yeah,' he said. 'Me Gran sent me to that boat kids' school a few times when I were a little 'un. But that were afore Miss Roberts took it over. It were back towards th' end o' ol' Miss Watts's time, when the school were on a ol' boat! Real strict, she were. You didn't dare put a foot out o' line wi' 'er, or she'd take the slipper to your backside! Mind, the cut were a lot busier in them days, o' course, so I never spent a great lot o' me time there, but I did learn to read an' write a bit, like. So, yeah, you carry on wi' it all, girl, an' good luck to you! An' don't you go worryin' your 'ead about me, cos I shan't say nuthin' to your Dad about it, neither. It'll be a little secret 'tween the two on us.'

'Thanks!' Izzie was relieved. She enjoyed reading and re-reading her limited library and there seemed to her to be fewer new words to struggle with, so the new arrangement suited her very well. With George steering *Aphrodite*, when she had finished her other jobs she was able to carry on with her studies in the butty cabin, away from her father's gaze.

George was a good butty steerer. He watched carefully what Bill was doing with *Zeus* and reacted intuitively to his movements. Occasionally he glanced down into the cabin at Izzie, and when their eyes met he gave her a smile and a conspiratorial wink. 'Tha's jus' like me Mam used to do!' she mused, a lump coming in her throat. 'George is all right, but I do miss me Mam!'

George proved himself to be an excellent cook. From when he first came on board it was agreed that he would do the cooking.

'I dunno nuthin' about cookin',' Bill had said. 'Maggie allus done that.' Although she had learned much from her mother, Bill thought Izzie was old enough to help with meals, but not to manage independently.

Like Maggie, George could do the cooking while steering

Aphrodite at the same time. Even Bill had to compliment him on his culinary abilities.

'You're been cookin' us some fine meals, George, me boy!' he exclaimed one evening, having cleared his plate.

'Well,' George replied, 'when I were a nipper I used to watch me Gran doin' the cookin' an' I sort o' got interested in it. An' when I growed up a bit she learned me 'ow to do it so's I could 'elp 'er, like. So after she died I allus done all the cookin' for me an' me Grandad. I sort o' jus' got used to doin' it.'

'Well, I'm real glad as you did! But nobody won't never be as good as my Maggie were.' Bill sighed and looked away.

The coal contract to the pickle factory continued throughout the winter. Although the canal froze over on a number of occasions and they were sometimes a day or two late arriving at the works or getting to the coal yard, Bill never suggested moving the boats after dark. On some winter nights, as they lay in bed, they would occasionally hear a pair of boats chugging past them, travelling in the freezing darkness. Bill would rouse himself and say, almost to himself, 'Dear God, look after 'em. Look after 'em.' And Izzie would add her silent 'Amen' to his prayer.

Unloading at the works took less time now because George helped with the shovelling. He would start cooking, then leave Izzie in charge of the meal and preparing endless mugs of tea for the men at the same time. John and Dick were as complimentary about their midday meals as they had been about Maggie's.

'You two's nearly as good cooks as what Mrs 'Orne were,' Dick said one day.

'That's true,' John added, 'but 'er meat pies – well – they was really good, they was!'

'Me Mam 'ad 'er own special way o' doin' 'em,' Izzie said. 'I don't reckon I can git it quite right yit.'

'You keep at it. You'll git it in time,' George encouraged her.

Winter turned into spring. George was a good man to be with. As his confidence grew he started to tease Izzie unmercifully, but she did not mind in the least. She soon learned how to tease him back and they always ended up laughing until their sides ached. She realised that she was beginning to like him very much.

She imagined that having George around was a bit like having an older brother. Everything in her life had improved immeasurably since that dark hour when she had stood on the wet towpath at Braunston, looking deep into the darkness of the tunnel, the threat of having to leave the cut hanging over her head. Not only had the grief for her mother still been raw, but she had also been worried by the fear of the unknown.

Life was good for her again now. She still missed her mother terribly, but, thanks to George, she and her father were still living and working on *Zeus* and *Aphrodite*. That was the most important thing as far as she was concerned. They had not been forced to leave the cut – the only life they knew – and go to live in a house on the bank. They both got on well with George and he liked being with them. There seemed to be an increase, albeit a small one, in regular work for the boats. The pickle factory coal contract looked as though it would keep them occupied for the next few months at least, and sometimes they were fortunate enough to get a return load. Bill was always overjoyed when this happened because of the higher wages he received when they were travelling loaded. He and George looked on it as an occasion to be celebrated at the pub!

If the return load was any sort of foodstuff, however, it meant more work. Soon after the last shovelful of coal and been thrown up onto the canal-side, all of them had to be down in the hold, hard at work with mops, buckets and scrubbing brushes. Every last trace of coal dust had to be removed from both boats. If food was to be carried, the holds had to be spotlessly clean before they could even think about going to load up.

Looking back, Izzie realised that it was only ever a matter of time. It had to happen one day. And it did. Despite all her best efforts to avoid it, one day Bill caught his daughter studying her books. She was absorbed in what she was doing – reading words and copying them into her notebook, then covering them up with her hand and trying to write them again from memory – just as Miss Roberts had shown her. They had tied up for the evening and her father was busy checking the engine as he usually did at the end of the day's run. 'I'm only got a few more words afore I gits to th' end o' the book, so I got plen'y o' time to finish it while 'e's busy with th' engine.' Or so she thought!

On that day it took him far less time than she imagined, and before she could hide her book away in the knife drawer she felt the boat heel over as he stepped onto the counter. Coming down the steps into the cabin he stopped and looked first at the open book in her lap, then at her. He was about to say something, but before he could open his mouth, Izzie looked up from her book and met his gaze. The look on her face was so serious that, for that moment, Bill was unable to speak. Izzie knew that this day would come eventually, so she was ready for him. She knew exactly what she was going to say.

Very quietly and very firmly, she said, 'Now listen Dad! Don't you say nuthin' about me learnin' me readin'. Jus' you remember this. It's summat as me Mam wanted me to do, an' cos she wanted me to do it, I'm gonna carry on doin' it, whatever you say!'

Her father had merely nodded and said, 'Right.'

After this, although he may have complained about 'bloomin' book learnin'' to other people, he never again said anything about it to her.

Chapter 9

Excitement and sadness

One afternoon at the beginning of May, Izzie was sitting on *Aphrodite*'s roof, chatting happily with George, when she suddenly lapsed into silence. George could see that she was lost in her own thoughts, which, from her face, he could see were not happy ones.

'Anythin' up?' he asked at last.

'I were jus' a-thinkin'.' She looked over the side into the water.

'Thinkin' about what?'

'Well, it's me birthday nex' week.' She faced him.

'Why the sad face, then? Your birthday's s'posed to be a 'appy time, ain't it?'

'Yeah, I know it is, but... Well, it's gonna be the first birthday as I'm 'ad wi'out me Mam bein' 'ere, ain't it?' she replied.

'Ah!' said George. 'I see what you mean.' Izzie remained silent.

'Well,' George continued after a few moments, 'if it's any sort o' comfort to you, I don't remember much about me Mam an' Dad cos I were only a nipper when they died, like, but I do remember 'ow I felt when me Gran passed away.' He paused. 'Yeah,' he said, 'I remember that awright! That first year after she'd gone, that were the worst! See, everythin' as 'appens in that first year after you're lost somebody – it's 'appenin' the first time wi'out 'em bein' there, ain't it? An' it's 'ard. I knows as it's 'ard. So, like I say, if it's any comfort to you, I'm been through it, so I knows 'ow you're feelin'.'

'Oh, George!' Izzie touched his free hand. 'You're such a kind, thoughtful fella!'

'I'll do the best as I can for you. You knows that.'

A week later Izzie awoke with a mixture of excitement and sadness. On the one hand she was excited. It was her eleventh birthday. On the other hand she was sad. 'Me first birthday wi'out me Mam!' she thought.

As the day of her birthday had come closer she had realised it would be different this year. Yes, she had been looking forward to her birthday. She was growing up. "Leven! Tha's nearly growed up!' she thought. But she was anxious. She did not want to face the day without her mother there.

She reached up and, unhooking her bag of treasures, took out the handkerchiefs her mother and father had bought for her a year ago. She remembered with a little smile how they had teased her by pretending they had forgotten that it was her birthday. She held them to her face. She could almost smell her mother. She traced the embroidered 'I' with her fingers, remembering how her mother had checked that she had chosen the right letter. She drew her knees up under her chin and balanced the hankies on top of them. 'I'll allus keep these,' she said out loud. She looked through the porthole at the water, dappled in the sunshine. 'I bet me Dad misses me Mam,' she thought. 'An' George – poor ol' George,' she mused, 'though 'e 'ardly knew 'is Mam an' Dad afore they was killed – an' then 'e 'ad to go through it all again when 'is Gran died. 'E's had worse 'n me to put up with, an' 'e's come out on it awright, so what am I got to be so miserable about?' She squared her shoulders. She felt braver, ready to face the day ahead.

As the three of them were finishing breakfast in *Aphrodite*'s cabin, George suddenly put his arm round Izzie and gave her a peck on the cheek.

"'Appy birthday, Izzie!' he said. 'Oh, an' I got you this.' He reached through the cabin doors and handed her what she first thought was a folded-up newspaper. On closer inspection she saw it was a story paper, especially for girls, called 'Crystal'.

'Wi' you bein' so keen on your readin' I reckoned as you might enjoy it. I 'ope as it won't be too hard for you, wi' you bein' still learnin', like.' Izzie's eyes lit up as she unfolded the paper and looked at its contents. There were a number of short stories, all with a picture alongside the title.

'Oh, thanks ever so much, George!' she said, putting her arms round his neck and giving him a hug and a kiss. 'I reckon as I'll really enjoy lookin' at that. I might even be able to read some on it!'

'Oh, git on wi' you!' George laughed at her show of affection in front of Bill. 'It's only a sort of a comic when all's said an' done. An' it weren't that dear, neither. I reckon it comes out every week, so you might wanna buy yourself one some time.'

Bill had watched with the trace of a smile on his face. He knew his daughter's birthday this year was going to be difficult, so he was very pleased to see George doing his best to make things easier for her. He was certainly not going to spoil it by adding any comments about 'bloomin' book learnin'! Not today. He let Izzie look at 'Crystal' for a few moments, and when she put it down he spoke.

'I got summat for you an' all, Izzie, love. You know that there bag o' yourn as you keeps your treasures in, as you call 'em?' he began. 'Well, I'm noticed as it's gittin' a bit the worse for wear – an' not only that, but it looks to me like it's gittin' a bit small for all o' the stuff as you're keepin' in it an' all,' he continued as he reached back through the curtain and picked something up. 'So I reckoned as 'ow I better make this for you!' He held out his hands to show her a beautifully made wooden box, decorated with painted roses. It was complete with a hinged lid and a little lock with a key in it. Izzie was overwhelmed.

'Oh, Dad!' she exclaimed. 'It's lovely!' She opened the lid. The inside surfaces had been varnished so that they shone brightly. "Owever did you find the time to do all this?'

'That's for me to know an' for you to find out!' He tapped the side of his nose.

'No. Go on, 'ow did you?'

'Well, some o' them nights as you reckoned me an' George was down the pub all evenin'? Well, we wasn't! We'd sneak back 'ere a bit early – wi' a bottle or two o' course – an' 'opin' as you'd be in the land o' Nod! Then we'd git on the motor an' I'd git to makin' up that box for you. 'Ad to work quiet, though, jus' in case we woke you up!'

'That's why the joints in that box is all glued!' George chuckled. "E daren't use no nails in case you 'eard 'im 'ammerin' an' waked up!'

'An' you're painted it so nice, an' all!' she said, turning the box round in her hands.

'Yeah,' said Bill. 'I'm a bit sorry about the paintin' really. See, I can only do roses an' castles.'

'That ain't nuthin' at all for you to be sorry about, Dad!' his daughter placated him. 'Awright, so p'raps you can only do roses an' castles – but you do 'em really nice!'

She finally stopped admiring the box and put it down on the table next to 'Crystal'. She stood up and gave her father an enormous hug.

'Steady on, gel!' he protested. 'I shan't 'ave no ribs left at this rate!'

'Thank you ever so, ever so much, Dad! I reckon it's the most beautiful thing as I'm ever seen – well, apart from them 'ankies as you an' me Mam give me last year.' She paused. 'I weren't lookin' forward to today very much – what wi' me Mam not bein' 'ere no more an' that. I reckoned as I were goin' to be … well … a bit sad, like. I s'pose I am sad, really … a bit. But you two's made me really 'appy an' all. So, I s'pose what I'm sayin' is "Thank you" – not jus' for me presents – which is both lovely – but for 'elpin' me to feel … well, 'appier 'n I ever thought as I were gonna.' Bill and George both put their arms round her.

'That's awright, Izzie, love,' said her father.

'That were a grand little speech!' added George. Bill looked at his watch and got up from the table.

'Ah, well,' he said, 'birthday, or no birthday, it's time as we was gettin' 'em ahead!'

Chapter 10

Next job

The pickle factory contract eventually finished in June. The Government contract – if that was, indeed, what it was – had come to an end. Tom Speechley explained: 'We're finished that big order we 'ad, so we won't be needin' so much coal now, Bill. My blokes are all moanin' cos they've got used to the overtime an' you've lost a reg'lar job. It's sad, but there you are. What coal we need for our usual orders, we can get local.' They all shook hands with Tom, John and Dick, then set about preparing the boats to leave the canal by the factory for the last time.

'If we get that big order again I'll be sure to put the work your way!' Tom called as they pulled away.

'Thanks!' Bill shouted back.

After so many months of regular work it was worrying not to know where their next job was coming from. An air of despondency hung over them all as they made their way back to the Wharf, a mood that was not helped as there was no return load on this run either.

'It's a pity that there job's finished. It were a good reg'lar run – an' they was a decent bunch o' blokes at that works,' Bill said to George after they had stopped for the night.

'Yeah, that Tom were a good sort, an' Dick an' John was a couple o' 'ard-workin' lads an' all.'

'I 'ope Mr Roberts 'as got summat else for us. I don't fancy the idea o' spendin' too much time tied up there, waitin' for orders. It'll come 'ard after 'avin' a reg'lar run all this while.'

'It's gonna seem a bit strange,' George agreed. Izzie knew that her father was concerned. The regular run had entitled him to maximum pay and they had become accustomed to the extra income.

The following day Izzie was in her usual position on the cabin roof chatting with George.

'Cor blimey!' he suddenly said. 'Look at that!'

Izzie looked over her shoulder. They were approaching a bridge where a main road crossed the canal. Crossing the bridge was a long convoy of vehicles, all painted the same shade of dark green.

'That's the third load o' army wagons we're seen this run!' George commented.

'Why d'you reckon they're suddenly so busy, movin' stuff about, then?' Izzie asked.

'I dunno. P'raps it's on account o' this 'ere war as they reckon's goin' to 'appen.'

'Me Dad says as he still reckons tha's all jus' a rumour.'

'Well, I ain't so sure. Seein' th' army so busy, I reckon there mus' be summat 'appenin'.'

Izzie was quiet for a moment, then she asked, 'Wha's war like?'

'Well,' said George, 'I don't really know. I mean, the last 'un were all over a couple o' year afore I were born. But me Grandad, 'e were in it. 'E never talked much about what it were like, though.'

'Did you ask 'im?'

'Oh, ah. When I were a nipper, like. I mean, young boys is allus keen on playin' at wars an' fightin' an' that. Course, at that age you don't sort o' realise that in a real war you don't get up again when your been shot dead.'

'No. Didn' 'e never say nuthin' about it then?'

'Oh, 'e sometimes said a bit to shut me up after I'd pestered 'im about it. 'E said as it were 'ard in the trenches – cos that's 'ow they was fightin', see? There was our trenches an' there was the Germans' trenches an' the bit o' ground in the middle was what they called "no man's land".'

'What was the trenches like?'

'They was like long narra 'oles dug in the ground – 'bout eight foot deep. That's where they 'ad to live when they was fightin'. Be'ind 'em was a load o' big guns as was firin' at the Germans' trenches, an' when they'd finished, me Grandad an' his mates 'ad to climb out the trench and go across this no man's land an' capture the Germans' trenches.'

'An' was the Germans shootin' at 'em?'

'Course they was! Loads an' loads o' blokes was killed. You're seen them stone crosses as they put up in the towns an' villages wi' them lists o' names on? They're called war memorials and them names is the blokes as was killed.'

Izzie thought for a moment, remembering the lists of names she had seen. 'It don't sound very nice, war don't!' she said at last.

'It ain't,' George replied. 'It definitely ain't!'

✳

'There are no more regular contracts at the moment, Bill,' Horace said as Bill and George sat in his office in the afternoon after their last return run from London.

'That don't sound so good!' Bill replied.

'I agree,' said Horace. 'We seem to be scratching around a bit for orders of any sort at the moment.' Just then his telephone rang.

'Excuse me,' he said as he answered it. He picked up his pen and began making notes.

'Yes, of course,' he said to the caller. 'I'll get it in tonight's post for you. Thank you. Bye!' He replaced the receiver.

'That might be your next job if it comes through!' he said.

'Thank you, Mr Roberts,' Bill said as they stood up to leave.

'I reckoned as all this talk o' war were gonna mean a bit more work for us!' he said to George as they made their way back to the pair.

'Ain't seen none on it yit, are we?' came the reply.

'This is the first time we're been waitin' for orders since you're been wi' us, ain't it?'

'I knows what you're gonna say, Bill!' George interjected. 'It were the same when I worked for me Grandad, an' it's no more nor less 'n I expected. You're gonna git paid less for sittin', tied up 'ere, so your gotta pay me a bit less an' all. I understand all that.'

'Good!' said Bill, sounding relieved. 'I wondered if I might 'ave a mutiny on me 'ands!' They both chuckled at that.

'I understand an' I don't mind. Jus' as long as you pay me summat.'

'Ah, I will. But as long as you understand it won't be a lot.'

Izzie, on the other hand, was pleased to be back at the Wharf for a while. While they had been travelling she had read and re-read the books Emily had lent her until she could almost quote them all by heart. They had rarely stopped at the Wharf, and then usually overnight when the school was closed.

As George and her father had stepped off the boats to go to the office, she had gone into the schoolroom. Emily was, as always, delighted to see her. Thomas Johnson was the only other pupil that afternoon.

'Where's your brother?' Izzie asked.

''Elpin' me Dad clear the mudbox,' he replied.

'Typical o' Ray Johnson,' thought Izzie. 'Anythin' to git out o' goin' to school!' She could see from the look on Thomas's face that even though everyone hated clearing the mudbox on a boat, he would rather have been helping his father too.

In order to engage her young pupils' interest, Miss Roberts had brought in a box of tin soldiers and a tray of sand. Between them she and Thomas had created a battle scene. It looked to Izzie as if there were a lot of casualties!

'Now, Thomas,' said Miss Roberts, 'while I help Isobel, you write a sentence or two about your battle.' At this point Thomas's interest suddenly waned, and he doodled aimlessly on the paper while Emily devoted her attention to Izzie.

Izzie explained to Emily the latest change in their pattern of work and, beaming, said, '...so I'm gonna be in 'ere a bit more now!'

'Good!' Emily said. 'Now, let's see what progress you've made while you've been away!'

As Izzie was so confident, she decided to introduce some simple comprehension exercises. She gave Izzie a book in which each page had a picture, under which was a short passage followed by some questions. Emily explained that she had to use the information in the passage and the picture to answer the questions. The first piece was about a boy and a girl who were playing on the beach at the seaside. Izzie read the passage aloud.

'What's the seaside?' she asked when she had finished. Miss

Roberts explained about Britain being an island, and about coastlines and seashores. She showed Izzie a map of Britain. She showed her a piece of sea that was called the English Channel and explained that on the other side of it, off the map, there were other countries called France and Germany.

'We calls the deep bit in the middle o' the cut "the channel",' Izzie said.

'The English Channel's a lot wider than the cut!' Emily said.

'I can see it is,' Izzie agreed as she continued studying the map. 'So France an' Germany is down 'ere somewhere?' She pointed at the wall below the map.

'Yes,' said Emily. 'A long way down there.'

Izzie paused.

'George says as there's a-gonna be a war wi' Germany,' she said.

'I think he may be right,' replied Miss Roberts thoughtfully, 'but I pray he'll be wrong.'

'That's what George says.'

Emily returned Izzie's attention to the exercise.

'Now, Isobel, remember. You have to answer the questions using complete sentences,' she instructed. 'Read the first question.'

'"What is John doin'?"' Izzie read.

'And what is he doing?' Emily repeated.

'Doin' summat wi' the sand. What is it?'

'It's called a "sandcastle". He's building a sandcastle.'

'Oh yeah. I can see it looks like the castles as we paint on the boats – only it's made o' sand.'

'So, what is John doing?'

'Buildin' a sandcastle.'

'Is that a complete sentence, Isobel?'

'Er … no. Sorry! John is buildin' a sandcastle.'

'Good! Now read the second one.

'"What is Mary doin'?"' she read.

'And what is Mary doing?' Emily asked.

'She's in the sea,' Izzie answered.

'Who is in the sea?'

'Mary.'

'Complete sentence?'

'No, sorry, I forgot. Mary is in the sea.'

'But what is Mary actually doing in the sea, Isobel? Look at the passage again and pick out the important words. You've already found "Mary" and "sea". What else is there to help you?'

Izzie scanned the passage. 'Ah! Got it! Mary is paddlin' in the sea!' she exclaimed exultantly.

'Well done!'

'We 'as paddles on the cut too,' Izzie said. 'On the locks. Ain't it funny 'ow it's the same word but it don't mean nuthin' like the same thing?' Then she added. 'Me Mam got stuck in a paddle 'ole.'

'Yes, she did, Isobel,' said Miss Roberts. 'I'm sure that she would be so pleased that you are continuing with your schooling. She would be very proud of you.'

'I know,' Izzie answered.

The exercise was completed and she did two more before the end of the school day. As she was leaving, Emily said, 'Take the comprehension book with you, Isobel, and try the next exercise at home. You can write the answers in your notebook and bring it with you tomorrow.'

'Righto, Miss Roberts,' Izzie replied, picking up the book.

As soon as she was back on board, she took a pencil from the knife drawer and proceeded to answer the questions on the next exercise, which was all about a visit to a zoo. 'I ain't never been to a zoo afore,' she mused, 'but it looks like fun!'

The next morning, when Emily had checked her answers, she suggested to Izzie that she could also use her notebook to write some stories of her own.

'I dunno if I could do that.' Izzie was hesitant. 'What could they be about?'

'That's the beauty of writing your own stories, Isobel. They can be about anything you like, anything at all that pops into your head. It doesn't matter what they're about and it doesn't matter if they're long or short. They can be fast-moving and full of action or they can be slow with lots of description. It doesn't matter. You write about anything you feel like.'

'Right!' said Izzie, 'I'll 'ave a go.' She paused, then said with a chuckle, 'P'raps I'll write about goin' to the seaside – or the zoo!'

❄

Fortunately, Horace's 'next job' came through. A week later he called Bill and George to the office.

'What sort o' job is it?' Bill asked.

'Wholesale builders' merchants. They've noticed that they have a number of their customers working on sites close to the cut, so they're wondering if it might be more economical to deliver by boat than by road.'

'What – bricks an stuff like that?' George asked.

'From what he said it would be mostly bags of cement. You'd load at their depot near Rugby and take it to whichever site had ordered it. It wouldn't be a regular run like the one you've just finished because, obviously, you'd be taking the loads to different places.'

'I understand that,' Bill said.

Horace filled out the paperwork for the first load and handed it to Bill.

'Thanks again, Mr Roberts,' Bill said as they stood up to leave.

They set off for Rugby the next morning. Because of the nature of the job, Horace had explained, they would not be away from the Wharf for long periods and, to Izzie's delight, they were sometimes waiting there for new delivery instructions for several days. This enabled her to be at school regularly, to make great strides with learning, and to impress Miss Roberts with her progress.

Chapter 11

War

While they were waiting at the Wharf one morning in August, Horace asked them all to go into the office. As they entered they saw a pile of small cardboard boxes stacked against the side of his desk. He picked up three of the boxes and placed them on his desk.

'Now,' he said as he sat down, 'these boxes contain gas masks. Everybody in the whole country has to be issued with one and shown how to use it.' George smiled to himself. Mr Roberts was off on one of his explanations!

'Is this summat to do wi' all this talk about a war as we keep 'earin'?' he asked.

'I'm afraid it is. The Government is concerned that the Germans might launch gas attacks on our civilians, hence the masks.'

'I still reckon it's all rumour – that an' Gover'ment propaganda!' said Bill.

'Well, rumour or not, these are your gas masks and this is how you put them on.' He took another mask from his desk drawer and demonstrated. He pulled the mask down over his head until the filter part was over his nose and mouth, then he tightened the straps at the back.

'Now, you try!' he said, as he pushed three of the boxes across his desk towards them. His voice sounded very muffled and strange from inside the mask, and it was all Izzie could do not to burst out laughing.

They all put their gas masks on as he had shown them, Horace checking the straps to see if they were tight enough. 'They smells awful!' thought Izzie. 'A 'orrible rubbery smell! An' it's 'ot – an' I can't see nuthin' neither!' The acetate eye panel was starting to mist over.

'You don' 'alf look daft!' said George, his voice muffled and distorted by the mask.

'You ain't no oil paintin' yourself wi' that on!' Izzie retorted.

When they had all removed their masks and packed them back into their boxes, Horace picked up a leaflet.

'Now,' he said, 'these masks are to be carried with you at all times, so that they are there ready to use wherever and whenever a gas attack takes place.'

"Ow are we gonna know when there's a gas attack, Mr Roberts?" George asked. 'I mean, by the time as we smells it, it'll be too late, won't it?'

'It says here that wardens will travel around affected areas blowing repeated blasts on a whistle. So when you hear the whistle, take out your gas masks and put them on – double quick!'

"Ow the 'ell are we goin' to 'ear a bloody whistle out on the cut?" scoffed Bill.

Undeterred, Horace continued. 'It might be a good idea to practise putting them on and taking them off, so you'll be ready in an emergency – like when you are tied up in a town.' He looked at Izzie. 'But why am I reading you all this from this leaflet? If half of what my daughter tells me about you is true, Izzie, you can make sense of this and explain it to your father and George.' Horace handed her the leaflet, making her feel very important indeed. She looked at it. By looking at the pictures she was pleased with what she could understand. She was soon brought back down to earth, however, as her father said, 'I still reckon as it's all bluff – rumour, propaganda an' bluff!'

'Well,' said Horace, 'I've done what I'm obliged to do according to the law. I've issued you with your masks. I've shown you how to put them on, and I've told you the orders are to carry them with you always. Oh, and I've also told you what the signal for a gas attack is going to be. Now, whether you do all that is your affair – but it could just as easily be your funeral!'

They stood to leave the office, carrying their gas masks.

'Jus' a minute, Mr Roberts,' George said, sitting down again. "Ow's this warden bloke gonna be able to blow a whistle if 'e's wearin' one o' these things? Cos if 'e ain't wearin' one 'e's gonna git gassed, ain't 'e?'

Horace was silent. It was the first time they had ever known him to be stuck for words.

'I don't honestly know,' he said at last. Then quickly added, 'But that's not our problem, is it?'

'Rumour!' said Bill as they returned to the pair. 'Nuthin' but bluff an' rumour!'

George thought differently. 'I reckon as I'm gonna keep mine close at 'and. I mean ... you never know!'

'An' I reckon as I'm a-gonna do that an' all,' Izzie agreed. 'Look,' she said, 'these 'ere boxes 'as got a string through 'em so's you can wear it round your neck!'

'Very 'andy when I'm got me 'ead down the engine 'ole, I'm sure!' muttered Bill. Izzie and George exchanged a smile.

The longer she spent in George's company, the happier Izzie was that he had joined them. As an only child, she had never known the company, the fun, the teasing – and the arguments – that came from having brothers and sisters. She felt that George treated her like a younger sister. He was very kind and thoughtful towards her and she was beginning to like him very much. She was content with her life, but little realised the impact that an announcement made that September day would have on her life and her new-found happiness.

Horace was waiting for them on the Wharf as they returned after making a cement delivery.

'I don't suppose you'll have heard,' he began, as Bill turned off the engine. 'We've declared war on Germany!'

'Oh!' Bill was shocked. 'So it weren't no rumour, then?'

'No, Bill, I'm afraid it wasn't. Mr Chamberlain was on the wireless earlier today. He was saying something about the Government having sent a note to the Germans telling them that they didn't much like what they were getting up to in Poland. Do you remember? I told you about what Winston Churchill thought Hitler was intending to do there, didn't I?' Bill nodded. 'Well, it would seem that he was absolutely right, because that's exactly what he's gone and done!'

'Don't them Germans never learn?' George asked. 'I mean, we showed 'em who were boss in the last lot, didn't we?'

'Well, we won the war, as far as that goes. Perhaps this is Hitler trying to get some sort of revenge for what happened then. I don't know.'

'From what I'm 'eard folk sayin' about 'im, an' on the wireless in the pub, I reckon as that's jus' the sort o' thing 'e would do. Nasty piece o' work, 'e sounds like!'

'You're right there, George, he is! But whatever his reasons, it's happened. We're officially at war, and we've all just got to get on with it.'

'Can't say as I'm that surprised, really,' said George. 'We're seen so much o' th' army on the move these las' weeks. An' the wireless said as they're buildin' bomb shelters some places cos they think they're gonna git an air raid.'

'Yes, I read about that in the *Express* the other day. I suppose there's no harm in taking precautions, is there?'

'We seen some lorry loads o' sandbags bein' took round an' all. What d'you reckon, Bill?' George asked. 'You're been a bit quiet.'

'Ah,' said Bill, 'I were thinkin' about our Bert.'

'He was your older brother, wasn't he?' said Horace.

'Killed on the Somme in the last war, 'e were! Only eighteen. What a waste o' life that were!'

All three fell silent. After a while, Bill asked, 'So what d'you reckon that'll mean for us over 'ere then, Mr Roberts?'

'Well…,' Horace thought for a moment or two. 'There might be a few bombs falling, particularly in the big cities. You'll have to watch out for yourselves if you're tied up in any large built-up areas. But otherwise, I can't see that there'll be too much of a change really. That's as far as I can tell you at the minute anyway … except, of course – well, you never know – it might even mean there'll be a bit more work for the boats!'

'That definitely won't go amiss!' Bill replied.

'Might even git a few more back loads!' George added.

'You never know your luck!' Horace said, returning to his office. 'Wait there a minute,' he called. 'There's something else I need to give you.'

At the mention of falling bombs, without even thinking about it, Izzie cast a worried glance up to the sky. She did not like the sound of that at all.

Just then, Horace reappeared carrying some pieces of black material. 'I've been instructed to give these out to all the boats,' he said. 'They're to fix up against your portholes before you light your lamps at night, and you've also got to remember to put all your lights out before you open your slide or your doors after dark. It's particularly important when you're in or near a town or a city.'

'What's all that for, then? asked Bill.

'It's so German aircraft can't see where you are.'

'An' what if we don't?'

'You could be in trouble! There are people called Air Raid Protection Wardens, and it's their job to go round after dark and make sure that nobody's showing a light anywhere.'

'Bloomin' busybodies!'

'No, come on, Bill!' George protested. 'Think about it! If you was a German bomber an' you was lookin' down on England an' you see no lights, you wouldn't know where to drop your bombs, would you? Then, if someone opens a slide an' you seen that one light, shinin' out in the dark, well, that's where you're gonna let 'em go, ain't it?'

'I s'pose there is that to it,' Bill reluctantly agreed.

As Horace returned to his office, Izzie made her way to the schoolroom. It was getting towards the end of the afternoon session and Miss Roberts was reading her class a story. As Izzie entered, she looked up.

'Hello, Isobel!' she said. The other children greeted her as she sat down at an empty desk at the back and Emily continued with the story.

Soon it was the end of the school day and, as the other pupils went back to their boats, Izzie returned her books.

'You know, Isobel, you really are getting on very well with your reading.'

'Am I?' Izzie was not so sure.

'Yes, you are. Look, I've got a few minutes before I need to go home. Why don't you pick one of the books you've read recently and read some of it to me?'

'Awright!' Izzie looked at the bookshelf and found one she had particularly enjoyed.

'I'll read a bit o' this 'un.' She opened the book and began to read. Apart from a few words where Emily had to correct her pronunciation, Izzie read the first two pages with no problems.

'You really are my star pupil when it comes to reading, Isobel!' her teacher enthused.

'Thank you, Miss Roberts.' She paused. 'Wha's all this talkin' about a war, Miss Roberts?'

'Well, there's going to be one.'

'Mr Roberts were jus' tellin' me Dad an' George about it, an' we seen summat about it on a newsreel at the pictures th' other week. I don't like the sound on it! Bombs an' guns an' things! Why do people 'ave to start doin' 'orrible things like that?'

'If I knew the answer to that I wouldn't be a teacher!' Emily chuckled. 'I think I'd have a top job in the Government. It's hard to know why people start wars. This one is because the Germans want to take over part of another country called Poland and make it part of Germany. And because Britain is friends with Poland, our Government don't think that's a good thing to do, so they've said we'll go to war with Germany to help Poland.'

'It's 'ard to understand, ain't it?'

'Look, here are some more books for you to take with you – and don't you worry about the war. People are saying that it'll all be over by Christmas.'

'Thank you, Miss Roberts. I really 'ope as it is!'

'Mind you, that's what they said about the last one – and that went on for four years!'

From the look of horror on Izzie's face, Emily realised she ought not to have added that. She quickly changed the subject.

'I know what you could do, Isobel.'

'Yes, Miss Roberts?'

'Do you know what a diary is?'

'Is it like a book, where you write down things as you're gotta do?'

'It can be,' Emily explained as she opened her desk drawer and took out a small notebook. 'You can also write in it the things you have done each day. When you do that it's also called a journal,' she said as she opened the book. 'You know how to write the days of the week and the months of the year – all you need are the dates.' Emily delved into her desk once again and produced a small calendar.

'You've seen one of these before, haven't you? It's a smaller version of that one hanging on the schoolroom wall. It shows you all the numbers for all the days of every month of the year.'

'Tha's clever!' said Izzie. 'Does that mean as they 'as to print new 'uns every year, then? Cos the dates ain't gonna be on the same days, is they?'

'That's quite right. This one is this year's. As soon as I get one for next year, I'll keep it for you, because I think that you have come on so well with your reading and your writing that at the end of each day you can write in it the day and the date and then you can put down all the things you have done that day – like where you have travelled from and to, whether you have been loading or unloading – and, of course, anything you get up to when you're away from the boats.'

'Tha's a good idea, that is!' Izzie smiled. 'I will. I'll write a bit in it every day!' she said, as she picked up the notebook. 'Thank you, Miss Roberts.'

In December they received the good news that the contract for coal from Coventry to the pickle factory was starting again, and because they had impressed Tom Speechley so much the previous year he had specifically asked for them to have the job again. Horace was always pleased when he received good reports of one of 'his' crews, and was pleased to agree.

At this news, Izzie went to tell Emily Roberts that they would soon be on the regular Coventry to London run again.

'Fine!' said Emily. 'We'll manage it the same as we did last year. I'll lend you some books to take with you when you are off on the run, and when you call in here you can give them back to me and I can give you some more. It works rather like a library.'

'Like a what?' Izzie asked.

'A library. Most towns and cities have a place called a public library. It's a building with lots and lots of books, all arranged on shelves, and people can join the library and borrow the books for a set number of weeks. They take them home to read them and bring them back either when they've finished them or when the time's up.'

'So they gets to read all them books wi'out 'avin' to buy 'em?'

'Yes.'

'That's a good idea, 'ooever thought on it!' said Izzie.

'It was an American man called Andrew Carnegie.'

'Well, 'e were very clever, comin' up wi' an idea like that.' Izzie thought for a moment. 'So why does we 'ave bookshops an' all, then?'

'Well, sometimes, you don't just want to borrow a book, read it once and take it back again. If it's a book you particularly like – a book that's special to you for some reason or other – then you might want to keep it. So rather than borrowing it from the library, you'd go and buy it from a bookshop.' Again, Izzie was quiet for a moment as she remembered fondly the bookshop next to the butcher's in Birmingham.

'I see,' she said, then she smiled. 'I'd really like to join your library, then, please Miss Roberts!'

The cement deliveries were given to another pair and *Zeus* and *Aphrodite* were soon on their way to the coal yard near Coventry to collect their first load.

'I 'ope as that John an' Dick's still workin' there to 'elp with the unloadin',' said George as they were waiting, breasted up, in the queue for the hopper.

'They might o' been called up,' Bill said.

'I 'ope not,' George replied. 'They're good 'ard-workin' lads, them two.'

✳

At first the war hardly seemed to interfere with their lives at all. With the pickle factory contract having started again, they were busy between Coventry and London. Over the next few months they occasionally saw groups of aircraft flying in the sky, although they were never sure whether they were German planes or RAF. Then one night, when they were tied up at the pickle factory, they heard the sound of bombs falling somewhere in the distance. Fortunately, the pickle factory was long way from the London Docks, which seemed to be the bombers' target.

But, like everyone else, they were subject to food rationing. Having received a message from Horace, they tied up at the Wharf late one afternoon and he called them all into the office.

'I have to give you these,' he said. 'They're what are called Ration Books.' He picked up a handful of books and ticked off Bill's name on a list.

'They arrived here yesterday, so I'm giving them out to each crew as they arrive.'

'What's it all about?' Bill asked.

'Well, as you might have guessed, it's because of the war. Apparently, there are some shortages of lots of different sorts of food – the stuff that we import from abroad, mostly. So the Government has brought in this rationing scheme to try to make sure that everyone gets their fair share of what food there is available.'

'Sounds like good sense,' George said. Horace showed them the Ration Books and explained how they worked.

'Who's going to be responsible for your shopping?'

'I reckon that'll be our Izzie,' Bill answered. 'She's been lookin' after us since we lost 'er Mam, 'aven't you, love?' Izzie nodded and Horace handed her the books.

'Now, Izzie.' Mr Roberts turned his attention to her. 'You must remember to take these books with you whenever you go shopping for food. If you don't have them with you, you won't be able to buy any of the food that's on the ration. Not only do you have to take them with you, but you have to go to the same shops all the time. I know that won't be possible when you're on a run, so I suggest you have a chat with the shopkeepers where you usually go and have one set of shops in London and another in Coventry while your Dad's on this pickle factory contract. But you have to remember that you won't be able to buy any of the rationed stuff from any of the shops anywhere else during your run, so you'll need to stock up with the maximum you're allowed at each end. Do you follow me?'

'Yes, Mr Roberts. I won' forgit to take 'em wi' me.' She paused, thinking. 'So that means as I'll 'ave to stock up in London an' Coventry for the whole o' the run?'

'Yes, it does. Can you cope with that?'

'I reckon so,' she said, taking the books.

When she was back on the boats, Izzie looked at the books in more detail. She was pleased with how many words she could recognise. Reading the instructions about how to use the books, she was happily surprised by how much she could understand. She was about to say, "Ere, Dad! I can read most o' these 'ere words!' But then she remembered his attitude to 'book learnin''. She also remembered what her mother had said all that time ago when she had first begun to learn to read – about her father being jealous of her abilities. She decided to keep it to herself and say nothing at all. 'They ain't as interestin' as the books as I gits from Miss Roberts,' she thought, as she put the books away safely in the ticket drawer, 'but I better git used to usin' 'em if we're gonna eat!'

After a few shopping expeditions in London and Coventry she soon managed to get to grips with using them. She explained her situation to the shopkeepers in both cities, and they were happy to oblige. She found that her youth gave her something of an advantage over the other customers. She was on good terms with the shopkeepers and they knew that she was getting all the provisions to feed two grown men who were helping the war effort. Some of the shopkeepers had a soft spot for this young girl and her great responsibility. If they could spare it, they would slip a little extra into her bag. On these occasions Izzie would smile broadly and whisper, 'Thank you ever so much!'

Bill was sometimes known to visit the 'Boatman's Garden'. It was said that the garden stretched the whole length of the canal! After dark, the boatmen would sneak over the fence into someone's garden and return with a freshly cut cabbage – or whatever else was needed for the following day's meal. Izzie sometimes found a cabbage or a few carrots appearing in her basket. Nothing was ever said, but they were enjoyed by all.

As she was putting the Ration Books back in the drawer one day, George complimented her on how well she was managing with shopping for them all and coping with the Ration Books as well.

'It's jus' as well as I can read a bit!' she said. 'I couldn't do anywhere near as good if I couldn't. You're gotta make sure as they cut the right number o' coupons out the right bit o' the book for what you're bought. An' it 'elps an' all, cos I can read some o' the signs as they 'as up in the shops.'

'Good for you! You keep on wi' your readin' and we'll all 'ave full bellies!'

They laughed, then Izzie suddenly remembered something. 'George,' she said, suddenly serious, 'what's "call-up papers"?'

'Where are you 'eard that?'

'When I were in the greengrocer's th' other day. One o' the women who was there was sayin' as 'er 'usband'd 'ad 'is call-up papers.'

'Ah!' George explained, 'it were on the wireless in the pub a few week back. They was sayin' as 'ow they need more men in the military, so they're introducin' what they calls "conscription".'

'What's that?'

'Well, as I understand it, they can call on any able-bodied bloke in the country an' make 'im join th' army or the navy or th' air force.'

'Hang on!' Izzie said. 'You're an able-bodied bloke, ain't you?'

'Yeah, I am,' George said, 'but I ask the landlord when I 'eard it. I said, "Could that be me?"'

'What did 'e say?' Izzie was getting worried.

''E said as the Gover'ment 'ad a list o' what they call "reserved occupations", an' 'e were sure as boatman was on it.'

'What's reserved occupations?'

'It's them jobs as the Gover'ment reckons is important to the country, 'specially when there's a war on. Things like coal-minin' an' dock-workin' – an' transport, an' that means me!'

'That's awright then.' Izzie was reassured. She thought, 'I don't want George to 'ave to go off fightin' in no war!' She noted this conversation in her journal as she wrote it up that night.

She was pleased to find that, not only was she able to read many of the signs she saw in the shops, she was also able to understand the posters that were appearing on the billboards she passed. She understood what the 'Dig for Victory' poster meant, although their nomadic lifestyle prevented them from following its advice. She also realised what another poster meant, the one that said 'Careless Talk Costs Lives'. She told her father and George about it after they had eaten one evening. 'So jus' watch out for anybody as might be listenin' to you in the pub!' she warned them. They both nodded, but whether they took her warning seriously, she was not so sure.

Chapter 12

Only a girl

Izzie was relieved to see how well George and her father got on together. Bill was always kind and gentle to her, and she knew he loved her as much as she loved him. But he could be determined, stubborn and strong-willed. He was used to getting his own way, although both Izzie and her mother knew how to get round him – most of the time. The two men enjoyed each other's company. George treated Bill with respect, asking his advice and opinions, and Bill treated George like the son he had never had.

Sometimes, after they had tied the boats up for the night and enjoyed one of George's truly excellent dinners, Bill and George went for a pint or two together at a nearby pub. One of Bill's favourites was The Running Horse, and he tried to time their runs to London and their return trips so that they were able to stop close by it overnight. He had often stopped there with Maggie, and Izzie remembered sitting on the wall outside with the other boat children, drinking a bottle of mineral water through a straw.

"E keeps a decent boozer, does Alf,' Bill often said when referring to 'The Horse', 'an' 'is lad, Alan. 'E's a good barman.'

'The Horse' was one of the many pubs that stood on the towpath. They had been built there many years before, not long after the canals opened, so that the boatmen could slake their thirsts after long days at the tiller. Back then they also had stabling for boat horses. It was a classic two-room house – a public bar where the men drank if they had gone to the pub on their own, and a saloon bar for when they took their wives and children with them.

As the evening wore on, one of the customers would produce a fiddle, a concertina or a melodeon, and very soon the whole pub would be singing – boatmen and locals alike – not only the popular songs of the day but also the folksongs of the cut, songs that had been passed down from generation to generation of boat people. The later the sing-song went on, the bawdier the songs became! Many a boatman would awake in the morning after one of these sessions with both a hangover from drinking too much and a rather hoarse voice as a result of his fortissimo efforts of the night before.

Sometimes Izzie would go along with them for a glass of lemonade, or, when her father allowed her, the odd half pint of shandy. But more often than not she preferred to stay with the boats. She realised soon after George had joined them that if the two men went to the pub on their own they enjoyed their evenings a lot more. It was easier for them to chat with the other boatmen without having continually to try to involve her in the conversation, and some of their conversation was not suitable for the ears of an impressionable young girl!

On those occasions when George and Bill went to the pub without Izzie, Bill always made sure that someone else on a boat tied up close by was aware that she was on board on her own and that Izzie, in turn, knew who to go to if she needed help. As Bill said, 'You never know what might 'appen – what with a war on, an' all.'

Izzie did not mind in the least being left alone on the boats at night. When it was cold or wet she busied herself with her beloved books, reading, writing or drawing, or she would do a bit of mending, knitting or crochet. But when the weather was fine and warm she often sat up on the cabin roof looking out along the canal as the dusk gathered.

There on the roof, just sitting and watching the cut at night, she always felt a deep sense of peace. There was something very special about the gathering darkness, the atmosphere of tranquillity, the stillness of the cut, the quietness of the moored boats with their flickering oil lamps and their dim reflections in the muddy water. It was something – a feeling – that she did not yet have the words to describe. But it was a feeling that seemed to put her mind at rest and actually pervade her very soul with such an aura of peace that it felt so real and so tangible. She imagined she could actually touch it with her fingers and physically feel its texture. 'It's like I can feel the dusk sort o' gatherin' around me ... like a big, soft, comfortin' blanket,' she thought.

Sitting, watching the canal on these evenings, she often thought that these wonderful feelings were something really important; so important that she ought to try to find the words to describe exactly how she felt and write them down. 'I wonder if should write down them words as say 'ow I feel? I wonder if I should write 'em down in a book, then other folks could read 'em an' then they'd know how good it is to feel them feelin's. I wonder if anybody else ever felt them same feelin's when they been sat on the cabin roof, all quiet-like, of an evenin'? If they 'ave felt 'em, I wonder if they ever thought as them feelin's was important enough to write down in a book. An' if they 'ave, I wonder if it might be one of them 'undreds o' books I seen in that bookshop agin the butcher's, waitin' for me Mam that day in Brum.'

Sometimes she would take her box of 'treasures' up there with her. She would take them out of the box and look at them. She would arrange the pebbles, shells and trinkets into patterns on the roof. She would look at her 'special treasures' – her copy of 'Crystal' and, of course, the two lace handkerchiefs with her initial embroidered on them – the last birthday present her mother had bought for her. Looking at them still made her sad because she missed her so much, but in other ways they were a comfort, a link with her mother. She pressed them to her face, closed her eyes and remembered the things they had done together.

The evening would pass so quickly, and she would get so wrapped up in her thoughts that she lost all track of time. Her reveries would suddenly be interrupted by a boatwoman's voice from one of the neighbouring pairs.

'Ain't you in bed yit, young lady? You'd better git a shuffle on, or your Dad'll be after me for not keepin' an eye on you proper!' Izzie would smile back, say she was sorry and that she was just on her way to bed. More often than not there would follow the offer of a cup of tea, '...cos I jus' got a brew on.'

Most nights Izzie was fast asleep by the time her father and George returned from an evening at the pub. Over the years of sharing the tiny cabin with her parents she slept deeply enough not to hear them moving about. Usually Bill was able to enter the cabin and get himself into bed without waking his daughter, but in truth she was a light sleeper.

Sometimes, when George and her father had a conversation on the towpath before turning in, she would rouse sufficiently to hear what they were saying. On one such night, she woke to hear her father and George having a discussion that was not altogether – well – friendly! She realised that George was proposing an exchange of steering duties. He had had the temerity – fortified by a pint or two at 'The Horse', no doubt – to suggest to Bill that it might be a good notion for him to have a go at steering *Zeus* for a change! Predictably, Bill was not quite so sure.

'I only ever seen you steerin' the butty on your Grandad's pair,' Bill stated firmly. Izzie recognised his 'I'm right!' voice.

'That's only cos the stubborn ol' bugger wouldn't never let me steer the motor, neither!' George countered. 'I asked 'im an' asked 'im. I asked 'im loads o' times but 'e allus made some excuse why I shouldn't.'

'Well, I dunno…,' Bill mused. 'Ol' Man Andrews', as George's grandfather was known by everyone on the cut, was renowned for his legendary stubbornness – and Bill suddenly realised that if he was not careful, he was about to be tarred with the same brush.

'Go on, Bill.' George interrupted his thoughts. 'If I never git the chance to try wi' the motor I ain't never gonna learn 'ow to do it, am I?'

'Well, I s'pose there is that to it,' Bill had to agree. Neither man spoke for a few moments. It was Bill who broke the silence.

'Awright, George, me boy. I'll let you 'ave your chance. If there ain't too much wind about tomorra, you can 'ave the motor.'

'Aw, thanks, Bill!' George replied. Izzie could hear the happiness in his voice. 'You won't regret it! I'll not let you down, I promise.'

'You better not!' was Bill's parting comment as he stepped onto the counter.

Izzie pretended to be asleep as her father came aboard, but really she was laughing silently to herself. She clearly remembered a conversation with her mother many years before when she had been a little girl. 'I knows why 'e don't wanna gi' up the motor! An' it's the same reason why Ol' Man Andrews didn't wanna gi' up 'is 'un!

✳

It had occurred one morning while they were tied up at the Wharf, waiting for orders. She had been out playing with some of the other boat children, when one of the boys had implied that there were certain things in life that she would never be able to do because she would never be strong enough.

'And why won't I never be strong enough?' she had asked

'Cos you're only a girl!' had been the reply.

All the other boys had backed up one of their own, and as she happened to be the only girl there on that occasion Izzie had sensibly thought it wiser not to argue. Later, however, when all the children had gone back to their boats, she had asked her mother if it was true.

'Mam, is it right that boys is stronger 'n girls?'

''Ow do you mean, love?'

'I mean, is men stronger 'n women? Is there things as men can do what women can't?'

Her mother stopped stirring the saucepan, simmering on the range, and turned to face her. 'Well,' she began, 'wi' a lot of folk, 'specially folk on the bank, I s'pose that might be true. A woman, gen'rally speakin', ain't got the stren'th of a man. But then it all depen's.' She returned to her stirring.

''Ow do you mean, Mam? Depen's on what?' Izzie asked.

'Well,' her mother explained, 'it sort o' gits altered around some'ow by what you does, an' by what you gits used to doin'. Take workin' on the boats, f'r'instance. We women as works on the boats, we gits used to doin' all the same sort o' work as what the men do. An' we starts doin' it when we're still young, still growin' really. So all o' them years as we're doin' that sort o' work, we're buildin' up our stren'th, an' our muscles an' that, till we're pretty near as strong as what the men are. You jus' think. You're been openin' an' shuttin' 'eavy ol' lock gates since you was a little girl, ain't you?' She continued stirring, then stopped all of a sudden, and looked at Izzie. 'But I'll ask you summat! When you're got a man an' a woman steerin' a pair, when did you ever see the woman on the motor an' the man on the butty?'

'Never,' Izzie answered.

'That's right! Never! An' neither didn't I, an' neither didn't nobody else – well, not very often, any'ow! But I tell you summat. I reckon as 'ow it's a bloomin' sight 'arder steerin' a butty 'n it is a motor. You need to be a lot stronger in th' arms for a start – an' you need to keep your wits about an' all! You're gotta watch where the butty's goin' o' course, but you gotta keep an eye on what 'e's doin' wi' the motor an' all. An' you'll 'ave seen me rowin' on that 'eavy ol' tiller when we're goin' round a tight turn. That take some strength, I can tell you. An' on the butty, remember, you ain't got no engine to 'elp you out, to put the boat where you wants it to be.'

Maggie again returned to her stirring before suddenly stopping again.' All that, an' git all the cookin' done at the same time!'

Izzie realised as she grew older that this had been one of her mother's favourite 'hobby-horses', an issue she was always prepared to argue about with anyone who cared to listen – except, of course, her husband!

'So,' Izzie thought, smiling to herself as she lay in bed, pretending to be asleep, 'come the mornin', me Dad's gonna need a lot o' strength in 'is arms, an' 'e's gonna need to keep 'is wits about 'im an' all – but 'e won't 'ave to do the cookin' at the same time! Not now George 'as learned me 'ow to cook – I can do all that.' A worrying thought occurred to her. 'I wonder if this changeover's gonna make it 'arder for me to carry on wi' me readin'?' She wondered if her father might think it strange if she suddenly changed her habits by spending more time aboard *Zeus* than *Aphrodite*. She decided to continue studying on *Aphrodite*. 'So what if me Dad does see me readin'?' she asked herself. 'After all, 'e don't never say nuthin' to me about me "bloomin' book learnin'" no more. Not since I tol' 'im as I were carryin' out me Mam's wishes.'

❄

George was a natural motor steerer. In no time he had learned the finer points, quickly becoming adept at controlling the engine speed and using reverse gear. He was soon forging ahead as if he had been steering a motor all his life. Within a short time he looked almost as practised as Bill – not that anyone would ever say so! Izzie noticed, though, that it took her father rather longer to remember how to handle the butty – something he had not done since his youth. On more than one occasion she noticed his hand move towards the place where the speed control or the reverse lever would have been. Realising his error, he cursed quietly under his breath, then went back to wrestling with the tiller – much to Izzie's amusement.

After a few days they arrived at the ideal situation where each man would happily steer either boat, so they took it in turns.

It was soon after this that Izzie had a thought. 'I'm gonna ask me Dad if I can 'ave a go at the motor an' all. After all, I can steer the butty awright. I done it lots o' times when me Mam were 'ere an' I'm done it when George or me Dad's been busy doin' other stuff an' all.'

It was the end of a day, a day or two later, when George had been steering *Zeus* all day and she had been on *Aphrodite* with her father. She had spent some of her time preparing and cooking the mutton hotpot that all three of them had just eaten, and as they sat in the butty cabin, drinking their cups of tea, she decided that the time was right.

'Dad, I been a-thinkin'.'

'Thinkin' what, Izzie love?' Bill asked.

'Well,' she began, 'seein' as 'ow you two can both steer the motor an' the butty now, I were jus' wonderin'. I can steer the butty, so d'you think you could let me 'ave a go with the motor some time?'

'Now see what you're done!' Bill said to George, chuckling. 'I let you 'ave a learn on the motor an' now me little girl wants to 'ave a go at it an' all!'

'I'm ever so sorry, Bill,' George mocked

'Well now, young lady!' Bill said. 'I reckon as you're about ol' enough – though the Company wouldn't 'ol' wi' it, o' course. What d'you reckon, George? D'you reckon as we should gi' 'er a go?'

George smiled. 'I reckon she'd soon pick it up.' He put his hand to the side of his mouth to speak to Izzie, pretending he did not want Bill to hear. 'It ain't that 'ard, honest!'

'That's settled, then,' Bill said, ignoring the jibe, and the following day Izzie was at *Zeus's* tiller.

Her father explained, 'This 'ere wheel is what it makes 'er go faster an' slower, an' this is what makes 'er go for'ards an' back'ards.'

'Dad!' she said, 'I'm been watchin' you fiddlin' wi' them controls since I were a babby. If I don't know what they does by now, I ain't never gonna know!'

'Right,' Bill said. 'Off you go then – but careful, mind!'

Once she had got the hang of the speed control and the gears, she found looking after the motor easy after her experience on the butty. The only scary moment was when she met the Cox's pair, *Eros* and *Clotho*, on a really tight bend. Bill, who was with her on *Zeus's* counter, was about to grab the tiller from her, but he stopped when he saw that she was doing exactly the right thing to avoid a collision.

'Well done, our Izzie. You're a natural!' he told her. 'But don't you go lettin' on to Mr Roberts as I let you steer the motor, now, will you?'

'Course I won't, Dad!' she chuckled as she increased the speed. 'This'll be summat to write in me diary tonight!' she thought.

Chapter 13

Such a lovely day

For Izzie's twelfth birthday the boats were tied up at the pickle factory. They had been emptied late the previous evening and she had expected that they would be turned round and heading off back to Coventry on her special day.

While they were eating breakfast Bill announced to his daughter that he had no presents for her birthday this year.

'What?' she asked, a forlorn look on her face.

'No,' her father replied. 'Instead, me an' George is goin' to gi' you a day out goin' round London!'

'What?' she asked again, her face now a picture of excitement. 'You mean, we ain't goin' back today?'

'No,' said Bill. 'For once we shan't worry if it takes us an extra day to git back to Coventry!'

Izzie could hardly contain her excitement as they set off for the Underground station.

'Don't forgit your gas mask, Dad!' Izzie called as her father was stepping off *Aphrodite*. Bill cursed under his breath as he went back for it.

Although she had travelled many miles in her short life her experience had been limited to the narrow stretch of water with a bank on either side and the small villages they had passed through. Even her excursions into the bigger towns had been limited to the streets in close proximity to the canal. She had never been on a train before, although she had often seen them steaming along where the lines ran close to the cut.

Her father bought the tickets and Izzie proudly showed hers to the ticket inspector as she passed through the barrier and walked onto the platform. It was bustling with men and women in uniform mingling with commuters and shoppers, all heading for the middle of London. As the train approached, Izzie looked confused. "Ow's that train goin'?" she asked. 'It ain't go no engine on it!' 'No,' Bill explained, 'these train's run on the 'lectric.' With a squeal of brakes the train came to a halt in front of them and – another surprise for Izzie – the doors slid open by themselves! They found three seats, and Izzie sat transfixed as the train pulled away from the platform, drinking in the sights and sounds of her journey.

The train eventually arrived at a large, busy station and many of the passengers got off. More people got on and the train pulled away, immediately entering a tunnel. After a while Izzie said, 'This 'ere's a long ol' tunnel, ain't it?'

'Ah!' said Bill. 'All these 'ere 'lectric trains is in tunnels in the middle o' London. They calls it the Underground.' Izzie was amazed. After a few more stops they arrived at Kings Cross St Pancras and Bill, despite his 'pride' in being unable to read, recognised the station name.

'This is where we gits off,' he said, standing up. They followed him off the train and joined the flow of people making their way off the platform. Turning a corner they were confronted by two staircases side by side. It took Izzie a few seconds to realise that the people were not climbing the stairs, but the stairs themselves were moving – one side up and the other side down. Her father watched her carefully as she wobbled unsteadily, stepping onto an escalator for the first time. George followed.

They gave up their tickets and walked out of the station onto Euston Road.

'Blimey!' Izzie exclaimed. 'I ain't never seen so many cars an' lorries – an' so many folks all hurryin' along!'

'Busy ol' place, London,' her father agreed.

Although George had been to London on many occasions with his grandfather's boats, he, like Izzie, had only got to know the streets close to the canal. It seemed to him that Bill knew a lot more about where he was going and had appointed himself their tour guide.

Izzie noticed that all the cars and buses had what looked like hoods attached to their headlights. She was about to ask what they were for when she remembered the pieces of black material that she had to put over the portholes at night. 'I bet that's cos o' the blackout,' she thought, 'so as them 'eadlamps don't show up too much.'

'Now, we needs to catch a bus. It's a number 91 as we're lookin' for – if they ain't changed the numbers,' Bill said. They found the right bus stop and only had to wait a few minutes for a number 91 to appear. They had to stand up as the bus was crowded, and Bill asked the conductor, "'Ow much is it to Trafalgar Square for two an' a young 'un?" He paid the fares and the conductor took three tickets from the rack on his belt and, punching them with his machine, handed them to Bill.

Izzie looked on. 'So many new things as I ain't seen nor done afore!' she thought. 'I'm gonna 'ave a lot to write in me journal tonight. That's for sure!'

At Trafalgar Square they got off the bus. Izzie stood still, transfixed by the sight in front of her. She had never seen anything like it before.

'Look at them big lions!' she exclaimed. 'An' wha's that big tall thing in the middle?'

'It's called Nelson's Column,' her father said, 'an' that fella stood right on the top on it – that's Nelson. 'E were a famous navy man back in the past.'

'An' them fountains! They're lovely, ain't they! An' I ain't never seen so many pigeons!'

Bill smiled at his daughter's delight. They crossed the square and walked under Admiralty Arch.

'This 'ere road's called "The Mall" an' that big buildin' up there,' Bill pointed towards the end of the road, 'that's Buckin'am Palace. That's where the King lives.'

'Ooh!' Izzie cried. 'Can we go an' 'ave a look at it?'

As they walked up The Mall, George commented on the large area of parkland. 'I allus reckoned as London were all buildin's,' he said as he looked around. 'I never thought as they'd 'ave a park like this the middle on it.'

'There's a number o' parks in London,' Bill informed him. 'This 'un's called St James's Park. One o' th' others 'as got London Zoo in it.'

'Oh!' Izzie exclaimed. 'Can we go the zoo?'

'All in good time, young lady. All in good time,' Bill replied, smiling at her. A woman passer-by stopped.

'I couldn't help overhearing what you were saying,' she said. 'The zoo's not a good idea at the moment, because a lot of the animals have been moved to somewhere up in Bedfordshire. It's in case they get bombed. I only tell you because I wouldn't want your daughter to be disappointed.'

'Thank you, Missus,' Bill said, touching his cap. 'Well, it looks like we'll 'ave to leave the zoo till the war's over and they bring all th' animals back.'

'Oh!' Izzie was disappointed.

'Never mind!' Bill said. 'We'll find summat else as is jus' as good!'

They continued walking along The Mall when Izzie, pointing towards the Palace, suddenly shouted. 'Look at all them!' Coming towards them along the road were some men on horseback. As they approached it became obvious that they were soldiers. Izzie could not take her eyes off them.

'Ain't them 'orses beautiful? They're a bit different from the ol' boat 'orses!' she exclaimed. 'An' them soldiers – don't they all look smart? Where d'you reckon they're goin'?'

'I dunno,' said George.

'Me neither,' said Bill as they watched the troops trot away.

Eventually, they arrived in front of the Palace.

'It's 'uge!' Izzie gasped. 'An' that's where the King lives?'

'It is,' her father answered.

''E must rattle around a bit in there!'

'Ah,' said her father. 'It's a bit bigger 'n our little cabin on the butty, ain't it? But don't forget, there's 'im, an' there's the Queen, an' there's the two little Princesses, 'Lizabeth an' Margaret Rose. An' then, o' course, there's all the servants as they 'as to look after 'em.'

''Ow d'you know so much about 'em?' George asked.

'Ah, well,' said Bill. 'That were Maggie's doin'. Very keen on the Royal Family, she were.'

'Wha's them soldiers doin', walkin' up an' down like that?' Izzie asked.

'They're guardin' the King in case anybody tries to git into the Palace an' do 'im 'arm.'

'I s'pose tha's cos 'e's important, like, ain't it?'

'Most important man in the country!' George said. Looking up at the Palace, Izzie noticed a cluster of barrage balloons in the sky. She had seen them in the distance when they had been tied up at the pickle factory, but she was much closer to them now.

'I never realised as them balloon things was so big!' she said. 'An' they're s'posed to stop the German planes from gittin' through to drop bombs?' she asked.

'Tha's the idea,' George replied.

They turned left and walked along Birdcage Walk.

'That great big buildin' over there,' Bill pointed, 'tha's Parliament, that is. Tha's where the Gover'ment is.'

'Is that where that Winston Churchill bloke lives – 'im as Mr Roberts were talkin' about?' Izzie asked.

'No,' her father replied. 'That ain't where 'e lives, it's where 'e works. An' that big tower wi' the clocks on it…'

'I seen pictures o' that!' Izzie said. 'Ain't that Big Ben?'

'You're right, Izzie, love. It is.'

They walked on further and turned left towards Whitehall. As they passed one of the many tall stone buildings they noticed a parked lorry with men unloading what looked to Izzie like small, well-filled sacks.

'Is them sandbags, like what they use to stop breaches on the cut?' she asked.

'Yeah,' her father replied, 'but they ain't stoppin' no breaches 'ere, are they?'

They watched for a few moments as the men piled the sandbags against the wall of a building.

'I reckon they're to 'elp stop damage from bombin',' George commented. 'I seen summat about it on the newsreels. It's to stop the blast 'itting the buildin' full on, like.'

'An' I reckon you're right,' Bill agreed.

A little further along Whitehall they came to the Cenotaph.

'What's that thing there in the middle o' the road?' Izzie asked.

'It's called the Cenotaph. It's what they put up after the last war

– like a memorial to all them as died in the fightin'. Your Uncle Bert were one of 'em.'

'I never met me Uncle Bert,' Izzie said to George. ''E were killed in the war afore I were born.'

''E were my big brother,' Bill said to George. 'Boatin' man, o' course! But when the war come 'e said as 'e wanted to see a bit o' the world beyond the cut. Always 'ad a bit o' the ol' wanderlust, did Bert.'

''E were killed on the Somme, weren't 'e?' George said.

'What's the Somme?' Izzie asked.

'It's the name of a river in Belgium. There were a big battle near it in the last war. Thousands on 'em was killed there – thousands. An' your Uncle Bert, 'e were one on 'em.' They all looked at the Cenotaph in silence for a few moments.

'I'd like to 'ave known me Uncle Bert,' Izzie said at last.

'I reckon as 'e would 'ave liked to 'ave known you an' all, Izzie love,' her father said. 'But that's what war does – mucks up families.' He changed the subject. 'Let's walk a bit further up 'ere.'

They walked on to Downing Street, and Bill showed Izzie and George where Number 10 was. 'That's where Mr Churchill lives now,' he announced.

'What about th' other bloke?' Izzie asked. 'What were 'is name … Chamberlain?'

'Dick were tellin' us while we was unloadin' yesterday. Chamberlain ain't the Prime Minister no more. It's Churchill now. 'Appened a couple o' days ago.' Now Izzie understood the billboards she had noticed outside the newsagents' shops saying things like 'Churchill – New PM' and 'Winston in No 10'.

Further on they arrived at Horse Guards, and on each side of the gates they saw one of the soldiers on horseback they had seen earlier.

'What d'you reckon they're doin'?' Izzie asked.

'Guardin' summat, I s'pose,' George answered.

'But guardin' what, though?'

'Dunno!' Izzie walked right up to one of the mounted guards. She even plucked up the courage to pat the beautiful horse he was sitting on.

'You're got a nice 'orse, Mister!' she said to him. The soldier did not reply, but remained staring straight ahead, although Izzie was sure she could see the trace of a smile on his face.

After their early start they were all beginning to feel hungry. When they arrived back at Trafalgar Square they found a Lyon's Corner House in the Strand.

'It's big, ain't it?' Izzie commented, 'an' there's such a lot o' people!'

Bill led the way upstairs where there were several different restaurants on different floors. Bill and George selected one they thought they could afford.

'I reckon this'll do us,' said Bill. As they entered Izzie looked around at all the people sitting and eating. She had never been anywhere as grand as this, and it made her feel quite important. Finding an empty table, they sat down and George handed Izzie a menu.

'There y'are, Izzie,' he said. 'You read out to us all as it says on there.' Izzie took the menu from him and was amazed to discover it was a list of all the different meals and drinks, together with the prices.

'You can git all this lot in 'ere?' she queried.

'Ah,' said her father, 'if you can pay for it, that is.'

Izzie read out what she could and they decided on their meals. 'I s'pose if it weren't for the ration there'd be even more dinners to choose from,' she said.

'Yeah,' said George. 'I reckon places like this are on the ration like everybody else.'

A few moments later, a lady in a smart black and white uniform came to the table and asked what they would like. Izzie felt even more important as she ordered for all three of them and the lady wrote the orders on her pad. When she had gone Izzie casually mentioned to her father that had she not been able to read, they may have asked for the wrong thing.

'I reckon as I could o' made 'er understand what I wanted wi'out no book learnin'. Any'ow, I don't come in posh places like this that much, do I?' George and Izzie smiled at each other.

When they had finished and paid for their meal they left the restaurant. They walked along Northumberland Avenue, then crossed over Victoria Embankment. Looking over a stone wall, Izzie saw a wide stretch of water.

'This 'ere's the River Thames,' Bill announced. 'The cut joins it a bit further upstream.'

'Ain't it wide!' Izzie exclaimed. 'Our pair'd be lost in the middle o' that!'

As they walked downstream they saw lighters and barges going backwards and forwards on the busy river, with some larger ocean-going vessels tied up at the docks and wharves. The road eventually led them away from the river, and when they came to a crossroads Bill turned right.

'This way,' he said to the others. The road took them onto a bridge over the Thames.

'This 'ere's London Bridge,' he announced.

'Me Mam learned me a rhyme about that when I were little,' Izzie said. 'It were fallin' down!'

'That were th' old bridge. They built this 'un in it's place.'

Izzie looked downstream over the side of the bridge. 'That next bridge is a funny lookin' thing,' she said.

'That's Tower Bridge,' Bill informed her, 'an' that big stone place as you can see next to it is the Tower o' London.'

Izzie continued to look at the bridge. Approaching it from the far side was a large cargo vessel. She expected the tugs to manoeuvre it into one of the docks she could see downstream on the other side of the bridge. To her horror, however, the ship was heading straight for the bridge!

'That ship!' she shouted. 'That ship! It's gonna crash into the bridge – with all them cars an' buses goin' over it!'

Bill chuckled. 'It won't crash. You jus' watch an' see what 'appens.'

Izzie was still convinced that the ship was going to collide with the bridge. But then something happened she had never expected. She could not believe what she was seeing.

'Look! Look!' she exclaimed. 'That bridge! It's sort o' split itself in 'alf! So the ship can git through it wi'out crashin'!'

'Clever, eh?' her father said.

George, too, was watching open-mouthed. 'I'm 'eard about that, but I never thought as I should see it 'appen!' They all watched as the ship passed through the bridge and the two parts of the road came back down and the traffic over it resumed.

'I 'ope none o' them cars 'n' lorries was in a 'urry!' Izzie laughed.

It was time for them to head for home. They caught an Underground train from Tower Hill back to Kings Cross St Pancras, where they changed to another to take them back to the pickle factory and their boats. As the train made its way back above ground, George turned to Bill.

'I gotta ask you, Bill,' he said. "Ow come you knows your way around London so well? I mean, you're been on the cut all your life like I 'ave. 'Ow 'ave you got to know so much about it?'

'Ah,' said Bill. 'When I were a nipper, me Mam 'n' Dad 'ad a reg'lar run down the Regent's Cut. That's the one as goes through Regent's Park – not far away. So when we was tied up for the night – when I were old enough, in me teens, like – I used to take meself off an' find me way around. That were afore the last war, though.'

'Well, we'd 'ave been a bit lost wi'out you today, an' that's a sure fact!' George said.

It was late in the afternoon when they got off the train at the station near the pickle factory. As they walked along the street they passed a little tea room. Bill and George stopped and looked through the window.

'See anybody in there as you know, Izzie?' George asked. She peered through the window. Sitting at a table for six were Tom Speechley, John and Dick, all smiling and waving at her. Tom got up and came to the door.

"Allo, Izzie!' he said as he stood aside for her to enter. 'Many 'appy returns, an' welcome to your birthday tea party!' As the three of them joined the others at the table, Izzie could see that there were sandwiches and trifle – and in the middle, a birthday cake with twelve candles.

'When your Dad told us it were goin' to be your birthday today, we thought we ought to do a party for you. To say "thanks" for all the meals and the cups o' tea you've made for us.'

'But 'ow did you git all this wi' the rationin'?' Izzie asked.

'We all put our coupons together and told the caff to do what they could.'

'Well!' said Izzie. 'It's all lovely. Thank you very much, all on you.' And with that she gave all three of them a kiss on the cheek.

Later, with the sound of their voices singing 'Happy Birthday' still echoing in her ears, Izzie sat with her father and George in *Aphrodite's* cabin.

'D'you know?' she began. 'That's one o' the bestest birthdays as I'm ever 'ad! I'm really enjoyed it! I'm 'ad such a lovely day an' I'm seen an' done so many new things! Thank you ever so much, both on you!' With that she gave her father and George a big hug.

''As it been better 'n a birthday when you're 'ad some presents as you could keep, then?' George asked her in mid hug. 'I mean, like, you're 'ad a good day an' everythin', but you ain't got nuthin' to show for it, like, 'ave you?'

'No, I ain't. That's true,' she replied. 'But I'm got me memories, ain't I? An' I sometimes reckon as memories – well, some memories any road – is more important nor things.' She gave him a kiss.

'The thing about memories,' said her father, 'is they don't git old, they don't git spoiled, an' nobody can't take 'em away from you.'

'That's true enough!' George agreed.

Later, as she lay in bed, Izzie started to write up her journal. 'So many new things!' she thought. 'I don't know where to start!' She wrote down everything she had seen and done on that day. When she had finished it was the longest entry in her book. At last she put down her pencil and fell asleep, dreaming of soldiers on horses, trotting along The Mall.

Chapter 14

Jean

Although Izzie was now twelve and was beginning to think of herself as a young woman rather than a child, her father still regarded her as his 'little girl'. Consequently, he rarely, if ever, discussed with her what he considered 'grown-ups' business'. Whenever she asked him about such things, his reply was always, 'There ain't no need for you to worry your pretty little head about things such as that, Izzie love!'. So the only way she got to know anything was from overheard conversations between him and George. More often than not, like the one about George steering the motor, they happened just before they parted company after an evening at the pub.

On one night they were moored near The Running Horse on their way to London when Izzie roused to hear George say, 'Pity Alf's lad's been called up to the military.'

'Ah, 'im an' Mary'll miss 'im – that's for sure ... an' they'll worry about 'im!' Bill replied.

'Yeah, but I reckon as 'ow that there new barmaid's took a bit of a shine to you, you know, Bill!'

'Who?'

'That Jean.'

'Git off!' Bill scoffed.

'No! Serious!' George replied. 'You didn't see the way she were lookin' at you while you was playin' that game o' darts.'

'Git away wi' you!' Bill scoffed again.

On their way back to Coventry they stopped at 'The Horse' again and Izzie awoke to hear another conversation as they returned. Her father asked George, 'Do you reckon as she were serious about it, then?'

'She sounded pretty serious to me, Bill!' George replied.

'But she don't know nuthin' about boatin',' nor the life on the cut, nor nuthin'!' protested Bill.

'She didn't know nuthin' about barrin' neither afore she went to work at Alf's pub,' George continued. 'An' she can do that awright, can't she? I reckon as she picks things up pretty quick – fast learner, like.'

'But the cut! I mean ... well, it ain't like no ordinary job, is it? It's more like a way o' life, ain't it?' Bill argued.

'I know that! But think on this. She wouldn't be the first woman to come off the bank an' take to the life, now would she? My Gran 'adn't never been on a boat afore she met me Grandad,' said George.

'I s'pose there is that to it.' Bill was forced to agree. 'Ah, well. We'll see! Sleep tight. See you in the mornin'!'

'Goodnight, Bill.'

Izzie was not quite sure what to make of this little snippet of conversation, but she decided it need not concern her at the moment and soon drifted off to sleep again. As nothing more was said about it, Izzie came to the conclusion that she must have either dreamed that she had heard it or had misunderstood what she had heard.

The coal runs from the yard near Coventry to the pickle factory in London continued throughout the summer, and the first months of the war hardly affected them at all. Whenever they were tied up they noticed a number of people in uniform, and the talk in the pubs was nearly all about the war. Izzie noticed that all the vehicles had headlamp covers. 'Jus' like in London,' she thought.

Not long after her birthday Izzie heard two women in one of the shops arguing about something called Dunkirk. One was saying what a setback it was, while the other was grateful that so many soldiers had been brought home. She did not know what it was about and asked George to explain it to her. Otherwise, apart from the blackout and rationing, life on the canal was much as it had been before.

Later in the summer they became aware of aircraft flying overhead more often, and Izzie heard a customer in a shop talking to the shopkeeper about the "Battle of Britain". She listened intently to the conversation and gathered there was a lot of fighting between aeroplanes in the skies to the south. She remembered the map of Britain that Emily had shown her. 'I'm glad we don't 'ave to go no further down that way than London!' she said to herself.

One October evening they had stopped again at The Horse on their way to London. While the men had gone for a pint Izzie was sitting on the cabin roof watching the stillness of the water as the warm autumn day gave way to the dusk of evening that slowly gathered around her. Looking up along the towpath, she spotted someone just outside the door of the pub. She could just about make out the figure of her father walking towards the boats. As she looked she saw he was not alone. There was someone else with him, but it was not George. 'Besides,' she thought, 'it's ages yit afore closin' time!'

As they came closer, Izzie could see that the person with her father was a woman and that they were chatting happily together. Bill called to his daughter. 'Izzie! You remember Jean, don't you? You're seen 'er workin' be'ind the bar at "The 'Orse".'

'Oh yeah. I remember you,' Izzie replied.

'Well,' her father continued, 'Jean's been sayin' for a while as she's served no end o' beer to no end o' boatin' folk, but she ain't never seen what th' inside of a boat looks like.'

'Never been on one, I ain't!' said the woman, as she threw the remains of a cigarette into the water.

'Well, the pub ain't too busy tonight,' Bill continued, 'so Alf said as she could come up 'ere an' 'ave a quick look at ourn. Jean, this is our Izzie, me daughter – well, Isobel, really.'

'Lovely to meet you, Isobel,' said the woman.

'Hello,' Izzie replied, recalling the overheard and partly forgotten conversations.

'This is *Aphrodite*. It's what we calls "the butty". It's where me an' our Izzie lives,' Bill said proudly as he stepped onto the back deck. 'Move your legs out the way, Izzie, so Jean can 'ave a gander inside.' Izzie obediently moved out of the way so that the woman could look through the doors.

'Ooh, my Gawd!' Jean exclaimed. 'Ain' it tiny?'

Izzie noticed that her accent was similar to Tom Speechley's and his men from the pickle factory, and realised that this Jean must also be a Londoner. Izzie was able to get a good look at her. She was older than she first appeared – mid-forties, Izzie guessed. Face powder and skilfully applied make-up gave her the appearance of being younger. The blonde hair, Izzie saw, was dyed. Mousy-grey roots were visible as she bent down to peer – rather nosily, Izzie thought – into what was, after all, their home. She noticed that the woman was not very tall; she did not have to bend down far to see into the cabin. 'You're a bit overweight an' all!' Izzie thought.

'Me an' me Dad manages in it awright,' Izzie said.

'We're never known no different, you see,' explained Bill.

'An' you do all your cookin' an' eatin' an' everythin' all in that one tiny little room?' Jean asked, disbelievingly.

'Ah.' Bill replied. 'We're got everythin' as we need. It's all in there.'

'Where do you kip, then?' Jean asked – rather pointedly, Izzie thought.

'Our Izzie sleeps on the side bed – that's what you can see down there on your right, an' I 'as the cross bed as lets down out the left side o' the cabin jus' through there in what we calls "the bed 'ole",' said Bill, pointing.

'I bet it gets real cosy in there of a night time, though, don' it, eh?' Jean mused.

'Ah, it does that,' replied Bill.

'Well, I best be gettin' back,' she said, looking at her wristwatch and taking another cigarette from her packet. 'Alf said as I should only be a few minutes.' But, despite her haste, she paused. Although Bill did not smoke, he always had a box of matches with him for relighting the range. He struck one and lit her cigarette.

'Ta,' she said, inhaling the smoke. 'You know summat? 'Avin' seen inside one o' these 'ere boats for the first time ever in me life, I reckon as it were right what I said to you that time. I could live on one of 'em, I could. Really, I could. Like you say, you've got everythin' you need in there, ain't you? An' it's all so close to 'and, ain't it? Nice to 'ave met you, Isobel – an' nice to 'ave 'ad a little butchers at your boat,' she continued.

'Bye,' Izzie replied, then under her breath, 'Nobody 'cept Miss Roberts calls me Isobel!'

As she watched them walking back to The Running Horse, Izzie decided that, although she could not put her finger on it, there was something about this Jean woman that she did not like, something about her that she did not like at all. 'This must be what me Mam used to call 'er "woman's intuition",' she thought. She remembered again that conversation when George had said someone at 'The 'Orse' called Jean was a 'bit fond' of her father.

'He certainly seems 'appy in 'er comp'ny,' Izzie thought. 'They're chattin' an' laughin' together walkin' back down to the pub. But then, she thought, they only ever sees each other when 'im an' George goes to "The 'Orse".' Then she noticed something else. 'What's she doin'? It looks like she's sort o' leanin' in towards 'im. Is she tryin' to link arms wi' 'im?' She noticed Bill pull his arm away, pretending he needed to take off his cap to scratch his head. But a little further on Jean tried again. This time Bill accepted and linked his arm with hers.

What really concerned Izzie was what she had said about being so sure that she could live on a boat! Especially after she had only just seen inside the cabin of one for the very first time in her life.

"Ow could she 'ave made up 'er mind about summat like that so quick?' Izzie wondered. The last thing she wanted was for someone else to come along and upset the life that the three of them now enjoyed so much. Of course, it was not the same as when her mother had been alive. There was no way that it ever could be, but with her father and George around, life was all right.

She managed to put this thought to the back of her mind as she got ready for bed. Drifting off to sleep, she heard another pair tying up for the night behind *Zeus* and *Aphrodite*. Later, she roused when her father and George returned from the pub.

'We're got company,' she heard Bill say as he noticed the lights from the other boats.

'I reckon as 'ow the cut seems to be gittin' a bit busier every day,' George replied.

'An' we'll not complain about that!' said Bill as he climbed aboard. They wished each other a good night and went into their respective cabins. Izzie was relieved that there was no further mention of the Jean woman.

A couple of weeks later, as they were working a lock near Watford on their way to London, the lock-keeper called George over and passed on a message from Horace. George looked rather concerned and went straight over to Bill in *Zeus*'s counter.

'Bill, you know me Grandad's livin' at me Auntie Connie an' Uncle Tom's? Well, Mr Roberts 'as 'ad a message from me Auntie sayin' as 'e's a bit poorly, like. She reckons as I ought to go an' see 'im.'

'I see,' Bill replied. "Ow long d'you reckon you'd be away?"

"Ard to say. I mean, I dunno 'ow poorly 'e is till I git there, do I?'

'If you can 'ang on 'ere till we're unloaded most o' this coal – say, late tomorra – then you can git a bus to the station. I doubt as we'll git a back load so Izzie can 'ave the butty on the way back. 'Ow's that?'

'That'll be fine. Thanks, Bill.'

✳

When George had gone, Izzie was surprised by how much she missed him. But she spent more time with her father, which they both enjoyed.

'You an' young George git on awright, don't you?' he said to her one day.

'Yeah,' she replied. "E's a good bloke!'

'Ah. 'E is that,' her father agreed.

They tied up for the night by The Running Horse and Bill asked Izzie if she would like to go with him for a drink. It was a dark dismal evening with a threat of rain, so she agreed.

'So, you're brought your daughter wi' you tonight then, 'ave you, Bill?' Jean cooed as they entered the bar.

'She ain't a big drinker, but she's come wi' me cos young George is away visitin' 'is Grandad.'

'What can I get you?'

'Usual for me an' a lemonade for Izzie.'

'I'm glad you've come in tonight,' Jean said as she drew Bill's pint. 'I wanna word wi' you.'

'What about?'

'Well, I gotta few days off, startin' tomorra, an' I was wonderin' if I could come on your boats wi' you. I'll pay you summat for your trouble. Which way are you goin?' she asked. Izzie's heart sank.

'We're on our way to the coal yard up by Coventry.'

'I ain't never been up that way. It'd be nice to see a different part o' the country. What time'll you be startin' off in the mornin'?'

'I reckon we'll be gettin' 'em ahead about seven. You can come along for the ride if you like. It'll be good to 'ave some company wi' George bein' away, won't it Izzie?' Izzie's heart sank even lower.

'An' when will we be back 'ere, d'you reckon?'

'Jus' over a week – give or take.' Jean thought for a moment or two.

'I'll be along just before seven o'clock then, Bill.'

Izzie was dismayed. 'A 'ole week wi' 'er! I really don't like 'er at all. Oh, Dad! What're you doin'?

True to her word, at about five to seven the next day Jean was standing on the towpath next to *Aphrodite* with a capacious handbag in one hand and another bag in the other.

'Mornin', Jean,' said Bill as he emerged onto the butty counter. 'I'll show you the motor cabin where you'll be sleepin' so you can put your bags in there.'

'Ta!'

Izzie stood on the steps and watched as they disappeared into the motor. A few seconds later Bill reappeared and stepped down into the engine hole. The sound of *Zeus's* engine starting up soon broke the relative quiet. Suddenly, Jean's worried face appeared at *Zeus's* hatch. 'What in Gawd's name's that bleedin' row?' she asked.

'That's the engine,' Izzie shouted as if she were talking to a small, slightly stupid child. 'It's what makes the boats go. Cos we don't use 'orses no more,' she muttered as she stepped down out of Jean's sight.

Having paid Bill some money for her 'holiday', Jean considered that she could happily spend her time on the pair as a lady of leisure. With George away, there was more work for both Bill and Izzie. Bill looked after the motor while Izzie steered the butty full time and also prepared the meals for the three of them. Fortunately, most of the locks on the run to Coventry were broad, so the boats could be taken through breasted up. It upset Izzie when Jean did not even offer to help with washing up after they had eaten, but her father did not seem to notice. 'It's only till George gits back from seein' 'is Grandad,' she consoled herself.

One night they tied up a few miles north of the entrance to the arm leading down to Northampton. It was a cool November evening and they were sitting in *Aphrodite*'s cabin, eating their meal, when they heard the sound of aircraft engines. This was nothing unusual as they had often heard aeroplanes flying overhead. But this time was different. This time there seemed to be so many more of them than they had ever heard before. The sound of the engines just went on and on until they wondered if it was ever going to stop. Bill opened the slide and the doors and looked out.

'Look at this!' he called to the others. They all gathered in the hatch and on the counter, looking upwards. The darkening sky was black with aircraft, row upon row of dark shapes droning across the sky, all heading in the same direction.

'Where do you reckon they're goin', Dad?' Izzie asked.

'I dunno,' Bill replied, 'but Coventry's over that there way, somewhere.'

Eventually the noise of the engines faded away. They were about to go back down into the cabin when the noise of the aeroplanes was replaced by the distant rumble of explosions. As they turned and looked in the direction of the sound, they saw that the sky far to the north-west was lit up by an eerie glow.

'Yeah,' mused Bill, 'it looks like Coventry's gittin' it tonight awright! Poor buggers!'

Izzie felt very sad for the people of Coventry, suffering under the bombs. Then she noticed Jean's face. 'It must' be cos it's dark an' I can't see 'er face proper!' she thought. 'It mus' be a trick o' the light or summat, but I could swear as she's got a smile on 'er face!'

As they approached the coal yard a few days later, it was apparent that Bill had been correct about the bombers' destination. Although they only had to go to the coal yard on the outskirts of the city, there was plenty of evidence of the damage the bombs had caused. While they were waiting to load, Bill chatted to the man in the hut about the bombing.

'Terrible night it was!' he said. 'Me and the missus spent the whole night in the cellar. You know the Cathedral's burnt down, don't you?'

'No!' Bill could not believe it. 'They'd never bomb a cathedral, would they?'

'Well, they 'ave – incendiaries,' came the reply. 'Almost the 'ole o' the city centre's either blown up or burnt down. It's terrible!'

'Cor blimey!' was all Bill could muster as a reply.

It was the first time either Bill or Izzie had seen bomb damage on such a large scale. Izzie tried not to think what it must have been like during the raid. 'Them poor folks just sittin' there wi' all them bombs fallin' around 'em! They musta been real scared,' she thought.

As Jean spent most of her time on the motor with Bill, Izzie was able to keep out of her way most of the time. When they were together for meals and during the evenings she managed to remain civil to her even though she still did not like her.

They had just finished their evening meal one night on their way back from Coventry when Jean suddenly announced she was going for a walk. Bill got to his feet.

'I'll come wi' you.'

'No! You're all right, Bill. I'll be OK on me own. I need to walk me dinner down, an' like I told you, I ain't never been up this way before, so I'll just take meself off an' 'ave a bit of a shufty.'

When she came back, the news she brought was not what Izzie wanted to hear.

'While I were out I seen a phone box, so I thought I'd phone Alf an' see 'ow the pub were doin'.'

'An' 'ow're they copin' wi'out you?' Bill asked.

'Well, 'e said as they wasn't that busy an' they was managin' fine, so I could stay on 'ere wi' you a bit longer if I want.'

'That'll be nice!' said Bill.

'Whereabouts in London do you take this 'ere coal, Bill?' Jean asked.

'It's a pickle factory, somewhere near Park Royal.'

''Ow long do you stay there then?'

'Normally it's only a coupla days, but wi' George not bein' 'ere I reckon as it'll take three days at least to git unloaded.'

'Oh,' replied Jean. 'If I come wi' you, I could go and see me sister.'

'Where's she live, then?'

'Poplar – I can get a bus.'

Stopping briefly at The Horse as they passed so that Jean could 'collect a few o' me bits,' they carried on towards London. The prospect of Jean being with them for the rest of the run was another blow for Izzie. She was impatient until they were tied up outside the pickle factory and she had seen Jean walk off to catch a bus to visit her sister. As she watched her disappear, she heaved a sigh of relief.

'Yes, it's a lot 'arder wi'out George – an' I'm missin' 'im summat awful – but it'd be a lot easier wi'out 'er. I wouldn' miss 'er one bit!

Jean arrived back late in the afternoon two days later, just as the last of the two boats was being emptied. Izzie had gone into the works to use the telephone, to receive the familiar answer – no return load. Horace had, however, heard from George. His grandfather was getting better and George would be waiting for them at The Running Horse on the return trip. When Izzie heard this her heart leapt.

She was much more cheerful as they set out northwards the following morning, knowing that it would be only a matter of days until George would be back on board with them. Sure enough, as they approached the pub a couple of days later, George was standing there on the towpath, waiting to catch the rope she threw from the butty. Jean had already packed her bags and stepped off *Zeus* as soon as the boat was secured.

'Jean's 'ad a sort of a 'oliday wi' us,' Bill called to George by way of explanation.

'Ah,' he replied. 'Alf said as you'd been off wi' 'em for a run.'

'I've really enjoyed it too!' Jean piped up. 'P'raps I could come wi' you again some time?'

'Any time you like,' was Bill's reply.

'I 'ope not!' Izzie thought.

Jean leaned over and gave Bill a quick peck on the cheek. 'Ta-ta!' she called as she headed back to the pub, clasping her bags tightly.

Chapter 15

Different company

That Christmas they could not get back to the Wharf, so Bill managed to time their run so that they would be at The Running Horse for Christmas Day. There were a number of pairs tied up there, including the Thomases', who worked for the same company, and others, all of whom they knew. Alf had managed to get hold of a couple of chickens, everyone chipped in with their rations, and the 'Boatman's Garden' provided a generous supply of vegetables. Mary, his wife, had made a passable Christmas pudding. There was no sign of Jean.

'Jean not about for Christmas, then?' George asked Alf.

'Gone to stop with 'er sister down London,' came the reply. 'Pity really! I could 'ave done with 'er 'elp, but I suppose it's a time to be with your family, ain't it?'

After lunch, Mary organised some games for the children to play while the adults got down to the serious business of drinking. Izzie felt as if she was getting a bit too old for the children's games, so instead she spent her time sitting with her father and George, listening to their 'grown-up' conversation.

After Christmas their life returned to normality and, despite the weather being particularly cold, they continued with their runs from the coal yard near Coventry to the pickle factory in London. They were pleased when the days began to lengthen and the sun was warmer on their backs.

One spring day they had just come through the top lock at Stoke Bruerne on their way back to Coventry.

'Are we stoppin' 'ere the night, Dad?' Izzie asked. Bill looked at the sky.

'I reckon we'll git through the tunnel afore dark an' tie up by

Blis'orth.' He lit the headlamp and set off into the darkness. It was almost dark when they emerged from the other end, and Izzie was glad they were tying up for the night.

They had heard bombs exploding at various places on many of their runs, as well as in London and Birmingham, but that night Izzie was awakened by a loud 'crump' that sounded all too close. It was followed by three more loud explosions and she could see flashes of light around the edges of the blackout material over the portholes. She felt the boat rock from the vibrations the explosions caused, and the roar of the bombers' engines overhead was deafening. Not a little frightened, she sat up in bed. She waited and listened. There were no more explosions, only the sound of aircraft getting quieter as they flew away. Her father was awake too. He came through from the cross bed and sat down next to her. Putting his arm round her, he asked, 'Are you all right, Izzie, love? That were a bit too close for comfort!'

'Yeah, I think so. That's the closest we're ever 'eard bombin'. What d'you reckon they'd wanna bomb a little village like this for?'

Her father thought for a moment. 'Well, I reckon as they wasn't aimin' for the village – they was aimin' for the tunnel. They missed it – but not be far!'

'Why'd they wanna bomb the tunnel?'

'If you think about it,' Bill said, 'if that there tunnel was collapsed, you couldn't git no boats through neither way, could you? So anythin' as was bein' took be boat'd 'ave to go be road or the railway, wouldn't it? An' from what I 'ear folk sayin', the roads an' the railways 'as already got more 'n they can do with.'

'So if they'd 'it the tunnel it would 'ave upset things good an' proper, then?'

'I reckon it would.'

A few days before Izzie's thirteenth birthday, George received another message to say his grandfather was ill again. Knowing it to be a usual stopping place, Horace Roberts had phoned this message through to The Running Horse. Alf passed it on to him when they called in on their way to London. Izzie had gone with them on this occasion. She found she was joining George and her father on more and more visits to the canalside pubs. 'I jus' likes bein' wi' George,' she reasoned.

'I'm sorry, but I'll 'ave to go and see 'im – see 'ow 'e is, like,' he said to Bill. 'I can git a bus from the stop just outside 'ere in the mornin'.'

Jean overheard the conversation. 'Last time George were away was when I 'ad me 'oliday on your boats, weren' it?'

'Ah,' Bill replied as he put down his glass and wiped his mouth. 'It were.'

'Which way are you goin' this time?'

'On our way down to London wi' a load on.'

'I could do wi' goin' to see me sister again – see 'ow she's gettin' on wi' all the bombin' in London. That's why I moved out, see. To get away from the bombs. I wanted 'er to come wi' me, but she would insist on stayin' there.'

'If Alf'll gi' you the time off, o' course you can come wi' us. Be nice to 'ave some different company, won't it, Izzie?'

'Yeah,' was all the answer Izzie could manage. 'Fine birthday this 'un's gonna be!' she thought. 'No George – an' 'er instead!'

A little later George spoke quietly to Bill, then returned to the pair on his own.

'Where's 'e goin'?' Izzie asked.

'Where's 'oo goin?' her father replied.

'George, o' course!'

'Oh, 'im!'

'Yeah. 'Im! Where's 'e gone?'

''E's gone back to the boats to git summat.'

'Git what?'

'I dunno.' Izzie realised her father was being intentionally evasive, so she decided not to pursue the matter any further.

A few minutes later, George reappeared carrying a small brown paper bag. 'It looks like I ain't gonna be 'ere for your birthday, Izzie. So you may as well 'ave these now.'

'Thank you, George.' She took the bag from him and peeped inside. Her face broke into a smile as she pulled out a pair of beautiful red hair ribbons and a matching brush and comb.

'I 'ope as the colour o' them ribbons is all right for you,' he said.

'They're lovely!' Izzie said as she gave him a kiss. 'I'll keep 'em to wear for best – and the brush an' comb set's jus' smashin'!'

Jean intruded on her celebration. 'Alf says as they can manage wi'out me for a few days, so, if it's all right, I'll come to London wi' you.'

'That's all right, then,' Bill replied. For Izzie, it was anything but all right.

They arrived at the pickle factory the day before Izzie's birthday, and were tied up waiting to unload on the following morning. Jean had decided to put off her journey to Poplar until the following day as well.

That night saw one of London's biggest air attacks ever. Bill and his crew were used to the explosions of the bombs and the sound of anti-aircraft fire because they had recently sat through a number of air raids on London, but the raid that night was an exceptionally fierce one and far more intense than usual.

Izzie tucked her head under her pillow, but she still found it was impossible to get to sleep – not just because of the noise but because she was beginning to feel ... well, more than a little bit frightened! Her mind went back to the night they had heard the bombs at Blisworth. Tucked behind the curtain, even Bill, who had always bragged that he could sleep through anything, was finding it difficult to drop off. Hearing his daughter gasp at the sound of a particularly loud explosion, he called out, 'You OK, our Izzie?'

'That 'un sounded like it were a bit too close, Dad, didn't it?' she replied. 'Do you think we ought to go down into one o' them there air raid shelter things, if we can find one round 'ere, that is?'

'No, we needn't do that, Izzie love,' her father comforted her. 'Them bombs is still a fair way off, yit. It sounds like the East End. I reckon they'll be goin' for the docks again. Tell you what, though,' he said, trying to think of a way to take his daughter's mind off the noise outside, 'I could murder a cup o' tea!' As he said this, he got out of bed, pulled back the curtain, and lit the oil lamp.

'Good idea, Dad!' agreed Izzie, getting up and reaching for the kettle, very glad of something to do. She placed the kettle on the range and sat down. Bill sat down next to her on the side bed and put a protective arm round her. Listening to the raid outside, waiting for the kettle to boil, sitting there with her father next to her and the familiar, comforting sound of the kettle singing on the range, Izzie's fear seemed less. But she was still frightened enough to cuddle up to him and cover her ears at the loudest explosions, flinching as the boat rocked.

She had just poured out a mug of tea and passed it to her father when there was a loud, frantic knocking on the outside of *Aphrodite*'s cabin. They looked at each other, wondering who it could be. As Bill cautiously opened the hatch they heard Jean's voice.

'Can I come in there wi' you two? I wouldn' 'ave come, but I don' like listenin' to the sound o' them bleedin' bombs an' guns an' things, not sittin' in that little cabin all on me own, I don'!'

'Come on in, Jean, love!' Bill said as he sat down again so that Jean could step down into the cabin, pulling the slide shut as quickly as she could so as not to let any light show.

'Ta,' she said, sounding mightily relieved. 'Ta very much!' She stepped down into the cabin, her fur-collared coat wrapped tightly over her nightdress.

'Izzie's jus' got a brew on. Do you wanna cup?' Bill asked.

'Ooh yeah! Ta!' Jean replied as she sat down on the step and lit a cigarette. Izzie was not overly pleased that Jean had joined them, although she had to admit that she did look pale. Nonetheless, she reached for another mug and poured tea for her. As she did so, she thought, 'That's the first time I ever 'eard 'im call 'er "love"!' Again, she recalled the conversation between her father and George that night. But just at that moment there was another loud explosion from outside. It was so loud that it rocked the boat and made everything on board rattle. Izzie clung to her father, so scared that any other thoughts were driven completely from her mind.

'I moved out o' London to get away from bleedin' air raids!' said Jean, 'an' 'ere I am – back 'ere in London an' right slap bang in the middle of a bleedin' big 'un!'

It was nearly dawn before the raid ended. All three of them had spent the night in *Aphrodite*'s cabin, talking and talking and drinking endless cups of tea. Bill had recounted some of the more unusual and amusing incidents that had happened to him and other folk that he had met during his life on the water. Izzie had heard most of these stories many times before, but they were still funny when her father told them again, making her laugh. Jean, to whom they were new, laughed loudly at every humorous event he recounted. Bill was an excellent raconteur and, laughing at his stories, they managed to keep their spirits up, only flinching when a particularly loud explosion shook their enclosed little world, and almost forgetting the mayhem that was happening a few short miles away in another part of the city. Izzie was able, at least for a time, to contain her animosity towards Jean. They were all in this together.

Eventually the sounds of bombs exploding, engines droning and guns firing ceased. They had all come through the raid unscathed and in reasonable humour, but there was still a great communal sigh of relief when they heard the sirens sounding the 'All Clear'.

'Well, that's a good sound to 'ear!' Jean said, standing up and stretching. 'I'll go an' get a bit o' shut-eye before I 'ave to get up again an' get me bus to Poplar.' And with that she was gone.

Izzie and Bill, too, settled down for some sleep, knowing that it would not be long before John and Dick would arrive to begin unloading – air raid or no air raid.

Two days later it was Izzie's thirteenth birthday. She woke from a fitful few hours sleep, the noise of the previous night's explosions still reverberating inside her head. Opening the slide and looking around her, there was little evidence of the bombing. 'Me Dad were right,' she thought' 'They must 'ave been more over the east. Well, war or no war, it's me birthday. I'm thirteen!' She pulled herself up tall and ran her fingers through her hair. 'I'll put me new ribbons in today, an' I'm gonna wear 'em all day!' Going back into the cabin, she took the brush and ribbons from the bag. She brushed her hair and, drawing it back from her face, tied the ribbons loosely at the back of her head. 'Thank you, George,' she whispered.

Jean joined them for breakfast, still complaining about last night's raid. As they were finishing breakfast Bill reached behind the curtain and pulled out a large brown paper bag. ''Appy birthday, Izzie, love,' he said as her gave it to her. Out of the bag Izzie took a maroon hand-knitted cardigan.

'I seen as your ol' cardie were gettin' a bit worn round th' elbows,' he said, 'so I give Bet Johnson some money to git the wool an' knit you a new 'un.'

'It's lovely, Dad!' she exclaimed. 'I were meanin' to ask you for some money to git some wool an' knit one for meself, but I couldn't 'ave done these fancy patterns like Bet's done. Thank you, Dad!' She kissed him. 'I'll wear it today wi' these new 'air ribbons as George gi' me.'

'Oh! Is it your birthday today, Isobel?' Jean chimed in. 'If I'd 'ave knowed, I'd a got you summat meself.'

'That's all right,' Izzie replied. 'Knowin' you, it would 'ave been a bottle o' your cheap scent!' she thought.

'Well, I must be off,' said Jean, picking up her capacious handbag. 'I'll be back at teatime.' She stepped off the boat and headed for the bus stop.

The unloading proceeded as usual with John and Dick helping, although they missed George's extra pair of hands. There was no return load, but instead there was a message from George to say he would be waiting for them at The Running Horse as they made their way back towards Coventry. Needless to say, Izzie was delighted to hear this. Jean came back as the last shovelsful were being scraped from the butty's hold.

'Is your sister awright?' Bill asked.

'There's a lot o' bomb damage near where she lives but she's OK. I tried to tell 'er to get out o' London while the war's on, but she wouldn' listen. Well, it's 'er funeral!' She disappeared into *Zeus's* cabin.

As the pair pulled in to the towpath not far from the pub, Izzie caught sight of George walking up to meet them. As soon as she had helped her father secure the boats she ran down the towpath and flung her arms round him. George swept her off her feet and swung her round. When he let her go, she turned away from him so he could see her ribbons.

'I'm wearin' them new ribbons you gi' me!' she said over her shoulder. "Ow do they look?'

'I weren't sure about the colour when I bought 'em, but seein' 'em in your 'air like that, I reckon I chose right.'

'You chose exactly right. They're lovely!'

'Is that a new cardie, an' all?'

'Yeah – me Dad got Bet Johnson to knit it for me. It's nice, ain't it?'

'Ah, you look a right bobby-dazzler now all right!'

'Is your Grandad awright again now?' Izzie asked as they walked back to the boats from the pub.

''E's doin' awright for an old 'un.'

'But that's the second time as your Auntie's sent for you, sayin' as 'e's poorly, ain't it?'

'Yeah, I tol' 'er, I reckon as 'e puts it on a bit sometimes. I reckon as 'e sits there a-thinkin', an' when 'e reckons as it's time I went to see 'im, 'e makes out to 'er as 'e's poorly.'

As George stepped aboard *Aphrodite*, Jean was standing on *Zeus*'s counter, clutching her bags, ready to return to her work at the pub.

When she settled herself in bed that night Izzie thought how happy she felt. Despite the war, although her mother was dead and even in spite of Jean's presence, Izzie was content. She loved the life of the cut, and George was such a joy to be with – his kindness, his understanding, his sense of humour. She realised that the longer they spent together, the fonder of him she was becoming.

Chapter 16

A rum ol' job

The months passed and the war hardly interrupted their runs to and from the pickle factory. They saw the bombers and fighters overhead, and they kept up with events when they stopped at the Wharf or the pub. They saw bomb damage, but apart from rationing their lives followed a regular routine as the seasons changed.

Apart from saying 'Hello', Jean kept her distance on the occasions when they stopped off at The Running Horse. 'She don't seem so friendly now,' thought Izzie. 'I wonder why?'

They had received a message to go to the Wharf and, as they approached it on that early April evening, they were greeted by an empty scene. Not a single pair was tied up, waiting for orders. This could mean only one thing. All the boats were working!

'Well, damn me!' Bill exclaimed. 'I ain't never seen the Wharf this empty for a good few year!'

They had hardly finished tying up the ropes when Horace Roberts was out of his office and calling to Bill. There was a new job almost immediately. As Horace had predicted, the war was, indeed, creating additional work on the canals.

All three of them sat in Horace's office as he explained what their next job entailed.

'I'm taking you off the pickle factory job, Bill,' he said.

'Is there some problem, then?' Bill asked, a little nonplussed.

'No! No! No problem at all! Quite the reverse, in fact. I've had a request from the War Office.' He picked up a letter from his desk. 'It's rather a special job.'

''Ow do you mean, "special"?'

'Well, I can't actually tell you an awful lot about it, except that this one is definitely a Government contract and it looks as if it's going to be quite a regular run for you. The orders have come direct from the War Department and the whole thing's a bit "hush-hush". You're to pick up a cargo of sealed wooden crates from somewhere in Birmingham and carry them down to Kensal Green.'

'London again, then,' said Bill.

'Yes. Now, I'm not sure whether your pickle factory job was a Government contract or not,' Horace said, 'but this one certainly is,' repeating himself as he often did.

'So what is it that's in these 'ere crates then?'

'That's just it. I don't know. When the chap at the War Department was on the phone to me, telling me about the job, I asked him what the crates contained, but he wouldn't say. I told him I was not too happy about asking one of my company's boatmen to transport a cargo without knowing what it was he was carrying, but he simply said it was all covered by the Official Secrets Act, and he was, therefore – what was phrase he used? – "not at liberty to divulge". Obviously, from what little I've been told about this new job, it needs someone who is not only a competent boatman, but also someone who is transparently honest and trustworthy and can be guaranteed to deliver a cargo on time and intact, and you're the best boatman we have on all those counts.' Bill's chest swelled noticeably with pride.

'That's very nice of you to say, Mr Roberts,' said Bill, a little embarrassed.

'You know me well enough to know that I wouldn't say it if I didn't believe it was true.'

'But what about the pickle factory run?'

'I'm giving the pickle factory contract to Arthur and asking you to take on this War Office job.' Horace smiled. 'The thing is, Bill, are you happy about carrying a load of crates, but not knowing what's in them?'

'Well, it's a bit unusual, I'll say that. But I don't s'pose it's explosives nor nuthin' nasty like that – an' after all, it's a job, ain't it? An' you say as it might be reg'lar?'

'It certainly sounds like it could be.'

'Well! The way I sees it, in ordinary times, I might 'ave said

"No". At least, not till I 'ad some idea what were in them crates as I were gonna be carryin'. But these ain't ordinary times, are they? There's a war on, ain't there? An' that changes things a bit, don't it?' He paused. 'We'll take it.'

'I think you've made the right decision, Bill.'

'I reckon so too, Mr Roberts. Whereabouts in Brum are we loadin' 'em?'

'That's another strange thing, I don't know exactly! Like I said, I'm afraid it's all a bit sort of "cloak and dagger". The only information that I've been given is in this letter that came from the War Office a couple of days after I'd had the phone call.' Horace referred to the letter. 'It says here that it's somewhere up Smethwick way. Someone – I presume someone from the War Office – will be waiting to meet you at the top of the Farmers Bridge flight. He'll come aboard your boats, and then he'll direct you to wherever it is that you have to go to load.'

'It's a rum ol' job, this 'un is!' George said. 'A rum ol' job for sure!'

'Oh, and you also have to sign this first.' Horace detached a piece of paper that was paper-clipped to the letter, 'and then you need to take it with you when you go. I should imagine that someone will need to see it when you get there. They'll most probably take it and file it when you arrive for your first load.'

'What's it say?'

'It's a lot of typical Government jargon, actually, but what it basically says is that you're signing to say that neither you nor any of your crew will attempt to break the seals or open any of the crates or tamper with them in any way, and that you will also do everything reasonable within your power to prevent anyone else from trying to open or tamper with them either.' Horace put the piece of paper down in front of Bill, his finger pointing to a dotted line. His other hand held out a pen.

'I ain't never 'ad a load interfered wi' yit, and I'll be buggered if anybody's gonna mess about with this 'un!' He took the pen and marked an 'X' on the dotted line. Horace took the pen and paper back and wrote against Bill's 'X' certifying that it was, indeed, his mark.

'You're due to load in three days' time, about mid-morning, they said,' Horace told them as he was writing.

'We'll git 'em ahead first thing in the mornin', then.' George and Izzie both nodded in agreement.

From what they had been told by Horace they realised that they should not be tempted to ask what the crates contained. It was agreed that this was definitely a case of 'the less they knew, the better'.

'There's a mighty load o' locks on that run,' George said as they made their way back to the pair. 'Them at 'Atton's not so bad. I know as there's twenny-one on 'em, but at least they're all broad 'uns, so we can breast 'em up. But there's the "Ol' Thirteen" at Farmers Bridge an' they're all narrow 'uns!'

'I know they are,' Bill replied. 'Izzie, you better eat up your grub an' git your stren'th up over the next couple o' days, love. There'll be a awful lot o' bow-'aulin' the butty up them narrow locks in Brum.'

'Don't you worry, Dad. I'll manage 'em.'

About mid-morning, three days later, the pair was nearing the top of the Farmers Bridge flight of locks in Birmingham, the 'Old Thirteen' as they were known. Izzie had, indeed, 'managed them', and had managed them very well – and right in the middle of a prolonged, heavy downpour at that!

Zeus was just leaving the top lock of the flight when, looking ahead through the driving rain, Bill noticed a man standing on the towpath and sheltering from the rain under the next bridge. From the way he was dressed it was obvious that he was not one of the folk whom one would normally expect to see standing on the towpath in this neighbourhood. He was wearing a bowler hat and a light-coloured mackintosh. He was also carrying a furled umbrella and seemed to be peering in the direction of Bill's boats. As the pair approached the bridge the man caught sight of the name of the motor written on the cabin side. A smile came over his face as he opened his umbrella and ventured out from under the bridge.

'Ah! *Zeus!*' he exclaimed. 'Steerer Horne?' From his accent he sounded as if he was what Bill would call 'a bit posh'.

'That's me,' Bill answered, managing to work into those two words all the habitual distrust of the boating fraternity for anyone or anything that either looked, sounded or smelled like any form of officialdom.

'My name's Hargreaves,' said the man in the bowler hat. 'War Department. May I ... er ... come aboard?'

'S'pose so,' Bill replied. Overhearing this exchange, Izzie thought, 'Somebody's at least learned that bloke summat o' the manners o' the cut. Askin' me Dad's permission to come aboard – an' callin' 'im by 'is proper title. That'll impress 'im a bit, any road!'

'But first,' Bill said, 'you can 'elp me crew bow-'aul the butty through this 'ere lock – if you don't mind, that is?'

'Oh ... er ... right ... OK!' Mr Hargreaves stammered, somewhat lost for words and obviously a very long way from his more accustomed environment, sitting at a desk and pushing a pen in a War Department office in Whitehall. But – and they all had to give him credit for it – he willingly grabbed hold of the proffered rope without hesitation. It was all Bill, George and Izzie could do to stop themselves laughing, however, at the sight of him as he tried desperately to hold his umbrella above his bowler-hatted head with one hand, while tugging manfully – though rather ineffectively – at *Aphrodite's* bow rope with the other.

'Is that all right, Steerer Horne?' he asked, smiling from under his umbrella.

'That's jus' fine,' Bill chuckled as *Aphrodite* emerged from the lock and Izzie closed the gates. 'But you better step aboard now an' tell us where it is we're got to go for loadin'.'

'It's not that far, actually,' said Hargreaves as he stepped onto the counter next to Bill. 'It's a warehouse on the ... er ... Icknield Port Loop, I believe it's called.'

Bill steered *Zeus* round a long right-hand bend, then turned sharp left to enter the loop. The Icknield Port Loop was one of three loops that had been created when the main line of the canal through Birmingham had been straightened out many years before in an attempt to cut journey times.

'It's just round this bend here, on the left,' said Hargreaves. As they were approaching the bend in the loop Bill had to turn the motor away to the right to avoid another pair coming towards them.

'That was the pair of boats just ahead of yours on our list,' Hargreaves said. 'You should be able to take your boats straight in now.'

'That's good!' Bill replied as the pair rounded the bend.

'It's in there,' said Hargreaves as he pointed to an undercover private wharf, one of many that had been built a century earlier into the structure of the factories and warehouses. Like most such private wharves, this particular one had been built wide enough to accommodate two boats, side by side.

'Breast 'em up!' Bill shouted to his crew, and proceeded to give Mr Hargreaves a masterclass in the technique of 'breasting up'. Slowing *Zeus's* engine speed, he gave a short burst in reverse so that the towline connecting *Zeus* to *Aphrodite* became slack. Bending down, he lifted the towrope loop off the dolly on *Zeus's* stern and threw it onto *Aphrodite's* bow. As *Zeus* began slowing down, inertia enabled George to steer *Aphrodite* carefully alongside. As the two sterns drew level with each other, George threw *Aphrodite's* stern rope to Bill, who duly made it fast. Izzie, meanwhile, had made her way round the outside of the cabin, run nimbly along *Zeus's* top planks and was now standing on the bow. She watched carefully as the fore end of *Aphrodite* inched nearer. When the gap between the two boats had reached manageable proportions, she grabbed the butty's bow rope and fastened it onto the dolly on *Zeus's* fore end. Throughout this entire operation, Hargreaves stood on *Zeus's* counter, staring open-mouthed, hardly able to believe what he had just seen with his own eyes.

'Is ... is that your daughter, Steerer Horne?' he managed to ask when he found his voice at last.

'Ah,' Bill replied. 'That's our Izzie.'

'As her father, aren't you just the slightest bit ... well ... concerned about her running along those planks like that, especially with them being so wet?'

''Ow do you mean?' Bill asked, bemused.

'Well, I mean to say, she only needs to slip on one of those wet timbers and she could easily fall over the side of the boat and into the canal!'

Bill looked at him and smiled. 'No, Mr Hargreaves. I don't never worry about that at all. I reckon as every kid as were ever born on a boat 'as learned to run along the tops very near as soon as they can walk.'

'Astonishing! Absolutely astonishing!' was all Mr Hargreaves could say.

Bill frowned slightly as he remembered how Maggie had died – she had not been so lucky.

'You'll 'ave to duck your 'ead a bit while I swing the tiller over to turn in 'ere!' Bill warned. Hargreaves dutifully obeyed, but forgot about his umbrella, which became entangled with the tiller bar.

'Sorry!' he called as he tried to extricate it. He succeeded, but when he examined the umbrella three of the spokes were very badly bent.

'Oh, bother!' he muttered.

'Couldn't 'elp it!' Bill sympathised.

'No! No! My fault entirely!' Hargreaves replied, somewhat breathlessly. 'Don't worry. I know somewhere in London where I can get it repaired.'

The pair was soon tied up in the covered wharf. Hargreaves stepped off and spoke to another, older but similarly dressed man who held a clipboard in one hand and a pen in the other. He looked up at Bill.

'This is Mr Jenkins,' Hargreaves said. 'He'll be dealing with you now.' He made his way back out into the rain, struggling to put up his broken umbrella.

'Steerer Horne with *Zeus* and *Aphrodite*,' Mr Jenkins said, half to himself. He flicked over two or three pages on his clipboard, then wrote something down.

'Have you got your chit, Steerer Horne?'

''Ave I got what?'

'Sorry,' said Mr Jenkins, realising that Bill had never come across the word 'chit' before. 'I mean the piece of paper you signed before you left your depot.'

'Oh, that! Izzie! Go an' git that bit o' paper as Mr Roberts give us, will you, love? I stuck it in the ticket drawer.' Izzie dutifully obliged and her father handed it over. The man glanced at it.

'That all appears to be in order. These gentlemen will help you to get loaded.' He pointed to half-a-dozen men who were wearing brown overalls and resting on sack trucks. Behind them were piles of wooden crates.

As the first crate was brought to the boat, Jenkins motioned to the man in brown overalls to stop. He turned to Bill.

'As you will see, Steerer Horne, these crates are all sealed – here.' He pointed to an official looking seal on the nearest crate. 'So any tampering of any kind will not go unnoticed.'

'Like I tol' Mr Roberts when I signed that there paper,' Bill replied, 'I ain't never 'ad a load interfered wi' yit, an' I'll be buggered if I'm gonna start now!'

'Quite!' said Mr Jenkins, smiling. 'Quite!'

The men in brown overalls set about loading the crates under Bill's direction and he was given specific instructions by Jenkins that the cargo was to be clothed up immediately the loading was finished, before they left the wharf, and that the cloths were not to be removed until immediately before unloading after they had arrived at their destination in Kensal Green.

When the loading was complete, Bill was asked to 'sign' against the names of his boats on a list to confirm that the pair had been correctly loaded and the cargo was now his responsibility. This done, *Zeus*'s engine was fired up and the pair reversed back out onto the canal. The ropes were quickly reorganised for towing and, as they made their way back to the top of the locks, they got a cheerful wave from Mr Hargreaves, as he walked along the towpath, still struggling with his umbrella.

❈

That evening, after they had eaten, they sat in the cabin and tried to imagine what the contents of their sealed crates might possibly be.

'I'd say its probably summat for the military – guns per'aps!' George suggested.

'You reckon?' Bill queried.

'Could be. What wi' us not bein' tol' what's in 'em like, an' not to open 'em neither. Could be guns for the troops.'

Bill thought for a while. 'No, I don't reckon it's that. I reckon th' army's got enough lorries to take its own guns about wi'out using boats.'

'What do you reckon it is, Izzie?' George continued.

'I dunno. I s'pose it could be guns or summat, couldn't it?'

'It could be trumpets an' things for them there military bands,' George suggested. He said it with such a straight face that Izzie could not make out whether he was being serious. Then he grinned and she realised he was not.

'Oh, you!' she exclaimed. 'They ain't gonna be playin' no trumpets while they're out there fightin' the Germans, are they?'

'I dunno. They could allus defeat 'em by deafenin' 'em, couldn't they?'

'D'you reckon it might be apples for the 'orses?' Izzie asked.

'What 'orses?' George asked.

'Them 'orses as we seen them soldiers ridin' down London as you took me to see on me birthday that time when we was waitin' for that back load. You remember, we got a bus to near that big 'ouse where the King lives and they was ridin' down the road near there. I reckon them 'orses'd probably like a few apples now an' again.' She paused. 'I'm jokin', o' course. I ain't got no idea what's in 'em really.'

'I dunno neither,' said Bill. 'Could be anythin'. Bits for aeroplanes, bits for them big field gun things as they 'ave, anythin'!' He paused. 'To be honest wi' you, I don't really wanna know what's in 'em.'

'Why's that then? Ain't you jus' a bit curious, like?' enquired George.

'Well,' he said, 'it's plain as the Government don't want nobody knowin' what's in 'em, ain't it? So let's jus' say if we ain't got no idea what's in 'em, then we can't go tellin' nobody else what's in 'em, can we? An' as there's a war on, that's probably all for the best.'

'An' I reckon as you might be right at that. Like they says in them newsreels at the pictures, "Careless talk costs lives"," George agreed.

'That's what it says on them posters as I told you about an' all,' Izzie added. The subject of what might be in the crates was dropped and never referred to again.

Chapter 17

Read us summat

They arrived at Kensal Green about mid-morning. Bill knew that they had found the right place when he was hailed from the bank by yet another man wearing a bowler hat and holding a clipboard. The man looked at *Zeus*'s nameplate, then quickly referred to his list. 'Ah, Steerer Horne is it?'

'It is,' Bill replied.

'Good! Good! My name's Thompson. You can tie up here. We'll get you unloaded this afternoon.'

'Righto!' Bill nodded. They tied up alongside an open space of concrete on which a Nissen hut had been erected. This appeared to serve both as an office for the War Ministry officials who supervised the unloading of the boats and also as a mess room for the men in brown overalls who actually did the work.

Bill spoke to Mr Thompson. 'Weren't there a buildin' 'ere? I reckon there were a red-brick place 'ere last time we come by?'

'Bombed!' came the reply. 'We think they were aiming for the railway over there.' The man in the bowler pointed backwards over his shoulder. 'The incendiaries started the fire and the high explosives did the rest.'

That afternoon four large vans arrived and parked next to the Nissen hut. Immediately after their rear doors were opened, Bill was asked to remove the side cloths from his cargo. The seals on all the cases were carefully checked as they were unloaded from the boats by the gang of men in brown overalls, who put them straight into the vans. As soon as the vans were fully loaded, the doors were closed and secured and they were driven away again.

'I'm afraid we don't have a lot of space for you to stay moored up here,' Thompson said as the last crate was being lifted out of

Aphrodite's hold, 'and we have another pair of boats already on their way. They should be here soon.' He consulted his wristwatch. 'There's a place where you can turn round a bit further on,' he continued, sounding a little agitated and pointing in a southerly direction. 'If I were you, I think I might start back for Smethwick straight away.'

Bill thought for a few moments. 'Yeah, I knows the windin' 'ole you mean. We'll go on down there an' wind 'em, an' then we'll git 'em ahead for Smethwick, I reckon.'

'That's fine. I may see you again on your next trip.' He looked relieved as he waved them off.

And that was the way their lives were to continue. They spent their days travelling between Smethwick and Kensal Green with their 'secret loads'. Izzie was thrilled when once they got a return load that needed delivering somewhere near the Wharf. She was able to see Miss Roberts and show her her journal.

'My, Isobel!' Emily said. 'You've almost enough here to write a book!' Izzie was delighted to receive such praise and was even more thrilled when Miss Roberts gave her some 'proper' books to read.

'You don't need children's primers any more. Try these short books. They are full of interesting facts as well as stories.'

Bill, as always, was keen to see Horace and check on any new developments.

The Running Horse had become a regular stopping place as it fitted well with their schedule. On their next run from Smethwick, as the evenings became lighter and warmer, Izzie was sitting on the cabin roof with her thoughts while Bill and George had gone for a pint. 'I'm gonna be fourteen soon!' she thought. 'I wonder if I'm gonna feel any diff'rent than I do bein' thirteen?' She casually cast a glance towards the road that ran along the far side the pub, and saw Jean waiting at the bus stop. After a few moments a bus came along and she boarded it. Later, as they returned from the pub, she heard George comment to her father, 'Jean weren't there tonight.'

'No,' Bill replied. 'Accordin' to Alf she were gittin' the bus to London to go and see 'er sister again.'

'That's odd!' Izzie thought. 'That bus as she caught weren't goin' London way at all. It were goin' north!'

They all carried out their usual duties on the morning of her birthday, but this year they did not pretend they had forgotten it.

'We 'ope as you don't mind too much, our Izzie,' her father said, 'but me an' George is givin' you some money this birthday. With this crate run we ain't 'ad no time to git to no shops.'

'It's better, in a way,' George added, 'cos then you can git what you want wi' it, can't you?'

'I knows as you're both been real busy an' you ain't 'ad no time to git off the cut. So, thank you both very much for the money. The next time I goes shoppin' I'll buy summat wi' it, an' then I can show you both what you're bought me.' She thanked them and hugged and kissed them both in turn. As she kissed George, she suddenly realised that being hugged by him was a most enjoyable experience. She remembered the lovely box her father had made her for her birthday some years ago to keep her treasures in. 'I reckon as me birthday's as good a time as any to 'ave a look through 'em an' sort 'em out!' she decided. 'I'll do that later.'

That evening it was cool, even for early May, and there was a constant drizzle, so she stayed inside the cabin and, sitting on the side bed, opened her treasure box. 'You're fourteen now,' she said to herself as she looked at the contents. 'You ain't a little gel no more. You're gittin' to be a growed-up woman, so what do you want wi' eggshells an' pebbles? Kiddies' stuff they are! An' that ol' cloth bag as I made is jus' about wore out. She carefully put all the eggshells and all the pebbles except one – a particularly pretty one – in the cloth bag. Then she did the same with most of the trinkets and oddments. She put the bag to one side ready to throw it out with the rubbish. She decided to keep her grandmother's brooch and the piece of lace from the ear protector of her other grandmother's boat horse. These she put carefully back into her box, together with the two initialled handkerchiefs – her mother's last birthday present to her – and the copy of 'Crystal' that George had bought for her the same year as her father had given her the box.

The following day she was out shopping while the pair was being loaded with another consignment of crates. She was anxious to spend her birthday money, so she stopped and looked in the taped-up window of a ladies' clothes shop. Besides the dress, skirt and blouse on display there were some headscarves. My ol' 'eadscarf is gittin' so thin in places as it'll soon be wore through,' she thought, and, without more ado, entered the shop. The shop assistant explained that shortages as a result of the war meant that there were not many to choose from. Izzie said she understood that and selected a scarf with a red and blue diamond pattern. She handed the Clothing Book to the assistant who proceeded to cut out of it sufficient coupons to cover the headscarf and handed it back. Izzie paid for her purchase and left the shop.

Looking at her reflection in a shop window to make sure it looked all right, she put it on her head and tied the ends under her chin just before she arrived back at the warehouse. Proudly, she strutted into the warehouse to show her father and George.

'Is that what you bought wi' your birthday money, our Izzie?' her father asked.

'Yeah, it's a nice 'un, ain't it?'

'It certainly is, Izzie, love! You look like a real young lady in that!' he said.

'A real bobby-dazzler!' George added. Mr Jenkins and some of the men in brown overalls loading the boats were very complimentary too!

Izzie found that she was spending more time sitting on the roof of whichever of the pair George was steering rather than with her father. Bill did not seem to mind and George seemed to enjoy her company.

On one occasion George asked her how she thought she was getting on with her reading.

'Well,' she said, thoughtfully, 'I reckon as I'm doin' awright, an' Miss Roberts, she reckons I'm doin' awright an' all, so I s'pose I must be, mustn't I? She said as I'm gittin' too good for them primers an' I can read real short books.'

'See, I'm 'ad an idea,' said George. 'One o' these days, why don't you git one o' them books o' yourn an' read us summat – while we're gettin' 'em ahead, like?'

'Yeah! I reckon as that might do me some good, wouldn't it? I mean, wi' you bein' able to read a bit an' all, you could tell me if I were sayin' it wrong.'

'Hang on!' George warned her. 'The main thing you said there was "a bit". It is "a bit" an' all. I ain't never really learned to read proper.'

'No, but you can 'elp wi' the words as you know – an' I can probably 'elp you wi' some on 'em as you don't.'

The following day Izzie sat on the roof and read to George from one of the books Miss Roberts had lent her. It was called *Children of the Empire* and consisted of a series of chapters, each about the life of a child in a different country of the British Empire.

'I'll read you all about "Gupta from India",' Izzie announced, and proceeded to work her way, haltingly, through the chapter. George was impressed and helped her with a few of the words. Some words neither of them knew!

Reading to George became almost a daily occurrence.

'Together we're learnin' a thing or two,' George remarked. She had a number of books from Emily Roberts's 'library'. Some days she would read him poems from a book called *The Joy of Poetry*. On others it would be a story from a book of children's fairy tales. They learned a lot about famous people – artists, scientists, inventors and heroes and heroines.

Sometimes Izzie looked up from the book she was reading to George and catch her father looking at them. As their eyes met he would toss his head and avert his gaze. 'Ah, well,' Izzie thought, 'it's a good job as George is 'appy for me to read to 'im, cos it looks like me Dad ain't changed 'is mind!

Chapter 18

Called up

During those summer months Izzie realised that her feelings towards George were changing. When he had first arrived, soon after her mother's death, he had just been one of the lads from off another pair of boats. Living and working together over the months, she had come to look upon him as a kind of older brother. They got on well together. When they were working the narrow locks at Farmers Bridge, having made sure that *Aphrodite's* bow was in the entrance to the lock, George would often jump onto the towpath and help Izzie bow-haul the heavy boat into the lock, then close the paddles so that Izzie could open those in the other gate.

He was always ready to help and encourage her. If a lock gate was particularly stiff or heavy he would leap off the counter and help her to push it. They shared the cooking duties too. Most of the time George decided what they would eat, and he would cook it with Izzie's assistance. Occasionally, though, their roles would be reversed.

'Cook us summat as your Mam used to make,' he would say, then help her with the preparation.

There was precious little leisure time to be had as they were busy with the Government contract, but what little they had they tended to spend together – except when the two men took themselves off to a pub in the evening. George enjoyed a game of cards, a pastime that Bill and Maggie had indulged in only rarely. In no time he had taught Izzie how to play knockout whist, rummy and cribbage. Of all of the games the one Izzie enjoyed most was cribbage – 'crib' as she learned it was usually called. She always giggled when the appropriate Jack turned up and she was able to say, 'One for 'is knob!'

And now they had a new pastime – one that they could enjoy while they were working – that of Izzie reading aloud to George. 'Yeah,' she had often thought to herself "e's jus' like 'e's me older bother. 'E certainly teases me like I reckon most older brothers do!'

But now … now Izzie had a sense that things were somehow changing. There was a kind of a difference. Day by day, and almost imperceptibly, she began to realise that her feelings for this tall young man with the uncontrollable shock of fair hair were becoming somehow stronger, somehow deeper. She felt herself strangely… attracted – yes, that was it, attracted to him. She sometimes found herself just looking at him, watching him, for no better reason than – well, she just wanted to. When he then noticed her looking at him, she would smile at him and look away. She had begun to notice some of the little things he did, like the way he wrinkled his nose when he was thinking hard, and the way he stuck his thumbs in his belt when he was walking.

She had never experienced feelings like this before. 'Could this be what they mean in them films I seen at the pictures?' she mused to herself. 'Could this be what they call "love"?' She loved her father and she had loved her mother, whose memory she cherished dearly, but this … this emotional upsurge was so totally different from anything she had ever felt for anybody – ever! It was so different that, at first, she had great difficulty in understanding it, and it was only after some weeks that she had come to the conclusion that, yes, she was slowly but surely falling in love with George Andrews!

George, on the other hand, did not appear to share her feelings in any way, shape or form. He seemed completely oblivious to the emotional turmoil that she struggled with inside. He carried on in his usual, joking, brotherly fashion. Izzie could not understand it at all. Here was she, totally convinced that she was falling head over heels in love with this man, and there was he, seemingly immune from it all. She wondered whether she should tell him how she felt, but quickly dismissed the idea. "E'd think I were bein' daft!" she reasoned. 'If only me Mam were still 'ere,' she wished. 'I could 'ave asked 'er what to do – an' she'd 'ave knowed.' She shared her dilemma with her journal that night.

❋

Acting on a message from Horace Roberts, passed on by Mr Jenkins, they returned to the Wharf rather than going directly to London. When they arrived late the following afternoon, a serious-faced Horace asked all three of them to step into the office. 'Now,' he began, 'I'm not sure what this is going to mean to you all, but I have a fair idea and I don't think it's going to be good news. I've got a letter here for you, George. It looks as if it's come from the War Office and I've a pretty shrewd idea what's in it.'

George quickly opened the envelope and looked at the letter. 'I can make out some on it, Mr Roberts, but can you tell us what it all means?' he solemnly asked.

Horace took the letter and scanned its contents. 'It's exactly what I thought, George. You've been called up for the army,' he said, sadly.

'Oh, no!' groaned Bill. Izzie was too dumbstruck to say anything at all, or listen to his long explanation.

'But some o' the blokes was sayin' as 'ow none of us was gonna git called up cos what we're doin' already is a sort of war work,' George protested.

'That's what we all thought, George. That's what they thought at the Company office too,' Horace explained. 'The Government put out a list some time ago of what they called "reserved occupations". These were people who they said were in what you might call protected employment. Those on the list wouldn't be called up for military service because the work they were already doing was important for the war effort. This list, it had jobs on it like merchant seamen and railway workers, and so we all assumed that it would cover you boatmen as well, but apparently either it doesn't, or they've had to revise their thinking. I've had to give out a number of these letters to you younger chaps this week. Reading between the lines, it seems they're getting so short of men now that even some of the people in the so-called "reserved occupations" are being called up. My next-door neighbour's a guard on the railway and he's had his papers too.'

'What do I 'ave to do, Mr Roberts?' George asked, resignedly.

'It says here they want you to report to some barracks at a place called Catterick a week on Monday,' Horace told him, looking at the letter.

'That's Yorkshire way, ain't it?' asked George

'Yes,' Horace confirmed. He then turned to Bill. 'The main problem this poses for you, as you may have probably already realised, Bill, is that it leaves you a man short to work your pair.' Shocked into action, Izzie opened her mouth to speak. 'And before you say anything, young lady,' Horace turned to her, 'I'm sorry, but you're too young to take on the responsibility of working a pair of boats just with your father.'

'But...' Izzie's protest was cut short by a stern look from Bill.

'Is there anybody else as you know of as could take over from George?' Bill asked quietly.

'Nobody I can readily think of,' Horace replied. 'Most of the likely candidates have either already been called up, just like George, or I've got letters here to give to them when they get back off their runs.'

Izzie simply glared at the floor, not only horrified at the thought of losing her George, but also wondering again what the future might hold for her and her father.

'You ain't got one o' them there letters for me, then?' Bill asked.

'No,' Horace replied. 'I've been thinking about that and I guess there might be a couple of reasons why they don't want you, Bill. One is that you're quite a bit older than George, although I know that some of the men nearly your age have had them. The other reason – and I think this is really why – is that your situation is a bit different. You're a widower and you have what the Government would call "a dependent minor" – young Izzie, here. I mean to say, what would happen to her if you had to go into the forces?'

'Hmm...,' was Bill's only reply.

There was silence for half a minute or so. It was broken by Bill.

''Ang on a minute! If George ain't got to go to th' army till a week Monday, it's only Tuesday today. We can git another run in afore 'e 'as to go.'

'You can that,' agreed Horace.

'Then we'll 'ave another look at it when we gits back,' said Bill. He, George and Izzie got up to leave.

'In the meantime,' Horace said, 'I'll keep my ear to the ground and see if I can find a boatman looking for a job – but I'll be honest with you, I don't hold out a lot of hope.'

'Thanks, Mr Roberts,' Bill called back over his shoulder. 'I know as you'll do your best!'

As they walked back to the boats, Emily Roberts was just leaving the schoolroom to go home.

'Isobel!' she called as she caught sight of her. Izzie ran over, her fears about their future temporarily put to one side as she saw her teacher again for the first time in months.

''Allo, Miss Roberts,' she said. 'I'm sorry I ain't been at the school much lately, but we're been ever so busy!'

'I know,' Emily replied. 'Since the war started I haven't had many pupils at all. Are you still working at your reading?'

'Every spare minute as I gits!' said Izzie. Emily could see from the look on the girl's face that her enthusiasm for her subject had not dimmed one iota. 'I'm finished all them books as you gi' me last time. I'll go an' git 'em for you.' With that she ran off to *Aphrodite*'s cabin, reappearing a few moments later with the books in her hand.

'I been readin' 'em out loud to George,' she said as she handed them over. 'We're got through all on 'em.'

'You'll be needing some more, then,' said Emily.

'I dunno,' said Izzie sadly, as the reality of their precarious situation overtook her again. 'George is got to go in th' army, an' if Mr Roberts can't find no one else afore we gits back off our next run, I dunno what'll 'appen to me an' me Dad.'

'Oh dear!' Emily said. 'Well, let's look on the bright side. I'll give you some more books anyway.' She turned and headed back to the schoolroom with Izzie in her wake. As she replaced the returned books in the cupboard she asked Izzie, 'Did you have any difficulties with those?'

'I could read most o' the words, an' George 'elped me wi' some on 'em,' Izzie replied, 'but there was a few on 'em as neither on us didn't know what they meant.' Emily carefully selected some more books from her cupboard.

'Try these,' she said, handing them to Izzie. 'They're a little more difficult than the last ones you had. In fact, they are the most difficult I have! These two are collections of short stories.' She showed Izzie a book called *Ten Minute Tales* and another called *Tales of Robin Hood*. 'These ones are just one long story from beginning to end,' she added as she gave Izzie two more books. They were *Winnie the Pooh* and *The Velveteen Rabbit*. 'Oh, and I think you ought to take this one with you as well,' she said as she picked up a very old-looking, dog-eared book from another shelf.

'This is a rather different sort of book,' she explained. 'It's called a dictionary. It doesn't tell a story like the other books, it's just a long list of words – see?' She opened the book and showed a page to Izzie. 'And written down alongside each word is what it means – it's what's called a "definition". All the words in the book are in the same order as the alphabet that you learned all that time ago when you first started to learn how to read. So now, when you come across a new word in the book you're reading, you can just look it up in here and then you'll be able to see exactly what it means!'

'That's clever, ain't it?' said Izzie in amazement. 'Jus' think! Somebody must 'ave sat down an' writ out all them words to put 'em in this 'ere book! That must 'ave took 'em a long ol' time!'

'I'm sure it must have!' Emily chuckled. 'But you'll be very glad that they took the time when you come across a new word.'

Izzie was thumbing through the dictionary. 'There's loads an' loads o' words in 'ere as I ain't never seen afore!' she said, looking a little worried.

'Don't worry about that,' Emily comforted her. 'There are very few people in this world who know all the words that there are. That's why they make dictionaries like this so that even people who can read very well can look up the words they haven't come across before. I have to use a dictionary sometimes because I occasionally find a word that's new to me.'

'Thank you, Miss Roberts. Thank you ever so much for all the books as you've let me take on the runs an' for this 'un 'specially,' said Izzie, smiling at her teacher.

'Thank you, Isobel,' Emily Roberts replied. 'It's not often I have a student who is as keen to learn as you are. How are you getting on writing in your diary?'

'I does it every day – well, nearly every day. Some nights I'm jus' too tired. Sometimes I does it in the mornin' then, but sometimes I forgits.'

'Well, there's another little exercise you can do to help with your writing. When you have finished reading a book you can write what's called a review. In it, you write a bit about where the book is set and a little about the main characters. But most of a review is really about what you thought about the book – whether you thought it was believable, if it's a story, and how well you thought you had got to know the characters in it. If it's a book about a real person then you say whether you thought it told you enough about them and about what they did. Do you see?'

'Yes, Miss Roberts. I'll enjoy doin' that.'

'Are you going to be here long this time?'

'I don't think so,' Izzie replied. 'Me Dad an' George is sayin' as 'ow we should git another run in afore George 'as to go in th' army, so I reckon we'll be gittin' 'em ahead for Brum first thing tomorra mornin'.'

'But there's no one about who can take over from George?' Emily asked.

'No. Mr Roberts says as 'e's gonna see if 'e can't find somebody for when we gits back, but 'e said it were gonna be real 'ard to find anybody.' Izzie paused. 'So me an' me Dad ... well ... we might end up 'avin' to go on the bank after all,' she said, sounding totally depressed. 'An' I'm gonna miss 'im an' all!' she added, almost without thinking.

'You've grown quite fond of George, haven't you, Isobel?'

'Yeah, I 'ave. I ... I reckon ... I reckon as I might 'ave ... sort o' ... fell in love wi' 'im!'

Emily stared at the confused young girl standing in front of her. 'Does George know how you feel?' she asked, quietly.

'No. Least I don't reckon so. Well, I ain't tol' 'im, any road.'

Emily immediately recalled having similar feelings for a boy with whom she had been at school. He was a year older than her and during her final year he had been articled to a local solicitor. They had spent many happy hours together during that year, but then she had left school and gone to college. Although they wrote to each other frequently, when she came home for the holidays and they met up again, they both realised that, emotionally, they had moved on and the old feelings were no longer there.

'Well, if that's the case, then being apart for a while may not be a bad thing,' she said.

"Ow do you make that out, Miss Roberts?' Izzie was appalled.

'Well, sometimes, people only think they're in love. And then they find that absence – rather than making the heart grow fonder – it does just the opposite. When they meet up again they find that they feel quite differently about each other.'

'But what if when they meets up again they still feels the same?'

'Well, then, I think that means that it probably is love after all – true love.'

Izzie sighed. 'Thank you for tellin' me all that,' she said. 'It don't really make me feel a lot better but I can see what you mean.'

'Good. But you mustn't feel too sorry for yourself – this war is doing a lot of terrible things to a lot of people.'

'Yeah. It might put me an' me Dad on the bank for a start!'

'I hope for your sake, and for Mr Horne's, that it doesn't come to that. I look forward to seeing you again when you're back this way,' said Emily, as she prepared for home.

She and Izzie said their goodbyes and Izzie walked back to *Aphrodite*. Stepping down into the cabin, she saw George, sitting on the side bed, his face thoughtful as he looked through his call-up papers. Her father was nowhere to be seen. 'Where's me Dad?' she asked.

"E's gone back to Mr Roberts's office to use the phone,' George replied. They sat in silence for nearly a full minute.

'Are you lookin' forward to goin' in th' army, then, George?' Izzie asked.

'In one way, I s'pose I am. I mean, like, we're all got to do our bit for the war an' that, but I reckoned as I were doin' that already, workin' on the boats. But I s'pose the Gover'ment reckons as a bloke like me'll do more good in th' army than on the boats. I expect I'll git to meet a lot of new people – an' I might even git to go abroad.'

'An' me an' me Dad might git to go on the bank!' Izzie shouted, angrily.

'Now look 'ere, Izzie!' George said, taken aback by her tone. 'I never asked to go in th' army, did I? It ain't like I wanna go off an' leave you both in the lurch, is it? But I ain't got no choice! I been called up for th' army an' … well … I got to go. That's 'ow it is, see? The Gover'ment says as they wants you to go an' fight for your King an' country an' you 'as to go. You can't write back to 'em an' say, "Sorry, I can't come, I got other things I got to do." As far as they're concerned, they're called me up an' I'm duty bound to go.'

'What if you jus' didn't turn up, like? What if you jus' said as you'd never 'ad that there letter? Give us it 'ere. I reckon I can read enough to understand it.' George passed the letter to her and she studied it.

'Now you jus' stop an' think about it, Izzie. There's a war on, right? The Gover'ment's writ to me sayin' as 'ow it wants me to go in th' army an' fight. Now, if I didn't go – well, that'd be agin the law, wouldn't it? They'd probably call it treason or some such an' I could end up bein' sent to prison for it.'

'I s'pose you're right. It says 'ere that failin' to join your unit on the app-summat date will make you an ab-sent-ee and you will then be – a word I dunno – to be arrested – summat else I dunno – a Court of … summat or other. I don't know them words!'

'So, then I'd 'ave to go to court, an' then I'd be in prison. Neither way, I wouldn't 'ave a leg to stand on, would I? An' as for sayin' I never 'ad the letter? Well, they'd know as it were delivered to the Wharf 'ere, so if I said as I'd never 'ad it, then Mr Roberts'd be in trouble for not givin' it to me, wouldn't 'e?' George said, looking straight at her. 'Like I said, I ain't got no choice. I got to go!'

'I know,' said Izzie, her voice softening. She placed her hand on the back of George's. 'I ain't angry at you, George. It's jus' … its jus' it don't seem fair! We nearly 'ad to go on the bank when me Mam died. We would 'ave done if you 'adn't come along. Now you got to go in th' army an' unless Mr Roberts can find us somebody else to 'elp work the pair, then me an' me Dad's really got to go on the bank this time! I dunno what 'e's gonna do. 'E don't know nuthin' 'cept boatin'! 'E'll 'ave to git a job o' some sort though, won't 'e?' George could see that Izzie was trying very hard not to cry. 'An' I'm gonna miss you. I'm gonna miss you a awful lot!'

'I'm gonna miss you an' all, Izzie.' He looked at her very seriously and, for a brief moment, she honestly believed he was about to confess his love for her, but instead his face suddenly split into a grin. 'But all dependin' on this 'ere phone call as your Dad's makin' – right this minute – you an' 'im might not 'ave to go on the bank after all.'

'What?' Izzie asked, surprised.

'You jus' wait an' see,' George smiled. 'I ain't a-gonna tell you no more!'

'What?' she repeated, her voice rising in excitement.

'You'll find out soon enough when 'e gits back. Make us a cuppa, Izzie.' Despite her asking repeatedly who her father was talking to on the telephone, George refused to say any more and insisted that she wait until he returned.

'Me lips is sealed!' was all she could get out of him. At last, and not a moment too soon for Izzie, the doors opened and Bill stood on the counter, beaming from ear to ear.

'She says as 'ow she'll give it a go!' he exclaimed.

'Who says she'll give what a go?' Izzie asked, totally confused.

''Ave you said owt to her?' Bill asked George, nodding in Izzie's direction.

'Nary a word. Me lips is sealed,' George said again.

'Izzie,' Bill began, 'you remember Jean, don't you?'

'Yeah!' Izzie replied. 'I remember 'er all right.' She rose and put the kettle on the range. She knew full well that at their first meeting she had taken an instant dislike to Jean. She still could not put her finger on the reason, but there was something about the woman that she did not like, something about her that she felt she could not altogether trust. Izzie had been so busy during the summer on the Birmingham to London run and wrapped up with her feelings for George that thoughts of Jean had not entered her head. They had stopped at 'The Horse' a couple of times but each time Izzie had stayed on the boats, and each time, whether by accident or design, neither Bill nor George had mentioned Jean on their return.

'She were sayin' to me an' George when we was in there last run that while she's been workin' at the pub she's got talkin' to a lot o' boatin' folk, an' from what she's 'eard an' from them few days she 'ad on the boats wi' us, she reckons as 'ow boatin's definitely the life for 'er. Reckons as she were never really cut out for pub work,' Bill explained. 'I jus' been talkin' to 'er on the phone now, an' she says as 'ow she'll give it a go.'

Izzie's heart sank. Not only was she losing her George, but that woman was going to take his place. 'I don't like it!' she thought. 'I do not like it! But better 'n goin' on the bank, I s'pose…'

'What did Mr Roberts 'ave to say about it?' asked George.

'Oh, 'e went on a bit about 'ow she ain't bin on this 'ere Gover'ment scheme thing for trainin' women, so she ain't been taught proper. But I ask' 'im, I said, "If I can't learn somebody 'ow to steer a pair an' work a lock after all this time, then I dunno o' nobody as can." An' anyway, I says, "Don't you know there's a war on?" That done it! 'E agreed!'

Bill and George laughed while Izzie digested the news with very mixed feelings, very mixed feelings indeed. But on the other hand, if it meant that she and her father could stay on the boats… 'Per'aps…,' she thought, 'per'aps I might manage to git on wi' 'er well enough for 'owever long it takes for this 'ere war to be over an' for my George to come back to me.'

'What are we doin', then?' George asked.

'We're pickin' 'er up on the way down to London. George sleeps on the side bed o' the motor, so she can 'ave the cross bed,' Bill explained.

'I hope the curtain's awright!' interjected George, smiling. 'I ain't never pulled it acrost since I'm been in there on me own.' He was referring to the curtain that could be pulled across to mask the bed hole from the rest of the cabin.

'Perhaps she ain't too squeamish about that sort o' thing,' retorted Bill, 'an' she's ol' enough to be your mother, but we'll check on it any'ow. Like I say, we'll pick 'er up on the way down an' we can learn 'er what she 'as to do all the rest o' the way down to Kensal Green. An' then again on the way back up till we gits as far as "The 'Orse". Then we can all sit down an' see where we are.'

'What if she don't like it?' Izzie asked.

'Well, then we 'ave to think again, don't we?' replied Bill. 'But we're got to do summat, our Izzie, or otherwise this could well turn out to be our last run! If we don't git summat worked out, you an' me'll be on the bank for sure.'

Chapter 19

Welcome aboard, Jean

'She said last night as she'd be along 'ere about 'alf past seven,' Bill said as he threw his shaving water over the side. Izzie was busy with the breakfast, and the smell of frying bacon had brought George along from *Zeus*. The pair was tied up about a quarter of a mile along the canal from The Running Horse, where the men had spent the previous evening.

'What time is it now?' Izzie asked.

Bill looked at his pocket watch. 'Jus' gone quarter past,' he answered. The three of them ate their breakfast, and while Izzie was doing the washing up George and Bill checked the load and the engine. Then they all sat and waited – and waited.

'I don't reckon she's a-comin'!' said Izzie at last.

'She'll be 'ere!' her father replied.

Sure enough, at ten minutes to eight Jean emerged from the front door of the pub and proceeded to scurry along the towpath. Her progress was impeded by the large suitcase that she was carrying in her right hand, while her left held her capacious handbag. Her gas mask in its box bounced around her neck as she walked.

'Where's she reckon she's gonna stow that there case?' Izzie asked.

'We'll find somewhere,' said Bill, 'An' if she decides she's gonna stay on 'ere per'aps we can drop it off at "The 'Orse" on the way back an' they can look after it for 'er.'

Jean arrived at the boats and climbed aboard. She stood on *Aphrodite*'s stern, breathing heavily from the effort of hurrying along the towpath with all her luggage.

'Welcome aboard, Jean,' said Bill, standing up to greet his new crew member.

'Sorry I'm late, Bill!' she muttered between gasps. 'Couldn't make up me mind … what to bring … an' what not to… Then it took me ages … to get me bleedin' case shut… Ended up bleedin' sittin' on it, I did!'

'Well, you're 'ere now, an' that's all as matters,' said George. 'I see you're brought your 'andbag. Do you wanna come an' see where you're gonna be sleepin' so as you can stow your stuff? Like I said last night, it ain't ideal, but we're gotta make do, what with the war on an' all.'

'I'm sure it'll be fine,' she said, regaining her breath. She followed George back along to *Zeus*.

A few minutes later, George was back in *Aphrodite*'s cabin. 'I'm left 'er to stow 'er things,' he said as he rejoined the others.

'Is she 'appy with the sleepin' arrangement?' Bill asked.

'Reckon so,' George replied, then, in a conspiratorial whisper, 'She give the curtain a good ol' lookin' at from both sides, though. Then she said as she thought as it'd be awright cos you couldn't see through it!' He and George chuckled quietly. Izzie smiled bleakly.

Bill consulted his watch again. 'It's gittin' on,' he said. 'Time we was gittin' 'em ahead. We're runnin' late awready!'

With that, George disappeared into *Zeus*'s engine hole, and after a few moments they heard the sound of the engine bursting into life.   By the end of her first day, even Izzie had to admit to being more than a little impressed by how quickly Jean had got to grips with steering *Aphrodite*.

'She's a natural!' Bill kept saying. 'Took to it like a duck to water, she did!' Their newest crew member had even insisted on having a go at working a lock herself. She had chosen a lock with particularly stiff paddle gear. Izzie gave a satisfied grin when she saw Jean's face as she realised not only how heavy the gates were to open and close, but also the amount of effort involved in winding the stiffer paddle gear. After they had worked through the entire Marsworth flight, Jean had sat down, lit a cigarette and spluttered, 'I'm bleedin' pooped, I am!'

'You'll git used to it, after a while,' Izzie had nonchalantly replied as she put the kettle on the range.

176

*

After the boats had been tied up for the evening they sat down together to enjoy the hotpot Izzie had prepared. The men went outside to check the side cloths on the load and Jean was sitting on the side bed in *Aphrodite*'s cabin. She lit a cigarette then, delving into the depths of her huge handbag once more, she produced a Mills & Boon novel and began reading it while Izzie was washing the dishes. Having read a couple of paragraphs, she stopped and looked up at Izzie. 'Don' s'pose you've ever learned to read, 'ave you, Isobel?' she asked with a superior smile on her face.

'Yes, I 'ave,' Izzie replied, curtly. 'An' I'm called "Izzie" – awright?'

'Show us one o' your books, then, Izzie!' Jean snapped.

Putting down the tea towel, Izzie took *Winnie the Pooh* from the knife drawer and proudly held it up in front of Jean, who took it to have a closer look. 'Oh, I see!' she scoffed dismissively, handing the book back. 'It's only little kiddies' stuff, that is! It ain' a proper book – not a proper grown-up's book.'

'Well,' said Izzie, a little defiantly, 'we're all got to start somewhere, ain't we?'

'S'pose so,' Jean replied and went back to her own book. Izzie finished drying up and was pleased to get out of the cabin to join her father and George. 'Well, 'ow are you gittin' on wi' 'er, Izzie, love?' Bill whispered, putting his arm round her shoulders. Izzie was about to blurt out the truth – that she did not like the woman at all – not one little bit. In fact, she really hated her! But, with a supreme effort, she managed to stop herself just in time as she remembered what the consequences might be if she were to say what she really thought. 'If she ain't gonna be on the pair wi' us, then we won't be on 'ere neither.' With that sobering thought in her head Izzie decided that it would be the lesser of two evils if she at least appeared to be getting on reasonably well with the newcomer.

'She's awright, I s'pose,' she began, 'It's jus' ... well ... different. That's all. I mean, like, we ain't never 'ad another woman on the pair since me Mam, 'ave we? Well, not countin' them few days as she spent wi' us last year. I s'pose it'll jus' take me a while to git used to 'er bein' 'ere, like.'

'Course it will, love. Course it will,' Bill agreed, 'But you will git used to 'er ... in time. I knows as you will.' Izzie returned his smile with a little weak one of her own.

'Looks like she'll make a boater, any'ow,' said George.

'Ah! Took to it like a duck to water, she did,' Bill said for the umpteenth time that day.

✳

During the remainder of the run a kind of uneasy truce developed between Izzie and Jean. They spoke civilly to each other when they needed to and Jean certainly did her fair share of the work, even cooking the meals and washing up on some days. Bill decided he was confident that she would make an adequate replacement for George after they had finished this run and it came the time for him to leave for the army. He wasted no time in telling Jean so, making sure at the same time that Izzie heard him too.

Gradually, Izzie came to terms with the fact that Jean was there to stay, at least until George came back from the army, or until she, herself, had reached the magic age of sixteen – but that day seemed to her to be simply ages away, and no one could say how long this war would last, or when George would come back – if he ever did. She had tried not to think about the possibility of anything happening to George while he was away, but the thought of having to spend so much of her future with Jean on board made her think about it now. She had heard people talking about the thousands of soldiers who had lost their lives in the Great War. She had to face the facts. She knew that there were a number of them who had survived but were badly injured, having lost limbs, or who were blind. She had also heard what had happened at Dunkirk. 'Any o' them things could 'appen to my George, an' if they did 'e wouldn't never be able to come back an' work on the boats!'

So she came to a decision. She reasoned that as she considered herself to be almost a grown-up – despite what her father might still think – she decided that she would be very grown-up about the situation. She knew that it would be better for all concerned if she were always to keep her true feelings about Jean to herself, so that was what she would try to do. She was rather pleased that she had noticed that any signs of affection from Jean towards her father were not reciprocated, even though the memory of that late-night conversation that she had overheard between him and George all those months before often surfaced in her mind. It appeared to her that, as far as her father was concerned, Jean was a member of his crew – and that was as far as it went.

They arrived back at the Wharf on the Sunday afternoon prior to George joining up. During the last part of the journey Jean had steered *Aphrodite* while George had been busy packing up his few belongings. Jean had made him a gift of her battered old suitcase, which had spent the run sitting on the roof of *Zeus's* cabin because there was no space in either of the tiny cabins to keep it. It was so old and worn that any additional damage the weather may have inflicted upon it during the run was hardly noticeable.

After the boats had been tied up at the Wharf, George quickly changed out of his working clothes and was soon ready for his journey to Yorkshire. Izzie gave him a tearful hug and told him that now she could read and write, he could write letters to her. 'But don't you go usin' too many o' them big words, will you!'

'I dunno none on 'em neither!' was his reply. 'An' you can write to me an' all. As soon as I knows the address I'll write an' let you know.' Jean gave him a peck on the cheek and Bill shook his hand.

'You kept me an' our Izzie on the cut, boy,' he said, 'an' I can't never thank you enough for that! Take care o' yourself, me boy!'

'I dunno what else I'd 'ave done if I 'adn't worked for you, Bill,' he said. Horace emerged from his office and locked the door. He walked over to the boats and Bill introduced him to Jean. Horace asked her how she was managing with her new job and her new way of life on the boats.

'Well,' she replied, 'it's bleedin' 'ard work, it is. I'll say that. But I ain' never been afraid o' 'ard work, I ain'. An' I 'ave to tell you as I'm really enjoying the life!' Bill and George both confirmed how well she had taken to steering the butty and working the locks. Horace smiled. Izzie stayed silent.

'Good! Good!' said Horace, then after a pause, 'Are you ready to go, George? Your train leaves in ...' He consulted his watch. '... just over twenty minutes.'

'Ah, ready,' George replied. 'Thanks for givin' us a lift to the station, Mr Roberts. I really appreciate it.'

Horace waved the thanks away as the two of them walked round to his car. 'It's the least I can do for a soldier of the King!' he replied.

There was a flurry of waving hands and George was gone. They all stood in silence, watching Horace's old Morris as it disappeared along the Wharf road and turned right at the main road on the way to the railway station. Then Bill said, 'Ah! That's that, then! What're we eatin' tonight, Izzie, love?'

She hardly heard him. All she could feel was a cold, lonely emptiness inside. George – her George – was gone. He had gone to fight in a war and none of them knew how long it would last and how long he would be away. She hoped and prayed that he would come back safely, but she had to face the fact that he might get wounded or, worse still, that he might not come back at all. She tried to put these thoughts to the back of her mind as she trudged sadly back to the boats to prepare the meal.

From the door to the schoolroom Emily watched with a tear in her eye. Apart from Izzie, only she herself knew what the poor young girl was suffering inside.

Chapter 20

Proper family

The three of them quickly fell into a routine not unlike the one that had existed when George had been on board. Having mastered *Aphrodite*, Jean began dropping hints that she wanted to learn how to steer *Zeus*.

'All in good time!' was Bill's answer. 'All in good time!' While he always took charge of supervising the loading and unloading as well as maintaining the engine, Izzie and Jean looked after the meals and the general housework.

There was one job, however, that Jean had always insisted on doing on her own as soon as she had become a permanent member of the crew. This was doing the shopping. She had been shopping with Izzie once in London and similarly in Birmingham to get to know 'which shops take our Ration Books', she said. But thereafter she had always insisted on going alone. The reason she gave was that with the food shortages caused by the war, if anybody could talk a shopkeeper into selling a bit more of something that was off ration but in short supply then she could!

'Are you sure you don't want our Izzie to come wi' you – for company, like, – 'elp you carry the bags an' that?' Bill asked.

'No ta! I'll do better if I'm on me own,' she replied – much to Izzie's relief! The shopping trips they had done together had been a nightmare for her. They had hardly spoken to each other from the moment when they left Bill on the pair to when they had returned, other than for Izzie to show Jean which shops to use and to introduce her to the shopkeepers. But now, having established that she would do the shopping alone, no sooner had the pair tied up in either Birmingham or London than Jean would appear on *Zeus*'s counter, a cigarette dangling from the corner of her mouth, her gas mask in its cardboard box round her neck, holding her large handbag and a shopping bag, and announcing that she was off to the shops.

After the first few of these solo shopping expeditions, it occurred to Izzie that it seemed to take Jean far longer to do the shopping than it had ever taken either her or her mother. Initially, Izzie put this down to the fact that she probably did not know her way round the districts as well as she did. She knew that the wartime shortages meant that she might need to go to more than one shop to find what she needed, and then probably have to queue for a long time to be served. With regard to the rationed food, customers were supposed to use only one butcher, one grocer, and so on, but because of the nature of living and working on the canal this was not always possible.

The Birmingham to London contract with the sealed crates, as Horace had predicted, was proving to be long-term. Bill and Jean would spend some of the autumn evenings in a canalside pub, and occasionally Izzie would go with them. More often than not, though, she would spend this time with her books. She found that the dictionary Emily Roberts had given to her was beginning to look even more scruffy and dog-eared because of all the use she had given it. 'I 'ope as Miss Roberts won't mind!' she thought every time she picked it up to look up a word. 'It looks like it's gonna fall to bits any minute!'

These days they stopped at the Wharf only when they needed something. On one such occasion they arrived only a few minutes before Emily was due to leave for home. Izzie quickly helped her father and Jean to secure the ropes, then, picking up her books and the pieces of writing she had completed, she ran to the schoolroom. Emily was just putting on her coat. 'Isobel! How wonderful to see you!' she exclaimed.

Izzie smiled. ''Allo, Miss Roberts! I'm brought them books back, an' 'ere's some stories as I wrote.' Emily took the proffered books and pieces of paper from her. Leaving the written work on her desk, she went to the cupboard, exchanged the books, and picked up the work that Izzie had left with her the last time they had met. Handing the fresh selection to Izzie, she said, 'You know, Isobel, these little stories you have written are really getting very good.'

'Thank you!' was all Izzie could say.

'I particularly liked the one about the air raid in London. I could almost hear the bombs falling as I read it,' Emily continued.

'It were 'orrible!' Izzie said. 'We all sat in the butty, jus' chattin' an' drinkin' tea all night! Not one of us got even a wink o' sleep!'

'You can certainly write well from your own experiences and you obviously have a good imagination, judging from the other stories you have written. Your spelling is improving too. You really are progressing very well.'

'Thank you, Miss Roberts.' Izzie beamed.

'I must be going now, Isobel.' Emily looked at her watch. I have to get home before it gets too dark now they don't light the street lamps any more.'

'I know! It's as dark as on the cut in London. Why are they done that? Is they runnin' out o' gas or summat?' Izzie asked.

'No, it's not that. It's so that the German bombers won't know whether they're flying over a town or over the countryside. That way the Government hopes that the towns and the cities might avoid being bombed.'

'Well, it didn't the other night!' Izzie replied. 'I'm sorry if I made you late, Miss Roberts. But I ran in 'ere jus' as soon as we'd tied up,' Izzie apologised.

'No, that's fine,' Emily said. 'I'll take your stories home with me and we can look at them if you're still here when I get here in the morning.'

Izzie said goodbye and made her way back to the boats. When she returned, her father and Jean had gone into the office to see Horace. Even though there was now no need for secrecy, she still kept her reading and writing materials in the back of the knife drawer where they had always been, if only to keep them from Jean. She carefully placed her new supply in it.

She sat down on the side bed and thought over what Miss Roberts had said to her. She realised that she was quite unusual – a boat girl who wanted to read and write, and now she could do so reasonably well. Miss Roberts said so! She knew her father still believed that all the effort had been a complete waste of her time.

'But that's me Dad for you!' she sighed contentedly. 'Me Mam would 'ave been proud o' me, though,' she thought.

She still firmly believed in her heart of hearts, as she always had, that at some time in the future – she did not know exactly when – but one day she had an appointment with a bookseller in a particular bookshop next to a butcher's in a street in Birmingham. Then she would buy her own book.

Izzie couldn't help but notice the growing affection between her father and Jean. Jean had called him 'Darlin'' for a while, but her father had started to address her as 'My love'. She had also seen them holding hands together as they walked to and from the pub.

One day they were tied up in Kensal Green and Jean had set off on her lengthy shopping expedition. Izzie was cleaning *Aphrodite*'s brasses and thinking about nothing in particular when her father called to her from inside the cabin. 'Come in 'ere an' sit down a minute, our Izzie. I wanna a quiet little word wi' you.'

Izzie left the brass she was cleaning, stepped down into the cabin and sat on the stool. As she did so, she recalled the last time her father had wanted a 'quiet little word' with her. It had happened on the day after her mother's funeral when he had warned her that they might have to go on the bank. It was, therefore, with some trepidation that she looked up and met his gaze.

'What's up, Dad?' she asked, thinking, 'At least 'e's smilin', so it can't be all bad news!'

'Well, we was thinkin', like, me an' Jean, that is. We was wonderin', 'ow would you like to 'ave the motor's cabin all to yourself, like?'

Izzie allowed this to sink in for a moment, thinking, 'Yes, it would be good to 'ave some space o' me own – but that means that me Dad'll be sharin' the butty cabin wi' ... wi' that Jean woman!'

'What?' she began. 'An' ... so Jean'll move in 'ere wi' you?'

'Er ... yeah,' he replied a little sheepishly.

'An' she won't be sleepin' on no side bed neither, will she?' Izzie said, anger creeping into her voice.

'Well…,' Bill hesitated.

Izzie cut him off. 'Look, Dad! I ain't a little girl no more! I knows as you reckon I still am, but I tell you, I ain't! I knows what's what, an' I knows why you're wantin' 'er in 'ere wi' you, an' I knows what the two on you will be gittin' up to in 'ere at nights an' all!'

'Well,' Bill started again, 'I'm only a 'uman bein' – an' so's she. We're kind o' got … well … a bit fond o' one another, like, an' … wi' your Mam gone … well…' He tailed off.

Izzie let the silence hang between them for a few moments. Then she put her hand on top of her father's. She spoke, her voice softening. 'I s'pose … I s'pose I don't mind – not really, I don't. It jus' come as a bit of a shock, like, that's all. You jus' comin' out wi' it like that, I mean.'

'Perhaps I could 'ave put it a bit better, Izzie love,' Bill apologised. 'I ain't never been no good wi' words.' For a few moments they looked at each other in silence.

'Jus' so long…,' Izzie began, falteringly. 'Jus' so long as you still got a special place in your 'eart … for me Mam,' she said, almost in a whisper.

'Oh! Course I 'ave, Izzie love! Course I 'ave! Really, I 'ave – allus will 'ave. Jean won't never replace your Mam in my 'eart. Never!'

'That's awright, then,' said Izzie. Then, after a moment, 'So when are we shiftin' round then?'

'When Jean gits back from gittin' the shoppin', if you like,' he answered.

'I'd best git me stuff packed up, then,' she said, standing up.

'Right,' said Bill, and left the cabin to leave room for his daughter to get her possessions together.

Jean returned about twenty minutes later to find them sitting in *Aphrodite*'s cabin with a mug of tea each and Izzie's clothing lying in a bundle on the side bed.

''Allo, my love,' Bill greeted her as she stepped down into the cabin and sat on the step. 'I'm tol' our Izzie about the new sleepin' arrangement an' she's quite 'appy wi' it.'

'Oh, good!' Jean replied with a smug grin.

'I'm collected me stuff together so's you can move yourn in when you want,' Izzie said without looking at her.

'I'm ever so pleased you don' mind me an' your ol' man sharin' a cabin. Makes us seem more like a proper family some'ow, don' it?' Jean said. Izzie said nothing.

'An' you'll 'ave all o' the motor cabin to yourself,' Bill added.

''Ere!' Jean suddenly said. 'I know what'll make us feel even more like a real proper family! I've 'ad a really good idea, I 'ave, Izzie! If we're gonna be a real proper family, you can start callin' me "Mum"!' Then, seeing the look on Izzie's face, she added rather lamely, 'If you want … that is …'

The silence that ensued hung so heavily in the air that it could have been cut into slices with a blunt knife. Izzie's face was like thunder, and Bill, immediately realising that Jean had said too much, became suddenly fascinated by the laces in his boots.

The silence was finally broken by Izzie. 'Listen!' she began in a quiet, precise tone that her father recognised as the voice she used when she was struggling desperately to keep her temper under control, 'Listen!' she repeated. 'Me Mam's dead. She drownded in Buckby locks three year past.' She paused, struggling to keep her anger in check. Then she took a deep breath, swallowed and, looking at the floor, she spoke again. 'I loved me Mam. I really loved 'er, an' I misses 'er. I misses 'er a lot – even now.' She raised her eyes to look straight at Jean. 'Now, you might be sharin' a cabin – an' a bed – wi' me Dad, but that don't make you me Mam! You won't never, ever … never in a million years, ever … be me Mam – never! An' neither won't nobody else!'

'I jus' thought…,' said Jean flustered.

Izzie interrupted her. 'That's all there is to it!' She said this with such force that it was obvious, as far as she was concerned, the subject was closed and would never be referred to again. She pushed past Jean and went back outside, picked up her cloth and continued polishing the brasses – rubbing even more furiously than usual. As she did so, she heard Bill whispering to Jean, 'Thought an awful lot of 'er Mam, she did! So don't git too upset, love.'

A few minutes later Bill came out onto *Aphrodite's* counter. 'Are you awright, Izzie, love?' he asked.

'I'll take me stuff out an' put it on the roof o' the motor so's she can pack 'em up an' put it in 'ere,' she said, and with that she disappeared down the steps into the cabin. With not so much as a glance in Jean's direction, she picked up the rolled-up blanket that contained all her clothing and other worldly goods and climbed out again.

✳

During the next few days Izzie managed to get rid of the smell of Jean's cheap perfume and cigarette smoke from *Zeus*'s cabin. She cleaned the entire cabin thoroughly from top to bottom and determined that she was always going to keep it absolutely spotless. She realised that, unless Jean's standards of cleanliness and tidiness improved somewhat, and improved quickly, her father would soon notice a deterioration in the cleanliness of *Aphrodite*'s cabin.

Then she arranged the tiny space the way she wanted it. She no longer needed to keep her books, her pieces of paper and her pencils in the knife drawer. She made the decision that she would sleep on the cross bed. She put her books and papers in the cupboard so that when she pulled down the door, it formed a table top as her desk and the side bed was her seat.

The new sleeping arrangement obviously meant that she spent less time with her father, but as he steered *Zeus* and Jean *Aphrodite*, she made up for this by staying on the motor as much as she could during the daytime. Although they had lost some of their easy comfortableness, she still felt happy to be with him and to keep away from Jean.

A few days after the cabin changeover, as they made their way back to Birmingham with a return load of tinned goods, she was sitting on the cabin roof. They were both wearing their thick winter coats and scarves against a biting cold wind, and Izzie could tell that her father wanted to say something to her but was not quite sure how he should start. To help him out, she looked at him and smiled encouragingly.

'You know, our Izzie?' he began, 'you was right what you was sayin' the other day.'

'When I said what in partic'lar?'

'The other day, when you said as you ain't a little girl no more. You ain't, are you?'

'That's what I were tryin' to tell you, Dad.' She paused. 'What is it as 'as made you suddenly realise that?'

'Well … when I first tol' you about as 'ow Jean an' me wanted to start sharin' the butty. I mean … well, you never got all upset about it an' took to bawlin' nor nuthin'. I'll be honest, I reckoned as 'ow you might 'ave. Fact is, I damn near expected you to.'

'What made you think as I might do that, then, Dad?' Izzie asked, playing dim as her father struggled for the right words.

'Well,' Bill continued, 'I didn't reckon as 'ow you'd think much o' the idea of … another woman … in the same bed as I used to share wi' your Mam.'

'You mean the same bed as I were conceived in?' said Izzie.

'Well … yeah … since you come to put it like that,' Bill said quietly. 'But you … you kinda … you accepted it. You kinda accepted what I tol' you, like … well, like a growed-up woman – cos that's what you're gittin' to be now, ain't it? A growed-up woman?'

'Course I am!' Izzie replied. 'I growed up after me Mam died.'

'I jus' wanted to say "Thank you" to you for bein' – well – for bein' so growed-up about it, like.'

It was obvious to Izzie that her father was not only very grateful to her, but he was also very relieved to have got this matter off his chest. She pondered on what he had said. 'Yes,' she thought, 'I talked it over wi' 'im an' then I accepted it like a adult, I didn't throw no tantrums nor nuthin', like some little kid might 'ave done, cos I reckon as I knows what it's like to love someone.'

'That's awright, Dad.' She smiled at him again. 'Jus' so long as she don't never ask me to call her "Mam" no more!'

'Oh, no!' Bill assured her. 'I'm already tol' 'er as she overstepped the mark there. She knows as that won't never 'appen – never!'

'Good!' Izzie said. 'You know 'ow much I loved me Mam – an' I still loves 'er, even though she ain't 'ere no more.'

'I know as you do! She were a fine woman, awright, your Mam were,' Bill mused. He reached up and hugged her with his free arm.

He looked down into *Zeus*'s cabin. By his face Izzie could tell he admired the way she was keeping it spick and span, just as she had kept *Aphrodite*'s cabin clean and tidy. He smiled at her. 'You're your

Mam's daughter awright, our Izzie! A true boatin' woman! Jean'll never be a real boatin' woman.' And that made her feel very proud!

Izzie looked back at Jean on *Aphrodite* and thought to herself, 'I don't really like the idea o' you bein' in me Dad's bed, but if that's what it takes to keep me Dad 'appy, and if that's what it takes to keep us both workin' on the cut, then I reckon as 'ow I can put up wi' it. At least till this 'ere war's over an' George comes back from th' army.' She saw that Jean's face was pinched and red from the cold. She was wearing her winter coat too. Izzie noticed that, typical of Jean, it had a fur collar, but it was so obviously fake fur.

Chapter 21

Nearly twice as long

One thing Izzie still failed to understand was why it seemed to take Jean so long to do the shopping whenever they were tied up in Birmingham or London. Even though she had been getting their groceries for a number of months now, she still took nearly twice as long as Izzie had done in the days before she arrived. 'What does she find to do as takes 'er so long?' Izzie could not help wondering. Sometimes Jean would announce, 'I'm to 'ave me 'air done.' But that did not explain all the other times. During the next of Jean's lengthy shopping absences, while they were tied up at Kensal Green, Izzie mentioned the matter to her father.

'I don't know why it allus takes 'er so long. I mean, she's been doin' it for a good few month now. She ought to know where all the shops is by now, shouldn't she?' she asked.

'Well,' Bill replied, 'you know what they says about these 'ere Londoners – "You supply the food an' they'll supply the chatter!" I reckon as 'ow she spends a lot o' time gassin' wi' the shopkeepers, a lot longer than you ever done, any'ow.'

Izzie said nothing more at the time, but she was not convinced by her father's answer. Her curiosity deepened over the ensuing run back up to Birmingham. No matter how hard she tried, Izzie could not put it out of her mind. The question kept gnawing at her and would not go away.

As soon as the pair was tied up at the top of the 'Ol' Thirteen' at Birmingham, waiting to go and load first thing in the morning, Jean, as usual, immediately put on her hat and coat, lit a cigarette and, picking up her enormous handbag and the shopping bag, made her way onto the towpath .

'I'll be off to git the shoppin' then, Bill, darlin',' she called.

'Righto, my love,' he called back from the depths of the engine hole. Out of sight in *Zeus*'s cabin, Izzie was already putting on her own hat and coat. She gave Jean about half a minute's start, then she too climbed across onto the towpath.

'Jus' goin' for a walk, Dad,' she called nonchalantly, as she set off in the same direction as Jean. At the next bridge she climbed up the path onto the road and looked round to see if she could spy her quarry. She spotted Jean almost immediately, picking her out by the big fake fur collar on her coat. She was walking quite quickly towards the row of shops where Izzie had purchased the provisions back in the days when it had been her responsibility. Izzie started to follow her, making sure that she kept a safe distance behind so that she would not be seen.

But Jean walked straight past all the shops, without even looking in the windows. 'She must 'ave made arrangements to use them Ration Books at some other shops, then,' Izzie thought. But why? Jean, however, did not appear to be looking for any shops at all. Instead, she was heading in the direction of the railway station at New Street. Sure enough, when she arrived at the station she walked inside. 'Why's she goin' in the station?' Izzie wondered. 'She ain't got no time to go nowhere on a train!'

Izzie's assumption proved to be correct because, on entering the station, Jean ignored the booking hall and the platforms and made straight for the station buffet. Izzie was still following and found it fairly easy not to be spotted in the crowded station concourse. The buffet was bustling with people, many of them in uniform, sitting, eating and drinking. She managed to find herself a position quite close to the entrance to the buffet where she could peep round a pillar and get a good view of what was happening inside. She could also quickly duck back out of sight, should the need arise.

'Why on earth is she in 'ere?' Izzie thought. 'What's she doin'?' But nothing, however, could have prepared her for what she witnessed next. Izzie could hardly contain her surprise – then her anger.

As she entered the buffet area, Jean stopped at the doorway and scanned all around the tables as if she was looking for someone. A man, sitting at a table near the back, looked up and smiled at her.

Jean smiled back at him and made her way straight to his table. On the table there was a cup and saucer and the newspaper he had been reading. As she approached the table, he rose to his feet, then hugged her and kissed her on both cheeks.

The man was tall, bald, with a pinched face framed by wire-rimmed glasses. He was smartly dressed in a khaki-coloured gabardine raincoat, which was unbuttoned to reveal a check sports jacket with a collar and tie underneath. Izzie thought he would be about forty years old.

Greetings over, Jean sat down at the table – fortunately for Izzie, with her back to the buffet entrance where she was hiding. The man went to the counter and returned with a cup of tea for her. Jean took her cigarettes from her handbag and lit one. The man returned to the table and sat facing her. He leaned forward. Jean leaned forward too, their heads almost touching, her hands around her cup, her eyes looking intently at his. They obviously did not want anyone at the adjoining tables to hear their conversation – not that they were likely to amid the noise and bustle of the refreshment room. Jean dropped her hand to the table. The man reached out and patted it reassuringly. 'She's two-timin' me Dad, the 'ussy!' Izzie nearly exploded inside. 'No wonder she don't never want nobody to go out shoppin' wi' 'er!'

The few minutes of earnest, whispered conversation was drawing to a close. The man let go of Jean's hand and reached into an inside pocket of his jacket. Having taken hold of something, he paused and looked very carefully all around the room before removing it. When he was satisfied that he was not being watched, he produced a large brown envelope and quickly passed it over the table to Jean, who grabbed hold of it with equal speed and immediately deposited it deep inside her capacious handbag. Then he passed her something else, something too small for Izzie to see what it was. They both then looked around again as if to make doubly sure that no one had been watching their movements. Confident that their actions had passed unnoticed, they smiled at each other a knowing smile. 'So that's why she needs such big 'andbag!' Izzie realised. Jean stubbed out her cigarette in the ashtray and they both stood up. Izzie then realised – to her horror

– that in order to get a better view of what was happening she had moved away from her hiding place behind the pillar.

Jean and the man embraced and kissed each other on the cheek. Izzie quickly ducked down behind a soldier's kitbag and pretended to tie her bootlace as Jean swept past her without, fortunately, looking in her direction. The man sat down and picked up his newspaper. Izzie breathed a sigh of relief as she watched Jean cross the concourse to a row of telephone boxes. 'Now what's she up to?' she thought as she picked her way through the luggage, following her at a safe distance. She paused as Jean put the bag carefully on the floor between her feet and picked up the receiver. She watched as Jean made her call and carefully replaced the receiver before picking up her bags and making her way straight out of the station by the same route that she had entered. Izzie continued to followed her.

Making her way back to the canal, Jean visited all the usual shops that Izzie frequented. She called at the baker's, the grocer's and the butcher's as she passed by. Izzie afforded herself the luxury of a brief glance through the window of her bookshop next door to the butcher's, but only a brief one, as she needed to keep her eyes on Jean and to make sure that she was not spotted.

If she had been puzzled before, she was very puzzled now – very puzzled indeed! At first, when she had seen the friendly way in which Jean and the bald man with the wire-rimmed glasses had greeted each other, she had jumped to the conclusion that Jean was cheating on her father and that these extended shopping trips in Birmingham were her way of seeing 'the other man' without Bill knowing anything about it. But that, she soon realised, could not be right, because apart from the cursory pecks on both cheeks when they had met and again when they had parted, and the reassuring patting of Jean's hand during their whispered conversation, they had done nothing that could be described as romantic at all! And then there was the business with the large brown envelope – and the telephone call. What was all that about? 'There certainly weren't nuthin' romantic about that!'

Her purchases completed, Jean retraced her steps to the boats. Izzie followed her onto the towpath, then walked away in the opposite direction for a while. As she walked she pondered what she should do with her new-found knowledge about their newest crew member. 'Should I come straight out wi' it an' ask 'er what she's up to?' she thought. 'Should I ask 'er when me an' 'er's alone, or when me Dad's there?' She tried to envisage what might happen if she were to ask Jean about it directly. 'No!' she decided. 'I'll 'ave a word wi' me Dad about it first. I'll tell 'im all about what I seen 'er doin' wi' the bloke at the station an' then 'e can decide what's to do about it.' Her decision made, she turned and made her way back to where the pair was tied up.

She had only walked a few yards when she suddenly stopped as another thought occurred to her. 'It takes 'er jus' as long to git the shoppin' when we're down London. What does she git up to when we're down there, I wonder?' She decided that before she spoke to her father on the subject she would investigate Jean's shopping trip again when they got to Kensal Green.

When Izzie arrived back at the boats, Jean was just finishing putting the shopping away in the cupboard and chatting with her father quite amiably.

'Ah, there you are, our Izzie,' he said as she stepped onto *Aphrodite*. 'Jean's jus' got back from doin' the shoppin'.' He stepped across onto *Zeus*, went into the engine hole and started cleaning the engine.

Jean asked, 'You've been for a walk, then, 'ave you?'

'Yeah,' Izzie replied. Although she tried very hard to make it sound nonchalant, there was more than a little suspicion in Jean's tone as she asked, 'Which way did you go ... on your walk?'

'Oh, jus' down the towpath a little way down there,' she pointed down the locks, in the opposite direction to the shops, 'an' then back again.' Jean sounded quite relieved as she replied, 'Oh! Nice walk, was it?'

✳

The run back down to London passed without incident and almost as soon as they were tied up Jean was again standing on the towpath, cigarette in mouth, handbag and shopping bag in hand.

As before, Izzie announced that she had decided to go for a walk and donned her coat. She waited until Jean was out of sight, then, as she had done in Birmingham, she set off in the same direction.

Again, she followed as Jean walked quickly past the grocery shops without so much as a glance, and instead went beyond them until she arrived at a small café. Jean opened the door and went inside, A bell jangled loudly as she closed it behind her. Izzie hesitated. 'It won't be as easy to watch 'er 'ere like it were in Brum,' she thought. She inched closer to the window, scared that Jean would see her. She spotted the fake fur collar. Jean was sitting at a table near the window, fortunately with her back to it. Izzie quickened her pace to get past the café before Jean would have time to turn and notice her. Apart from Jean there were only two men in overalls sitting at one of the other tables. She surmised that the builder's lorry parked in the road outside belonged to them.

The shop next door sold ladies' clothing. It was a double-fronted shop with a deeply recessed door in the middle and, unlike many of the shops in the road, it had not suffered bomb damage and its windows were not boarded up. Izzie slipped inside the recess and cautiously peered around the window. She noticed a smartly dressed man walking along the street towards her. She noticed his dark blue overcoat, his trilby hat and his briefcase. The smartness of his clothes and his tall well-built appearance attracted her attention. She suddenly became very interested in the only dress in the window and started to admire it intently. With half an eye she watched his reflection in the shop window as he walked behind her and disappeared into the café. 'Dare I risk another walk past the caff to see if 'e's sat down wi' 'er?' she wondered.

She reasoned that, if she approached the café from the road, the builder's lorry would hide her while she looked inside. Slipping out from the dress shop doorway, she walked a short distance in the opposite direction before turning round. Pulling the collar of her coat around her face, she walked back on the edge of the pavement. 'It's jus' like in them secret agent films!' she thought as she stepped off the pavement and walked behind the lorry. She stopped and glanced through the cab windows, then ducked down and pretended to tie her bootlace. She peeped around the lorry and stole another quick glance through the windows.

Yes! She had guessed correctly! The smartly dressed man was sitting at the same table as Jean! She stood watching them for as long as she dared. The inside of the café was rather dimly lit and she could not see the man clearly. He was a big man, and she could see that he had placed his hat and briefcase on the table and was stroking his moustache with his fingers. "'E's what me Mam would 'ave called "dapper",' she thought.

She bent down quickly again as she thought the man looked in her direction, and retied her bootlace. When she dared to look up again she was just in time to see Jean shutting her large handbag. The man was busy fastening his briefcase. Jean stubbed out her cigarette in the ashtray and they both stood up. Realising they were about to leave the café, Izzie stood up and hurried across the pavement into the recessed doorway of the dress shop. From there, if she looked at an angle through the two panes of glass of the shop windows, she had a clear view of the pavement immediately outside the café. First the man emerged, quickly followed by Jean. There was no hugging and kissing this time, just a brief handshake and the man raised his hat before turning smartly, crossing the road and walking back in the direction from whence he had come. Jean, holding her bag tightly to her, started back towards the canal.

Again, Izzie followed her at what she considered to be a safe distance. She assumed that Jean would now go shopping as she had to go past the shops on her way back to the boats. This she did, but not before having stopped to make a short call from a telephone box along the way.

Izzie tried to make sense of what she had just witnessed. She was now thoroughly confused. 'Two different men! One in Brum an' one in London. An' what were all that business wi' that envelope?' Try as she might, she could find no logic in Jean's encounters with these two strangers. There were no romantic liaisons, she knew that much now. The meeting in the café had been brief and business-like. She headed back to the boats, following Jean at a safe distance, with what she had seen still tumbling around in her mind.

Chapter 22

Spying on people

As she lay in bed that night Izzie kept going over and over the situation in her mind. 'Should I really tell me Dad? An' if I do, what am I gonna say to 'im? I'm pretty sure that Jean woman's up to summat – but what? I'm seen 'er wi' one bloke in Brum an' wi' another bloke in London. Wi' both on 'em, I seen 'em meet up an' 'ave a chat an' a cup o' tea together. The bloke at the station give 'er an envelope. So what 'appened to that?' Then she remembered that when she had looked up from behind the lorry, Jean had been shutting her handbag and the man had been doing the same with his briefcase. ''Ad she jus' give 'im the envelope?' Izzie had not actually seen the envelope change hands, but that could be one explanation. 'Or perhaps it weren't nuthin' to do wi' that. Perhaps it were jus' a coincidence as they was both shuttin' their bags at the same time! This ain't the real world!' she said to herself. 'It ain't my world o' the cut an' boats an' wharves. It's like watchin' a film.'

She thought long and hard about what she should do throughout two long wet and rainy days as they headed back up the canal towards the Midlands. On the third day the weather brightened up a little and, having polished the brasses and whitened the ropes, Izzie was sitting on Zeus's cabin roof, chatting happily with her father as he steered along a lock-free stretch. Suddenly, she looked at him very seriously.

'Dad,' she began, 'I'm found out why it takes Jean so much longer to do the shoppin' than it used to take me or me Mam!'

'An' is it what I said it was?' he replied. 'Is it she spends so long gassin' to the shopkeepers?'

'No. It ain't,' said Izzie

'What then?'

'She meets up wi' blokes! She met one at the railway station in Brum and she met another 'un in a caff in London.'

'What?' Bill was suddenly serious. 'Are you tellin' me as you're been follerin' her, then?'

'Yeah,' Izzie said quietly.

'What!' He was speechless for a moment. 'You done what? You followed 'er? Well, I ain't 'appy about that!' There was anger in her father's eyes. 'I ain't 'appy about that at all! You don't go around follerin' folk – an' spyin' on 'em! You jus' don't do that sort o' thing! You hear me?'

'But I...' Izzie started to say something.

'But nuthin'!' Her father cut her off. ''Ow dare you even think o' doin' a thing like that? That were a bad thing, that were!' He paused. Izzie was too shocked by his reaction to speak. 'I'm ashamed as a daughter o' mine should sink so low as to even think about doin' such a thing as that!'

Izzie opened her mouth to speak, but again her father got in first. 'I'll 'ear no more about it!' he said. 'Spyin' on people! What next?'

Surprised by his reaction, Izzie reasoned that it was best to keep out of his way for a while, so she went back down into the cabin. As she went down the steps her father called after her, 'That there bloomin' book learnin's give you some funny ideas if you reckon as it's awright to go around follerin' folk an' spyin' on 'em!'

She opened a book and tried hard to read, but the words did not seem to mean anything to her. She could not concentrate on it because she was still smarting from the telling off her father had just given her. 'He gets cross sometimes, but I ain't never see 'im as angry as that afore!' she thought. She had tried to protest. She had wanted to tell him that she knew that what she had done was wrong, but that she had done it for all the right reasons. 'I'm sure that Jean's up to no good, but I wish I could find out jus' what it is she's doin'!' In her frustration she thought round and round the problem. It was obviously no good attempting to broach the subject with her father again. But try as she might, she could not come up with a solution.

She remained in the cabin. They ate in silence and as soon as she could Izzie made her excuses and spent the evening in her cabin. They soon got under way the next morning. Izzie carried out her morning chores in silence, then went down into *Zeus*'s cabin. For once, she did not feel like reading. She just sat and thought. When they had been travelling a while Bill called her up out of *Zeus*'s cabin. 'I need a word wi' you, young lady!' he said sternly as Izzie climbed up to stand on the step.

'Now then!' He looked angry. 'I 'ad a talk wi' Jean last night about that there story o' yourn about 'er meeting blokes in stations an' caffs an' what not. An' she swears to me as 'ow it's all jus' a pack o' filthy lies! She tells me the only reason it takes 'er longer to do the shoppin' is what I said all along. She spends a long ol' time gassin' wi' the shopkeepers.'

'But I seen...'

'Don't you go tellin' me no more o' your filthy lies, now!' Bill stopped her. 'Jean's swore to me as that's the truth on it, an' I believe her!'

Izzie could not accept this without making some show of protest. 'So, you believe what that woman says agin' your own daughter, do you?'

'I do when me own daughter's tellin' me a pack o' filthy, bloomin' lies!' said Bill, his face angry. 'Me an' your Mam, we never brought you up to be a bloomin' liar!'

'I ain't a liar!'

'Well, I says as you are – ashamed enough as I am to say it. Look, my girl! I know you don't git on wi' Jean. That's as may be. But I like 'er. Fact is, I'm beginnin' to like 'er a lot, so you better git used to it! An' you jus' remember this! It's only 'er bein' 'ere as is keepin' us off the bank! So it don't matter what you think of 'er, do it? You made me real ashamed o' you, you 'ave! Ashamed o' me own daughter, me own flesh an' blood!'

Her father's angry gaze left hers and concentrated on the length of canal ahead of the boat and Izzie realised that it was pointless for her to even try to continue to protest her innocence. Anything else she said would similarly be met with her father's total disbelief. As far as he was concerned, he had made up his mind. He had told her what he believed – and the matter was now closed. 'She got 'im wrapped round 'er little finger, she 'as!' Izzie thought. She really wanted to cry. She wanted to cry so badly because her father had been wrongly convinced that she had lied to him. She wanted to cry because it meant that Jean had won. But most of all she wanted to cry because of the sheer frustration of it all! 'But I ain't gonna bawl,' she told herself. 'I ain't gonna let me Dad see me bawlin' – an' I certainly ain't gonna let 'er see as I'm been a-bawlin' neither!'

For the first time since her mother had drowned on the flight, Izzie was relieved to see Buckby locks ahead of her. She waited until her father pulled the boat briefly to the side and, jumping off with her windlass in her hand, she made her way to the first lock.

✳

That evening, Bill and Jean walked along the towpath to the nearby pub. Although it was cold, the weather was clear and, having put on her thick coat, Izzie decided to take up her favourite position, sitting on the cabin roof. 'Perhaps I might be able to sort out what to do, sittin' up there with it all calm round about me,' she reasoned. The pleasant feeling of tranquillity that always overwhelmed her when she sat there helped to calm the turmoil in her head, although not with as much peace as she usually felt. She was lost in her thoughts as she sat in the darkness. Suddenly, she felt the sharp jab of a finger in the middle of her back.

'You're a bloody nosey little bitch, ain' you?' she heard Jean's voice as she turned round to face her adversary, who was standing on the towpath with anger written all over her face.

'What're you doin' back 'ere? Where's me Dad?' Izzie blurted.

'You do like shovin' your little nose into other folk's business what don' concern you, don' you? As it 'appens I tol' your Dad as I needed to come back 'ere to get a 'andkerchief. Not that that's none o' your bloody business, neither!' She stepped onto *Zeus*'s counter to get closer to Izzie. 'But what I really needed to come back 'ere for was to talk to you when your Dad weren' around. I needed there to be jus' the two of us here, so as we could 'ave a cosy little chat – an' I could give you a piece o' my mind, you schemin' little brat!' she shouted at her and blew a cloud of cigarette smoke into Izzie's face, causing her to cough.

'What d'you mean?' Izzie spluttered, frightened by the vehemence of Jean's outburst.

'You know bloody well what I mean! Follerin' me about in Birnigum, an' then follerin' me about again in Kensal. You're a little busybody! That's what you are!'

'But I did see you meetin' up wi' them blokes.'

'So you might 'ave done! So you might 'ave done! But what I do, an' where I go, an' who I meet, that's all my business, that is – not yours. Now jus' look 'ere, madam! I know as you 'ate me. You've always 'ated me an' you probably always will 'ate me, for all I know. Well, as far as it goes, I bloody well 'ate you an' all, so there! So we're quits, ain' we? But jus' you listen to me, young lady, an' you listen to me bloody good!' She continued, pointing her finger and waving it in Izzie's face. 'Don' you never, ever try to cross me again. Do you hear me? An' don' you never try to come between me an' your Dad ever again. Got it?' Izzie remained silent.

'Got it?' Louder this time.

'Yeah,' Izzie almost whispered.

'I reckon I must be gettin' a bit mutt an' jeff in me ol' age. I never quite caught what you said jus' then!' As she said the word 'then', Jean took hold of a handful of Izzie's hair and pulled it hard, jerking her head back and causing her to squeal. Jean threw her half-smoked cigarette into the canal and placed her free hand over Izzie's mouth. Her other hand gripped the hair tightly as she put her face so close to Izzie's that the girl felt overcome by the smell of drink and tobacco on Jean's breath.

'What was that you said? Say it again – only a bit louder this time!'

'I said "Yeah"!' Izzie almost shouted through the hand covering her mouth, her hands scrabbling round the back of her head in an attempt to release her hair from Jean's grip.

'Good! Good!' Jean released Izzie's hair and uncovered her mouth. She smirked as she spoke. 'I'm so glad! I'm glad cos I can see we kinda understand each other so much better now. See, the thing is, I've managed to convince your Dad as you was lyin' to 'im about all that stuff as you tol' him you'd seen me doin'. An' that means that from now on, 'e's always gonna believe what I tell him again' anythin' you say. So from now on you better watch your bloody step, Miss nosey bloody Parker! An' you better not do nuthin' to upset me, neither. Cos I can make up whatever stories I bloody well fancy about you. An' all I got to do then is to tell 'em to 'im. Cos when I tell 'im, 'e'll believe every bloody word I say. 'E'll believe every little thing I say to 'im about you, whatever it is I decide to say, so jus' you be bloody careful, madam! You picked on the wrong one when you thought you could get the better o' me, young lady!'

Jean stepped across the counter and down into *Aphrodite*'s cabin, emerging a few seconds later, dabbing her nose with a clean handkerchief. 'Oh, an' another thing!' she began. 'You won' be able to tell 'im nuthin' about this – what shall we call it? – this "friendly little chat" as we've had together neither. Cos I shall deny that it ever 'appened – an' now we both know which one of us 'e'll believe, don' we?'

She smiled a cruel smile of self-satisfaction and turned away. After two or three steps along the towpath she turned round. 'I damn near forgot to tell you the most important thing. It's this. You better not try follerin' me around no more, neither. Cos from now on I'll 'ave me eyes peeled an' I'll be lookin' out for you. Understand?'

'Yeah,' Izzie replied.

'Now, get yourself back to your little kiddies' books an' stay out o' my bloody way! Or else!'

With that, Jean flounced off back down the towpath, lighting another cigarette as she went. She returned to the pub. Izzie stayed, motionless, for a few minutes, gazing into the murky water of the canal, her evening idyll shattered. Eventually, she went inside and made herself ready for bed where she sobbed herself quietly to sleep.

❈

The next morning they continued their journey north towards Birmingham. Uncertainty and unease hung in the air. Bill was angry with Izzie. Jean was furious with Izzie. Izzie cared little about

Jean, but it hurt her inside to think that her father believed Jean against her and would not trust his own daughter.

'You take the motor,' he said as they prepared to set off. After starting the engine he climbed aboard *Aphrodite*, took hold of the tiller and waited for Izzie to pull away from the bank. Jean busied herself in the cabin.

It was a cold, raw November day and Izzie tied her scarf tightly round her ears. 'Oh George!' she sighed, remembering how he had smiled at her when she had strutted into the warehouse on her birthday. 'A real bobby-dazzler!' he had said. 'Oh George, you'd know what to do!'

Trying to lift her spirits, she thought back over the books she had read since she last saw Miss Roberts. She had read and re-read them all. She craved the excitement of beginning a new book, of not knowing where the story was going, the joy of discovering how it ended. She had wondered whether her father would let her have some money to buy a book while they were in Birmingham. 'But I don't s'pose 'e'll let me do that now!' she thought.

She saw the arched entrance of Braunston Tunnel in the distance and pushed all thoughts of her father, Jean, George and her books to one side as she concentrated on the tunnel and the locks that lay ahead.

❋

'We'll pull over for a brew on the Puddlebanks,' her father shouted to Izzie as she positioned *Zeus* to go under the arched bridge at Braunston Turn. She was working the boat round the bend when she was surprised to hear a voice, a man's voice, shouting her name.

'Izzie! Izzie! Up here!'

She looked up to the footbridge above her. 'George!' she shouted back, waving frantically with her free hand. 'Look, Dad! It's George!' she shouted, all thoughts of past arguments forgotten. Bill looked up and waved. George ran down from the bridge and hopped onto *Zeus*'s counter as Izzie brought the motor through the bridge hole.

'Oh, George! It's lovely to see you! But what are you doin' 'ere?

Ain't you supposed to be off fightin' a war somewhere?' Izzie appraised the young soldier standing beside her. 'And don't you jus' look the part in your smart new uniform?' she said as she grabbed him with one hand while steering with the other.

'I 'ad a few day's leave due, so I went to see me Grandad at me Auntie's, then I went an' asked Mr Roberts whereabouts 'e thought as you might be. 'E reckoned as you'd be 'ere about now, so 'ere I am! I wanted to git to see you afore Christmas.'

'It's so good to see you again, George.' Izzie smiled and hugged him as best she could while keeping the motor on a straight course.

'An' I got summat for you an' all,' George said. He opened the kitbag he had been carrying over his shoulder. 'Miss Roberts said as I were to give you these.'

Izzie looked down. In George's hand were five new books! Izzie's eyes widened with delight.

'She said as you can take 'em back wi' th' others as you're got when you're finished wi' 'em.'

'George Andrews! If I weren't steerin' this 'ere motor, I'd give you an even bigger 'ug than what I jus' did, an' I'd kiss you into the bargain!'

'I can allus wait till you're tied up!' George smiled and they both laughed.

''Ow come you're on the motor, any'ow? It ain't like your Dad to wanna steer the butty. I can remember all them battles I 'ad wi' 'im afore 'e'd let me steer this 'un.'

'It's a long story, George,' she said, and was about to launch into telling him what had happened in the past few days. But she changed her mind. 'Not yit,' she thought. She said, 'Jean's doin' the dinner today, so me Dad's stayed on the butty wi' 'er.' George looked confused. 'Oh, yeah. She lives on the butty wi' me Dad now, an' I'm on 'ere on me own,' she explained.

'Oh, I see.' There was a pause, then George said, 'It don't sound like you're gittin' on wi' 'er no better then?'

'No, I ain't!' Izzie was about to say more when Bill's voice suddenly shouted from behind.

'Izzie! Pull over an' we'll git that brew on. It ain't every day as we 'as a visitor, is it?'

Minutes later they were sitting on *Aphrodite*'s back deck, each with a mug in hand.

'So 'ow long 'ave you got then, George?' Bill asked between gulps of tea.

'It's what they calls "embarkation leave", Bill. We're done all the basic trainin' an' then I 'ad to go for artillery trainin'. I got to be ready to go on a ship out from Liverpool next Friday.'

'Whereabouts are you goin'?' Izzie asked.

'That's jus' it,' said George. 'We none of us don't know. They ain't tol' us yit. An' even if they 'ad, I couldn't tell you – "Careless talk costs lives", an' all that!'

'So 'ow did you know we'd be 'ere?' asked Bill, changing the subject.

'I seen Mr Roberts, an' 'e said 'e reckoned as you'd be about Braunston either late yesterday or today, so I 'itched a lift down 'ere from the Wharf an' I got 'ere late yesterday mornin'.'

'Where did you sleep last night, then?' Izzie was concerned.

'I 'ad a few pints at the pub in the village an' the landlord said seein' as I were off to fight for me King an' country then the least 'e could do was gimme a night's bed an' breakfast for nowt.'

'That was lucky for you!' Jean said. 'Mind you, we pub folk are always kind an' welcomin'.' She shot a dark glance at Izzie.

'So are you plannin' on bein' wi' us for a few days, then?' Bill asked hopefully.

'That's what I was 'opin', Bill – if you'll 'ave me, that is!' George smiled.

'We can allus use a extra 'and, an' that's for sure!' he smiled. 'Our Izzie sleeps on the motor now. Neither of you minds sharin', do you?'

'I 'as the cross bed,' said Izzie, staking her claim.

'Side bed's fine wi' me,' George said. 'I see you're runnin' empty.'

'Ah,' Bill replied. 'Not many back loads – a few more 'n afore the war started, but still not many. We're still on that there Government contract wi' them sealed crates from Smethwick as we started jus' afore you left.'

'You still don't know what's in 'em then?'

'No, an' I still don't wanna, neither.'

George picked up his kitbag. 'I'll stow this 'ere on the motor, then,' he said.

'You jus' make sure as you keeps that cabin clean an' tidy, George Andrews!' Izzie warned. 'An' pull that curtain across!'

'I wouldn't dare do no other!' he laughed back.

That night all four of them went for a drink. On their way back to the boats they noticed another pair had tied up behind them.

Izzie thought that it was wonderful to have George back on board again. His presence – and his sense of humour – did so much to lift her heart that she almost forgot about her experience with Jean and the fact that her father was convinced that she was a liar. She almost forgot about them – but not quite. She temporarily locked them away in a little dark place right at the back of her mind. She would not think about them. Not now. One day she would have to go back and think about them. But not now! For now, none of that mattered. For now, George was back – even if only for barely half a run!

When George had first joined them at Braunston, she had nearly told him the whole sorry story. But she didn't. She would have plenty of opportunity as they were going to be sharing *Zeus*'s cabin, and she knew that, of all people, George would understand. He knew both her and her father better than almost anyone else. Then, one evening, when the pair was tied up for the night, Izzie was already in bed when George came aboard from talking with Bill and Jean on *Aphrodite*. She was still awake and she heard him moving about behind the curtain, getting ready for bed. She almost started to tell him everything, to get it all off her chest and to ask him for his advice on what she should do next, to ask him how she could convince her father that she was not lying and that Jean was up to no good. But she didn't. Just before she opened her mouth she was struck by the thought, ''Ere's 'im, goin' off to fight in a war – an' 'e don't even know where 'e's goin'! An' 'ere's me about to add my troubles onto 'is! I can't do that to 'im, can I? It jus' wouldn't be fair!' So, instead of pouring her heart out to George, she remained quiet and kept her thoughts and her worries to herself.

Chapter 23

Government scheme

'Bill! Bill! Are you awake yit?' It was first light on the following day and George was hammering on the doors of *Aphrodite*'s cabin, Izzie standing just behind him. Bill, in the middle of shaving, stuck out an arm and unbolted the door. 'What's up?' he asked.

'That pair as tied up be'ind us last night! You couldn't tell in the dark, but now I see as it's *Worcester* an' *Dolphin* – it's me Grandad's boats! What the 'ell are they doin' 'ere?' George was obviously upset.

'Damned if I know!' Bill replied. 'Let me git this 'ere soap off me face an' we'll go an' find out.'

A few minutes later, with Izzie watching from the hatchway, the two men marched up to the other boats. At that moment the sliding hatch of *Worcester*, the motor, slid back and a young woman's tousled blonde head appeared. 'Good morning!' she called in what sounded to Izzie like a very posh accent.

''Ow do,' replied Bill. He looked carefully at the boats. 'These is Ol' Man Andrews's pair!'

'Sorry?' the woman replied, looking and sounding a little confused.

'These boats,' Bill repeated, accusingly. 'They're Ol' Man Andrews's!'

'Ah!' she said, suddenly realising what he meant. 'They probably are.' During this exchange *Dolphin*'s sliding hatch had also opened and the heads of two other young women had appeared, one with short black hair and the other light brown, tied back in a bun. 'Allow me to introduce us all,' the first woman continued. 'My name is Susan and those two are Carol…' The dark-haired woman nodded and waved, '…and May.' The brown-haired woman did likewise. 'We're on a trial run for a Government scheme that's going to train women to work the boats on the canals. So many of the boatmen have been called up for military service, you see.'

'But what are all you a-doin' on me Grandad's boats?' George asked.

'That, I'm afraid, I can't tell you because I don't know,' Susan replied. 'All we know is that we were trained by a lady called Kit. Kit Gayford? Perhaps you know of her?'

'Never 'eard on 'er,' Bill said.

'Well, after we'd been trained, we were shown these two boats and told that they were the ones we were to have.' She paused, then turned to George. 'Why is your Grandfather not working them then, if they are, indeed, his boats?' she asked.

"E's been in the 'ospital – 'e's 'ad to 'ave a operation,' George snapped.

'I'm sorry, but that explains it,' Carol said. 'The way we've been given to understand it, the Government is so desperate to get cargo moving on the waterways that they're urging all the boat companies to bring every single boat they can get their hands on into service.'

By this time Jean had appeared on *Aphrodite*'s counter.

'I see you're got a load on. Where are you 'eaded?' Bill asked.

'We're taking this scrap iron to Birmingham.' May spoke for the first time.

'That's what we calls "spelter" on the cut,' Bill appraised her, pointing at their load.

'Did you pick that up from down London way?' George asked, having still not come to terms with the fact that these well-spoken young ladies were living and working on the pair that had previously been his home.

'No,' Susan replied. 'We had to go up to Slough for it – right up to the end of the arm. Why do you ask?'

'I were jus' wonderin',' said George. 'I wondered if it might 'ave been a back load for us, like. But we wouldn't 'ave 'ad time to go all the way up the arm to Slough.'

'Whom do we have the pleasure of addressing?' This was May. It took Bill a few seconds to realise what she meant.

'Er... Oh! I'm Bill 'Orne an' this 'ere's George Andrews.'

'Very pleased to meet you both!' Susan replied.

'Is there many o' you women's crews on the cut, then?' George asked.

Carol replied, 'Not yet. As I said, we're a kind of trial run, but if we're successful, there'll probably be more and more being trained in the future because they keep calling up more and more boatmen for the forces.'

'I know,' muttered George. 'I'm on what they calls embarkation leave. I sail out o' Liverpool on Friday.'

'Oh, I'm so sorry,' said Susan. 'You must be having a farewell time with your family. We're sorry if we've spoiled it for you.'

Bill looked at his pocket watch. 'Humph! Well, it's time we was gittin' 'em ahead, George.' He turned to Susan. 'An' didn't you ought to be gittin' goin' an' all?' Without waiting for an answer, Bill started *Zeus*'s engine and they were soon under way.

'Load o' silly girls!' he muttered. 'What do they know about boatin'?'

A little while later, *Zeus* and *Aphrodite* made their way along the canal, with everyone munching on Izzie's bacon sandwiches. She had used her week's ration especially for George. He and Izzie were talking on *Aphrodite*.

'Seems a bit funny, like,' George said, 'complete strangers workin' me Grandad's pair. I mean – I grew up on them boats. They're me 'ome!'

'Bet it does,' Izzie agreed. 'I s'pose it's better that your Grandad's boats is bein' used, though – rather than jus' lyin' idle, like. I mean, at least they're bein' looked after. An' like them women said, if they're usin' all the boats as they can git 'old on, it's gotta be good news for us, ain't it? Cos it must mean there's plenty o' work about.'

'Yeah, but it still don't seem right. I mean, they could 'ave asked.'

Izzie laughed. 'Don't seem like they ask much when there's a war on! Did they ask us if we wanted to carry them sealed crates?'

'Well, Mr Roberts did ask your Dad.'

'But if me Dad 'ad said "No", Mr Roberts'd 'ave 'ad to gi' it to someone else, wouldn't 'e? An' did they ask you if you wanted to join th' army?'

'No. They didn't. It's all cos o' this bloomin' war, innit?'

George happily took care of *Zeus*, which suited Izzie very well. He had certainly not lost his sense of fun and it did her a power of good being teased by him again. She had not laughed so much or so often for a long time. Life for her was almost as good as it had been before that dreadful day when George had been given his call-up papers – before Jean! Before the argument with her Dad. Before Jean spoiled everything. But she would not think about that now.

Eventually they arrived once again at the warehouse on the Icknield Port Loop in Smethwick. Once there, they had to wait for another pair to vacate the private wharf before they could go in. George used the time to collect his things together and repack his kitbag. They were now well-known to all the men there. The man in the bowler hat greeted them and the loading crew all called 'Hello' as the boats entered the covered wharf.

Just before Izzie went to see George off on the train to Liverpool, Bill thanked him warmly for his help and the two men shook hands.

'It's been good to see you, George. Now, take care o' yourself, me boy – wherever it is you're goin'!'

'Been like ol' times!' George said.

After George had said goodbye to Jean, he and Izzie left the warehouse as the men in brown overalls were beginning to load the boats. He finally got his big hug and his kiss on a platform at New Street station. The train was already in and the platform was awash with uniforms – khaki, navy and air force blue. Many of the servicemen were boarding the train. George dropped his kitbag on the floor and pulled Izzie to him, sweeping her off her feet as he twirled her round. He planted a kiss firmly on the tip of her nose.

'Take care, our Izzie,' he said. 'I'll be back soon!' He stepped onto the train and slammed the door. He let the window down by its leather strap and leaned out.

'Now don't you go worryin' yourself too much about that Jean!' he admonished her.

''Er with the big 'andbag!' Izzie laughed, trying to make light of it for both their sakes.

'D'you know?' he said. 'She even takes it to bed wi 'er?'

'She don't!'

'She does! Honest! I seen 'er wi' me own eyes when we did that London run together afore I 'ad to go away!'

Then there came a shrill blast on a whistle. Izzie looked up to see a man in railway uniform waving a green flag. There was an answering whistle from the engine and, with much noise, steam and billows of thick, black smoke, the train slowly moved off. Izzie and George both waved until they were out of sight of each other. It was only then that Izzie noticed that she had tears in her eyes. 'Poor George,' she thought, 'off on a ship to God knows where – an' 'e don't even know if 'e's ever gonna come back! Come back to me, George! Come back to me!' she whispered.

Drying her eyes, she turned and started to walk back to the boats. Her route passed the station buffet. Unconsciously, she glanced inside. She walked a few paces and stopped suddenly, so suddenly that a woman behind her, carrying a heavy suitcase, nearly walked right into her.

'Sorry!' Izzie apologised. The woman grimaced and carried on walking towards the exit. 'It were 'im! Nothing had been further from her mind than Jean and her secret meetings as she had said farewell to George. She had only caught the merest glimpse of the man as her eyes had absent-mindedly scanned the people sitting in the buffet area. But there was absolutely no doubt in her mind that it was the very same bald-headed man with the wire-rimmed glasses. She turned again and walked back a little way. Yes! It was definitely him! He was even wearing the same clothes. He was sitting in the exact same seat at the exact same table where he had been sitting when he had met Jean, and he was looking towards the entrance – just as if he was expecting someone. 'Jean, I bet! That's who 'e's waiting for!' Izzie thought. Sure enough, as she walked out of the station, she caught sight of Jean making for the buffet. Fortunately, their eyes did not meet in the crowd. Izzie again watched furtively from a distance as exactly the same ritual was played out in the station buffet. This time Izzie left before Jean had finished her cup of tea.

❊

As it was nearly Christmas, Bill decided to make a detour to call in at the office to ask Horace whether there was anything that they needed to know.

'No, Bill,' Horace said. 'Carry on as normal. Just watch out for bombs!'

'We're 'eard a few on 'em!'

'I bet you have.'

'Oh, another thing!' Bill said. 'We seen some women on George's Grandad's pair.'

'Ah, yes,' Horace said. 'They're a pilot for some Government scheme or other. So many of you chaps are being called up for the forces that they're bringing in a...' He searched through some papers on his desk. 'Here it is.' He extracted a letter from a pile of papers and read, '"The Boat Women Training Scheme".'

'Bet I can 'andle a boat better 'n any on 'em,' Izzie said almost to herself.

'Izzie!' her father glared at her.

'I don't doubt that's true, Izzie,' said Horace, 'but the fact of the matter is that you're only – what? Thirteen?'

'Fourteen now!' said Izzie defiantly.

'Fourteen,' Horace repeated. 'That crew you saw are all grown women. I'm afraid that you need to be sixteen before you can steer a boat – it's Company policy, I'm afraid.' He gave a knowing look at Izzie, who quickly changed the subject.

'Is Miss Roberts in next door?' she asked.

'Yes, she is,' Horace replied, 'and I'm sure she'll be very glad to see you.'

When Izzie entered the schoolroom with a pile of books under her arm, Emily, who only had two pupils that day, looked up and smiled. She set them some work to do on their own and beckoned Izzie to her desk.

'I'm brought these back, Miss Roberts. It's so long since we're stopped 'ere, I reckon as I'm read 'em all at least four times!' Izzie said as she put the books on the desk. 'Oh, an' thank you for sendin' them others wi' George.'

'Well, I knew you must be needing some more books, and as he was coming to see you it seemed a good idea.' She paused. 'How is he … that young man of yours?'

'I seen 'im off on the train jus' afore we left Brum. 'E's goin' off on a ship to fight in the war an' 'e don't even know where 'e's goin'!' Emily could hear the sadness in her voice. 'I 'ope as 'e's gonna be awright!'

'We must pray that he will be,' said Emily, trying to comfort her.

'I best be goin',' Izzie said. 'Me Dad don't wanna lose too much time comin' up 'ere.'

'Bye then, Isobel.'

'Bye, Miss Roberts.' Izzie made her way to the door, stopped and turned.

''Appy Christmas, Miss Roberts,' she said.

'And a Happy Christmas to you too, Isobel,' Emily replied.

As Izzie closed the schoolroom door, she suddenly thought, 'P'raps I should tell Miss Roberts about Jean an' me Dad. She's clever – she'll know what to do!' She put her hand on the doorknob. 'But she ain't like family – an' she ain't a boater. She prob'ly wouldn't understand.' She let go of the doorknob and went back to the boats.

✳

That Christmas was the unhappiest Izzie could ever remember. They spent it at The Running Horse. Over the years since her mother's tragic death she had reconciled herself to Christmases without her, but this year she was without George. She felt guilty when she realised that she missed him more than her mother. When they arrived at the pub there was a pleasant surprise waiting for her. As they entered the bar Alf's wife gave her an envelope addressed to her, care of The Running Horse. Eagerly, she opened it. It was a Christmas card from George! Inside he had written, 'To My Izzie Happy Christmas With Love from George'. He had posted it in Liverpool before he had boarded his ship. It was the first Christmas card she had ever received, and tears pricked her eyes as she read it. It lightened her mood a little, but made her miss him all the more. She tucked it into her cardigan pocket, glad that neither her father, nor especially Jean, had seen it.

After Christmas lunch, they sat round drinking and chatting to the other boat families who were there. But when Jean stood up and positioned herself under the mistletoe that Alf had fixed to the ceiling and said, 'Come on, Bill, darlin'! It's time for me Christmas kiss!' it was just too much for Izzie to bear. She made an excuse of not feeling too well and returned to the boats.

She sat in the motor cabin and buried her head in her hands. She took out George's Christmas card, tears welling up in her eyes. She came to a decision. 'I'm gonna write to 'im!' There was a British Forces' address on the Christmas card envelope, so she knew she could send it to him. She took paper and a pencil from the cupboard and proceeded to write a long letter, pouring out her heart to him, telling him everything about Jean, about her Dad, about her. When she had finished it she felt much better. The act of writing down how she felt had, somehow, lifted the weight from her shoulders.

But when she re-read it later before she went to bed, she realised that it would be unfair to burden him with all her worries. She put the letter with the Christmas card in her box of treasures and wrote a shorter, happier letter to George, thanking him for his card and hoping he was all right and had enjoyed Christmas. She put it in the envelope and held it to her cheek. 'Keep safe, George!' she whispered. Just before they left the following morning, she took her letter to Alf and asked him to post it for her.

Chapter 24

That's all there is to it!

They spent New Year's Eve in a pub just north of London. Izzie stayed long enough to see in the New Year, then went back to the boats, leaving her father and Jean to carouse with the other boating families. Back on *Zeus*, she took out her journal and turned to the next new page. '1st January 1943,' she wrote, thinking, 'You're s'posed to make New Year Resolutions today. The only resolution I wanna make is to convince me Dad as I ain't a liar!'

Unable to put pen to paper, she put the book away and got herself ready for bed. Once tucked beneath the blankets, she lay in the darkness thinking about how things had been between her and her father since she had told him of her suspicions about Jean. On the surface things seemed to be back to normal. Gradually, since that day, they had begun to talk to each other again and life had settled down almost to what it had been before. But there was still that niggling doubt in her mind, and she knew it was still in her father's mind too, that she had lied to him. 'But I ain't!' she said aloud to herself. 'An' I only wish I could git 'im to see as I ain't!'

She thought about it long and hard, wondering whether she should mention it to him again. Doing so might lead him to believe her, then everything would be fine. He would know that it was Jean who had lied and not her. 'On the other 'and,' she mused, 'it might put us back where we was!' She decided that if she had the opportunity she would broach the subject again, although she would try to do it in such a way that it would not make him angry. 'I ain't sure as 'ow I'm gonna manage that, but I'm a-gonna try.' And with that thought in her mind, she drifted off to sleep.

It was a cold afternoon in February and they were tied up at

Kensal Green when her chance came. Jean had gone 'shopping', and Izzie and her father were sitting in *Aphrodite*'s cabin awaiting her return.

'I don't reckon as she'll be out long in this weather,' Bill said.

'Unless she's found a nice warm caff to sit in,' Izzie answered.

'Now, don't you start goin' on about 'er meetin' men in caffs again! I told you afore, I ain't gonna believe none o' your lies.'

'All right!' she almost shouted. 'All as I meant were if she got cold out there she might go in a caff for a cuppa. I never sad nuthin' about 'er meetin' nobody!' She thought, 'This ain't workin' out like I 'oped it would.'

Bill started to speak. 'I thought you was…'

Izzie cut him off. 'Well, I weren't! But even if I were, I still says as I weren't lyin' to you. Why do you believe Jean more 'n me?'

''Cos Jean's a growed woman an' knows what's what, an' you're actin' like a little kiddie over this. You're never liked 'er, ever since that day as she wanted you to call 'er "Mam". An' you're out to git even wi' 'er. That's why I don't believe you, our Izzie. It jus' ain't fair on Jean. She's doin' 'er bit, an' she got us out of a 'ole. That's all there is to it, so we'll just leave it at that.'

After a few moments Izzie stood up. 'I got some tidyin' up to do on the motor,' she said as she climbed up the step.

'All right,' her father replied as she left.

Back in her own cabin she realised that it had been a mistake to raise the matter again. 'An' if I 'adn't said nuthin' about not lyin' it would 'ave been all right. Why did I 'ave to say that?' she asked herself. The answer was because being branded as a liar by her own father had wounded her more deeply than she had realised. It rankled in her and would not go away.

She came to the conclusion, however, that there was no way out of it. 'I'll jus' 'ave to grin an' bear it!' she thought. ''Cos there ain't no point in talkin' to 'im about it no more.'

❉

During the weeks that followed the uneasy truce returned. Jean only spoke to Izzie when necessary, and Bill did not seem to notice that anything was amiss. It seemed to Izzie that only she was still troubled by what had happened.

One afternoon in March they were again making their way south to Kensal Green with a full load of crates. Bill was steering *Zeus* while Jean was on *Aphrodite*. It was mild for the time of year and Izzie was sitting on *Zeus*'s roof enjoying the spring sunshine on her face. As they were negotiating a tight bend they met a pair of boats coming towards them.

'What the... ?' Bill exclaimed as he threw *Zeus* into reverse. 'There ain't nobody steerin' that motor!'

The two women on the approaching butty were shouting, and the motor was heading straight for *Zeus*. Bill tried to steer away but the other motor smashed into *Zeus* and pushed her bows onto the mud at the side of the canal, the impact almost tipping Izzie into the water. *Aphrodite* then collided with *Zeus*'s stern and pushed her further onto the mud with Izzie hanging on for dear life!

A dark-haired head appeared from the hatch of the other boat.

'I am so sorry...,' the steerer began. Izzie then realised what boats they were and who was steering.

'It's *Worcester* and *Dolphin*! You're Carol!'

The steerer also realised who she had crashed into. Her face fell. 'Oh, it's Mr Horne, isn't it?' she spluttered. 'The stew was boiling over on the range. I only stepped down for a moment to move it off the heat! I really am very sorry!'

'So you bloody well ought to be, Missus!' Bill replied, angrily. 'You're got us well an' truly stemmed up now! Knock 'er out o' gear for God's sake!'

Carol followed his instructions and *Worcester* drifted back away from *Zeus*. Izzie took the long pole from the cabin roof and pushed *Aphrodite*'s bows away from the motor stern so that Bill could attempt to reverse off. To their credit, May and Susan had the sense to use their pole to bring *Dolphin* into the towpath on the far side.

While Bill gunned the engine Carol continued to repeat how sorry she was. Despite Bill's best efforts with the engine and Izzie's pushing against the bank with the pole, their motor would not budge. He gave up and throttled back. Carol started to cry. From the bank Susan called, 'Is there anything we can do to help?'

'You could gi' us a tow off for a start!' Bill shouted.

Carol sniffed and wiped her eyes on her sleeve. 'Sorry,' she said. 'I'm not sure what I have to do?'

Bill groaned. 'Take the long snubber off the dolly, put the short snubber on an' chuck me th' other end!' Carol looked blank.

Susan, who seemed more experienced and knowledgeable, translated for her. 'Carol, untie the towrope and throw it to me. Then get the shorter one out of the locker and tie it on. When you've done that, throw the other end to Mr Horne.'

'OK.' Carol was better at following instructions than steering. Bill untied his own rope and threw it onto *Aphrodite*'s bows, then grabbed the thrown rope and attached it.

'Now, put 'er in gear an' build 'er up slow.'

She understood this, and as *Worcester*'s engine speed increased slowly, very slowly, *Zeus*'s bows slid off the mud and back into deeper water. Bill untied the rope and threw it back to Carol. She was not expecting it, missed the catch, and it fell into the water, splashing up and soaking her leg.

'Serve's the silly cow right!' Bill murmured, turning to see what had happened to *Aphrodite*. The gentle breeze had blown the butty over to the towpath and Jean was on the bank, holding onto a rope. Motors were re-attached to their respective butties and the pairs moved off, the three women still apologising profusely.

'Takes a real boatwoman to cook a dinner an' steer a motor at the same time!' Bill shouted as they departed. 'Can you believe that?' he asked Izzie. 'Leavin' the tiller on a bend like that! Bloomin' Gover'ment Scheme! They oughta leave boatin' to boatin' folk if you ask me!' Izzie said nothing.

They were continually on the move between Smethwick and Kensal Green. Jean was still taking ages over the shopping, and although Izzie now knew the reason why, she knew she was unable to tell anyone. She knew that if she did so, and her father found out – and within the close community of the canal it was a certainty that he would find out – she would be in very serious trouble, very serious trouble indeed.

On one run they had a back load that took them near the Wharf, so they stayed there the night. Bill caught up with the news from Horace, and Miss Roberts was pleased to see Izzie again.

'I'm still writin' me journal,' Izzie told her.

'Good!' Emily replied. 'Is it the sort of journal you would let other people read, or is it the sort that you keep only for yourself?'

'Jus' for meself, definitely!' said Izzie. 'I write things in there as I wouldn't want nobody else to see. It kind o' 'elps me, writin' down things as is worryin' me.'

'Well, that's a good thing, isn't it?' Emily replied. 'Now look, Isobel, I brought some books in from home that I thought you might like, in the hope that you would be calling in here some time. She opened her cupboard and took out three large books. 'These were given to me as presents when I was about your age.' She showed Izzie the books. 'They're all part of a series called the "Wonder Books",' she said. Izzie looked at them. There was *The Wonder Book of Animals*, *The Wonder Book of Bible Stories* and *The Wonder Book of Nature*.

'They're lovely books, ain't they?' Izzie said. 'An' I can see as you're looked after 'em cos they still looks like new.'

'If you promise me – as I know you will – that you'll look after them as well as I have, you can borrow them, if you like.'

'Oh, I would like to, Miss Roberts! I would like to very much – an' I will look after 'em, I promise! Thank you, thank you very much.'

Emily handed her the books. 'It's going to be your birthday soon, isn't it? How old will you be? Of course, fifteen! You're a real young lady, Isobel. You should be proud of how you've looked after your father, looked after the boats and how you've learned to read. Have a very happy birthday, Isobel!'

'Thank you, Miss Roberts,' said Izzie as she left the schoolroom. Miss Roberts had made her feel proud. 'If only I felt 'appier inside!' she thought.

They spent her birthday in Birmingham. Bill again gave her some money as they were having breakfast.

''Appy birthday, Izzie love,' he said. 'That's from me an' Jean.'

''Appy birthday,' Jean echoed with a smile that Izzie knew she did not mean. She thanked them and put the money in her pocket.

'I'll git summat next time I go to the shops,' she said.

Jean was even longer at the shops. 'Got to 'ave me 'air done,' she announced as she set off, bag in hand, and true enough she returned with her hair tightly curled under her headscarf. 'I dunno 'ow she affords it!' Izzie mused. 'Me Dad don't gi' 'er that much an' I knows it costs a bob or two at the 'airdresser's cos I'm looked in the window an' seen the prices. So where's she gittin' the money from?'

Chapter 25

A bout of the 'flu

I t was a few weeks later, when they were on their way north from London, that Jean began coughing and sneezing. 'I reckon I'm gettin' a 'ead cold,' she spluttered as they were tying up for the night near The Running Horse. When Bill asked if she was going to the pub she said she thought she ought to go to bed instead.

'You're probably right at that,' he said. 'You don't look too good, and that's a fact. I won't go neither.'

'She mus' be feelin' bad not to wanna go to the pub,' Izzie thought.

The following morning Jean decided that it would be better if she stayed in bed.

'She's feelin' a bit rough,' Bill said to Izzie. 'Do you reckon as you can steer the motor? It's been a long ol' while since you done it.'

'I reckon so, Dad.'

'Best I stay on the butty so as I can keep an eye on 'er, like,' Bill added. Izzie was happy with that, and she was more than happy for Jean to be tucked away in *Aphrodite*'s cabin.

They made steady progress on their way back to the Midlands. Bill looked down into *Aphrodite*'s cabin at regular intervals to check on Jean's health and shouted a progress report to Izzie. Izzie was not in the least bit interested, but replied with an 'Oh, good' or 'Tha's nice' in order to keep her father happy and not antagonise him further. ''E mus' really think a lot on 'er,' she thought. ''E don' often suggest as 'e should steer the butty!'

Izzie cooked the meal that night in *Zeus*'s cabin. Bill collected a mug of tea for Jean.

'She says as she ain't 'ungry,' he said, 'an' she don't look too good neither. I reckon as we ought to stop off when we git to Stoke an'

221

ask Sister Mary to 'ave a look at 'er. It won't do 'er no 'arm.' He spent the whole evening ministering to Jean's needs while Izzie stayed on *Zeus*.

Highly respected by the boat people, Mary Ward had developed her skills nursing in convents across the world. She had been born in Stoke Bruerne, and she returned to the family home at the side of the canal to nurse her sick father. She knew the boat people and they trusted her and her medical knowledge. They sought her advice as they passed through the village, so much so that the Canal Company appointed her as 'Consultant Sister' to the boatmen and their families.

They had arrived at Stoke Bruerne early in the afternoon and made the pair secure between the top lock and the tunnel. Bill asked Izzie to go back along the towpath and ask Sister Mary to come and take a look at Jean. Izzie walked along to Sister Mary's house and knocked on the door. A lady in her late fifties, not much taller than Izzie and wearing a nurse's uniform, answered it.

'Izzie! Come in!' Sister Mary smiled as Izzie walked in. 'You've grown up since I saw you last! Quite a young lady now. And your father?'

''E's fine,' said Izzie.

'So what can I do for you today?'

'It's Jean, me Dad's er…'

'Lady friend?' Sister Mary interjected helpfully.

'Yeah, lady friend. She thought she were gittin' a 'ead cold last night, but she's been in bed all day today an' me Dad's a bit worried about 'er.'

'It could be the 'flu, but people usually get that in the winter. Let's go and have a look at her.'

Taking a bottle of medicine from her cupboard, Sister Mary picked up her bag and followed Izzie back to where the boats were moored. Bill was standing by *Aphrodite*, waiting for them.

''Allo, Sister. Good to see you again,' he greeted her.

'It's good to see you again, Bill. Now, where is my patient?'

'Jean's in 'ere.' He stood aside and held out his hand to help her on board. As he and Izzie waited on the towpath, neither of them spoke a word. A few minutes passed and Sister Mary emerged from the cabin.

'It's what I thought – it's a bout of the 'flu. I've left a bottle of medicine with her. She's to have two teaspoonsful, three times a day. Apart from that, all she needs is bed rest for a few days and to try and keep herself warm. She should start to feel better in about a week or so.'

'Thank you, Sister,' said Bill, putting his hand in his pocket and drawing out some coins.

'There's no need for that,' Sister Mary smiled. 'And how are you and Izzie getting on these days, Bill?' she enquired.

'Oh, we're awright! We jus' keep on ploddin' on, much the same as usual. We're gotta reg'lar run on at the moment, so some good's come out o' this 'ere war. But it's 'ard times for all on us.'

Sister Mary agreed. 'Good! Well, if Jean's no better next time you're passing, you know you only have to knock on my door and I'll come and see her again.'

'Thanks again, Sister.' Bill turned to Izzie. 'Are you gonna walk back wi' Sister to 'er 'ouse?'

'Oh, there's no need,' Sister Mary protested.

'No,' said Izzie. 'It's awright, Sister. I'd like to.'

Bill shook Sister Mary's hand, and she and Izzie retraced their steps to her house. Mary Ward had watched Izzie grow from being a baby and she noticed that this normally cheerful, chatty girl was unusually quiet.

'And how are you getting on with Jean?' she asked, sensing this could be the reason for her melancholy.

'Awright ... I s'pose.'

'You ... you don't really like her very much, do you?'

'No! I don't!' Izzie stopped walking and stood still. 'I reckon she's up to summat be'ind me Dad's back, only 'e won't 'ear a word agin' 'er.' Izzie managed to stop herself before she said too much.

Sister Mary stopped too. 'Well, your father certainly seems to be very fond of her. I know it was a terrible shock for him – for you both – when your mother died.' She paused. 'Perhaps Jean gives him a little bit of the comfort that he must surely miss.' They started walking again and neither of them said anything more until they were almost back at Sister Mary's house. She turned before she entered and faced Izzie.

'Now listen to me, Izzie Horne! Don't let bad feelings get at you. You're a naturally cheerful girl – well, young woman now – and I'm sure I didn't bring you into the world to see you get all eaten up by ill-will, now did I?'

Izzie smiled. 'No, Sister... You didn't. Thanks.'

Sister Mary put her hand on Izzie's shoulder. 'It'll all work out all right, don't you worry. Now go back and look after your father. You know that men are no good with illness!'

Izzie walked slowly back to the boats, Sister Mary's words echoing in her ears. But inside, Izzie was still hurting.

Sister Mary's prognosis proved to be correct. Jean did not move from her bed for the next few days, and Izzie steered *Zeus* as they continued their journey back to Smethwick.

Chapter 26

What's she up to now?

When they reached Birmingham, Jean was still huddled in bed although it was warm and sunny. Izzie had to admit that she did look ill and her coughing reverberated around the cabin. The single locks of the 'Old Thirteen' at Farmers Bridge were hard work with only Bill and Izzie to work the pair through. When they arrived at the warehouse Bill suggested that Izzie should do the shopping while the pair was being loaded.

She did not know why, but as she walked towards the shops she felt an urge to go again to New Street station. She bought a platform ticket out of the money her father had given her for the shopping and walked onto the platform. She stood there for some minutes, oblivious to the people scurrying around her. She remembered vividly the last time she had been there. She recalled every word of the conversation she had had the last time she had been there with George. She felt her body quiver slightly as she relived the kiss and the cuddle he had given her before he had boarded the train. She felt tears rolling down her cheeks. 'Where are you now, George?' she thought. 'What are you doin'? Do you remember bein' 'ere? Do you think about me?'

'Excuse me, Miss.' A man's voice brought her back to the present. 'Can I get by?'

Izzie stepped aside to let a soldier with his kitbag on his shoulder get past her.

'Ta, love.'

She smiled at him. That could be George, she thought, then turned and made her way back to the barrier.

As she handed in her ticket another thought struck her. I wonder if that bald-'eaded bloke's here today? She looked in at the buffet. Yes! There he was sitting at the very same table, and again looking towards the doorway as if he was expecting someone. 'Well! 'E's gonna 'ave a long ol' wait for 'er today cos she's stuck in bed on the butty wi' the 'flu!' She walked out of the station exit with a suggestion of a smile on her face, as if she had won a little victory.

When she returned to the boats the loading was almost finished, and Jean was sitting on *Aphrodite*'s side bed, listlessly eating some porridge that Bill had made for her.

'She says as she's feelin' a bit better, so I said as she ought to try an' git some food down 'er,' Bill told Izzie as she stepped onto *Aphrodite*. 'She ain't ate nuthin' for a few days.' Izzie looked into the cabin and Jean gave her the weakest of smiles. As the day progressed, Jean appeared to recover remarkably quickly. By evening, although she said she felt tired, she was more her usual talkative self.

'I reckon I'll be all right to do a bit o' steerin' tomorra, Bill, darlin',' she said.

'Now, don't you go rushin' into nuthin',' he admonished her. 'Me an' Izzie can manage awright till you're good an' fit.'

'No, I'm really feelin' a lot better now. Any'ow, it'll do me good to get a bit o' that fresh air in me lungs.'

'If you're sure you're awright!' Bill was not certain.

'I'll be fine,' Jean answered. Izzie was not so sure. It seemed to her that Jean's face was very pale and she still both looked and sounded quite ill.

'You still don't look too good to me.' Bill was obviously concerned.

'No! Honest, I really am feelin' a 'ole lot better. I'll be fine doin' a bit o' steerin' tomorra. I'll wrap up warm. I'll be all right, an' it's about time I started pullin' me weight again. Like I said, it'll do me good to get some fresh air.'

Still looking and sounding 'like death warmed up', and against Bill's better judgement and advice, true to her word Jean took over *Aphrodite*'s tiller first thing the following morning. The sun was shining brightly and it promised to be a warm day. They had had a good road down the Farmers Bridge flight and had come through the bottom lock by lunchtime. Izzie was having a break after bow-hauling *Aphrodite* down the narrow locks on her own, as they had agreed that it would be too much for Jean to try to help with the locks. Izzie had followed Sister Mary's advice and, although hurting inside, she was more cheerful with Bill and more civil to Jean. She sat on *Zeus*'s roof, enjoying the sunshine and reminiscing with her father.

Looking back over Bill's shoulder, she could see Jean standing on *Aphrodite*. She was still wearing her thick winter coat with the fake fur collar, even though the weather was actually quite warm. 'She really oughta be in bed,' Izzie thought to herself. 'But she would insist on steerin' today!'

At that moment, *Zeus* went through a bridge hole and, as the stern was about to slip under the bridge, out of the corner of her eye Izzie thought that she detected some movement on the towpath to her right. But then the boat was under the bridge and the brickwork of the arch obscured her view. However, as *Aphrodite* approached the same bridge, she noticed that Jean was making some sort of hand signals to someone, obviously hidden from view on the far side of the bridge. Then Izzie saw Jean working hard with the tiller to get the butty's stern to come in as close to the towpath under the bridge as it would go. 'What's she up to now?' Izzie thought. At that moment a figure dodged out from behind the cover of the bridge and passed something – something that from that distance looked very much like a large brown envelope – over to Jean, then shot back again behind the bridge. Izzie only saw him for the split second that he was visible in the bridge hole, but she was absolutely certain that it was the same man, the bald-headed man with wire-rimmed glasses, the man from the station buffet. Without thinking, Izzie pointed and shouted to her father, 'Dad!'

'What, Izzie love?' Bill turned to look in the same direction. The man was gone.

'Oh, nuthin'!' Izzie said. Bill turned back. Jean glared at Izzie and gave her a self-satisfied smirk – looking straight at her, she drew the thumb and forefinger of her free hand across the width of her mouth, indicating that Izzie should keep her mouth shut about what she had just seen. Izzie glared back. She knew it – and Jean

227

knew it. They both knew that it would be absolutely pointless for Izzie to relate to her father what she had just seen. ''E never believed me afore, so why should 'e believe me now?' she thought to herself. It looked very much to Izzie as if Jean had her beaten at every turn.

When they had tied up and were eating their meal that night, Jean could not eat very much at all. 'I reckon you was right, Bill, darlin',' she said. 'I reckon I done a bit too much a bit too soon. I'm feelin' a bleedin' sight worse than I did before.'

'Then you jus' git yourself back off to bed, my love,' he replied. 'Me an' Izzie'll see to things till you're good an' fit again. I tol' you as you wasn't well enough, but you would insist.'

'I know!' Jean croaked. 'I should 'ave listened to you, shouldn' I?' And, as if on cue, she went into a paroxysm of coughing.

Izzie wondered about this sudden relapse. 'Anybody could see as she weren't well enough to do no steerin' today, so why did she 'ave to make 'erself do it?' she thought, then the reason suddenly dawned on her. 'She 'ad to git that envelope off the bald-'eaded bloke, cos she 'adn't been able to meet 'im at the railway station!' Izzie suspected that whatever those brown envelopes contained that were passed around between Jean and her men friends, it must be something very important. 'Important enough for 'er to git up an' do a full day's work when anyone could see as she were still full o' the 'flu. That must be really important!' she thought. But try as she might, she could still make no sense of it.

Chapter 27

Treason

Jean stayed in bed for most of the next week while Izzie and her father steered the pair onwards towards London. The days were long, and they travelled late into the evening. When they stopped and tied up for the night, Bill said he would go and sit with Jean. He had done so every evening while she had not been well.

The evening was warm and Izzie decided to go for a stroll along the towpath before going to bed. She walked along slowly, enjoying the last rays of the sun as it slowly sank below the horizon. After about half a mile or so, as she rounded a bend, another pair of boats came into view, also tied up for the night. 'I wonder if that's anybody as we know?' she thought, walking towards them. As she drew nearer she could see that it was *Worcester* and *Dolphin*, George's grandfather's pair with its crew of women 'trainees'. They, too, were making their way towards London. The blonde woman was sitting on *Worcester*'s cabin roof, trying to read a magazine by the failing light. She looked up as Izzie approached. 'Hello, there!' she called. 'It's Izzie, isn't it?'

'You're got a good memory for names an' faces, Miss!' Izzie smiled.

'Before the war started, I used to work in a busy solicitor's office. You had to remember who was who there, or you could get into serious trouble,' Susan smiled back.

'I'm tryin' 'ard to remember your name, Miss,' said Izzie. She paused a moment. 'Is it Susan?'

'You've got as good a memory for names as I have!' Susan laughed.

'Is them other two ladies still wi' you?'

'Carol's here. She's in the other cabin, writing letters to her cousins. I've never come across anyone with such a large family as she has! But May's had to go home because of her Mama.'

'Is 'er Mam poorly, then?'

'Oh no, nothing like that. Probably worse ... in a manner of speaking.' She patted the cabin roof. 'Come and sit up here with me, Izzie,' she said.

"Ow d'you mean ... probably worse?" Izzie was intrigued. She settled herself beside Susan.

'Well,' Susan began, 'May's Mama is a war widow. Her Papa was killed at Passchendaele in the last war, so she tries to make a little bit of extra money by taking in lodgers – you know – paying guests.'

'You mean they pays 'er some money to stay in 'er 'ouse, like?'

'Yes, that's right, and she gets their meals for them as well.' Izzie nodded. 'Well, it seems that she'd had this chappy living there for some weeks, so I understand. He seemed pretty OK to her. Apparently he spun her a yarn that he came from somewhere up north and was working locally for a few months and he needed somewhere to stay. He was very polite to her, and to her other lodgers as well, and he always paid her on time, so as far as she was concerned everything was tickety-boo.

'But then one night – quite late – there was a knock at the front door. May's Mama went to see who was there, and when she opened the door standing there were two policemen!' Izzie gasped. 'Yes, it must have been quite a nasty shock for her, very nasty indeed! It turns out that this lodger chap wasn't from the north at all. He was really a German agent! A spy! He had lied to her about everything. He wasn't even English! Of course, May's Mama had believed everything he had told her and had absolutely no idea that he was up to no good. She thought he was just an ordinary fellow who was needing somewhere to stay.'

'So why's May 'ad to go back to be with 'er, then?' Izzie asked.

'Well, not only have they arrested this spy chappy, but the police are also investigating her Mama! Apparently, she's been warned that they might arrest her too!'

'What would they wanna arrest 'er for?' asked Izzie. 'She ain't done nuthin' bad, 'as she?'

'There's a law that only ever comes into force when the country's at war. It says something like it's illegal to give aid and comfort to an enemy – or words something like that. Apparently, the courts treat it really seriously. They look on it as if it's treason. Anyway, May's gone home to be with her poor Mama to sort of … well, to try to help her convince the police that she would never have given any sort of help to an enemy, particularly a German. Not after what they did to her husband.'

'What's givin' aid an' comfort to a enemy mean?'

'It's things like providing food and a home for someone who is actually working for the other side in a war – in this case, the Germans. It's a very serious crime when there's a war going on. If they put May's poor Mama on trial and the jury decides that she is a traitor and find her guilty, then she would definitely go to prison – or worse! Treason is a terrible thing. It's all quite frightening, really.'

'What is treason?' asked Izzie.

'Treason? Well, it's working for the other side when your country's at war – being a traitor.'

'But if she didn't know 'e were spyin' for the Germans, she weren't bein' a traitor, were she?'

'No, she wasn't. Well, I don't see how she could have been, anyway. But you never know. I mean, if they say, for instance – oh, I don't know – if they say perhaps she should have noticed if he spoke with a strange accent, or if they say she should have possibly realised that he was acting a bit suspiciously, then she could easily be in really serious trouble. The police have given her a good telling off, saying that she should have asked him to provide her with some references, and that's what she must always do in the future. But I suppose she's the sort of trusting soul who never thinks badly of anyone.'

'You said as she could end up bein' sent to prison – or worse. What could they do to 'er as is worse than sendin' 'er to prison?' Izzie asked.

'Well,' Susan spoke slowly, 'I really don't like to think about it very much. It upsets me so. But, apparently, according to the law, well … they could hang her.'

''Ang 'er?' Izzie asked in a mixture of surprise and horror.

'Yes! It seems that everything changes when there's a war on. All the safe, sensible things that we are happy and familiar with in peacetime, they all disappear and there are only the mad and dangerous things left. It all goes completely topsy-turvy somehow. The whole dratted world seems to go utterly insane!'

'D'you reckon as you oughta be tellin' me all this?' Izzie asked. 'I mean, they say as "Careless talk costs lives", don't they? I'm seen loads o' posters wi' it on.'

'No! Oh dear! I don't suppose I should have! Me and my big mouth!' Susan's hand flew to cover her mouth. 'But you look like an honest, trustworthy girl. I hope so, anyway…' Her voice tailed off as she gazed into the distance. Izzie thought she looked as if she was going to cry, so she decided to change the subject.

'Is that a good book as you're readin'?'

'It's *Jane Eyre*.'

'What's it about?'

'I thought everybody…' Susan suddenly realised that the world of literature was closed to many of the boat people. 'It's about a girl – an orphan – who has a very difficult time growing up. Her aunt and her cousins who she lives with are really nasty to her. Then she gets sent away to school, where things aren't much better.

'After some years, she leaves to be a governess – that's like a private teacher – to a young girl who is looked after by a rich man called Mr Rochester. After a series of adventures, she ends up marrying him.'

'That's a real good story, that is!' Izzie said.

'I know it is. I must have read it at least three times already, but I keep coming back to it.'

'I'm learnin' to read,' Izzie smiled.

'That's good!' Susan replied. 'There are so many really good books with such good stories – like this one! You can sometimes get so lost in a story that you forget where you are and what you're supposed to be doing.' Izzie liked the sound of that.

''Ow are you managin' the pair wi' jus' the two on you, then? Are you gittin' on awright?'

'It took a bit of getting used to, I must admit,' Susan said, turning to face Izzie again. 'We've been trained to run them as a trio, so

Carol and I had to kind of share out the jobs that May used to do between us, but we're just about managing to cope now. But I'm forgetting my manners.' She lowered herself onto the counter. 'Please, come inside, Izzie. Would you like a cup of tea?'

Izzie accepted the invitation and they sat in *Worcester*'s cabin, Susan telling Izzie about the work she had been doing before the war. She was happy to learn from Izzie about her adopted profession. Izzie was keen to pass on a few 'tricks of the trade' to help Susan and Carol as they were working the pair two-handed.

However, Izzie was troubled by what Susan had said, and she could not get May's mother off her mind. She was so concerned that she brought the conversation back to the subject.

'Is May's Mam in prison now?' she asked.

'No, but she's been informed she should not leave her house for any length of time without informing the police and leaving them an address where she can be contacted.'

Izzie looked thoughtful. 'It's a terrible thing,' she said

It was now quite dark.

'I better be gettin' back,' said Izzie. 'Me Dad might be worryin' where I am – although I dare say as 'e's still busy lookin' after Jean.'

'I'm so sorry!' said Susan. 'I've been so wrapped up with my own problems, I've forgotten to ask after your parents.'

'Oh, me Dad's OK,' replied Izzie. 'An' Jean ain't me Mam!'

'I'm sorry if I've said the wrong thing. I didn't know ... I thought...'

'No! It's awright,' Izzie interrupted. 'Me Mam got drownded in Bugby locks about four year back. Jean's a friend o' me Dad's as is 'elpin' us out while George is way in th' army.'

'Of course, I remember George,' said Susan.

Izzie was about to say, 'An' there's summat fishy about Jean!' when she thought better of it and got up suddenly instead. 'Thanks for the tea. Might see you again on another run.'

Izzie walked back to the boats, her head still full of the conversation with Susan. 'Treason? Spies? Prison? The p'lice? I don't understand!' she thought.

They had an early start the next morning. Susan and Carol watched them go past as they prepared breakfast.

'Have a good run!' Susan called.

'You an' all!' Izzie shouted back with a friendly wave.

❋

It was late one afternoon the following week when Jean finally rose from her sickbed. She told them that this time she really was feeling very much better. Bill and Izzie could see from the way she looked and the returning colour in her cheeks that the worst of the 'flu had passed. They had stopped at Sister Mary's on their way through Stoke Bruerne and picked up another bottle of medicine for her, and over the next couple of days her health had steadily improved until, when they arrived at Kensal Green late one afternoon, she was almost back to her old self.

'Ah! Steerer Horne?' It was Mr Thompson. They had just tied up at the make-shift wharf.

'That's me!'

'I have a message for you from a…' He studied the piece of paper he was holding. 'a Mr H. Roberts.' He handed Bill the piece of paper. Bill looked at the marks on the piece of paper, but as they meant nothing to him, he handed it back to Thompson.

'Er … will you read it for us … please?' he asked, sheepishly.

'Oh! Er … yes, of course. Sorry!' Mr Thompson, a little embarrassed, took the piece of paper back from Bill and read.

'"Message for Bill Horne. I thought I ought to let you know about what has happened to George Andrews".'

'Oh my God! Don't say the poor devil's been killed!' Bill turned white. Izzie, who was listening, felt her heart freeze.

'Gi' us that 'ere!' she almost screamed, snatching the message from his hand.

'No, I don't think so,' Mr Thompson said as Izzie anxiously scanned the piece of paper.

'No! No, it don't say that 'ere!' she said, her heart thumping in her chest.

'Thank God for that!'

'No,' Izzie read. 'Mr Roberts says as George 'as been wounded – or summat – in North Africa an' 'e's on 'is way back to England.'

'Do 'e say 'ow bad 'e's been injured … what sort o' injury it is?'

'No,' Izzie replied. ''E don't say no more 'n what I'm told you.'

'I shouldn't imagine that he possibly knows that himself yet,' Thompson added.

'Well, thanks for lettin' us know, any road,' Bill replied.

'That's no problem. Now,' Mr Thompson looked at his watch, 'we shan't have time to unload you today, so you can stay tied up here overnight and we'll start first thing in the morning.'

'Right you are!'

'Poor George! I wonder what's 'appened to 'im!' Izzie felt herself starting to cry. She wiped her eyes on her sleeve. 'Oh, I do so 'ope as 'e ain't 'urt too bad!'

Jean insisted that, as she felt so much better, she would be quite able to resume her shopping duties. Despite Bill's protests, she picked up the shopping bag and, together with her large handbag, disappeared along the towpath towards the shops. After she had gone, Bill said he would go and find a telephone box to ring Mr Roberts and find out if there was any further news about George. Izzie went with him.

Waiting outside the telephone box she could think only of George. He had looked so smart and handsome in his khaki uniform, his beret set at a jaunty angle, when she had seen him off at the station in Birmingham. She had been the only one there to wave him off. She knew his parents had both died in a boating accident when he was only a baby and he had been brought up by his grandparents. Now his grandmother was also dead and his grandfather was very old. ''E ain't got nobody else 'cept me an' me Dad – apart from 'is Auntie 'n' Uncle.' She hoped and prayed that George's injuries were not serious.

After what seemed like an age, Bill emerged from the telephone box, looking grim-faced.

'Well? 'Ow is 'e?'

'Mr Roberts says, accordin' to what 'e's been told, George is lost 'is leg an' 'e's on 'is way 'ome in a 'ospital ship.'

'Lost 'is leg!' Izzie gasped. 'Poor George! 'Ow did it 'appen? 'E must 'ave been in a awful lot o' pain!' She tried to imagine what it would be like to lose a leg and shivered at the thought. 'I wish as I could go to 'im! Jus' be there wi' 'im, like!' she thought. She felt tears stinging her eyes. She clenched her fists tightly. She knew her father did not realise it but, in that moment, Izzie knew it for certain. She was, indeed, very much in love with George!

'Ah,' said Bill. 'It's bad ol' business!'

When they returned to the boats Izzie wanted to be alone with her thoughts. 'I'm goin' for a walk,' she called.

'You ain't goin' follerin' Jean an' spyin' on 'er again, I 'ope!?'

'No, I ain't!' Izzie answered angrily, and to make her point, she walked up to the bridge, onto the road and went in the opposite direction from that which Jean had taken. Her only thought was 'George'.

Chapter 28

Newspaper

She walked along the road for a while, past a row of very expensive-looking houses. However, wrapped up in her thoughts about George, she scarcely noticed them. She had missed him all the time he had been away, but was only now beginning to realise just how much she missed him. She missed his company. She missed his teasing, but most of all she missed ... well ... him!

A sudden thought struck her. "'Ow is 'e gonna manage on the boats wi' only one leg?" This was the cruellest stroke of all. He had not wanted to go into the army. He was already doing work for the war, work he had been born to, work he loved. Now, because he had been forced to join the army, he was injured. He had lost a leg, an injury that would stop him going back to doing the only work he had ever known. 'It ain't fair!' she thought. 'Even if 'e is on 'is way back to England, 'e won't be able to come back on the boats! Will 'e manage if 'e 'as one o' them tin legs? It means she'll 'ave to stay on the pair for ever! At least until I gets to sixteen, any road ... an' will she go then?' Having seen the way her father was with Jean, she doubted it. 'Bloomin' war!' she almost said out loud. 'We was doin' awright until the bloomin' war!'

She wandered aimlessly on down the road. There was little bomb damage along this stretch. The railings had gone, and cabbages were growing in one front garden! She stepped aside to avoid an elderly man walking towards her with a stick in his hand, tapping the pavement as he walked. 'Yes! Ol' Johnny Cox! Ray an' Tom's Grandad. 'E only had one leg. 'Is other leg had been blowed off in the First World War. 'E managed awright wi' Ray an' Tom's Dad an' their Uncle Fred 'elpin' 'im,' she thought. 'An' I'm bloomin' sure as George'll manage awright workin' a pair an' all, cos me an' me Dad'll be there 'elpin' 'im! Between us we'll bloomin' well make sure as 'e manages awright! If only she weren't around! What if me Dad marries 'er? I can't think about that!'

She suddenly looked around her. She had been so lost in her thoughts that she had walked a long way from the canal. 'I ain't never been down this way afore,' she thought to herself. She had walked past all the houses and past a parade of shops. Ahead she noticed the entrance to an Underground station. She had no desire to go back to the boats just yet. She knew that Jean would be out 'shopping' for some while. She decided to walk on a little further.

Standing outside the entrance to the Underground station a young boy was selling the early edition of the evening newspaper. She noticed that he was holding up a copy in front of him as he shouted the headlines. As she walked past him Izzie's eyes were suddenly riveted to the front page of the newspaper. Staring out at her from the page was a large photograph. It was not a very good photograph, but it was the photograph of a man – a man whom she was absolutely sure she recognised. It was not a very clear image, very grainy and under-exposed. 'That's 'im!' The thought pounded through her brain like a thunderbolt. 'That's the bloke as I seen Jean talkin' to in the little caff! I swear it is! It's 'im! The bloke wi' the 'tache!'

'Read all about it! Local news! German spy caught in North London! Nazi spymaster arrested!'

She knew exactly what she must do next. She felt in the pocket of her cardigan. Yes! She still had a few pennies left from the change she had 'forgotten' to give back to her father. She stopped and turned back. Clutching the money in her hand, she nervously approached the boy. Then she did something that she had never, ever done before, something no other member of her family had ever done before. She purchased a newspaper!

She walked away from the busy entrance and leaned against a wall. She looked closely at the front page. 'Nazi Spy Master Arrested in Hayes,' it read. Looking at the words carefully, she read slowly and out loud, 'Ronald Winterman is believed to be a German national. He has been charged with running a large network of enemy agents. It is thought that these agents are working in London, Birmingham and the industrial West Midlands.' Then a shiver went down her spine as she read on. 'The police are looking for his associates and are confident that they will make further arrests soon.' Although she was unsure of the meanings of some of the words, she knew enough to understand what the story was all about.

'So that's it! She's a bloomin' spy!' Izzie was certain as she folded the newspaper. 'Well, me Dad better believe me now! This 'ere's proof as she's up to no good!' Half running, she retraced her steps towards the canal.

She realised that what she had read in the newspaper was the final piece of the jigsaw – the piece that made everything else make sense. 'They must all be in it together,' she reasoned. 'Jean, the bald-'eaded bloke in Brum an' this bloke wi' the 'tache in the paper. She must 'ave been gittin' summat off the bloke in Brum in them envelopes an' then passin' 'em on to the bloke wi' the 'tache down 'ere. Summat secret an' all, I reckon.' As she continued to run, another thought struck her. 'If I 'adn't been learnin' to read I'd never 'ave knowed all this! Thank you, Miss Roberts!'

Breathless, she arrived at the boats. Bill was working on the engine, as she knew he would be. He always liked to give it a 'once-over', as he called it, at the end of each run. Izzie called out to him.

'Is Jean back yit, Dad?' She knew the answer to her question already.

'No, not yit, love,' came the reply. 'My! You're out o' puff. 'Ave you been runnin'?'

'Yes! Nor won't she be back – not for a while yit, any road.'

'You ain't been follerin' her again, 'ave you?' Bill said wearily as his head poked out of the engine hole. 'I tol' you afore you went...'

'No, I ain't!' Izzie said sharply. 'But I'll tell you summat. That bloke as she seen...'

'I tol' you afore, our Izzie!' Bill cut her off. 'I ain't listenin' to no more about 'er meetin' blokes in caffs. An' that's that!' He turned back to the engine.

'Well, Dad, all I gotta say is this! If you don't listen to me this time, you'll most likely finish up in prison – either that or summat worse!' she shouted at him as she climbed onto the counter.

Bill's head reappeared. 'What are you goin' on about, now? Prison?'

Izzie looked at him, took a deep breath, then spoke quietly, slowly and seriously. 'I said as if you don't listen to what I got to say to you this time, an' if you don't believe what I got to say to you this time, then you could well end up either bein' sent to prison – or worse still, you could end up bein' 'ung!' With this, Izzie made her way down into *Zeus*'s cabin while Bill climbed out of the engine hole and followed in her wake, wiping his hands on an oily rag as he went.

'What are you goin' on about, gel?' He now sounded worried. Izzie sat down on the side bed and said nothing.

'What are you goin' on about?' her father repeated as he stepped down into the cabin. 'Prison? 'Ung? What do you mean? I ain't done nuthin' wrong!'

'If I tells you what it is I got to say to you, are you gonna let me finish this time, Dad? Are you gonna let me git to th' end on it wi'out tellin' me to shut up wi' me lies?' she asked.

'I s'pose I better had.' Bill sat down on the step and put his hands on his knees.

'Right!' Izzie began. 'This bloke…' She held up the newspaper for her father to see. 'This bloke in this 'ere picture…' She pointed to the photograph, ''E's the same bloke as I seen Jean meetin' in that little caff jus' up the road from 'ere. I swear it is!' Bill was about to speak, but Izzie raised a finger, reminding him of his promise to let her finish.

'Now, it says 'ere, in this 'ere newspaper, as this bloke's been arrested by the police. An' it says as they've charged 'im wi' spyin' for the Germans. An' that ain't all, neither. It goes on to say as they're lookin' for … what do they call 'em?' She scanned down the page. 'Here, "'is known ass-o-ci-ates",' she read the last word slowly. 'The police is lookin' for all 'is "ass-o-ci-ates". That means 'er, Dad! That means Jean! She's one o' 'is "associates", cos I reckon that means 'is friends.'

There was a long pause while Bill looked carefully at the photograph. At length, he said a little uncertainly, 'Well, even if you did see 'er meetin' up wi' 'im – an' I still ain't sure as you did, mind – that don't make 'er a German spy an' all, now do it?'

'Oh, come on, Dad! Why else would she be meetin' up secretly wi' strange blokes in station buffets an' in little caffs – an' then passin' on big brown envelopes?'

'Envelopes?' Bill queried. 'You never said nuthin' afore about envelopes.'

'That's cos you never gi' me the chance to, did you? You wasn't interested! You jus' told me to shut up wi' me lies.' Bill said nothing. 'Well, I say what it says in this 'ere newspaper proves to you as 'ow I weren't lyin'!' Izzie looked at her father and he looked past her, his gaze fixed on nothing in particular. She broke the silence.

'She got you round 'er little finger, ain't she? You won't see nuthin' wrong in 'er, will you?'

'Well, what's all this about brown envelopes?' he asked, realising that his daughter had hit the nail on the head – then dismissing the thought immediately.

'Well, the bloke as she met in the station buffet in Brum, 'e passed a big brown envelope across the table to 'er, an' she put it away in that big ol' 'andbag of 'ern as quick as you like. An' they was both lookin' around while they done it, like they didn't want nobody to see what they was up to. Now, I never see that envelope again, so I ain't sure, but I reckon as she give it to this bloke…' She again pointed to the photograph in the newspaper. 'I reckon as she give it 'im when she met 'im jus' up the road 'ere in the little caff.'

Bill thought for a moment. 'Now look 'ere,' he said. 'Jus' supposin' you are tellin' me the truth – and I still 'ave to say as I can't really believe as you are, mind – Jean won't be gonna meet nobody in no caff today, will she? She won't 'ave no envelope to give to nobody today, will she? Cos she couldn't 'ave gone to no station buffet while we was tied up in Brum on this last run cos she never set foot off the bloomin' boat for the whole time we was there. She were too poorly! Remember? You done all the shoppin' for us while we was in Brum!'

Izzie was ready for this. 'Yes, I did. But you're wrong, Dad. While I were out doin the shoppin' I went into the station an' I see 'im there. I see 'im in the buffet at the station, awright. An afore that I see 'im when I went to say "Goodbye" to George an' all. 'E were allus sat in the self-same place at the self-same table. I dunno 'ow long 'e'd 'ave stayed there, waitin' for 'er last time, afore 'e realised as she weren't a-comin'. But now, you listen to me, Dad, cos I got summat to tell you as is important – really important!' Now, he really was listening.

'I see 'im again! It were while we was comin' out o' Brum, I see 'im. I see that same bloke as I see in the buffet. 'E jumped out from be'ind a bridge 'ole an' 'e give 'er an envelope – the same big brown sort o' envelope as 'e give 'er afore. I'm sure on it. Like I said, I see 'im sat in the buffet, waitin' for 'er, when I went to see George off on the train, an' I see 'im there again when I were out doin' the shoppin'. I reckon 'e must 'ave waited an' waited for 'er afore 'e realised as she weren't coming. But I reckon as they must 'ave already 'ad another arrangement planned for 'im to git that envelope to 'er in case she couldn't git to the buffet for some reason or other. That's why 'e were 'idin' be'ind that bridge 'ole while we was coming out of Brum. I see 'im! Jus' as the butty were comin' through the bridge 'ole', she steered it close to the towpath an' 'e dived out quick. 'E give 'er the envelope an' then 'e dived back in again so as nobody'd see 'im. But I seen him. An' I reckon as she knew as 'e were gonna be there at that bridge 'ole an' all.'

'I dunno!' Bill wiped his forehead with his hand. He was looking completely bewildered. 'If you reckon as you see 'im jump out from be'ind a bridge 'ole on the way out of Brum, why the devil didn't you think to say owt about it to me?'

"I did! Well, I tried, but 'e were gone back out o' sight again so quick you'd never 'ave seen 'im. An' ... well ... you 'adn't believed me when I tol' you about 'im afore, so I knew as you wouldn't believe me if I tol' you about 'im then neither.'

Bill's gaze was fixed on his daughter as he thought hard for a long moment or two. It seemed to Izzie that he was trying to decide from the look on her face whether she was telling him the truth, or whether she was lying.

'That were why she were so mad keen to git up an' steer the butty that day,' she said. 'You remember? That day when you an' me both knowed for a fact as she were still too poorly, but she went on about 'ow she were feelin' so much better an' she wanted to git up an' pull 'er weight. That were the day as it 'appened! That were the day as I seen 'im. She 'ad to make sure as she were steerin' the butty that day cos she 'ad to git that envelope off 'im some'ow afore we was away from Brum.'

'Awright,' Bill said after a pause. 'Jus' supposin' she is a German spy, like you say. That don't mean as I'd 'ave to go to prison an' all, do it?'

'But it do, Dad. I'm sorry, but it really do. That Susan, she were tellin' me. She were tellin' me all about May's Mam.'

'Susan? Susan who? An' who the 'ell's May?'

'You remember, Dad! Them women as is running George's Grandad's pair.'

'Oh, them!' Bill said dismissively. 'An' what the 'ell do they know about anythin'?'

Izzie explained to her father that before the war Susan had worked in a solicitor's office, then she proceeded to go through everything she had told her about May's mother and the problems she was having with her German lodger.

'You never know,' she said. 'It could even be the same bloke!' She tapped the photograph with her finger.

'Well...' Bill moved to sit down on the side bed, next to his daughter. 'I jus' don't know what to believe! I got to say as this time, you certainly don't sound like you're lyin' to me – an' you don't look like you are neither.'

Izzie grabbed hold of his hand and squeezed it. 'Oh, Dad! I ain't lyin', really I ain't! I ain't lyin' to you now, an' I weren't lyin' to you afore neither! It's jus' I don't wanna see you gittin' into no trouble ... gittin' arrested an' bein' sent to prison an' that. Apart from anythin' else, jus' think! What'd 'appen to me? I ain't ol' enough to steer a boat legal-like, an' I don't know 'ow to do no other work – anymore 'n you do!' This made Bill stop and think. He may have accused his daughter of lying to him, but she was still his 'little girl'. She was still his responsibility. Could he take the chance that she was being untruthful?

At length, he spoke. 'I jus' find it so 'ard to believe as Jean's been doin' all this ... all this spyin' stuff! She seem to me to be such a nice, kind-'earted sort o' person. I really can't bring meself to believe as she could do all this – not only agin' her country, but be'ind me back an' all!'

'Course she seems nice an' kind-'earted to you, Dad. Wouldn't be much good as a spy if she went around actin' all suspicious, now would she?'

'There is that to it, I s'pose,' Bill reluctantly agreed. Nothing was said for the next few minutes, and Izzie could see that her father was deep in thought. He was gazing at the porthole on the opposite side of the cabin and trying to work things out in his mind. Suddenly, he seemed to have decided on the course of action he should take. He turned to her and spoke.

'I tell you what we'll do, our Izzie. We'll sit an' we'll wait 'ere together for 'er till she gits back. An' when she does git back 'ere, then we'll 'ave a good talk wi' 'er. I reckon as I might 'ave come up wi' a bit of a idea as to 'ow we can sort this 'ole sorry, bloody mess out – one way or t'other – an' once an' for all!'

Izzie was tempted to ask him how he was going to do it but, seeing the look on his face, she decided it would be wiser not to. "E's come up wi' summat. I knowed as 'e'd know what to do!'

Chapter 29

Proof

As Bill sat in silence, immersed in his own thoughts, Izzie carefully turned the pages of the newspaper. She had looked at newspapers before – those that other people had discarded on tables in pubs, but this one was special. This one was hers. She had bought it.

Although she was anxious about Jean, anxious about her father and about what might happen on Jean's return, she soon became engrossed in her purchase. She was surprised at how much she was able to find out about what was happening in London. She read in the local news about a cinema that had been bombed and a lot of people killed. That made her sad. 'That could 'ave been me Dad an' me!' she thought. She read that Allied troops had landed in Sicily. She had an idea that this was near Italy, but she was not quite sure. Another article told of the RAF bombing Rome. 'That's in Italy for definite!' she thought. She enjoyed looking at all the advertisements. There were even letters that people had written. She found the cartoons quite funny.

'I reckon I might buy a newspaper again some time,' she said to her father as she folded up the paper and put it on her lap. Bill picked it up and looked again at the photograph of the German agent for a long time. Then he turned to her.

''Ere, our Izzie! You're the one wi' the book learnin'. Do you reckon as you can read us all as it says about this spy bloke in this 'ere newspaper?'

Izzie took the newspaper back from him. She refolded it in such a way that the whole of the headline story was visible. 'I dunno if I knows all the words,' she apologised, 'but them as I doesn't, I can look 'em up after. They should all be in 'ere.' She picked up the dictionary that Emily Roberts had given to her and placed it within easy reach.

'What's that there book, then?'

'Oh, it's what's called a diction'ry, Dad. Somebody as is real clever 'as took the time to write down all the words as there is. An' agin' all the words they've writ down what they all mean.'

'Oh, ah! So 'ow do you find the particular word as you're lookin' for, then?'

'That's easy. They're all writ down in the same order as a thing as is called the alphabet. That's the order as you says all your letters in.'

Bill nodded. 'The alphabet...,' he said, standing up. 'I'm 'eard o' that, I reckon, but I never knowed exactly what it were. Any'ow, while you're readin' it to me, I'll make us both a cup o' tea.'

Slowly, and a little uncertainly, Izzie began to read aloud the article in the newspaper. She had never read aloud to anyone before, except to George and Miss Roberts in the schoolroom. It seemed very strange to her to be sitting here reading aloud to her father – of all people – her father who had been so set against her learning to read from the start!

As she read further on into the newspaper story she became increasingly confident. She had read the story once outside the Underground station, and she managed to read it again, glossing over a few longer and unfamiliar words. When she finished, she started to look up the difficult words in her dictionary and, having read the meanings, she found that she could make sense of all the story.

Although his customary stubbornness would never have allowed him to admit as much, Bill had to confess that he was impressed with how well his daughter could read. He had not realised just how much she had learned. He looked at her again. Yes, she was almost a grown woman. He thought she was even beginning to look a little like her mother. Could he really believe that she had lied to him?

Teatime came and went, and Jean had still not returned. 'She'll still be sittin' in that caff, waitin' for 'im! Izzie thought as she looked again at the photograph on the front page. Bill took out his pocket watch, looked at the time, then heaved a heavy sigh. Izzie took this as a sign that he was possibly beginning to doubt Jean, but she said nothing. Outside, there was no breeze to speak of and the air in the cabin felt hot and heavy. Suddenly the stillness of the cut was broken by a loud clap of thunder. Streaks of lightning shot across the sky. Any rain, however, accompanying the storm was still far away. The air in the tiny cabin was heavy with expectation.

The thunderstorm was still rumbling on when Jean eventually returned. They felt the boat heel over a little when she stepped onto the counter. As she opened the doors and pushed back the slide a flash of lightning shot across the sky.

'Are you two all right, then?' she asked, smiling down at them from the top of the steps and gently lowering the full shopping bag together with her handbag down onto the rear deck.

'Cor! What a lousy storm, an' that's a bleedin' 'eavy bag today, it is!' She stood on the rear deck.

'You're very late,' Bill commented. His voice was quiet and remarkably calm. 'We was gittin' a bit worried about you – what wi' the thunderstorm, an' everythin'.'

'Ah!' Jean cooed, 'Worried about me, was you, Bill, darlin'? That's so like you, ain' it? Such a kind, carin' soul, you are! I'm OK, darlin'. I ain' been struck be lightnin' nor nuthin'.' She bent down, took a packet of cigarettes and a box of matches from her handbag and lit one. 'No, the reason I've been so long is I got chattin' wi' the bloke servin' in the greengrocer's. Could talk the 'ind leg off a bleedin' donkey, 'e could! 'E were goin' on an' on about 'is boy what's in the Navy. 'E were tellin' me about all the different places in the world as 'e's been. An' 'e were tryin' to explain to me about this code as 'is lad uses in 'is letters 'ome to let 'is dad know whereabouts in the world 'e is. They ain' allowed to say where they are in a letter, see, in case somebody sees it as didn' ought to. Then 'e were sayin' as 'ow this ship as 'is boy's on, 'ow it 'as to keep dodgin' them U-boat things.' She stopped, noticing the serious looks on the faces of the others, then quickly started again.

'What's the matter? 'As summat 'appened? Or 'as the cat got both your tongues?'

Izzie turned to confront her. 'No you wasn't!' She spat out the words. 'You wasn't talkin' to no greengrocer – well, only to tell 'im what veg you wanted an' to pay for it.'

'Oh, no? I weren', weren' I?' Jean sneered, a superior tone to her voice. 'What were I doin' then, pray, Little Miss Cleverclogs? Not as you'd know nuthin' about what I were doin' any'ow, cos I made doubly bleedin' sure as you wasn' follerin' me an' spyin' on me again!'

'No. I weren't follerin' you, but I bet you as I can tell you exactly where you was an' what you was up to.'

'What are you, then? Some bleedin' gyppo fortune-teller, or summat?' Jean chuckled. 'Got your crystal ball out, 'ave you? Come on, then! Out wi' it! Let's 'ear what that amazin' imagination o' yours 'as cooked up this time?' Up to this point, Izzie had not looked at her. Now she turned on the bed to confront her.

Jean smiled at Bill. 'Your daughter thinks she's so bleedin' clever!' Bill looked straight through her without returning her smile.

'I'll tell you,' said Izzie, confidence growing in her voice. 'You was sat at a table in a little caff in a street not very far from 'ere. You was sat there, drinkin' a cup o' tea. Fact is, you probably 'ad time to drink more 'n one cup o' tea. In fact, you probably 'ad time to drink the 'ole potful o' tea.' She paused 'Cos you was sat there waitin' for a bloke, a well-dressed bloke wi' a moustache. Only you 'ad a long ol' wait for 'im today, didn't you? Cos the bloke as you was sat there waitin' for never showed up, did 'e? That's what you was up to this afternoon!'

The smirk on Jean's face slipped – just for second – as she looked uncertain. She simply could not work out how Izzie could have known all this. To cover her uncertainty she replied angrily, 'Look 'ere! I thought I tol' you when you tried all this on before. It ain' no use you tryin' to come between your Dad an' me like this cos it jus' won' wash!' She looked towards Bill. He sat impassively. She drew breath and continued, oblivious to the thunderstorm that continued raging around them.

'You an' your bleedin' lies! Cos that's all they are, ain' they – bleedin' lies? Meetin' up wi' blokes in caffs, indeed! I tell you, you've got far too vivid an imagination, you 'ave, far too vivid by 'alf!' She paused. 'I s'pose it's quite clever o' you in a funny sort o' way, you makin' up all these bleedin' lies, all out your own 'ead! Yeah, you've got a good imagination, I'll give you that! If only you could read a bit better than them little kiddies' books you've got, you could even write some good stories o' your own with an imagination like that!' She laughed. Izzie ignored the insult and spoke again.

'You was sat at that table in that little caff, waitin' for 'im so as you could give 'im a big brown envelope, wasn't you? The big brown envelope as that other bloke give you by that bridge 'ole on the road out o' Brum.' Izzie paused again. 'Only 'e never showed up today, did 'e? You waited an' waited an' waited for 'im in that little caff – but 'e never turned up!'

Izzie could see it in her eyes. Jean was trying so very hard to work out in her mind how on earth Izzie could possibly know all this. She knew she had not been followed, so how could this girl possibly know? She did not have to wait long to find out. Izzie stood up with the newspaper in her hands.

''E never turned up to that caff today cos 'e couldn't! 'E couldn't cos 'e's locked up! The p'lice arrested 'im last night!' As she said this she let the newspaper unfold in front of her so that Jean could not fail to see the photograph and read the headline. Izzie did not miss the momentary look of horror, tinged with fear, that passed over Jean's face. Bill saw it too. Quickly, she regained her composure and went back on the offensive.

''Ow long are you gonna carry on wi' these bleedin' lies about me meetin' blokes in caffs, eh? An' what the 'ell's all this in this 'ere paper got to do wi' me? Not that you can believe nuthin' as you read in the papers these days, any'ow! Well, I'll tell you what it's got to do wi' me – nuthin'! That's what it's got to do wi' me! Nuthin' at all, that's what! I ain' got no idea who this bloke is. As far as I know, I ain' never seen 'im before, and I certainly ain' never met 'im in no bleedin' caff. So there!' She threw her cigarette end into the water and lit another one. Then, suddenly, she looked pleadingly towards Bill.

'Bill, darlin', you're quiet! You ain' said nuthin' at all to help me out while she's been goin' on at me with 'er bleedin' lies, 'ave you?

You're just sat there all quiet, ain' you?' Bill said nothing, so Jean spoke again.

'An' I reckon as I know why it is as you ain' said nuthin', I do. It's cos you're ashamed of 'er, ain' it? That's what it is, ain' it, Bill, darlin'? You're ashamed o' your own flesh an' blood! Ashamed of 'er cos she just goes on an' on, tellin' all 'er wicked, bleedin' lies about me? Just so as she can try to come between you an' me. So as she can try an' ruin what little bit of 'appiness as we've found with each other. An' now she's even trying to make out as there's some cock an' bull story or other in this paper as proves I'm a bad lot! I'm sure that's it, ain' it?' She paused. Bill said nothing.

'Oh, bless you!' she continued. 'You're too ashamed of 'er to say anythin' at all, ain' you? That's it, ain' it?' Bill sighed, but again he said nothing.

'Well ain' it?' she repeated with a little more urgency.

Bill broke his silence. 'I dunno what to believe, I'm sure! One o' you's got to be lyin' to me. That's for definite!'

'You surely don' think it's me, do you Bill, darlin'?' Jean adopted a wheedling, whining tone. 'It's 'er, I tell you! She ain' never liked me. Always 'ated me, she 'as! Right from the very start, right from that first time when I come an' 'ad that little look at your boats. Took an instant dislike to me, right then an' there, she did! An' now she's tryin' to come between us cos she don' like me bein' with you! She'll stop at nuthin' to see us split up an' go our separate ways! Nuthin'! You mark my words! It's 'er as is lyin', I swear to you!'

Izzie was still standing holding the newspaper in front of her. She slowly moved her gaze from Jean to face her father and, looking him straight in the eye, she spoke. She spoke very quietly and very calmly. 'Dad,' she began, 'I swear to you … I swear to you on … on me Mam's soul … I swear to you as I ain't lyin' to you now … an' I never lied to you afore, neither.'

No one spoke for a few seconds. Bill stared at his daughter. Then Izzie looked up at Jean, still standing at the top of the steps on the counter. She was bending down slightly to look at Bill, who was still sitting on the side bed, now carefully studying his boots. Jean was about to speak again when suddenly Bill raised his hand, cutting her off.

'As I sees it,' he began, seriously and thoughtfully, still studying his boots, 'there's only one way as we can sort all this sorry ol' business out, once an' for all.' He paused for a few seconds to let this sink in. 'Now, the way as I sees it is this.' He turned and looked at Jean. 'Jean. You're sayin' as you didn't pick up no envelope from no bloke by no bridge 'ole as we was comin' out o' Brum. You're also sayin' as you wasn't expectin' to meet nobody in no caff today so as you could give him an envelope. Well, if that's the case, then you won't have no envelope 'id in your 'andbag, will you? So, if you ain't got no envelope in your 'andbag, then I'll know for sure as it's you as is tellin' me the truth an' it's our Izzie 'ere as is lyin' to me. On the other 'and,' he turned to face his daughter, 'if there is an envelope in there, then I'll know as it's you as is tellin' me the truth, our Izzie, an' that it's 'er as is lyin' to me.'

He turned back to Jean. 'So, if you'll jus' empty out your 'andbag, Jean, we can clear all this sorry ol' mess up right 'ere an' now, once an' for all, can't we? It'll prove it – one way or th' other.' He let down the table. 'You can empty it out on 'ere, if you want,' he said.

'My Gawd!' Jean exclaimed. 'This is worse 'n bein' up afore the beak, this is! It really is!'

Izzie could see that Jean was panicking as it dawned on her that Bill had cleverly set a trap for her – and she had walked right into it! 'Well done, Dad!' she thought. Izzie marvelled at the simple ingenuity of her father's plan. It seemed to her that Jean had to opt for one of two choices. She could either empty her handbag out on the table, confess that she had been lying and that it was Izzie who had been telling the truth, or she would need to come up with a very good reason that would satisfy her father as to why she should not empty out her bag. Jean decided to brazen it out.

'Why should I 'ave to turn me bag out? Don' you trust me no more, Bill, darlin'? What do you need to see proof for? Can' you just take my word for it? Like I told you, it's only 'er an' 'er bleedin' lies!'

Bill's expression had not changed. 'Jus' show us what you're got in your bag, Jean, my love,' he said. Jean threw her cigarette end into the water and picked up her handbag. She made a move to open it, then stopped.

'No! No, I won'! I don' see why I bleedin' well should!' She clutched her handbag closely to her chest. 'A lady's 'andbag's private, it is! It's 'er own private affair. Nobody else shouldn' see what's in a lady's 'andbag, except the lady 'erself! It's private, a lady's 'andbag is!'

Bill spoke again, still quiet, still calm. 'Well, it's like this 'ere, Jean, my love. The way as I sees it is this. If you don't wanna show me what you're got in your 'andbag, then I shall 'ave to reckon as you're got summat to 'ide in it, shan't I? Summat in there as you don't want me to see!'

Jean glared at him for a moment. 'All right!' she shouted finally. 'So this is what it's bloody well come to, is it? Right! If it's proof you want, I'll give you some bloody proof!' She held her handbag in her left hand, opened it with her right and felt around inside it for a few moments.

'Jus' takin' stuff out o' your bag won't prove nuthin',' Bill explained. 'You're got to empty it all out so's I can see everythin' as is in it.'

Jean slowly withdrew her hand from the bag. Bill had no idea what he was about to see. Izzie thought it might be the large brown envelope, which Jean would then try to explain away to Bill with more lies. But neither of them expected to see what was in Jean's hand when she removed it from her handbag. Surprised and terrified in equal measure, they found themselves staring at the business end of a Luger pistol! And, right on cue, a clap of thunder broke overhead.

Chapter 30

Traitor

'What…? What are you doin'? What are you doin', Jean, my love?' spluttered Bill.

'Don' you "Jean my love" me, Bill 'Orne! Stay still – the both o' you!'

'But I thought…'

'What you thought don' count for nuthin'. I'm stood 'ere with a gun on you, so it's what I think as counts now!' She paused, then sighed. 'You really ain' got it yet, 'ave you? Gawd, they tol' me as you bargees was a bit stupid, but I never realised till now just 'ow bloody stupid you are!' She paused again, obviously thinking about something. When she spoke it was with a calm voice, a confident voice, a voice of decision.

'Well,' she began, 'I don' s'pose it'll make no difference now, so as it seems pretty obvious as you're too bloody stupid to work it out for yourself, I s'pose I better tell you everythin'. Cos when I 'ave, when I've told you everythin' as 'as really been goin' on these past months, while I've been on 'ere wi' you, then you'll see just 'ow much of a bloody fool you're been! An' I shall really enjoy seein' the look on your stupid face when you find all that out! Lookin' forward to that, I am!'

She looked down at the steps, considering whether to move down into the cabin or stay where she was. She decided that staying where she was, standing above them on the counter, was the more powerful position.

'Now listen 'ere, an' listen bloody good, Bill 'Orne! Your too-bloody-clever-by-'alf daughter 'ere – Miss Bloody Busybody – she 'ad me sussed nearly right from the beginnin'. But she only guessed a bit of it. She couldn' work it all out, could you?' She looked at

Izzie. 'I watched you when you was s'posed to be readin' your little kiddies' books. I seen you tryin' to work it out, tryin' to make sense o' what I were doin'. That's why you follered me, weren' it? You was good! I'll give you that. You was good, cos I never seen you! I never seen you in Birnigum an' I never seen you down 'ere!' With her left hand she took a cigarette from her packet.

'Light that for me, Bill 'Orne!' she ordered, tossing him the matchbox, all the time keeping the gun trained on him and Izzie. Bill lit the cigarette and passed it to her before throwing the matchbox to the floor. Jean scowled at him before starting to speak.

'There's information, see…,' she began. 'I dunno what it is, an' I don' need to know – but it's very necessary to get this information from Birnigum down to London – regular, like. An' it needs to be got 'ere in such a way as it don' raise nobody's suspicions, see? They could 'ave coppers watchin' out at the railway stations an' the bus stations, watchin' out for folks as is doin' the same journeys regular. I dunno if they 'ave or not, but it don' do to take no unnecessary risks. They wasn' sure 'ow they was gonna do it, but then somebody thought about the canals. They investigated an' they found out as there was a number o' boat companies as 'ad a regular traffic between Birnigum an' London – more so since the war started – so that suited their plans jus' fine.

'My orders was simple. I had to start off by gettin' meself a job in a pub somewhere along the canal between them two places. The next thing I 'ad to do was to get meself – what shall we say? – "involved" with a bargee who was on that run, regular. See, they'd already trained me 'ow to do bar work an' 'ow to steer one o' these 'ere boats an' 'ow to take it through a lock, so I knew as I'd be able do that all right.'

'No wonder you picked it all up so quick!' Izzie said. Jean ignored her.

'The rest of it was all so bloody easy. I 'eard talk in the pub as you'd recently lost your missus, so I decided to set me cap for you. You took your bloody time, but eventually you fell for me – 'ook, line an' bloody sinker! It nearly fell apart when you got took off the Coventry job an' put on this one. That pickle factory run suited me just fine. But this one? Well, it suited me even better. And who'd 'ave thought it, wi' you workin' for the Gover'ment an' all! I 'ad to make a special journey to Birnigum to sort that out.'

'That's when I see you gittin' on a bus when you was supposed to be goin' to see your sister. Only you was goin' the wrong way!' Izzie said.

'Oh yeah! 'Er – me sister – 'er as lives in Poplar?' Jean laughed. 'Fact is, I ain' got no sister!' She laughed again. 'I 'ad a brother. Useless idiot 'e was. 'E were on the dole when the war started so he volunteers for the Navy. 'E were sent to the *'Ood*. The *Bismarck* did for 'im – an' all 'is shipmates. "Sunk with all 'ands", that's what the papers said. Silly bugger!

'Now where was I? Oh, yeah, that boy George gettin' called up? That was a bloody Godsend, that was. I'd already told you I reckoned I could live on the boats an' I'd 'ad me 'olidays wi' you, so you put two an' two together, like I knew you would. You showed a bit o' nous for once in your life an' you rung me up. I can' tell you 'ow 'appy I was when I got that call. I'd 'ung around for so bloody long, I thought me contact would 'ave to take me off the job and move me to summat else. We was wastin' valuable time, see. So I got in touch with 'im straight away an' told 'im the job was on.

'Once I was livin' on 'ere, all I 'ad to do was make sure as nobody else come wi' me when I went off to do the shoppin'. I'd meet me Birnigum contact in the buffet at New Street station an' 'e'd pass me the information. Then I 'ad to make a phone call to confirm as I'd got it, so as they'd know to set up the meetin' 'ere in London. An' when we got 'ere I'd meet me London contact in the caff at Kensal Green an' pass the information on to 'im. Then I'd make another phone call to say I'd done it, so that me Birnigum contact would know that the information 'ad been delivered safe an' weren' lost, or fell into the wrong 'ands, or nuthin'. Also, 'e'd know what day we'd be back in Birnigum.'

Jean paused for breath, drawing on her cigarette and blowing the smoke into the air. Bill sat dumbfounded, staring at her in amazement. Izzie could not believe what she was hearing. She was about to speak when Jean started again.

'Course! It very nearly all went down the pan when I were laid up wi' the 'flu that time, didn' it? There wasn' no way I could get to

New Street then, but fortunately there was another plan, a plan what we called "the fallback". See, me Birnigum contact was to wait for me till six o'clock. If I 'adn' turned up by six, then the fallback plan was to come into action. 'E knew as 'e 'ad to be by a partic'lar bridge between certain hours on the follerin' day. I knew as 'e'd be waitin' by that bridge on the way out of Birnigum, so all I 'ad to do was make sure as I were steerin' the butty when we went along by it. That's why I told you both as 'ow I were feelin' so much better that day, when the truth was I was still feelin' bloody awful! Anyway, 'e were waitin' there, like I knew 'e would be, an' 'e give me the package. Miss Cleverclogs 'ere, she seen 'im 'andin' it over to me. But by then you thought your kid was a liar, didn' you, Bill 'Orne? I'd convinced you o' that. She couldn' say a bloody word, could she? Cos you wouldn' believe nuthin' she said, would you?' Bill winced.

She turned to Izzie. 'I were a bit too clever for you there, weren' I?' Izzie said nothing. 'So, directly after 'e's give me the package, 'e would 'ave gone an' made the phone call as I should 'ave made if things 'ad 'appened in the usual way. It were a good plan, a very good plan. It worked well. In fact, it worked bloody well – an' it could 'ave kept on workin' well for years an' years. 'Cept that of all the rotten bloody luck, I 'ad to go an' pick on the one bargee whose daughter knows 'ow to read well enough to read an' understand a story in a bloody newspaper!' She shouted this last phrase as she glared at Izzie.

Izzie, unflinching and unblinking, returned her stare. She managed to speak at last, her mouth dry, her voice hoarse. 'But you'd 'ave 'ad to stop it now, though, wouldn't you? With 'im bein' arrested, like.'

'Not on your life!' Jean retorted. 'No! We'd never 'ave 'ad to stop it – not altogether. You don' understand, see. In a few days time they'll 'ave sent somebody else out to take over from 'im.'

'But it says in the paper 'ere as the p'lice is lookin' for all 'is "associates", so there won't be no information to pass on no more, will there?' Izzie persisted.

Jean smiled. 'Don' you be so bloody sure, young lady! I tell you, they won' find that many of us, no matter 'ow 'ard they bloody well look!. That's another part o' the trainin', see. They know there's always the danger we'll be found out, an' they know it could 'appen any time, so we've all been trained in what to do so as we can just ... disappear! They'll probably find out where we was yesterday, but that most likely ain' gonna be the same place as where we are today! Oh no, they won' get 'old o' that many of us at all, I can tell you!' She paused.

'Still, it did work well while it lasted. I made it work. But like they say, all good things gotta come to an end some time. An' it was a good thing, a bloody good thing. I reckon as I've played my little part in 'elpin' a 'ell of a lot of information along on its way to Berlin. Although I dunno what information it was, I'm sure as it'll all be a real big 'elp to 'em when they're workin' out their plans for the big invasion o' Britain.'

'Berlin? Invasion?' Izzie's eyes widened.

'You ... 'elpin' ... what?' Bill sputtered.

'Oh, yeah! Won' be long now. You'll see. We wasn' quite ready in 1940. 'Itler 'ad made 'is plans but 'is generals wasn' quite ready. Them pilots of ours was brave in the Battle o' Britain, as Churchill called it. We landed a 'ole load o' spies over 'ere – an' no, they wasn' all dressed like bleedin' nuns!

'We might 'ave 'ad a bit of a setback in Sicily an' in Africa, an' that Eyetie coward Mussolini might 'ave gone – good riddance! But we're still just across the water there in France, just bidin' our time. We're just waitin' for the right time, an' when that time comes we'll be across that Channel so quick! Bloody England won' know what's 'it it. An' that lily-livered bunch of pansies in Westminster! They'll be quakin' in their bloody boots, they will! An' that Churchill? Well, 'e'll be the first to be shot, 'im an' the Royal bloody Family. You just wait an' see. Soon they'll see 'em! The mighty German Army of the Third Reich, marchin' along through the streets o' London, here, with 'Err 'Itler, the Mighty Führer hisself, ridin' along in the front of 'em. Now, there's a man! There's a real man! There's a man whose got the know-'ow – an' the guts – to get things sorted out! 'E'll get the whole o' Europe sorted out good an' proper, 'e will. 'E'll put us all on the right road!'

She paused for a moment, her eyes gazing into the distance,

appearing to be in some sort of reverie. Bill and Izzie watched her open-mouthed. After a few seconds Jean seemed to come back to reality and looked again at her two prisoners.

'It's a bit of a pity, really,' she laughed, in a matter-of-fact tone, 'that neither o' you's gonna be around to see none of it 'appen! Ahh!' she said in mock pity. 'It don' seem hardly fair, do it? 'Specially after you're done so much to 'elp me make it 'appen.'

'What d'you mean? What are we ever done to 'elp you?' Bill managed to find his voice.

Jean smiled. 'Gawd! You really are bloody stupid, ain' you? Think about it! You've give me food an' you've give me shelter, ain' you? You're provided me wi' transport, ain' you? Every time I got given the information in Birnigum, you've carried it down to London for me – on your boat! In my book that makes you nearly as much of a traitor to your bloody country as I am, Bill 'Orne! It would 'ave been the bloody 'angman's noose for both of us if I'd ever got caught. Cos don' think for a minute I wouldn' 'ave … what's that word them posh lawyers use? … "implicated"! That's it! Don' think for a minute I wouldn' 'ave implicated you in all of it! Cos I bloody well would 'ave!'

She turned to Izzie. 'An' what would you 'ave ad to do then, girl? Eh? What would you 'ave done wi' your ol' man inside – or 'anged? What would you 'ave done then, eh? You'd 'ave 'ad to give up your precious boats for a start. That's for sure! You'd 'ave 'ad to go an' live in a orphanage or summat, wouldn' you?'

Izzie ignored her. 'What do you mean? Me an' me Dad not being around to see it when the Germans come over 'ere?'

'Bloody 'ell!' Jean exclaimed. 'I thought you 'ad a bit more nous than your ol' man, but I can see you can be just as stupid as 'e is sometimes, can' you? It must be 'ereditary!' Another pause, another sigh.

'You surely must see it. You surely can' think for a second as I'd 'ave told you all that if I was intendin' to let either of you live for much longer, can you?' Another pause. The silence hung in the air. 'I mean, now I've told you all that, I really ain' got no option, 'ave I? The thing is, now you both know far more than is good for you. You know too much about what me an' me contacts 'as been doin' these past months, don' you? Both of you must see I ain' got no choice, 'ave I?' She stopped again and looked directly at them. 'I've gotta kill the both of you, ain' I?'

Bill gasped, the colour of his natural ruddy complexion draining from his face.

Izzie regained her composure first. 'Kill us?' she said.

'Got to, ain' I?' Jean answered. 'Can' 'ave you runnin' off to the law an' tellin' 'em all me little secrets, now can I? An' don' you go foolin' yourselves into thinkin' I can' or I won' do it, neither. They've trained me for that an' all – killin' people, I mean!' She waved the gun in their direction to emphasise her point.

'But somebody'll 'ear the gun goin' off.' Izzie was desperately thinking on her feet, anything to delay what Jean was planning!

Again Jean smirked. 'Jus' 'ave a look around out 'ere! Them Gover'ment men's all gone 'ome. There ain' nobody left around 'ere, nobody at all. The nearest 'ouse is a good way off an' with this 'ere thunderstorm rattlin' around there ain' nobody gonna 'ear a couple o' little pistol shots, now are they?'

Bill realised she was serious. 'An' what are you gonna do after you're done away wi' us both, then?'

'Oh! That'll be the easy bit! I'll grab 'old o' some o' that rubble as is lyin' around from when we bombed that factory over there, an' I'll stick it in the 'old o' the motor. Then I'll take us all out to some nice quiet spot, somewhere in the countryside, right in the middle o' nowhere. Then I'll weigh both your bodies down wi' the rubble an' I'll dump you both over the side. An' then? Well! Then I can do summat as I've been burstin' to do ever since I come on 'ere.'

'An' what might that be, then?' Bill asked.

'Well now, you might be quite 'appy an' content, livin' in ignorance an' not knowin' what's in them crates as we're carryin'. But me? I'm dyin' to know! So I'm gonna open one of 'em an' find out what this 'ere secret cargo is as we've been bringin' down 'ere all this while. I would 'ave 'ad a gander at 'em before, but all them bleedin' crates's got Gover'ment seals on 'em, an' if one of 'em was broke then there'd be 'ell to pay. Apart from anythin' else, they'd 'ave took you off the run. An' that wouldn' 'ave been no bloody good to me, now would it? But I'm damned sure as me friends in

Berlin would be really 'appy wi' me if I could tell 'em what's in them crates. Be a real feather in me cap, that would!'

Throughout all this Izzie had remained standing, holding the newspaper high in front of her, not daring to move. Now, holding the newspaper with her left hand, she used it as a shield to cover the movements of her right. Carefully, very carefully, very quietly, and very slowly, a quarter of an inch by a quarter of an inch, she began to open the knife drawer. She had no idea what she was going to do with the knife when she had it in her hand, but at that moment it seemed a better option than simply standing there doing nothing.

At the very last moment, just as her fingers were about to close round the handle of the big carving knife, Jean noticed the movement behind the newspaper. Swiftly swinging the gun round so that it was pointing straight at Izzie's head, she shouted, 'Oi you! Leave that bloody drawer alone. I can see your game! An' you can drop that paper an' put your 'ands up over your 'ead so as I can see 'em!'

Staring down the barrel of the gun, Izzie obliged.

Bill had been sitting motionless. He spoke quietly, in a measured tone. 'So, you're a traitor to your King an' country then, are you?'

'There's some as might say that, but I wouldn' exactly agree wi' 'em. See, I reckon as me country ought to be summat as I can be proud of, proud of its strength, proud of its position in the world. Great Britain? That's a bloody joke, that is! Nuthin' great about Great Britain now! We're got such a lily-livered load o' namby-pamby yes-men in the Gover'ment now as I'm ashamed o' me country, I am! Really ashamed of it!'

'Who would you rather 'ave runnin' the show, then?' Bill asked. 'This 'Itler bloke, a bloomin' foreigner?'

'There's only one Englishman could 'ave sorted this country out proper, like. 'E would 'ave let everybody know what's what, 'e would. If 'e'd been Prime Minister things would 'ave been a bloody sight different, I can tell you! An' a bloody sight better! They 'ad their chance! They could easily 'ave give 'im the top job. But did they? No! What did they do with 'im? I'll tell you what they done with 'im. That bloody Churchill, 'e stuck 'im in prison! That's what 'e done! It were one o' the first things 'e done when 'e got to be Prime Minister. An' d'you know why 'e stuck 'im in prison? Do you? I know for why. It were cos 'e were bloody well scared of 'im! That's why! Scared stiff of 'im, 'e was, an' all 'is lily-livered cabinet an' all! Cos they knew full well 'e were a better man than any of 'em. Worth ten o' them scaredy cats who we've got in power now, 'e is! You wait an' see. After the invasion, I reckon they'll let 'im out of prison an' make 'im President o' the country. 'E'll be 'ailed as a bloody 'ero, 'e will!'

'An' who might that be, then?' asked Bill.

'I don' s'pose an ignorant bargee like you's ever 'eard of 'im. But 'e's a fine man, 'e is! A real fine man! Sir Oswald Mosley is 'is name. Yeah! 'E's the man, all right!. I marched with 'im, I did, 'im an' the Blackshirts. Back in '36, we all marched together down the East End. Gawd! We showed 'em ol' Jew boys a thing or two, we did! An' it weren' before time, neither! An' I tell you this an' all, it were no more than they bloody well deserved! They'd all been livin' the 'igh life, they 'ad! The life o' bloody Riley, they 'ad! All of 'em, livin' it up, while the rest of us was damn near starvin'.'

While Jean had been haranguing them with her political exploits, Izzie had watched her carefully. She noticed that Jean was now leaning forward to get closer to her prisoners, so far forward, in fact, that her head was just inside the hatch doorway, and – more to the point, as far as Izzie was concerned – on a level with the open slide! Izzie continued to stand with her hands high above her head, as she had been ordered. Without raising Jean's suspicions she managed to slowly move her fingers so that they were resting against the wooden bar that was attached to the slide's underside. As Jean looked at her and her father with disdain, Izzie took a long, slow, deep breath, then, using every ounce of strength she possessed, she slammed the sliding hatch shut as hard and as fast as she possibly could.

Jean never saw what hit her. The edge of the slide caught her full force, right on the bridge of her nose. She screamed. In pain, her hands flew up to her face. The gun dropped from her fingers, clattering down the steps like a stone and coming to rest inside the cabin. Izzie moved quickly. She grabbed the gun as Jean fell backwards and collapsed into unconsciousness outside on the counter.

'Quick, Dad!' Izzie shouted. 'Go an' git that spare rope out the engine 'ole!'

Bill leaped up the steps, clambered over Jean's motionless body, and returned in no time with the rope.

'Tie 'er up afore she comes to, Dad!'

Bill tied Jean hand and foot, as a man who had worked with ropes all his life. They both knew that Jean would never be able to free herself from those knots.

'Let's shift 'er off the counter, so as we can git in and out a bit easier!' Bill said as he tightened the final knot. Jean began mumbling incoherently as, between them, they managed to manhandle her off the counter and onto the towpath.

Izzie held up the pistol. 'I'll keep this pointin' at 'er cos I reckon as she'll be comin' round in a minute.' She stepped back onto the counter. 'Dad, you best go an' phone the p'lice!'

'But you 'eard what she said, our Izzie! They might wanna arrest me an' all!'

'What else are we gonna do? We can't leave 'er 'ere, can we?'

'I dunno … I…'

'I reckon she were jus' tryin' to put the wind up you! I reckon she were bluffin'. It ain't like you knew what were in them envelopes, not that you knew anythin' at all about any envelopes till today!' She paused. She could see her father was still not convinced. 'Look Dad! We're got 'er all tied up, ain't we? When the p'lice gits 'ere we can prove to 'em as we're trapped another German spy – one o' that bloke's … what were that word in the paper? "Network"! One of 'is network as they're after. So they ought to be pleased wi' what we're done. I don't reckon as they'll be wantin' to arrest you an' stick you in jail after all this.'

Bill did not move. He stood there, uncertain. Izzie grabbed his shoulder, spun him round and gave him a push along the towpath. 'Get goin' Dad! Quick!'

Bill set off in the direction of the street.

✳

Her heart racing, Izzie watched as her father disappeared into the darkness. Tension and fear had driven all awareness of the storm from her mind. Now a flash of lightning lit the sky and the thunderclap that followed seemed to echo round the ruined buildings. It was then that the rain started. The driving rain fell like stair rods. The sudden soaking brought Jean back to consciousness. Izzie watched her as she stirred, tried to move, then realised that she could not do so because she was securely tied up. Izzie stood on the counter, motionless, and held the gun steady, pointing it straight at her head. Jean turned her head and noticed Izzie looking at her, pointing the gun at her.

'Izzie!' Her voice sounded thick and nasal, as it had sounded when she had been suffering from influenza. A trickle of blood slipped from her nostril and ran like a tiny river down her cheek. 'You won' shoot me, Izzie! No, you won' do it! You ain' got the guts! It takes some guts to pull that there trigger an' you ain' got 'em!'

'Ain't I?' Izzie questioned. 'Ain't I, now? Jus' think to yourself. A bit ago you said as 'ow I 'ated you. You said as I'd always 'ated you right from when I first clapped eyes on you. Well, you wasn't wrong there! But there's summat as you don't know. You don't know jus' 'ow much I 'ate you, do you, Jean? You dunno if I 'ate you enough to pull this 'ere trigger or not, do you?' She waved the barrel of the gun in Jean's direction to emphasise her point.

There was a long silence, then Jean spoke again, her voice wheedling and whining. 'I tell you what, Izzie... Why don' you just untie me? Untie me an' I'll walk away... I'll just disappear, like. You can tell your Dad as I some'ow managed to free meself while your back were turned, an' then I 'it you 'ard over the 'ead wi' summat an' run off before you could do anythin' about it... Go on, Izzie ... please! I need to get me to a doctor – or an 'ospital, I do... I reckon me nose is broke.' Izzie said nothing. Jean tried pleading with her again. 'Go on, Izzie ... just untie me an' let me go... If I get arrested, you know what they'll do to me, don' you? Eh? They'll 'ang me, they will! That's what they'll do to me, Izzie! That's what they does to folk they calls traitors. They 'angs 'em! Do you want that on your conscience for the rest o' your life, Izzie? Do you...? That you knowin'ly sent a woman to be 'anged ... just for doin' what she thought were the right thing for 'erself an' 'er country ... do you?'

Izzie looked thoughtful for moment or two, appearing to give full consideration to what Jean had said. She seemed to be turning over in her mind the course of action that Jean had proposed, wondering whether she should, indeed, untie her and let her go.

At length, it looked to Jean as if she had reached a decision. Still saying nothing, Izzie lay the gun down, carefully, on the roof of the cabin and stepped down off the boat. Smiling sweetly, she slowly walked over to where Jean lay on the towpath, stopping a foot or so away from her. Jean relaxed.

'There!' she said. 'I knew you'd see the sense of it. You're a clever girl, you are, Izzie! 'Ad me sussed from the start, you did, didn' you? I could see you was a clever one, even then I could. Now, if you just loosen this 'ere rope from around me wrists, I reckon I'll be able to do the one round me ankles for meself.'

Izzie moved and stood directly over her, staring at her. The smile had disappeared from her face to be replaced by a mask of hate. Without averting her gaze from Jean's face, she slowly and deliberately drew back her foot. 'This is for callin' me Dad a "bargee"!' she said, as she kicked Jean, as hard as she could, in the ribs. Jean cried out. 'An' this is for callin' 'im "ignorant" an' "stupid"!' Izzie kicked her hard again and Jean let out another yell. 'An' this is for tellin' 'im as I'd lied to 'im!' Izzie's boot connected with Jean's ribcage for a third time, bringing forth another yell.

'An' this...' Izzie's voice rose to a scream. 'This is for my George as is lost 'is leg on account of your German friends in Berlin!' Another well-aimed kick and another squeal of agony.

Jean's face was now contorted with pain and naked fear. Izzie turned and stepped back onto the counter. 'An' that's a sight less 'n you deserve, you lyin', two-faced bitch!' she shouted as she picked up the gun again. 'An' it won't do you no good tellin' nobody as I kicked you while you was tied up cos nobody ain't gonna believe you now, are they? Cos now they all knows you for a liar.' Izzie laughed. 'That's almost the same as what you said to me that night when you come back from the pub for a 'andkerchief, ain't it? "You can't tell nobody about it, cos now they knows you for a liar!" Bit different now the boot's on the other foot, ain't it? But you're more 'n a liar, you are! You're a liar an' you're a traitor!'

'What's gonna 'appen to me?' was all Jean could say. She was crying now, whether from pain or from the fear of what the future might hold, Izzie neither knew nor cared. She repeated it over and over again. 'What's gonna 'appen to me?'

After the fifteenth or sixteenth repetition, Izzie said, 'I'll tell you what's gonna 'appen to you. You're gonna be took from 'ere by the p'lice, in a p'lice car, when they come. Then they'll stick you in a cell down the p'lice station. Then you're gonna be tried in a court – an' then you're gonna be found guilty o' treason, an' then you're gonna be 'anged. You're gonna be 'anged cos you ain't worth nuthin'! You're nuthin' but a dirty, rotten traitor. That's what you are, an' that's what's gonna 'appen to you!'

"Ow comes a boat girl like you knows all this stuff about police an' cells an' courts an' everythin'?'

'A lady I know as is called Susan. She tol' me all about it. She used to work in a solicitor's office afore the war started, see? She knows all about it.'

Jean subsided into silence, the red rivulet still meandering across her cheek. Izzie stood, motionless, on the counter, the gun firmly in her hand, still pointing towards Jean. The rain lashed down on them as they awaited Bill's return.

Chapter 31

Arrested

A s Bill walked back from the telephone box, the bell of an approaching police car could be heard in the distance. Bill arrived back at the makeshift wharf shortly before it did. When the car arrived it sped onto the wharf and screeched to a halt. A constable and a sergeant got out, slamming the doors shut behind them, and shone their torches in the direction of the boats.

'Oh dear! Oh dear! And what have we here?' enquired the Sergeant, surveying the scene in the beam of his torch.

'Well, it were like this 'ere, Sir,' started Bill, looking at his feet. He was not comfortable being in the presence of police officers. 'Me an' our Izzie – me daughter 'ere...,' and he continued to explain to the policemen what had happened.

'We'll look after her now,' said the Sergeant and indicated to Bill to untie the ropes round Jean's hands and feet. Still moaning, Jean sat up and rubbed her ankles. Cautioning her, the constable snapped the handcuffs round her wrists. He held out his hand to help her to her feet.

As she did so she squealed and tried to grab at her side. Her blouse had come loose from her skirt and the light of the policeman's torch showed some livid red marks on her ribcage. The policemen looked questioningly at Bill and Izzie.

'Must 'ave caught 'erself on the cabin roof when she fell down,' Izzie said flatly. Bill looked at her quizzically. The policemen, however, accepted her explanation without further question.

While the constable led Jean to the police car, Sergeant Perkins of the Metropolitan Police picked up her handbag, which was still sitting on the counter.

'Come aboard, Sir,' said Bill, inviting him into *Zeus*'s cabin. Izzie followed them in, and passed the officer a towel so that he could dry the handbag.

'So you're pretty sure that I'm going to find an envelope in here with some sort of secret information inside it?' he said, drying the outside of the bag.

'Yes, I am, Sir,' Izzie replied.

'Well, let's have a look then, shall we?'

Bill indicated the table and the Sergeant proceeded to empty the contents of the bag onto it. Out tumbled Jean's purse, her lipstick, her powder compact, a handkerchief, a packet of cigarettes, a roll of bank notes – and a large manila envelope!

'Nothing written on the front of it,' the Sergeant said as he carefully opened it and removed a sheaf of closely typed sheets of paper.

'What d'you reckon, Sir?' Bill asked.

'I'm not sure,' said the Sergeant, thumbing carefully through the sheets of paper, 'but it looks important … aircraft production, possibly … you know – Spitfires and all that.'

Bill picked up the roll of bank notes.

'I'm jus' wonderin' where she got this lot from. I certainly never give it to 'er. There's more money there 'n I'd see in a year!'

'She probably got paid handsomely for her spying activities,' Sergeant Perkins said.

'That explains summat else,' said Izzie. 'I thought I seen the bloke as give 'er the envelope give 'er summat else an' all. It must 'ave been the money.' She paused. 'That's 'ow she were able to pay for 'er 'air-do's! I knew as she couldn't afford what she 'ad done on the money as me Dad give 'er.'

When Bill told him how Izzie had managed to disarm and disable Jean, Sergeant Perkins was full of admiration.

'That was an excellent bit of quick thinking on your part, young lady. You did very well. You should be very proud of your daughter, Sir!' he said to Bill.

'Oh, I am, Sir! Oh, you bet your sweet life I am!' Bill placed his arm, proudly, round Izzie's shoulders.

'Now young lady,' said Sergeant Perkins, sitting down next to her on the side bed. 'I need to ask you some questions. Don't worry!

Just tell me what you saw and what happened. I'll write it down in my notebook. Remember – tell me the truth because what you say might be used in court at the woman's trial.'

Bill spoke. 'Don't you fret about that, Sir! Our Izzie allus tells the truth. I knows that now.'

Izzie started to give him a detailed description of the man in the station buffet in Birmingham. She even drew him a little sketch map, indicating the table where she had noticed he usually sat, and she told him exactly what happened at the café.

'I'll ring that information through to my colleagues in Birmingham as soon as we get back to the station.' he said. 'If the Nazi scum's there tomorrow, they'll get him! You can be sure of that!'

After taking Izzie's statement and one from Bill, Sergeant Perkins looked around the cabin.

'I'll need to take all her things with me,' he said. 'There may be more evidence amongst her possessions.' He scooped up the contents of Jean's capacious handbag and shut it tightly.

'Wait till I tells George!' Izzie allowed herself a brief smile. "E allus wanted to know what were in it.'

'Where did she sleep, Mr Horne? Where are her possessions?' Bill led him to *Aphrodite*'s cabin without a glance at the waiting police car and its female occupant who was sitting in the back, holding a handkerchief to her nose. He helped the Sergeant collect Jean's belongings together, wrapping them all in her winter coat with the fake fur collar. The officer carried them out to the car.

After the policemen had returned to the station with their prisoner, Bill and Izzie were left alone in *Zeus*'s cabin to consider the evening's momentous events.

For a while they sat in silence, each of them with their own thoughts. So much had happened in the last couple of hours. So much had led up to tonight over the preceding weeks and months.

Suddenly, Bill turned to his daughter. 'Izzie, love!' He took hold of both of her hands in his. 'I'm been a prize bloody fool, ain't I?'

'No, you ain't, Dad!'

'I 'ave,' he reiterated. 'I let that bloomin' woman, that traitor! I let 'er make a complete fool out o' me! A complete fool! I let 'er make me think as 'ow she loved me. I let 'er make me believe as 'ow she were honest. An' worse of all, I let 'er make me think as 'ow it were 'er as were tellin' me the truth an' it were you as was lyin' to me... I honestly thought as you'd lied to me – me own daughter! Can you ... can you ever forgive me, Izzie love?'

Izzie could see the tears in his eyes as he spoke. She released her hands from his and threw her arms round his neck. 'O' course I can, Dad! O' course I can! You're me Dad, ain't you? I understand, see? I understand as you was real lonely after me Mam died, an' that. You was ... what were that word? I looked it up in me dictionary th' other day cos I weren't sure what it meant ... "vulnerable"! That were it! You was vulnerable, an' it seemed to you like she were the answer to all your prayers, didn't it? Cos she made out as she loved you, didn't she? An' she were good at it too, cos she'd bin trained 'ow to do it... An' you fell for it ... You reckoned as 'ow she really did love you ... and it made you feel a bit 'appier in yourself than you was afore she come along, didn't it?'

'But I believed what she said agin' you!'

'I knows you did, an' I don't mind tellin' you I were real angry wi' you at the time when you did that, real angry wi' you! It 'urt me, see? It 'urt me real bad, that did. But now I can see as it weren't really you as thought as I were lyin'. It were 'er as convinced you as I was. Like I said, now I can understand it, see?'

'Can you? Can you, really?' Bill whispered.

'Yeah, Dad. I can. You see, I reckon as it was cos you'd already lost me Mam. An' cos o' that, you didn't wanna believe nuthin' as 'd make it look like you was gonna lose 'er an' all. You'd got someone else to be with, someone else as you reckoned loved you, an' you could trust, an' you didn't wanna lose 'er.'

Bill was quiet for a moment. 'I reckon you're about right at that,' he breathed. 'Blimey! I reckon you knows more about me an' the way I thinks than I knows about meself!' With their arms tightly around each other they cried on each other's shoulders.

'Call it "woman's intuition", Dad,' Izzie said. 'I reckon that's what me Mam used to say it were.'

'It is, Izzie love! It is!' her father replied between sobs. The tension of the past months was released and everything between them was back as it had always been.

Eventually, Izzie looked up. 'I bet you could drink a cuppa.'

'I could that, Izzie, love. I could that.'

'Me too. I'll git a brew on.'

❈

Later that night, as she lay in bed, Izzie found it impossible to sleep. The events of the evening kept going round and round in her head. She had surprised herself that her quick thinking had enabled her to overcome Jean's threats. She was even more surprised at the blind fury she had felt when she had stood over Jean and kicked her. 'I ain't never been so angry!' she thought.

She thought back over the twists and turns her life had taken in recent years. 'It all started when me Mam died,' she mused. 'If she were still 'ere none o' this would 'ave 'appened. That Jean wouldn't never 'ave been on 'ere wi' us an' we wouldn't never 'ave got involved wi' no spyin' an' the p'lice an' all that!' She remembered how happy her life had been when her mother was alive. 'Why did she 'ave to go an' die?' she asked herself. But then another thought occurred to her. 'If she 'adn't died we'd never 'ave 'ad George on 'ere wi' us!' As she called to mind the happy times she had spent with him she suddenly felt guilty at the thought that her mother had to die in order for her to be happy with George. She thought about him coming home on the hospital ship. She imagined him lying in bed, and she hoped that his wound was not hurting him too much. She prayed that the ship would get back to England quickly and safely, and that George would soon be home again. Suddenly, the floodgates opened and the pent-up tears of the last few years tumbled down her face. Izzie sobbed – for her mother, for George, for her Dad, for herself – yes, even for Jean.

Eventually, emotionally exhausted, she fell asleep.

Chapter 32

'Eroine o' the cut

The morning after Jean's arrest, a strange atmosphere hung over *Zeus* and *Aphrodite*. The storm had cleared the air, but for Bill and Izzie their world seemed far from clear. They greeted each other with disbelief when they emerged from their respective cabins. Neither of them had slept well. Had last night's events really taken place? Had Jean really gone, taken away in a police car? Was she really a spy?

'Well, I s'pose I better ring the Wharf an' tell Mr Roberts what's up,' said Bill, drinking the mug of tea that Izzie had made for him. When he had finished, he made his way to the telephone box. As he approached it he saw that there was a man and a woman already waiting. When the man using the telephone came out, Bill was grateful to see them go in together. Their call was only short and Bill was soon posting his coins into the slot and dialling the Wharf Office number. As Horace's familiar voice answered, he pressed Button A and proceeded to recount the events of the previous evening. Horace remained silent until Bill had finished his tale.

'I wasn't sure about her when you came to me and said you wanted to take her on, Bill,' he said. 'But I certainly never thought she'd turn out to be a spy!'

'Neither didn't I,' Bill said. 'Still can't believe 'ow it 'appened.'

'So what are you doing now?'

'They're jus' unloadin' the crates at the minute.'

'Have you said anything to them about Jean?' Horace asked.

'I tol' Mr Thompson. 'E's like the 'ead man down 'ere.'

'And what did he say?'

''E made a phone call to somebody and then 'e said as 'ow 'e'd 'ave to make a report. 'E tol' me to come an' tell you first, an' then me an' Izzie'd 'ave to tell 'im all as 'appened last night.'

'And how are you and Izzie, Bill?'

'We're all right. Bit shocked, but I reckon as we'll do.'

'Good! I'll see you when you get back here.'

He finished the call and went back to see that Izzie had already invited Mr Thompson on board *Aphrodite* and was giving her version of events as he made notes. He looked up as Bill returned.

'Ah! Steerer Horne!' he said. 'That was an exciting time you both had last night!'

'Not the sort o' excitement I'd want to repeat,' Bill grimaced.

'Quite! Quite! Now your daughter, here – Isobel, isn't it?'

'Izzie,' she corrected him.

'Izzie has been telling me everything that occurred here last evening, and I have to say I think she is a very resourceful and a very courageous young lady.'

'She's that all right!' Bill beamed. 'I'm real proud on 'er!'

'And so you should be.'

'What 'appens now then, Mr Thompson?'

'Well, as far as we're concerned I'll need you to tell me what happened and see it agrees with what Iso ... what Izzie has told me. Then I've obviously got to check with my chaps that none of the crates has been tampered with, then you can make your way back to your base.'

'But we already gi' our statements to the p'lice,' Bill said.

'I know, but if we wait for them to send copies to us it'll take weeks. If I find out from you both what happened and make my own report it'll speed things up a bit.'

After another half-hour Izzie signed her statement and Bill made his mark on his. One of the men in overalls confirmed that the crates were all intact.

'Right, Steerer Horne, you can be on your way now.' He stepped onto the bank. 'I fear when you get back to your base, though, you may have to stay there for a while. There'll be a full investigation, of course, from our end as well as the police, and I should imagine you'll both have to come down to London again and give evidence at her trial.'

'I s'pose they can't be too careful when there's a war on,' Bill replied.

Mr Thompson stepped off the boat and headed back towards his office, their statements in his hand. Bill checked the engine and Izzie untied the ropes

'No, indeed. Treason's a very serious crime. Anyway, have a good trip,' Mr Thompson replied from the bank.

Bill eased *Zeus* away and, with Izzie steering *Aphrodite*, they began their run back to the Wharf. It felt good to be under way. Everything felt normal again. But not quite ... Izzie studied her father's back as he skilfully steered the pair out of London.

'It feels strange!' she thought. 'It's the first time we're been on the boats on our own. There's allus been somebody else afore – me Mam, or Jean or George. Oh, George! What a lot I gotta tell you! You won't believe all as is 'appened! 'Urry up an' come 'ome – I'm missin' you so much!

The news of Izzie's exploits spread quickly along the canal. Everywhere they stopped, everyone had heard about 'Young Izzie 'Orne capturin' a German spy'. They all wanted to ask her about it. How had she suspected Jean? What had made her certain? How had she overpowered her? When they arrived at the Wharf it was obvious that Izzie had become something of a heroine. Everyone she saw wanted to hear the story. Never one to boast, Izzie played down her part in the story, saying as she had all along, 'Anybody'd 'ave done it!'

The local police came to see her and Bill a number of times, and once they had two detectives from Scotland Yard who arrived with another man. He gave his name as 'Smith', but did not say where he was from. Together with all this there was the War Office investigation; most of it was carried out by Mr Hargreaves, who proudly showed Bill his repaired umbrella.

'Good as new!' he said.

While they were forced to stay at the Wharf because of the ongoing investigations, Izzie was eager to go back to the schoolroom. Although at fifteen she did not legally have to attend school, she was happy to join Miss Roberts's class. Now, however, Miss Roberts seemed to treat her more as an adult. She encouraged her to help the younger children and was pleased to spend time with her alone, explaining passages in books in more detail and encouraging her to develop her own thoughts and opinions.

On one particular afternoon she was the only pupil. She had not been there long when the door opened and Bill stood there. With a serious face he said, 'Excuse me, Miss Roberts, but your Dad wants to see me an' Izzie.'

'I bet we're in trouble over that Jean!' Izzie thought. She followed her father out of the door and was surprised to see Emily coming with them. At the door to the office, Bill stood aside to let Izzie go in first. 'That's odd!' she thought. "E don't usually let me go in afore 'im.'

Izzie entered the office and stopped dead! Expecting to see Mr Roberts, and possibly Mr Hargreaves too, she was amazed that not only was Horace there, but also the Coxes, the Johnsons and a couple of other families who were waiting for orders. As she walked in, followed by Bill and Emily, another man, who had been sitting on the edge of Horace's desk, stood up. Izzie had seen him before, but only on rare occasions. 'I knows 'oo 'e is,' Izzie thought. 'It's that Mr Prentice – Mr Roberts's boss from the big office. It mus' be summat mighty important for 'im to come down 'ere. Ah well!' she thought, 'at least everybody's smilin' so it can't be nuthin' bad!'

'Isobel Horne, or should I call you Izzie?' Mr Prentice chuckled. 'Mr Roberts and I, and all your friends from the Wharf, are here today to say how proud we are of you! We are proud because you, one of our people, and it has to be said one of our younger people, struck a great blow for freedom in helping, at great risk to yourself, to bring to justice an enemy agent who wished harm to this country that we love.'

He turned and picked up a small package from Horace's desk. 'I have come here from Company Office especially to present you with this,' he continued. 'I present it to you on behalf of the Company in recognition of your bravery in catching the German spy.' He beckoned Izzie towards him, held out his hand and shook hers warmly. 'You are a very brave young lady.'

'Thank you,' whispered Izzie, a little unsure of what to do. He handed her the small package, shook hands with her again, and everyone started clapping. When the applause died down Izzie carefully opened the little box. Inside, wrapped in tissue paper, she found a tiny model of a butty, made out of silver. Lifting it out and holding it up to admire it, she said, 'It's lovely!' Then, getting the feeling that everyone was expecting her to say something else, she cleared her throat.

'What I done weren't nuthin' special,' she began. 'Anybody'd 'ave done it. But there were summat as made me know as I 'ad to do it, an' that were what I read in a newspaper. Now, I couldn't never 'ave known what were in that paper if I 'adn't been learned 'ow to read. So I reckon as 'alf o' this 'ere belongs to you, Miss Roberts, for learnin' me.' She turned and showed the silver boat to her teacher, who smiled back at her. Bill was beaming too.

'You must be very proud of your daughter, Steerer Horne,' Mr Prentice said, shaking hands with him.

'Oh, I am, Sir! I am! She's my little 'eroine o' the cut, she is.' This brought another round of applause.

'Well,' said Horace, 'I think that deserves a little celebration. If you would like to accompany me, young lady, let's make our way down to The Boat.'

Inside the bar the landlord had laid out a plate of sandwiches, and his wife had baked a special cake. 'Everyone helped out and gave me their egg ration,' she said happily.

'Oh, thank you all, ever so much,' whispered Izzie, overwhelmed by everyone's kindness.

Later, back on *Zeus*, she took the little boat out of its box and looked at it again. 'It's really lovely!' she thought. 'They even got the mast an' the top planks on it – an' the little tiller moves.' She carefully re-wrapped it, put it back in its box, and put it safely in her treasure box. As she did so she noticed the copy of 'Crystal' that George had given her for her birthday, and the Christmas card he had sent her. 'I wonder what 'e's doin' now?' she mused. 'I wish 'e could 'ave been 'ere to see when Mr Prentice gi' me this. 'E'd 'ave liked that.'

✳

The next day Bill was called to the office again. Mr Hargreaves was there, wanting some further information about Jean.

'It's been a tough time for you!' he said. 'You did all you did in good faith. War throws so many different people together. If it hadn't been for the war I don't suppose I would ever have met you – or learned about the canals and the boatmen.' He paused. 'I'm pleased that I have, Bill. You don't mind if I call you Bill, do you?'

'Course I don't,' replied Bill.

'Good! My name's James.'

'Well, I reckon as I've told you all as I can. You're allus been fair to me – 'specially over this business. Can I ask you summat?'

'Certainly, ask away.'

'Well, it's like this. While I'm stuck 'ere in the Wharf I only gets "lay-in" pay, like when we're waitin' for orders. I'm losin' money!'

'I was coming to that, Bill,' James Hargreaves said. 'Horace Roberts mentioned it to me last week, and I've had a word with my office and they've agreed that since the reason you're not working is partly our fault, while we're writing up our report, they're going to make up your wages to what they would have been if you were still carrying the crates for us.'

'That's kind, an' it's a load off my mind, I can tell you!'

'I think it's only fair,' Hargreaves smiled.

'When this is all blowed over, shall we be back on the crates job again?' Bill asked.

'As far as I know, it's still going on, so there's every chance that you will be, but I'll liaise with Mr Roberts about it when the time comes.'

'Is that all you needs me for today, then?'

'I think so,' Hargreaves said, looking through his notes. 'Yes, that's all. Thank you, Bill.'

'Goodbye, Mr 'Argreaves.'

In the meantime, Izzie had gone to school, and had taken her silver butty so that Miss Roberts and the other children could see it more closely.

'Was you scared when she pulled the gun on you?' Ray Johnson asked.

'A bit, I s'pose,' she said.

Emily picked up the silver boat. 'You were right, Isobel. It really is lovely! And it was so sweet of you to say that half of it should be mine.'

'Well, it were you as learned me to read, Miss Roberts.'

'Let that be a lesson to all of you,' Emily addressed the others. 'You never know when being able to read is going to be important. Isobel never realised how important it was going to be until she read that newspaper. So let's have a bit more enthusiasm when it comes to learning your letters and words.'

As Izzie was leaving at the end of school, Emily stopped her. 'I've had an idea, Isobel.'

'What's that, Miss Roberts?'

'Do you remember – it must be almost exactly five years ago now, when you had just started coming to school – you told me why you wanted to learn to read ... about the bookshop next to the butcher in Birmingham?'

'Yeah, I remember!' Izzie smiled.

'And do you remember what you told me you were going to do one day?'

'I said as I were goin' there an' I were goin' to buy a book o' me own.'

'Well, I think you're ready to do that now.'

Izzie's smile broadened. 'D'you reckon so, Miss Roberts? D'you really think I could go an' git a book o' me own an' read it all the way through?'

'I'm sure you could!'

'I'm read all them little books as you lent me. But Jean allus called 'em "kiddies' books". She teased me about them books as I read. I wanna git a proper growed-up book,' said Izzie.

'The next time you go to Birmingham, ask your father to take you to the shop. I'm sure he won't mind. What is it he calls you now?'

'"Is "little 'eroine o' the cut",' said Izzie, embarrassed. She thought about Miss Roberts's suggestion for a moment. 'Yeah!' she said. 'I'll ask 'im.' Another pause. 'Miss Roberts...? D'you reckon as you could come wi' us ... to the bookshop?'

Emily clasped Izzie's shoulders. 'I should be honoured to come with you to buy your first book, Isobel!'

It was just over a month before they set out for Smethwick again, and their next cargo of crates. The police enquiries and the War Office investigation had dragged on and on until one day in early September Hargreaves told Mr Roberts that all enquiries were complete and that Jean's trial date had been set. However, he added, although both Bill and Izzie may well be called to give evidence, there was no reason why they should not resume work. He confirmed that the contract with the sealed crates was continuing and that *Zeus* and *Aphrodite* were expected in Smethwick as soon as they could get there. The only problem was that with Jean gone and George still convalescing, there was only Bill who could legally steer. To Bill's surprise, Horace solved the problem for him.

'I've contacted the insurance company,' he told Bill after he had called him into the office. 'They took a lot of persuading but I eventually got them to give a special dispensation allowing Izzie to steer the butty for the next few months up to her sixteenth birthday. After all,' he added, 'she is a special girl. I told the man at the insurance company, I said, "You can't tell me that a young woman who can single-handedly disarm and capture an enemy agent is incapable of safely steering the butty she was born on for a few months!" That convinced him!'

Before they left, Emily mentioned to Bill about Izzie's intended shopping trip. Bill had never known about what had happened on that day when she had waited outside the butcher's shop, the day she had looked in the bookshop window.

'Well, bugger me!' he said. 'Oh! Pardon me, Miss Roberts!' he grinned sheepishly. Emily smiled back – a conspiratorial smile. 'An' I thought th' only reason as she wanted to go to school was cos Maggie 'ad been on at 'er about it so much.'

Arrangements were made and, as the boats swung into the loading bay at Smethwick, Emily was waiting on the towpath.

'Good to see you again, Steerer Horne!' Mr Jenkins called, 'and your famous daughter too!' Bill secured the boats and, as they set out to meet Emily, Mr Jenkins said, 'Not staying to supervise today?'

'Not today,' Bill answered. 'Your blokes 'ave been doin' it long enough to know what they're about, an' any'ow I got a more important appointment today.' He smiled at Izzie, and she smiled back.

Chapter 33

Bookshop

Three people walked along a street in Birmingham. One was a woman of about thirty, and beside her a younger girl in her teens, wearing a headscarf, her fingers pulling at the knot under her chin – with nerves or excitement, it was hard to tell. Bringing up the rear was a middle-aged man. They walked with purpose, seemingly knowing exactly where they were going and also knowing exactly what they were going to do when they arrived at their destination.

Oblivious to the damaged shop fronts around them, they continued to walk until they arrived outside a particular shop. They halted. It was not just any old shop. It was a bookshop – a bookshop next to a butcher's. The frame round the window and the door next to it were painted green.

Izzie looked through the taped window, feasting her eyes on the books inside, then looked at Emily Roberts, her face alive with delight. Her father hung back a little. This was to be Izzie's day.

'I been looking forward to this day for years an' years an' years, Miss Roberts!' she exclaimed.

'I know you have, Isobel, I know you have! And now it's here, are you excited?'

'Yes, I am. But I'm jus' a little bit frit an' all. I ain't never been in a bookshop afore,' she laughed nervously.

'It was very kind of you to ask me to come along with you.'

'Well, I reckoned as you could 'elp me choose a book, Miss Roberts. There's so many on 'em in there, I wouldn't even know where to start!'

'You won't choose nuthin'!' Bill said. Izzie looked at him askance. 'Not till you gits in the shop, you won't, any'ow!'

They laughed as Bill's serious face split into a grin and he pushed open the shop door. A bell tinkled and he stood back to let Izzie go in first.

'Good afternoon,' the man behind the counter said.

'Af'noon,' Izzie replied. 'I'm come in 'ere to buy a book,' she blurted out.

'Well,' he smiled at her, 'I think you might just have come to the right place, don't you?' He spread his arms to indicate all the shelves full of books.

'Yeah.' Izzie did not move. 'I reckon as I might 'ave!' Her eyes surveyed the shelves. 'So many books,' she thought. 'I'm really glad Miss Roberts is 'ere to 'elp me out!

'Let's look at these books over here,' Emily suggested, leading her over to the section where there was a small notice, fixed to a bookcase with a drawing pin, which read 'Novels for the Older Child'. Izzie looked at some of the books. Emily picked out others and showed them to her. Izzie noticed that her father was standing by the door. 'You ain't gittin' bored, are you, Dad?' she asked, concerned.

'You take jus' as long as you want, Izzie love. I'm awright,' her father said. 'After all,' he added, 'you're my little 'eroine o' the cut now!' At this the man behind the counter looked up. 'This isn't Isobel Horne, the girl who caught the Nazi spy, by any chance, is it?'

'The very same.' Bill was justly proud of his daughter.

The man came out from behind the counter and walked over towards Izzie. 'I read all about you in the newspaper. Let me shake you by the hand, young lady.' He shook Izzie's hand and she blushed. 'That was a very brave deed you performed. I think that you deserve a medal or something similar for doing all that.'

'It weren't nuthin' really. Anybody'd 'ave done it,' Izzie replied quietly, embarrassed at the sudden attention.

'According to the *Post* the police picked up another one of them at New Street station the following day,' said the bookseller.

'Oh good!' Izzie said. 'I bet 'e were a bald bloke wi' glasses.'

Before the shopkeeper could reply, Emily called Izzie over. She had noticed the title of a particular book and pulled it out from the bookcase. 'Ah! Here's one I think you might like, Isobel.' She passed the book to Izzie. 'It's called *Black Beauty*. It's a story about a horse.'

'An 'orse!' Izzie sounded excited. She turned away from the shopkeeper. 'I like stories about 'orses.' She eagerly took the book from Emily, opened it and read the first page.

'I'm a-gonna buy this 'un,' she announced, and put her hand in her pocket to take out all the money she had managed to save up over the years. It was not much. She took it out of her pocket and with it in one hand and the copy of *Black Beauty* in the other, she approached the counter.

Her father walked up behind her. 'Put your money back in your pocket, our Izzie.' He reached into his own pocket. 'I'm gonna buy it for you. It's a present, like.'

As they approached the counter to pay for the book the shopkeeper said, 'Just a second!' and walked to a set of shelves at the other end of the shop. He returned with another volume in his hand.

'Here.' He handed the book to Izzie. 'It would be churlish of me not to reward a brave young lady like you. This is a book about another brave young lady. Her name was Edith Cavell, and she did some pretty brave things in another war many years ago.' Izzie again put her hand to her pocket. 'No!' said the shopkeeper. 'This one is with my compliments.'

'You mean, I don't 'ave to pay you nuthin' for it?'

'That's exactly what I mean!' he smiled. 'It's my great honour to have met you in person.'

'Thank you,' said Izzie. 'Thank you ever so much!' She looked at the others with an enormous smile on her face. 'I come in 'ere to buy one book wi' me own money, and I'm goin' out of 'ere wi' two books – an' I ain't 'ad to pay for even one of 'em!' she said excitedly.

Bill paid for *Black Beauty*, then they all bade the shopkeeper good day. As they were leaving the shop Izzie suddenly stopped.

'Jus' a minute!' They all looked at her.

'What?' Bill asked.

'I'm jus' thought o' summat,' she replied. 'Miss Roberts, you're gonna 'ave to 'elp me out.'

'Help you with what, Isobel?'

'Well, as I ain't spent none o' me own money, I jus' thought. There's another book as I want, but I can't remember what it's called.'

'Do you know what it's about?' Emily asked.

'Yeah, it's about a orphan girl as gits treated bad by 'er auntie an' then gits sent to rotten school. Then she goes to teach a little girl in a big 'ouse an' ends up marrying the bloke as owns it.'

'I know the one you mean!' Emily smiled. 'It's by a lady author, Charlotte Bronte, and it's called *Jane Eyre*.'

'That's it!' Izzie exclaimed excitedly. '*Jane Eyre*! That were the name on it!' She turned to the shopkeeper. 'Can I 'ave *Jane Eyre*, please?'

He went to a set of shelves that bore the label 'Classics' and removed the book. When she had paid for it, Izzie thanked him again and they left the shop.

'Tell me, Isobel,' said Emily as they walked back to the station. 'Where did you get to hear about *Jane Eyre*? I don't think I've ever mentioned the book to you. Although, come to think of it – perhaps I should have done. It's a very good book.'

'It were Susan – one o' them women as is workin' the boats cos o' the war. She were readin' it that evenin' when I see 'er an' she tol' me all about treason an' that. She said it were so good she'd read it three or four times.'

'It's certainly a very good story,' Emily agreed.

When they arrived at the station Emily saw that her next train was not for another hour. 'I know!' she said. 'Why don't we go to the buffet and have a cup of tea to celebrate Isobel's first books?'

'Good idea!' Bill replied.

As they entered the buffet Izzie looked around. 'This is where I seen Jean and the bald-'eaded bloke wi' the glasses,' she said as they sat down at a vacant table.

'They was sat at that 'un, over there.' She pointed to a table occupied by a middle-aged couple with a little girl and a young man in RAF uniform. She stared at the table, a sick feeling in her stomach, as she remembered all too clearly how she had witnessed Jean making her secret assignations with the bald-headed man.

Meanwhile her father and Emily went to the counter where they had a little argument about who should pay.

'I knows as it were your idea, Miss Roberts, but as I'm the only man 'ere, I should be the one as does the payin'!' Izzie overheard her father saying. Soon, however, they were all sitting at the table drinking tea and eating cakes, and all thoughts of Jean disappeared from Izzie's mind.

'Isobel!' Emily said as she wiped a cake crumb from her mouth. 'I almost forgot! I have something here for you.' She produced a letter from her pocket.

'That's George's writin'!' Izzie exclaimed.

'It arrived at Dad's office yesterday,' Miss Roberts said as she passed the letter to Izzie.

Izzie opened the letter and read eagerly. Bill and Emily looked at each other knowingly as they noticed a blissful smile appear on her face.

''E says 'e's gittin' on fine wi' 'is tin leg, an' the doctors is sayin' as they're gonna let 'im come 'ome soon!' she said, full of excitement.

'Do 'e say when?' Bill asked.

'No,' Izzie replied. 'They ain't told 'im that yit. 'E jus' says "soon" – some time after Christmas.'

'Well, that really is good news!' Emily sounded almost as pleased as Izzie.

'I reckon as this mus' be my lucky day,' Izzie said. 'I'm got three books o' me own, two on 'em as I ain't 'ad to pay for, an' now I knows as George'll be 'ome again soon!'

'I reckon you could be right at that,' said Bill.

Emily's train was announced and they made their way to the platform to see her off.

'Thank you ever so much for comin'.' Izzie hugged her teacher.

'I wouldn't have missed it for the world,' Emily said. 'The look on your face when we went into that bookshop made it all worthwhile!'

'An' thank you for bringin' that letter from George.'

'That's all right. I'm so glad it was good news.'

'I jus' wish as you'd let me pay for the tea,' Bill said.

'You can pay next time, Mr Horne,' she said, as she shook his hand and boarded her train.

As the train steamed out of the station, Izzie recalled watching another train depart – the one that had been taking her George away from her. 'I wonder when I'm gonna see 'im again,' she thought. 'But I knows now as I ain't got long too wait!'

Chapter 34

The same bloke

It was a cold November evening when they found themselves tied up next to *Worcester* and *Dolphin* outside The Running Horse. Although they had passed it a number of times on recent runs, Bill had never wanted to stop there. However, this time he changed his mind.

'Let's pull in at The 'Orse,' he said. 'Alf'll think it strange we ain't stopped there no more.'

As Bill and Izzie entered the pub they saw the three women from the boats already sitting at a table. Izzie was pleased to see that May had rejoined them.

Alf served Bill and the conversation inevitably turned to Jean.

'Never suspected anything!' said Alf.

'Me neither,' Bill agreed.

'She arrived here, saying she wanted to get out of London because of the bombing and had we got a job for her? I asked her which pubs she'd worked at before and she said she hadn't, but she'd worked in a shop and knew how to deal with customers and money. I was a bit dubious – with her having no experience – but the wife said we should give her a chance, so I did. She picked it up quicker than anybody I've ever known!'

'She done the same wi' boatin',' Bill said. 'An' d'you know why?'

'Why?'

'Cos she'd been trained!'

'No!' Alf was aghast.

'They'd planned it all real careful. She was to git a job at a pub on this cut, an' then git 'erself onto a pair. An' they'd already trained 'er for everythin' as she 'ad to do – steerin', locks, ev'rythin' – right down to the las' nut 'n' bolt!'

'The scheming buggers!' was all Alf could say.

'Izzie!' Susan called when she saw her, beckoning her to their table. 'Come and pull up a pew! You must tell us absolutely everything about your German spy! We heard about it on the towpath telegraph, but we missed it in the newspapers. We were unloading miles away from anywhere!'

Izzie told them the whole story from when she had first suspected Jean to when she had been arrested, carefully skirting round how Jean had got her bruises!

'It were only cos you tol' me about May 'ere, an' 'er Mam, as I knew if I didn't do nuthin' me Dad'd be in a lot o' trouble!' she finished. 'What's 'appened about your Mam, May? Is she OK?'

'Oh that! She's all right now, thanks. It was very scary at the time though! The police asked a lot of questions, but eventually they said they were satisfied that Mama had acted in all innocence. They agreed that she wouldn't knowingly have helped a German, especially since Papa was killed at Passchendaele. They just advised her very strongly to take up references for any lodgers she may have in the future.'

'Oh, tha's good!' Izzie said. 'What were 'e like ... the spy bloke?'

'Oh him!' said May. 'I met him a couple of times when I went home. He said his name was Ron and he came from somewhere up north and that he was working in the area and needed a place to stay. Seemed like a perfectly ordinary chap, really.'

'Ron?' Izzie queried. 'What were 'is other name?'

'He said it was Winterman, but...'

'That's 'im!' Izzie interrupted. 'That's the same bloke! The bloke as I seen in the paper! 'Im as Jean met in the caff! It said it in the paper, Ronald Winterman, but the p'lice didn't think it were 'is real name.'

'Well, the Winterman part was real enough – only, of course, being German, it was pronounced "Vinterman", but his real Christian name is Helmut.'

'So he was the man you saw with Jean?' Carol asked.

'Yeah!' said Izzie. 'The bloke with the moustache and the briefcase.'

'What a coincidence!' Susan exclaimed. 'You meet the three of us – completely by chance – and it turns out that May's Mama's lodger was the same man who was your Jean's boss!'

'Extraordinary!' Carol said.

May continued. 'You couldn't make that up, could you? Anyway, when it was all sorted out, Mama was very relieved that nothing else was going to happen and I was able to rejoin these two on the boats.'

'Yes, we were all very grateful to get our May back,' said Carol. 'They sent us a girl called Ann as a replacement, and she was absolutely hopeless, wasn't she, Sue?'

'Hopeless wasn't the word for it!' Susan agreed. 'But coming back to you, Izzie. You and your father must have been scared out of your wits when she pulled a gun on you and told you you were both going to be killed!'

'It were a bit scary, yeah.'

'Well, we all think you're very brave!'

'Anybody'd 'ave done it,' Izzie said for the umpteenth time. 'But I were goin' to ask you summat, Susan – wi' you 'avin' worked in a lawyer's office an' that.'

'What do you want to know? I was only a secretary, remember, not a solicitor!'

'I'm sure as you'll know. Now, Mr 'Argreaves, 'e's the bloke from the War Office, 'e were sayin' as me an' me Dad might 'ave to go an' gi' evidence at 'er trial.'

'I'm sure you will have to, yes.'

'What'll 'appen there? What'll we 'ave to do?'

Susan thought for a few moments.

'Well,' she began, 'as it happens, I do know a bit about this because I was so concerned about your Mama, May, that while I was on leave I went to the office and asked one of the solicitors to look some facts up for me. I think, given what this woman has done, they will try her under the Treachery Act, rather than going the whole hog for High Treason. I mean, it's not like she tried to shoot Churchill or the King, is it?'

'Well, she did try to shoot me an' me Dad!' Izzie exclaimed indignantly.

'And that's far more serious!' Carol joked, and they all burst out laughing, Izzie included. As the laughter subsided, Susan continued. 'I should think the trial will be at the Central Criminal Court. It's usually called the Old Bailey. Anyway, when you give your evidence, you're led into court by an usher who shows you to the witness box. That's where you have to stand. The first thing you have to do is to swear an oath on the Bible to say that the evidence you are going to give is "the truth, the whole truth and nothing but the truth".

'There'll be some men there wearing white curly wigs and gowns. The one sitting up high at the front is the judge, and the others are barristers – lawyers, they are. The barrister who is acting for the prosecution – that means the one who is trying to prove she is a spy – he'll ask you some fairly easy questions, all based on the statement you gave to the police. When he's finished, the other barrister will then ask you some trickier questions. You see, he's trying to prove that she's not a spy, so he's going to try and trip you up!'

'I don't much like the sound o' that!' Izzie said.

'No, it's OK, really. I've had to go to lots of trials, and if you stick to the truth, it'll be OK. If the barrister asks you something that obviously isn't a fair question, then the prosecution barrister will object to it. Then it's up to the judge to rule whether it's fair or not, and if he says it isn't fair then you don't have to answer it anyway. The other thing to remember is not to let him make you angry. That's the worst thing you can do!'

'Thank you ever so much, Susan. I'll git me Dad to come over later, if you wouldn't mind tellin' 'im all that an' all? 'E's a bit scared – like I am. Us boatin' folk try to keep out the way o' the law an' suchlike.'

'Of course I wouldn't mind. I'm only glad to be able to help you.' She paused. 'How's the chap whose grandfather's boats we're using? George, was it?'

'That's right,' Izzie said. ''E's lost a leg, fightin' in Tunis.'

'Oh, no!' the girls chorused in unison. 'Is he all right?'

''E's 'ad a tin 'un fitted, an 'e's in a 'ospital down south somewhere. It's a place as they sends 'em to git 'em to walk on 'em better.'

'Well, I hope he gets on OK and comes back to the boats soon,' Susan said. The others agreed.

Carol changed the subject. 'You'd never believe some of the stupid things we've done,' she said. 'Your Dad would have had a dicky fit!'

Izzie chuckled as Carol recounted their experiences with a windlass, a rope and a saucepanful of potatoes!

'Me Dad'd say, "You'll never be proper boatwomen, like me Mam were."'

Bill, who was standing at the bar with his fellow boatmen, looked over towards her and smiled.

It was surprising how quickly the evening passed. During a lull in the conversation Izzie turned to Susan. 'By the way, d'you remember that evenin' as I seen you – when you tol' me about May's Mam an' the spy an' everythin'?'

'I remember,' Susan said.

'D'you remember what book you was readin' when I come along the towpath?'

Susan thought for a moment. 'I can't recall exactly – but, knowing me, it was probably *Jane Eyre*. I just love that book so much!'

'It was!' Izzie exclaimed. 'An' now I got me own *Jane Eyre* book. I ain't started readin' it yit, but I got it!'

'Good for you!' Susan smiled.

'You'll love it!' said May.

'I must get round to reading it again some time too,' Carol agreed, and the conversation returned to the women's experiences as 'trainees'.

'We're seen some more o' you trainees – an' most on 'em is worse 'n you three ever was!' Izzie remarked.

'Don't worry, Izzie,' said Susan. 'We've always tried to look after George's Grandad's boats. We haven't sunk them or anything! I know it's not like this for you and your father. You're professionals – you were born to it. We're only amateurs. "Playing at boating", that's what some of the boatmen we meet say.'

'And that's putting it mildly!' Carol laughed.

'Do you remember the time we drained that pound?' said May – and off they went on another story.

At closing time Bill left his fellow boatmen at the bar and came over to join them. As she had promised, Susan explained to him what to expect at the trial.

When they were walking back to the boats, he said, 'I weren't sure about them women comin' on the cut an' workin' the boats, but I tell you, I'm glad that Susan were one on 'em. She's been a big 'elp in all this. She 'as, honest.'

'You ain't wrong there, Dad. It were 'er as tol' me about what might 'appen to you if you stuck wi' Jean. An' now, at least we knows what to expect when we goes into that court.'

When she was in bed she recalled the conversation with Susan and the other women about George, and it started her thinking about him again. Just before she went to sleep she whispered, 'Come back to me, George! Come back to me soon! You don't know 'ow much I'm missin' you! '

Chapter 35

The cut's a-changin'

Over the next few months Izzie and her father continued with the War Office contract. Christmas came and went. It was the fifth Christmas of the war and, although it had not affected the boat people's lives in the same way as those in the towns and cities, they, too, were fed up with rationing, shortages and queues. For some of them, like Izzie and her father, the war had come closer to home and touched their lives, and when the boatmen gathered the course of the war was as big a topic of conversation as trade on the cut.

During this time Izzie kept up a steady correspondence with George. She was both pleased and relieved to hear that he was progressing so well with his artificial leg. However, in one of his letters he told her that, although he was pleased she had been legally allowed to steer the butty, he wondered whether her father would want to employ him again when he came out of hospital with, as he put it, 'me being a cripple.' This concerned Izzie greatly too. She wanted George back with her on *Zeus* and *Aphrodite*. She wanted everything to be back the way it was before he went off to fight. She wondered how best to broach the subject with her father.

One evening soon afterwards, when they had tied up for the night on their way to Kensal Green, and were sitting in *Aphrodite*'s cabin, Bill gave her the opportunity to ask him the question that was on her mind.

"'Ow's' George gittin' on wi' that tin leg as 'e's got?' he asked.

'E's doin' fine! 'Is wound's stopped 'urtin' so much when 'e's got it on now, an' they're learnin' 'im 'ow to walk on it, an' 'ow to look after 'isself an' everythin'.' She stopped and took a deep breath. Next she asked him the big question. 'I been thinkin'.' She paused.

'Now Mr Roberts 'as sorted it out for me to steer the butty regular like, will you be 'avin' George back on 'ere wi' us?'

Bill smiled at his daughter. 'You think a lot o' young George, don't you, Izzie love?'

'Yeah,' she replied, looking down at her lap. She felt her face flush.

'Don't you worry, love. I won't see the boy wi'out a job. As soon as they let 'im out o' that 'ospital 'e can come back on 'ere – no trouble! After all, 'e 'elped us out after your Mam died, didn't 'e?'

Izzie gave him a big hug. 'Thanks, Dad!'

'That's awright,' Bill replied. ''E'd probably find it 'ard gittin' another job wi' only one leg, any'ow.'

Later that night, when she was back on *Zeus*, Izzie, with joy in her heart, wrote to tell George the good news. She received his reply when they called at The Running Horse the following week. He was mightily relieved to know that he would be rejoining them – and he had some good news as well. He was not sure exactly when, but he had been told by the doctors that he would soon be allowed to leave the hospital! Izzie was ecstatic as she relayed this news to her father. They hugged each other out of sheer joy.

They continued their journey towards Smethwick. Izzie carried George's letter in her pocket, and every so often she would touch it and sometimes draw it from its hiding place and hold it to her cheek. She would re-read the sentence, 'I'll soon be able to leave the hospital. Love from George xxx.'

'You'll soon be 'ome, George,' she would whisper to the passing breeze.

A day or two later they travelled through the tunnel at Blisworth, and as the pair emerged into the daylight Izzie caught sight of a young man in a suit and a trilby hat, with a suitcase, limping along the towpath towards them. She did not recognise him at first, but when she did she almost steered *Aphrodite* straight into the bank!

'George!' she screamed. At this, Bill also noticed him and

quickly brought *Zeus* to the edge of the towpath. The boats had hardly stopped before Izzie leapt off the counter and ran as fast as she could towards George. As she drew nearer he stopped, put down his suitcase, and spread his arms wide. She almost knocked him over as she threw herself into his embrace.

'Steady on, Izzie!' was all he could say as her lips met his in a long, passionate kiss. She was weeping, but these were tears of unbridled happiness, relief and joy. Her George was back! 'An' this time 'e's back for good!'

Bill shook his hand. 'It's good to see you again, George, me boy!' he said as George helped them tie up the boats. In the intervals between repeatedly hugging him and holding George's hand, Izzie managed to get the kettle on.

''Ow did you know we was gonna be 'ere?' Bill asked.

'I rung up The 'Orse an' asked when you'd left there, an' then I worked out as you'd be somewhere round 'ere today – dependin' whether you got a good road up Stoke or not o' course.'

'Well,' said Izzie, grabbing his hand yet again, 'we got a good road, an' we're 'ere, an' so are you!'

''Ow did you git 'ere?' Bill asked.

'They tol' me yesterday mornin' as I were goin' out in th' afternoon. So as soon as I got out I phoned The 'Orse an' then I made me way to the station an' got a train to Northampton last night. I kipped in the waitin' room an' then this mornin' I 'itched a lift wi' a lorry goin' to Oxford – an' 'ere I am.'

'I like your suit!' Izzie remarked. 'Very smart!'

'It's what they give us when we got demobbed from th' army. It's only a cheap ol' thing.'

'What's "demobbed"?' she asked.

'It's short for "demobilisation". It's just a posh word for sayin' as th' army don't need you no more.'

Later, when they were under way again, George was with Izzie on *Aphrodite*.

'From what I seen o' you so far, you look like you're doin' awright wi' that tin leg,' she commented.

'Yeah. The doctors said as I were one o' their best patients for adaptin' to it, like. There's some things as I can't do, like runnin' an' jumpin', an' there's some as I can do, but not as good as I used to, but all in all I reckon as I'll do awright.'

'I reckon as you will, an' all.'

Bill made sure that when they had tied up for the night there was a pub close at hand.

'Well!' he said. 'We're got summat to celebrate, ain't we?'

And what a celebration! There was so much to talk about and so much to tell. During the evening George asked, 'Which o' the pair am I sleepin' on?'

'I'm on the butty an' our Izzie's on the motor,' Bill said. 'So…'

Izzie cut him off. 'I want George on the motor wi' me!' she announced with a straight face.

George raised his eyebrows and looked pleasantly surprised, while Bill just smiled and nodded his head. 'That's awright,' he said, 'jus' so long as you two don't git up to nuthin' in there!'

'Dad!' exclaimed Izzie. 'We won't.' She smiled at George. 'It'll be like afore. I 'as the cross bed an' you can 'ave the side bed.'

'An' I won't forget to pull the curtain acrost!' George added.

'An' I'll 'ide your tin leg so you can't git up an' chase me round the cabin!' They all laughed.

'Bein' serious for a minute, though…' Bill brought the laughter to a halt. 'There's summat as I been meanin' to say to you, our Izzie, for some time, only I never seemed to be able to find the right time to say it. Well, now this young man's back wi' us, an' we're like we used to be, an' as I'm 'ad a pint or two, I reckon as this is the right time.'

'What Dad? What?' Izzie was concerned that the euphoric spell she was under was about to be broken.

'Well, I been thinkin',' he began, slowly. 'If your Mam 'adn't never sent you to that boat kids' school you'd never 'ave learned to read. An' if you 'adn't been able to read you'd never 'ave seen what you seen in that there newspaper. An' if you 'adn't read that, then God only knows where we might 'ave ended up!' Izzie thought she could see a little tear in the corner of her father's eye as he spoke. 'So, all I wanna say, really, is that even though I were dead agin' it at the time, I'm glad now as your Mam got you into that school. She were a lot wiser 'n what I am, your Mam.'

'So you don't think it was – what were it as you called it? – "bloomin' book learnin"? You don't reckon as it's such a waste o' time now, Dad?'

'No, it ain't. See, I never realised it afore, but the cut's a-changin'. I dunno whether it's cos o' the war or what. But things 'as never seemed important afore is gittin' to be more important now. I dunno where it's all gonna end.'

They sat in silence for few seconds, then George said, 'Another pint, Bill?'

'Ah! Good idea!'

'An' a 'alf o' shandy for the lady?'

'Thanks, George.'

When George returned with the drinks, Bill, now with some Dutch courage, asked the question they had both been dying to ask, but had not dared. 'So, 'ow did you come to lose your leg, George?'

Izzie glared daggers at him. 'George might not want to talk about it!' she said.

'No,' George said. 'I don't mind. I'll tell you. It were when we was takin' Tunis. We'd done pretty good – took a lot o' land back off the Germans. I were on a big field gun wi' a couple o' me mates – Mickey an' Slogger. Any'ow, even though we'd got 'em on the run, the Germans was still puttin' up a lot o' resistance, an' a shell landed right near our gun. I were lucky, I s'pose, cos I were on the other side o' the gun. See, it shielded me from the main blast, but it blew the gun right over an' it crushed me leg under it.'

'Poor you!' Izzie said.

'What 'appened to your two mates?' Bill asked.

George's face suddenly darkened. 'Mickey an' Slogger? Well, they was on the same side o' the gun as where the shell come down. They didn't 'ave no protection like I did...'

'They was both killed?' Izzie asked quietly.

'Good mates, they was.' George studied his glass. Bill stood up and made his way to the Gents. George looked at Izzie. 'You must 'ave 'ad a terrible time wi' that Jean!' he said.

'Yeah! See, I knew as she were up to summat, but I weren't sure what, an' me Dad were so besotted wi' 'er, 'e didn't believe me, an' there weren't nobody else as I could tell.'

'Spyin' for the Germans, though! 'Er, an English woman! But if only 'alf what you wrote me in that letter about what 'appened that night in London were true – you was very brave.'

'That's what everybody's said. That's what the bloke in the bookshop said. An' 'e gi' me a book!'

'Oh, yeah! Your trip to the bookshop in Brum. I wish I could 'ave been wi' you for that.'

'I wish you could 'ave been as well, George. It would 'ave been nice.'

'Never mind,' he said. 'Next time we're in Brum we'll go there an' I'll buy you a book too!'

'That'll be even nicer!'

'An' wha's 'appened to 'er now?' he asked.

'We 'ad to go to court an' gi' evidence, jus' like Susan said as we would. It were a bit scary!' said Izzie.

'An' did she go to prison?'

'I dunno an' I don't care!' said Bill firmly, changing the subject as he returned from the Gents.

That night, when they had returned to the boats, Izzie and George climbed aboard *Zeus*. Izzie tried several times to start a conversation, but George seemed preoccupied and did not appear to want to talk. In the end she asked, 'What's the matter?'

'I dunno!,' he replied. 'That is I do know, but it's a bit 'ard to put it into words.'

'Well try.'

He sat down on the side bed. 'Well...' He hesitated. 'Well ... when I were away in th' army, an' when I got them letters from you. Well, they was worth a awful lot to me, them letters was. They was like a link ... sort of ... like a link wi' 'ome. An' some o' them things as you said to me in them letters... Well, them things as you said ... they made me...' His voiced tailed off.

'What about them letters?' Izzie turned to look at him, puzzled.

'Well ... after I'd read some o' them things as you said in them letters, Izzie, I sort o' come to a decision, in me own mind, like.'

'What decision were that, then, George?'

'Well ... I decided ... I decided that when it were all over – the war an' everythin'... an' I come 'ome ... I were ... I were gonna ask you ... next May ... when you're old enough, like ... I were gonna ask you to marry me! There! I'm said it!'

Izzie thought this over for a moment. 'Why did you say as you was gonna ask me? What's stoppin' you askin' me now?'

'Well...'

'If you say 'Well' one more time, George Andrews, I'm a-gonna 'it you!'

'Well – sorry! Look, when I made that there decision, that were afore I got this.' He pointed down at his artificial leg. 'It sort o' changed everythin'. Fact is – I don't reckon as it'd be fair on you to saddle yourself for the rest o' your life wi' a bloke as is only 'alf a man – a bloomin' cripple!' His eyes were still cast downwards, afraid to meet hers. She sat down next to him and, putting one arm round him, she covered his hand with hers.

'Listen to me. I loves you George Andrews. I loves you – an' I'd still love you even if you 'adn't got no legs – nor no arms neither!'

'That's easy to say...'

'Look, I ain't jus' sayin' it. I means it. There ain't nuthin' in this world as I want more 'n to live wi' you for the rest o' me life!'

'But can you live wi' this?' George pulled up his right trouser leg, revealing his artificial leg. 'An' even if you can live wi' that, d'you reckon you could live wi' this.' He removed his artificial leg. Izzie stared. Just above where his knee had been was a stump. There were red marks where his artificial leg had been, and below them a ragged scar with marks each side of it where stitches had been. He looked at her, expecting to see a mask of shock and horror on her face. But instead, all he saw there was sympathy –sympathy and a little sadness. Slowly and deliberately, Izzie let go of his hand and ran her fingers along the line of his scar. Then she gently massaged the red marks away with her fingertips. When she looked up at him, she could see tears in his eyes.

'I can live wi' that,' she said quietly. 'You got that fightin' for your country – my country – our country. You got that fightin' for my freedom! So, I reckon as I can feel proud – real proud – o' livin' wi' that!'

He put both arms round her and hugged her to him, and as he buried his face in her shoulder, he cried like a baby. 'I thought ... I thought as … you wouldn't want me!' he managed to say between sobs.

'Well, I does!' she answered. 'God knows I does!'

When his weeping had subsided, he sat back. 'Well…,' he said again. She looked at him in mock anger.

'Well,' he emphasised, 'I'm still got one good knee, so I'm gonna do this proper, like.' He lowered himself to the floor, kneeling on his good leg, and, taking her hand in his, he looked up at her. 'Izzie 'Orne, when you git to sixteen, next May, will you do me the great 'onour o' bein' me wife? Will you marry me, Izzie?'

She helped him back onto the side bed. 'There ain't nuthin'! There ain't nuthin' in this 'ole world as'd make me 'appier 'n bein' Mrs George Andrews.'

He put his arms round her and pulled her close as she snuggled against him.

When Izzie awoke the following morning George was nowhere to be seen. She got up and relit the range before putting the kettle on. George poked his head through the slide.

'You're awake then? Sleepyhead! What's for breakfast?'

Izzie smiled at him. 'Only porridge again today! No more bacon till nex' week's ration.' She could see him standing on the counter and hear him, nervously drumming his fingers on the cabin roof. He was waiting for Bill to come along to check the engine over before starting up for the day's run.

He did not have to wait long. He heard *Aphrodite's* slide being pushed back and her doors being opened. Bill emerged and walked towards him, whistling.

'Mornin', George! You're up an' about early this mornin'. Mus' be all that army trainin'!'

Izzie stopped stirring the porridge and listened.

'Er … Bill, 'ave you got a minute? I got summat to ask you…'

Half Cut Theatre

Rupert Ashby is the nom de plume of Derek Harris. Under his other soubriquet of Half Cut Theatre, he has been performing canal-themed one-man shows in and around his home city of Peterborough since 2003. His repertoire consists of:

Up the Cut

An amusing and informative history of the canals of England and Wales, illustrated with songs, some involving audience participation.

Folk of the Cut

Similar in style to Up the Cut and looks at the people involved with our canal system from the early engineers to restoration by the volunteers of today.

Characters on the Cut

Told from the viewpoint of an observer at 'The Pub on the Cut', the audience is introduced to a variety of characters, past and present, who have been drawn to the canals of this country, including an 'Idle Woman' and a 'Gongoozler'.

A Cruise on the Cut

A slide presentation looking at the architecture and engineering of the British canal system.

Want to know more, or book a show? Visit his website at www.halfcuttheatre.com

- As to the origin of the name – Half Cut Theatre – the word 'canal' was rarely, if ever, used by the boating families back in the commercial days. The waterway was always referred to as 'the cut'. Add to this the fact that your author is rather partial to the odd pint of real ale, and it all seems rather obvious!